The Battle of Strasbourg

The Battle of Strabourg

by
Jules Lermina

translated, annotated and introduced by
Brian Stableford

A Black Coat Press Book

Edited by Peter Gabbani

English adaptation and introduction Copyright © 2014 by Brian Stableford.
Cover illustration Copyright © 2014 Yoz.

Visit our website at www.blackcoatpress.com

Introduction

La Bataille de Strasbourg by Jules Lermina, here translated as *The Battle of Strasbourg*, was initially published as a
43-part feuilleton serial in issues 25-67 of *La Terre Illustrée*
between 25 April 1891 and 11 February 1892, where it carried
the subtitle "*Histoire de l'invasion chinoise en Europe au XXe
siècle*" [The History of the Chinese Invasion of Europe in the
Twentieth Century]. It was subsequently reprinted in two volumes in 1895, without the subtitle, by L. Boulanger, the proprietor of the periodical in question. It was reprinted again as a
feuilleton in the daily newspaper *Le Matin* between 29 July
and 26 September 1900.

In its time, the novel was ground-breaking. It was one of
the earliest "immersive fantasies" set in the future—which is
to say, a story that adopts a hypothetical future viewpoint
without organizing any kind of transitional device, such as a
prophetic dream—and it is perhaps the earliest to do so
straightforwardly, with no other explanatory exposition than
its initial subtitle.

La Bataille de Strasbourg is by no means the first story
to depict a future war—there had been a brief glut of such
stories in the wake of the account of *The Battle of Dorking*
published in *Blackwood's Magazine* in 1871, inspired by the
horrible thought of what might happen if the Prussian armies
that had devastated France in the previous year turned their
attention to England and succeeded in crossing the channel.
That novelette had been rapidly reprinted as a pamphlet and
translated into several other languages, including French,
where *Bataille de Dorking: invasion des Prussiens en
Angleterre* (1871), with a preface by Charles Ynarte, went
through several editions. Most previous exercises in that vein,
however, had followed Chesney's example in focusing on the
deployment of contemporary weaponry and strategy, featuring

battles that might take place tomorrow or the day after. Lermina follows the more recent strategy adopted satirically by Albert Robida in *La Guerre au Vingtième siècle* (1883; different book version 1887; tr. as *War in the Twentieth Century*) in describing a war displaced into a sufficiently distant future for technology to have transformed the mechanics of mass murder, and depicting a conflict on a much larger scale than a squabble between neighboring nations: a conflict between entire races; a war embracing the entire world. In that respect, too, however, Lermina was innovative.

Historians of futuristic fiction, with the aid of hindsight, now credit *La Bataille de Strasbourg* with launching a small-scale literary fad that is generally known as "yellow peril" fiction; it is described in that context in an essay by Charles Moreau and Jean-Luc Buard entitled "*La Bataille de Strasbourg* de Jules Lermina et le Péril jaune" in a special issue of *Le Rocambole: Bulletin des amis du roman populaire* (nos. 43/44, été-automne 2008) devoted to Lermina.

It is, indeed, the case that the idea of a "Chinese invasion of Europe" did become a significant bugbear on the ragged fringe of future war fiction, luridly developed in the context of English feuilleton fiction by M. P. Shiel in "The Empress of the Earth," serialized in Arthur Pearson's *Short Stories* from 5 February to 18 June 1898 and subsequently reprinted (in abridged form) as *The Yellow Danger*, and the threat of Oriental plans for world domination subsequently fueled a very popular series of thrillers by "Sax Rohmer" (Arthur Sarsfield Ward) launched in 1913, whose villain, Fu Manchu, achieved a legendary status. The subgenre was imported into America, where a variant supplied the basis for one of the earliest successes of the science fiction genre in "Armageddon 2419 A.D." (1928)—which introduced the character of Buck Rogers, who achieved similar legendary status as a hero—and where the experimentation of the pulp magazine genre even produced a brief Rohmeresque yellow peril subgenre in a magazine featuring the dastardly exploits of *The Mysterious Wu Fang* (seven issues, 1935-36), who was then replaced by

Dr. Yen Sin (three issues, 1936). Jules Lermina had no idea that any such phenomenon might occur, however, and his novel involves a far more general Oriental uprising, which embraces India and the entire world of Islam as well as the Far East, so his imagined peril is by no means entirely yellow.

Lermina certainly cannot be exempted from the charge of lurid xenophobia, in which all fiction of this type participates, but he does have conscience enough to point out in the early chapters of his story that Chinese resentment against Europeans is largely a reaction to blatant white xenophobia and its political consequences. *La Bataille de Strasbourg* is thus one of the first future war stories to exemplify the notion that a worldwide military conflict was not merely feasible, thanks to the development of an embryonic global civilization courtesy of the concerted efforts of colonization and imperialism, but inevitable as a natural repercussion of such efforts.

Most subsequent images of the war in question—except, naturally, those that took aboard the notion of the "yellow peril"—imagined the global struggle as a conflict between imperial powers anxious to acquire a monopoly on the rewards of colonization, and only a minority envisaged new technologies of warfare playing key roles in such a conflict, but there were some notable examples of conflicts conceived in a broader context, including another British feuilleton published by Arthur Pearson, George Griffith's *The Angel of the Revolution*, which ran as a serial in *Pearson's Weekly* between January and October 1893 and was rapidly reprinted as a handsomely illustrated book. In Griffith's novel the heroes are a secret organization of self-proclaimed Terrorists who set out to use airships, submarines and new explosives invented by a young scientific genius to overthrow all the tyrannies in the world and establish world peace, along with liberty, equality and fraternity.

Both *The Angel of the Revolution* and *The Yellow Danger* became key works of the burgeoning British genre of scientific romance, their enormous success in serial form greatly assisting the more prestigious works of H. G. Wells to create

7

and popularize the idea of such a genre, and to persuade magazine proprietors and book publishers that it might have some commercial mileage. The idea of a similar genre was already being promoted in France by Louis Figuier, the editor of *La Science Illustrée*, who published a long series of feuilletons in the magazine under the rubric of *roman scientifique* [scientific fiction] between 1888 and 1900, which included reprints of three stories by Jules Lermina, thus tacitly crediting Lermina with being a pioneer of the genre, but the idea of the genre never caught on in France even to the limited extent that it did in England—and nothing like the extent, of course, to which it caught on in the U.S.A. in the 1920s, when pulp science fiction magazines achieved the kind of permanent market niche that yellow peril pulps conspicuously failed to achieve.

It is highly unlikely that George Griffith or M. P. Shiel ever read *La Bataille de Strasbourg*, but both considered themselves in 1892 to be devout socialists, and Griffith, at least, is likely to have been acquainted with some of the French Anarchists who sought refuge in London during the 1890s, when Paris became an unsafe place of residence for them. Those Anarchists would have been familiar with Lermina, who had long been active in their cause, and had been jailed for his propagandizing more than once. Indeed, writing popular feuilleton fiction had become a "refuge" for Lermina, much as exile in London was for comrades who did not have—as he did—a wife and daughters to support. It is not improbable that Griffith, a notorious borrower of other writers' ideas, knew about the serial version of *La Bataille de Strasbourg* when he was commissioned to write his own serial, and similarly possible that Shiel—who spent a lot of time in Paris—knew of its existence when he, too, decided that writing feuilleton fiction would be a useful way to battle his perennial financial difficulties.

If *La Bataille de Strasbourg* did play a slight inspirational role in the popularization of British scientific romance, it did so very obliquely. Whether it played any such role in the subsequent development of French futuristic fiction is equally difficult to determine, partly because its situation therein was curiously and rather enigmatically complicated.

One of the few locations in which Louis Figuier's rubric of *roman scientifique* was taken up was a periodical founded in obvious imitation of *La Science Illustrée*, the slightly more downmarket *La Science Française*, where it was similarly used on a series of feuilletons that did not last quite as long, and was somewhat narrower in focus. *La Science Française* was one of four magazines founded by L. Boulanger, the proprietor of *La Terre Illustrée*, in 1890-91. *La Terre Illustrée*, which was a "geographical magazine" imitative of the *Journal des Voyages et des Aventures sur Terre et sur Mer* was the third of the four, first appearing in November 1890, and *La Science Française* was the fourth, first appearing in March 1891. Boulanger entrusted the day-to-day editorship of the two magazines to the two editors who were already running the other two magazines he had recently founded, *La Revue Pour Tous* and *Le Monde de la Jeunesse*: respectively, Jules Lermina and Charles Simond.[1]

It was, perhaps, only natural that Boulanger should give the editorship of his popular science magazine to the editor of his children's magazine, as popular science magazines were regarded as didactic enterprises aimed primarily at the young, while appointing Lermina, a prolific *feuilletoniste* renowned for his imitations of the famous *feuilletonistes* of yore and the editor of his general interest magazine, as the supervisor of his magazine of travels and adventures, but it is not inconceivable that had the order of the last two periodicals' founding been reversed, Lermina might have been given the editorship of *La Science Française*, thus being specifically charged with the development of *roman scientifique*. There is no way of knowing what the relationship was between Charles Simond and

---

[1] The editorship of the latter magazine was subsequently taken over by Émile Gautier, another pioneer of French Anarchism who had followed Lermina's example by turning his hand of feuilleton fiction.

Lermina, although it might be significant that Simond never published anything by Lermina, and the "stables" of writers on which the two editors drew did not overlap.

Although Lermina did not write feuilletons for *La Revue Pour Tous*, contenting himself with routine editorial duties, he decided to supply *La Terre Illustrée* with serial fiction himself, at least to begin with—which, as a prolific and versatile *feuilletoniste*, he was well-equipped to do—and he probably welcomed the opportunity for a measure of self-indulgence that other editors did not routinely grant him. Three serials that ran simultaneously in the early issues of the magazine, all of which posed as the sorts of stories expected of a magazine of that sort, but all of which had idiosyncratic features, were his own work.

"Au Pays de Stanley: voyage dans l'Afrique équatoriale" [In Stanley Country: A Journey in Equatorial Africa], written under the pseudonym Dr. Julius Lumley (Lermina, all of whose work during the first few years of his career had been pseudonymous, had a particular fondness for English-sounding names), was published in thirty episodes from 8 November 1890 to 30 May 1891 and reprinted, under the same pseudonym, as *Voyage au pays de Stanley* in 1895. It includes an imaginative component that introduced an extra measure of exoticism into the African adventure.

"Le Mousse de l'amiral Courbet: campagne de l'Indo-Chine—Fou-Tcheou et Formose," [Admiral Courbet's Cabin-Boy: the Indo-China Campaign, Fou-Tcheou and Formosa] ran for twenty-six episodes from 8 November 1890 to 2 May 1891, and was reprinted in 1895 as *Le Mousse de l'amiral Courbet: récit dramatique, désopilant et pourtant véridique* [the subtitle translates as "A Dramatic and Hilarious but Nevertheless True story]. It is unusual both in its humor and its epistolary form, pretending—not very convincingly—to be a non-fictional account of events in the Sino-French War of 1884-85 as seen from the viewpoint of an innocent naval recruit.

"Les Drames de Constantinople" [The Dramas of Constantinople], signed Wohji-Aga, which ran from 15 November 1890 to 6 June 1891, and was also reprinted in 1895, under the signature Voghi-Aga, was an abridgment of an earlier work by Lermina that had appeared as a serial in *Le Peuple* in 1876 under the pseudonym Rutchli-Bey, that version having been allegedly translated from Turkish by "William Cobb"—the most frequently-employed of Lermina's pseudonyms—and ostensibly offering an insider's account of the improbable dramas in question.

La Bataille de Strasbourg overlapped all three of the earlier serials slightly and was itself overlapped very slightly by the much more orthodox "Terres des glaces et terres de feu: grand récit inédit de voyages et d'aventures" [Lands of Ice and Lands of Fire: A Great Unpublished Story of Voyages and Adventures] which ran from issue 66 to 109 (4 February to 1 December 1892). The latter was Lermina's final serial for the magazine, in which he also published nine short stories in 1890-91. He presumably ceased to edit the magazine some time during this period, as he never appeared in it again before it was bought by its competitor and combined with the *Journal de Voyages* in 1894. Boulanger continued reprinting material by Lermina for several years, and does not appear to have fallen out with him completely, but there does seem to have been a marked deterioration in the relationship. Whether or not that had anything to do with *Le Bataille de Strasbourg*, it is impossible to determine, but it might be significant that the work as published is very obviously not the work as it was originally planned, and that it gives every appearance of having been abruptly and drastically curtailed.

Although Lermina was recruited to the genre of *roman scientifique* by Louis Figuier in the pages of *La Science Illustrée*, he never published anything in *La Science Française*, even though it was owned by his own publisher. Almost all the fiction published in the latter magazine was supplied by two writers: Georges Espitallier, initially under the pseudonym Pierre Ferréol and subsequently as Claude

Manceau and G. Bethuys, and "Capitaine Danrit" (Émile Driant), and—in striking contrast to the fiction Figuier featured in *La Science Illustrée*—it was mostly future war fiction. "La Prise de Londres au XXe siècle" [The Capture of London in the Twentieth Century], signed Pierre Ferréol, ran there from March-December 1891, beginning a few weeks before Lermina's serial began; *Le Bataille de Strasbourg* might well have seemed to Charles Simond to be an imitation, or even a parody, especially given the fact that future war fiction seemed as conspicuously out of place in a magazine of travel and adventure as it must have seemed to some people to be in a popular science magazine.[2]

If Lermina was prompted to write his own future war story by Espitallier's serial in *La Science Française*, the other writer who subsequently contributed a long future war story to the latter magazine, "Captain Danrit," might have thought that both of them had taken some inspiration from him, and he certainly appropriated material from both of them. Danrit's *Science Française* serial was the fourth of four parts of an exceedingly long narrative eventually published in book form in eight volumes as *La Guerre de demain* [Tomorrow's War], the first volume of which had appeared in 1889. The particular war in question was between France and Germany, although it expanded over a larger stage than the two native territories. Danrit followed it up with the four-volume *L'Invasion noire* [The Black Invasion] (1895-96), the three volume *La Guerre Fatale—France-Angleterre* [The Fatal War: France/England] (1901-02) and the three-volume *L'Invasion jaune* [The Yellow

---

[2] The Ferréol story might have attracted Lermina's attention because the latter had previously published a story entitled "Ferréol"—one of his series of "*histoires incroyables*" in *Le Gaulois* in 1887 and might have thought that Espitallier had borrowed the pseudonym therefrom. Espitallier later mentioned in an interview, however, that it was the forename of one of his oldest friends.

Invasion] (1905-1906), the last two of which picked up the central themes of *La Prise de Londres* and *La Bataille de Strasbourg*.[3]

In fact, the references to the twentieth century in the titles attributed to both the Ferréol and Lermina serials imply that both of them were probably consciously following in Robida's footsteps, albeit in a more earnest vein. Another significant predecessor had appeared between the two versions of Robida's story in *La Guerre finale: Histoire fantastique* [The Final War: A Fantastic Story] (1885), issued under the by-line Barillet-Largargousse (*barillet* can mean gun-barrel, and a *gargousse* is a kind of cartridge), although that was closer in spirit to the ironic pacifism of Robida than to the earnest intensity of the fervently jingoistic and seemingly bloodthirsty Driant, who was a career military man.

Whatever the relationship was between Lermina and Charles Simond, it can be assumed that Lermina disapproved strongly of Espitallier and Driant, both of whom were at the opposite end of the political spectrum from his own Anarchist sympathies, and were not shy about showing it. It is not entirely clear where Lermina and Simond's employer stood but it might be worth observing that the first "Capitaine Danrit" novel had been advertised in 1887 as the work of the son-in-law of General Boulanger, whose meteoric political career briefly posed a threat to the stability of the Republic in 1888 before he fled the threat of arrest to England, where he committed suicide in 1891. Whether L. Boulanger was related to the general, and hence to Driant, it is difficult to tell—Jean-Luc Buard, who investigated his publishing activities for an article in *Rocambole* was not even able to discover his first name—but it is not inconceivable that the detail has some relevance to the curtailment of *La Bataille de Strasbourg*.

---

[3] More information about Captain Danrit can be found in the Black Coat Press' edition of *Undersea Odyssey*, ISBN 9781935558811.

The most glaring evidence that *La Bataille de Strasbourg* was initially intended to be much longer and more complex than it ultimately turned out to be is its title. Clearly, Lermina started the serial with the idea that the Battle of Strasbourg was to provide its climax, and the ultimate confrontation of the Oriental invaders and the defenders of France. In fact, no such battle occurs within the text, although the coda makes token mention of one, and the climax of the truncated story is provided by a blatant *deus ex machina*. The prologue and the first significant episode of the story set up a whole cast of characters, including a group of four in Paris and a larger group in Peking, with the obvious intention of tracking their stories individually in a multi-stranded plot of the kind pioneered in the heroic early days of feuilleton fiction by Eugène Sue. In the event, however, only two strands are actually developed, and those only partially. When they are eventually reconnected, rather crudely, to make way for a third, a huge chunk is missing out of one of them, and the subsidiary branches carefully established in the scenes set in Peking have been almost completely eliminated.

Had the logic of the narrative been followed scrupulously, *La Bataille de Strasbourg* would have been a much longer story, at least three times as long as the existing text, and perhaps as long as the thousand-plus pages of Danrit's *Guerre de demain*. Feuilleton fiction was essentially elastic, popular serials being spun out vastly by any means possible, and Lermina would have been prepared to go on for as long as necessary. By the same token, of course, serials that proved unpopular were always likely to get the chop, sometimes being required to wind up very rapidly, and it might have been the case that what happened to *La Bataille de Strasbourg* was simply a matter of responding to negative reader reaction. Then again, Lermina—who was attempting something radically new in more ways than one—might simply have discovered when he got stuck in his task that he had bitten off more than he could chew, and decided on his own accord to discontinue the narrative, cutting off most of his plot-threads and leaving many of his characters choking on their loose ends. There is, in consequence, no compelling evidence to suggest that his abrupt decision to abandon intimate storyline, retreat to a much greater narrative distance, and concoct a grotesque conclusion located hundreds of miles from Strasbourg, was the result of a stern command from L. Boulanger that led to his resignation from the editorship of the magazine, but one cannot help wondering...

At any rate, *La Bataille de Strasbourg* is undoubtedly a spoiled work, although it is significant that its eventual spoliation did not prevent it from being reprinted in *Le Matin*, where it must have reached a much vaster audience than it had in *La Terre Illustrée* or the Boulanger book edition, and where it must have seemed something of a novelty, immersive futuristic fiction not having been previously tried out there. The decision to reprint it in *Le Matin* was undoubtedly prompted by the so-called Boxer Rebellion, which reached its violent climax while the story was being serialized, the Legation Quarter of Peking having been attacked and besieged in June 1900. The actual siege lasted 55 days, considerably longer than the siege described in the story and slightly longer than the serialization of the novel, but the coincidence did give the reprint a bizarre topicality and lent its early chapters—but not the later ones—a vague implication of prophecy.

The eventual spoliation should not, in any case, prevent the story from being recognized as a significant pioneering work, not so much for its contribution to the myth of the yellow peril, which is one of the most despicable follies of the imaginative fiction of the period, but for its recognition of the difference that technological advancement and the globalization of politics might well make to twentieth-century warfare. It is difficult now to appreciate how much imagination that required in 1891, when very few people had yet arrived at that realization, and Lermina deserves credit for it in spite of the fact that his anticipatory efforts are tentative in some respects and ludicrous in others. Because he was writing before the development of wireless telegraphy and aviation, his images of future communication devices and heavier-than-air flight now seem to hover between the primitive and the bizarre, but his notions are not without a certain speculative flair.

It is equally difficult now to realize how awkward it seemed in 1891 to write novels set in the future which simple adopted a viewpoint further forward in time, without any elaborate explanation and without any apology at all. No one in England or America had yet done that, or would for another decade, and Lermina surely played some part, along with a handful of other pioneers, in enabling that narrative convention to take comfortable root in French fiction some time before it was able to do so in English-language fiction. In this respect, as in the particular technological innovations he envisages, Lermina's work now seems more than a trifle crude, because we have come a very long way in the interim, in terms of both the technological imagination and literary technique, but he was groping optimistically in the dark and can be forgiven a modicum of clumsiness. For all its faults, *La Bataille de Strasbourg* is a remarkable work, and its curtailment—whatever the reason for it might have been—is surely regrettable.

This translation was made from the version of the 1895 Boulanger edition reproduced on the Bibliothèque Nationale's *gallica* website.

Brian Stableford

16

PART ONE
THE STANDARD OF
THE FIVE HUNDRED GODS

I

On 5 February 19** there was great excitement in Paris. The Societé de Géographie was holding an extraordinary general meeting of its members at midday in the great amphitheater of the Sorbonne, to which all the illustrious individuals representing the new movement of the twentieth century had been invited.

Everyone knows that since the Treaty of Paris had restored the beloved lost provinces to France, and the fall of the German Empire had substituted the Germanic Confederation for the Hohenzollern autocracy, our fatherland, liberated from the burdens and anguish that had forced it to maintain excessive armaments for so long, had been able to devote all of its vital energy to intellectual studies, and merited more than ever the title of the World's Brain.[4]

In all branches of human knowledge, France had resumed its leading role; its literature, freed from the excess of a forgotten naturalism, was the most perfect expression of the ideas of the present and the hopes of the future. With no more internal shocks, Parliament was able to devote itself entirely to the reform of the Law and the great social questions on which

---

[4] Lermina could not know, of course, that there really would be a Great War prior to the 1920s, when his story is set, which would end in a German defeat, thus terminating the Hohenzollern Empire, and that one of its results would be the return of Alsace and Lorraine to France under the Treaty of Versailles, following a crucial French military takeover of the region that concluded with the occupation of Strasbourg.

universal wellbeing depends. The ordering of financial affairs, the momentum acquired by industrial enterprises and the renovation of our agronomic systems ensured the country a prosperity that nothing seemed able to compromise.

Great interest was, therefore, taken in new discoveries, especially when, as had been recently announced by the entire press, it was a matter of an application of electricity that might be even more marvelous than the telegraph and the telephone.

The invention that had impassioned all curiosity, the experimental demonstration of which was awaited with a quasi-feverish impatience, presented the very particular character that it was due, not to a conventional scientist, a qualified academician or a graduate of the École Polytechnique, but—unbelievably—to a simple poet...my God, yes!

Guy de Norès, who was not yet thirty, had revealed himself to the literary world in a little volume rather disdainfully welcomed at first, *Rêves vrais*, copies of which remained sadly stacked up on the publisher's shelves. Then, one day, a critic, the most respected and, to tell the truth, the least benevolent of the era, had devoted a two-column article to it, concluding thus:

Guy de Norès is better than a poet, better than a writer; he is a seer whose genius, engaging the unknown in hand-to-hand combat, has forced it to deliver its secret to us. In these few pages there is more real science than in the heaviest quarto volumes of our official doctors. This little book contains the scientific gospel of the twentieth century.

It was realized then, Panurge's sheep being eternal, that we were in the presence of one of the most original individuals, that the sculptor of rhymes was also a mathematician of the first rank, and that each of his short poems provided a hypothetical but possible solution to one of the great scientific problems.

Indifference had been succeeded by the most passionate infatuation; journalists had seized upon him as on a prey, his life had been searched in the hope of discovering alluring mysteries, but with great disappointment. Guy was a simple individual, working fifteen hours a day, going without pause from his study to his laboratory, simultaneously a chemist and a man of imagination, speaking all known languages, systematically deprived of all diplomas and refusing all distinctions. He was sincerely modest, patient and courageous, and above all, patriotic through and through, dreaming of giving his country the most beautiful of all glories, that which attaches to human conquests of nature.

For three years he had published very little: one semi-philosophical and semi-social novel, based on the influence of wellbeing on civilization and had enjoyed a *succès d'estime*. With the versatility that characterized the great city of Paris then as of old, people had begun to forget him; his friends, or those who claimed to be such, declared in hushed voices that he was finished—burned out, to use a popular nineteenth-century expression—when the announcement suddenly appeared in all the newspapers of the meeting organized by the Societé de Géographie, in which Guy de Norès would demonstrate the possibility of seeing, as clearly as in a mirror, what was happening a hundred, two hundred or a thousand leagues from Paris.

Curiously enough, the sympathy previously inspired by Guy, which had become somewhat dormant, reawakened with more force than ever; it must be said that the renown of the society that was sponsoring him, the indiscretion of reporters and anticipatory descriptions of the discovered methods, albeit vague, contributed to giving the promised experiment the most serious character.

Finally, to reveal all, what had perhaps contributed more than anything else to the universal benevolence was a sentimental story that had spread surreptitiously and which, given feminine sensibility, had in his favor disposed the weaker sex, both ladies and demoiselles alike.

This is it: Guy, having not yet made a fortune, was in love with a young woman whose name was not pronounced but who belonged, apparently, to one of the most highly-placed families in the scientific world. The father, it was said, had placed the condition on his consent that Norès must realize at least one of the items of progress of which he had made himself the apostle—but until then, he must remain separate from the woman he loved...doubly separated, since she was traveling with her father in the Far East.

People take an interest in these tender matters, and everyone wanted the young man to succeed. Generous hearts felt anxious. So, when Admiral Trécourt, who was presiding over the numerous assembly—nearly two thousand strong—that was crowded onto the benches of the Sorbonne's amphitheater, announced that Guy de Norès was about to commence the advertised lecture, a murmur of sympathetic curiosity ran around the hall.

"Mesdames et Messieurs," the Admiral added, "before handing the floor to our young colleague, may I be permitted to say one thing more: what is about to pass before your eyes will appear so strange, and so improbable, that some of you will be tempted to doubt the reality of the phenomena that you will witness. My presence, and that of several of my colleagues in the Académie des Sciences, is a guarantee that these experiments are not based on any subterfuge. We have only authorized these experiments—which I would call marvelous, if you were not all aware that miracles are not of this world—after having acquired the certainty of their astonishing perfection. You can, in total security of conscience, applaud the man that we are happy to call our friend...and, I will say, our master."

One can imagine the effect produced by this little speech, which the Admiral had made in an emotional voice. So, when the man whom the most illustrious were already calling a master advanced to the podium, there was such an explosion of curiosity throughout the auditorium that, within the blink of an eye, everyone was standing on the benches.

Guy de Norès appeared to be about thirty. Tall and very thin, he walked with a slight stoop, as if his head that seemed at first glance to be enormous were too heavy for his shoulders. His thick black hair surmounted a broad forehead of unusual amplitude. His eyes were large and wide open, his gaze escaping like a gleam. His nose was prominent, his mouth wide and his lips as red as those of a child. That ensemble, however, revealed such a vitality, such an exuberance of thought, and such a masculine energy, that a murmur of admiration passed through the room.

He had straightened up now, and after a slight bow, devoid of embarrassment or arrogance, he started speaking with a voice that was slightly muffled at first but gradually became clearer—magnified, so to speak—in a tone that was both sonorous and soft, whose harmony was an additional seduction.

With a few very sober words, in excellent taste, he thanked the admiral for the exceedingly benevolent words that had introduced him and applied the term of master, which he did not accept, judging himself only too glad to be welcome as a pupil of great French scientists.

"Permit me, however," he continued, "not to say any more about that; if you have been kind enough to respond to the appeal of the Society whose hospitality is for me an honor of which I am proud, you are all impatient to know whether it really has been given to me to lift a corner of the veil that nature extends so jealously over her secrets, and I ought not to delay any longer before satisfying your legitimate curiosity."

At the front of the stage was a table covered with a large sheet. At a signal from the speaker, and assistant lifted it up, and an instrument then became plainly visible whose form was strongly reminiscent of a star. The central point was constituted by a large copper ball, and the radii consisted of copper wires fixed to the copper ball at one end while the other was attached to a nickel circle forming an exterior circumference, fitted with as many buttons as there were wires.

"These wires," said Guy, "are in communication with the various telegraphic systems that put Paris in communication with the entire world. By putting pressure on this copper handle, I can open or close at will a current communicating with one of those wires, and, in consequence, with the telegraph wire of which it constitutes the first link."

21

Then he picked up a mirror, the foot of which he screwed into the copper ball.

"You have before your eyes, Messieurs, my entire apparatus, with the exception of the dry piles producing electricity, which are installed in the basement of the auditorium. Finally, I call you attention to the frame that you see suspended on the wall to the right of the hall, which, I declare to you immediately, is simply fitted with a screen designed to receive, in magnified form, the images that will shortly be produced in the central mirror."

These explanations, clearly given in a distinct voice, aroused increased attention. Not the slightest sound could be heard; everyone was waiting.

"Messieurs," the young scientist continued, "in the book that you might perhaps have forgotten, but which constituted the first phase of my research, I posed this problem. Already, thanks to electricity, human speech passes from one end of the earth to the other, either via the telegraph or the telephone, whose systems radiate throughout the whole world. In a few more years, it will be possible to converse from this very spot with the people of all the nations of Europe, Asia, America and Africa. You know that cables are being laid at present between Australia and the American continent, closing the circle enveloping the entire globe. Electricity has given you light and, thanks to the central beacon of the Hôtel de Ville, the magnificent apparatus that is the finest entitlement to glory of our great Sametel..."

As he pronounced that name, it seemed that the young man's voice suddenly weakened slightly; there was a slight interruption of which people took advantage to applaud the name of the man who had been nicknamed, in memory of the famous American, the French Edison.

Guy continued: "Electricity has given us heat, and, last winter, which was unfortunately too rigorous, the immense heater in Les Halles, suppressed suffering and misery, so to speak.

"Has electricity, then, said its last word, and must we renounce any further demand on that benefactor? Perhaps, if we had to rely solely on its power—but it is possible to provide it with an ally, to combine its energy with energies even more powerful than its own, and we can hope realistically to constrain it to produce new miracles. That is what I have attempted, Messieurs, and I can say without boasting, because the results are to hand, that I have succeeded...

"That idea is, as you have guessed, the magnetic force of the terrestrial globe, the seemingly so mysterious influence to which, for many centuries, the compass has owed its observed, but always unexplained, action.

"I shall content myself with that indication, the technical details of which will be set out in the brochure that will be handed to you at the end of the session.

"Having said that, permit me to draw your attention briefly to a fact whose first revelation was made in the final quarter of the last century, but which was not accorded the attention it merited.

"You are all familiar with selenium, the metalloid of the sulfur family whose electric conductivity, as Willoughby Smith discovered fifty years ago,[5] varies in accordance with the intensity of luminous radiation. That metalloid, which is produced by treating the mineral known as zorgite[6] with hydrochloric acid, could not be obtained in considerable quanti-

---

[5] Willoughby Smith published his paper on "The Effect of Light on Selenium during the passage of an Electric Current" in the 20 February 1873 issue of *Nature*, so this statement implies that the story is set in 1923, or perhaps, if "fifty" is assumed to be approximate, a year or two either side of that date. Given that Lermina deliberately plants this indicator and another a few lines thereafter, it is not obvious why asterisks are used in the dates specifically cited at the beginning of this story; I do not know whether the same convention had been used in the serial version.

[6] Copper-lead selenite.

ties until the recent discovery of zorgite mines in the United States of South America.

"Selenium is modified under the combined action of electricity and light, in proportion to the intensity of the current and the radiation that affect it. In addition, submitted to the action of terrestrial magnetism, which acts in its regard like photographic fixing agents, selenium retains the imprint of images that are communicated to it by the double influence of electricity and light, the former being, in a sense, the vehicle of the latter."

The orator then entered into a few considerations to which the audience listened with the greatest interest, which he summarized as follows:

"So, Messieurs, if you have understood me fully—or, rather, if I have been fortunate enough to explain myself clearly—this is the sequence of events that you are about to witness: at the initial point of the telegraphic lines whose network terminates here beneath my hand, a *camera lucida*, set up at a point where a part of the city is reflected on a screen, with its life and movement, is put in communication with the electric wire, which transports the fluid influenced by the light, in its various degrees of intensity; that fluid strikes the selenium mirror that you see here, fitted to the copper button, which itself contains a magneto-electric apparatus; and on that mirror will be depicted, in all their clarity, the scenes that are passing on to the screen of the *camera lucida* situated fifty or a hundred leagues away...and even further, as you will see shortly...

"These images will be reflected, thanks to an optical apparatus of the greatest simplicity, onto the framed screen that you see fixed to the wall, with the result being that in a moment, while being in Paris, you will see—see in their absolute, positive, living sincerity—the scenes that are unfolding at this moment in the capitals of Europe and...elsewhere."

Guy interrupted himself in order to drink a few sips of water. Everyone took advantage of that moment of silence to manifest their sentiments, and it must be admitted that they were not unanimously favorable to the orator.

"It's incredible!" said some.

"Impossible!" said others.

A peevish professor, who had never invented anything and declared himself incredulous in advance of all progress, even exclaimed: "This is charlatanism!"

Guy de Norès was still smiling, waiting for calm to be restored.

The president rang his hand-bell. "Mesdames et Messieurs," he said, not without irony, "those who speak of impossibility are in error; those who speak of charlatanism are committing an impertinence. But Norès will not take exception, sure as he is of his imminent triumph."

By virtue of one of the habitual mood changes of crowds, there was wild applause.

"Continue, Monsieur de Norès," said the Admiral.

The young man took out his watch. "It is one o'clock, Messieurs. From one end of Europe to the other, the difference in the actual time is more than two hours. In round numbers, it is one o'clock in London and two o'clock in Vienna, two-thirty in Constantinople and three o'clock in St. Petersburg, noon in Madrid and two o'clock in Stockholm and Rome. I'm reminding you of these facts in order that you will be able to explain the differences that you will observe in the atmospheric light of the various countries that will appear before our eyes. If you will permit, we shall commence with our neighbor on the far side of the Channel, whose Parliament finally voted two days ago for the construction of a tunnel that will link the French and English coasts—to London, then!"

He raised his hand and rang a bell; the room was plunged into darkness.

"Keep your eyes fixed on the selenium mirror to begin with," said Guy. "Then look at the screen."

After a few seconds, the surface of the mirror was seen to brighten with a singular blue-tinted light, which gradually turned red, while all beams of light seemed to spring forth from all its parts with such an intense vivacity that the eyes turned away to look at the screen on the wall.

A cry of surprise emerged from all throats.

On the white space, which measured about four square meters, the square of the Stock Exchange appeared, with its stupefying tumult of vehicles and its swarming crowds of people. The production was so bright, so clear and so vivid, the faces, the forms and the movements so perfectly rendered in their activity, that it was the very life of the enormous city that was before their eyes.

There was no more applause, so intense was the attention.

Two Englishmen, in a tangle of vehicles, picked a quarrel and hurled themselves at one another, fists raised; one of them, struck in the face, fell under the wheels of a cab. There was a cry of terror in the hall, but a policeman had leapt forward and had pulled the man away by the arm. The latter, now furious with his savior, belabored him with his fists...

It was not cold and dead photographic projection, but the absolute transportation of life itself.

"Now, Messieurs," said the clear voice of the demonstrator, I am putting the apparatus in communication with the telephone. Listen."

That was something else entirely: over that vast audience, transcending all encumbrances, an immense river of English voices now flowed. The reality of the scene took on fantastic proportions. The flood went on and on, with its own sound, making of a synthesis of all sounds. Sometimes, words stood out, including the cries of coachmen: "Keep left!" and other appeals: "Come here, boy!"

The effect was amazing.

"Now to Saint Petersburg," said Guy.

The English scene disappeared; the selenium mirror seemed to fade out. Then there was the click of a switch, and on the screen, the Nevsky Prospekt extended bleakly, covered with snow, with the occasional sleigh drawn by Ukrainian ponies, and muzjiks disappearing beneath their sheepskins, dragging themselves along, numb with cold.

"Twenty-nine degrees Réaumur,"[7] said Guy. "The Russians are at home around their enormous stoves."

All hands clapped: there was an enthusiasm tending toward delirium. Was it not a true miracle?

No criticism was possible; the solution had been found of the most curious problem that scientists had yet posed—and to what applications might such a discovery lead!

"To Vienna," said de Norès.

And it was the Prater that appeared. Then to Madrid, the Puerta del Sol with its swarm of idlers. An exceedingly pretty Spanish woman, with her head covered by a mantilla and her hair boldly curled, was swinging her hips as she went along, which earned a well-deserved applause. Then there was a silence. But as old Zorrilla,[8] the founder of the Iberian Republic, almost a nonagenarian, was passing in a carriage, the telephone reproduced the cheers that greeted him.

The scene disappeared. Then the lights in the hall were switched on again.

Guy was in his place, only slightly pale.

No man ever received such a vibrant ovation. The Admiral had come down from the stage and, taking the young man in his arms, embraced him effusively. More than ten minutes passed before calm could be reestablished; curious individuals had even leapt over the balustrades in order to examine the apparatus at closer range; it was extremely difficult to get them to resume their seats.

Finally, Guy began speaking again. "Messieurs," he said, "I can't tell you how touched I am by your expressions of

---

[7] This must be a mistake; it seems improbable that the author means minus 29°, so it is more likely that he means to indicate the Fahrenheit scale, on which 29 is three degrees below freezing.

[8] Manuel Ruiz Zorrilla (1833-1895) was twice Spanish prime minister, albeit briefly, in 1871-3, but failed to establish the Republic of which he dreamed; he would have turned 90 in 1923 had he lived.

sympathy; in my work I have done my duty as a Frenchman, and you are rewarding me beyond my merits..."

"No, no! Bravo! Vive Guy de Norès!"

"I hope to live long enough," he said, smiling, "to do better still. But permit me to show you one more experiment. Thus far, you have not left Europe. I want to take you further: to Peking."

There was an explosion of joyous laughter—not because there was any doubt now, but because the idea seemed particularly amusing to be a few steps from the Luxembourg and yet see what was happening in China, eight thousand kilometers from the towers of Notre-Dame.

A lady leaned toward her neighbor's ear. "His master Sametel is in Peking...and it's Sametel's daughter with whom he's in love...I hope he sees her..."

And as the whisper ran through the feminine ranks, more than one heart began to beat faster, perhaps with a little jealousy. Guy could have placed his affections much closer to home...

Meanwhile, the young man, having ordered darkness again, resumed speaking—although it was observable that his voice was trembling slightly.

"Messieurs," he said, "at this moment it is nine o'clock in the evening in Peking—which is to say that our apparatus is functioning by night. But I know that today, the fifth of February, is when the Chinese are celebrating their festival of the New Year, the first day of the month Li-Chun in their calendar.[9] The Chinese are masters in matters of illumination, and they must have produced a light akin to that of midday, inasmuch as"—he lowered his voice—"the great electrician Sametel will have deployed for the occasion all the resources of electric light. The apparatus is directed at the French Legation, where our compatriots ought to have assembled in order to enjoy the magical sight of the Celestial festival."

---

[9] The movable feast of the Chinese New Year fell on 16 February in 1923, but it fell on 5 February in 1924.

He fell silent. The effluvia, blue-tinted and then red and sparkling, emerged from the selenium mirror, and the screen brightened. A general acclamation greeted the scene that unfolded.

On the terrace of a pavilion, bathed in floods of electric light, there was an elegant crowd, very French, of ladies and young women, naval officers and young men in evening dress. In one corner, two young women, next to whom a Russian officer was standing, were chatting animatedly.

"The telephone! The telephone!" cried all the voices.

The young man seemed to hesitate.

The lady who was so well-informed said to her confidante: "You see those two young women. The blonde is Sacha Batowna, the daughter of Prince Batow, and the Russian officer, the military attaché Sandorf Wintscheff, is her fiancé. The other, the brunette, is Marguerite Sametel, the object of our great Norès' adoration..."

At that moment, not daring to resist the general will, Guy put his apparatus in connection with the telephone, and in the midst of the conversations of the guests of our ambassador in Peking, the voice of the Russian officer could be distinctly heard, saying to the young blonde: "I tell you that our dear Guy will succeed, and that I shall be a witness at your wedding..."

All the ladies, who were in the know, applauded.

At the same instant, however, an enormous, monstrous clamor sprang forth from the bright screen, mingled with cries of terror. All the women were fleeing in tumult. Sandorf had placed himself in front of the two young women, as if to defend them...and at the base of the terrace a hideous spectacle appeared: a whirlwind of people, shouting and running, while one of the wretches was carrying at the end of a blood-stained pike, suspended like an infamous trophy, the corpse of an old man, whose wrists were bound to his ankles by cords.

And the multitude of murders shouted: "Death to the foreigners! Death to the devils from overseas!"

Very few people in the auditorium of the Sorbonne understood the words proffered in Chinese, but they all divined the terrible meaning of that scene of horror.

The Chinese crowd rushed to assault the pavilion. Sandorf was seen to fire his revolver at the assailants. Then everything disappeared.

And in the hall, Guy de Norès, haggard, his fists clenched, shouted like a madman: "Help! Help! Marguerite...here I am...!"

And before anyone could stop him, he hurled himself at the wall, as if he wanted to pierce it in order to go to the rescue of the woman he loved.

The impact was so violent that he fell back, unconscious, into the arms of those surrounding him.

The Admiral shouted: "The wire to Peking has been cut. Oh, our poor Frenchmen! It's a massacre!"

Emotion was at its height. As the young man had collapsed into the surrounding arms, two screams had been heard, and two women, standing up abruptly in the first row of the assembly, had run toward him, cleaving through the crowd.

One of them, with a crown of hair as white as snow, dressed in the mourning that widows wear after the death of their husbands, was Norès' mother; the other, an adorable young blonde woman, was his sister.

Fraying a passage, they arrived beside him, and the mother, taking her son's head, set it on her knees, while Marie de Norès placed a bottle of smelling salts beneath his nostrils.

"We need to take him to the library," said a voice. "He needs air."

Vigorous arms grabbed the young man, and a few moments later, he was lying on a sofa, with the two women kneeling beside him, watching for signs of life.

A physician, Dr. Sabirat, who happened to be in the hall, administered his expertise.

In the crowd pressing at the door, comments flew back and forth.

In truth, they were still having difficulty believing that the scene they had just seen unfolding before their eyes belonged to the domain of reality. The effect was nevertheless prodigious, as the individuals evoked on the screen had all the appearances of life. It will be remembered, however, that it was a matter of events happening at that very moment at an enormous distance, beyond the deserts of Asia, beyond the sea, and they were wondering whether they might have been the victims of some astonishing trick.

Admiral Trécourt, however, imposed silence on the incredulous. "Once again, Messieurs, I remind you that I have given you my word—which is that of an honest man and a soldier, which I cannot suppose that you can doubt—that you have witnessed scenes that are, alas, only too real. At this very moment, the greatest danger is threatening our compatriots in the Chinese capital. I wish to God that it was only an illusion, but science does not lie..."

"My son is coming round!" cried Madame de Norès. "My child, my love!" she added, embracing him feverishly.

Indeed, Guy opened his eyes.

First of all he looked around haggardly, unable to remember where he was.

"Mother? Sister? What's happening?"

As he fell silent, in the fear of waking up too soon to dolorous memories, he suddenly put his hands over his face. Then he straightened up.

"Marguerite! Help! They're killing her, murdering her! Didn't you see? We have to run, make haste..."

He stopped abruptly. Then, with a burst of heart-rending laughter, he said: "Two thousand leagues away! Oh, accursed science...you've only revealed that catastrophe to me...are you impotent, then, to do anything about it?" He had drawn his mother and his sister toward him. "You, my dears, understand how I'm suffering..."

"Courage, Brother," said Marie.

"Yes, yes, you're right...a man doesn't have the right to despair while strength and life remain to him." He saw the

Admiral, and extended his hand to him. "Who would have supposed that my first experiment would bring me such pain? For you saw, as I did—didn't you?—that furious mob rushing toward the French ambassador, threatening the lives of all those we love. You don't doubt it?"

"No, unfortunately," said Trécourt. "Terrible events are occurring out there...but as you say, what can we do to prevent them?"

The young woman leaned in close to her brother's ear and whispered a few words to him.

Guy shook his head. "A very feeble hope," he murmured. "All things considered, though, I don't have the right to abandon it." He turned to the Admiral. "Can I count on your benevolence, Master?"

"Don't you know that I'm entirely at your disposal?"

"Well then, listen." He drew him to one side. "I've succeeded," he said, "in bringing scenes unfolding thousand of leagues from here before our eyes, but the distance is only apparently suppressed. I've attempted more, attacking a problem that's perhaps more astonishing still. Thus far, I haven't succeeded completely, but who can tell whether, at this critical moment, I might be able to find the desired solutions? I'm going to my laboratory; then, in a supreme adjuration, I'll ask the sphinx to yield me its secret. In the meantime, I beg you, send word to the Chinese Legation and the Russian embassy...to enquire...perhaps news has already reached Paris that might enlighten us in regard to this horrible tragedy...and, as quickly as possible, pass on the information that you've gathered to me."

"I'll make enquiries personally," said the Admiral, "and don't worry; I won't leave you without news for long. Go and work coolly. Remember that we have two battalions of marines in Peking, in the embassy itself. They're vigorous soldiers, and—who can tell?—but for that interruption of the telegraph wires, perhaps we'd have seen those wretched hordes driven back and chastised. Have courage, then...and confidence!"

The young man shook his head. In spite of those hopeful words, an atrocious vice was gripping his heart. That was because he loved Marguerite Sametel profoundly, with a love unique in his life. Before she had left for Asia with her father, the great physicist who had set forth to enable modern progress to penetrate the remotest corners of Asia, the two young people had exchanged the kind of vows that bind people together for life.

In truth, Sametel had not erected any serious obstacle to that affection; he professed for Norès the most sincere esteem and amity, and if he had demanded a delay before the two young people could marry, he had done so primarily because it would be too painful for him to be separated from his daughter.

That mission to China, to organize the entire telegraphic and telephonic network in the Middle Kingdom, was the last that he intended to accept. His formal plan was, as soon as he returned, to grant the wishes of the two fiancés and warm up his old age at the hearth of their happy youth.

Why must people always delay their own happiness and that of others?

"It's necessary to avoid the indiscreet crowd," the Admiral said to Norès. "Follow me. I'll get you out, along with your mother and sister, though the back door. That way, you'll be able to get home more rapidly."

"Do you feel better?" Dr. Sabirat asked.

"Oh, you're here, my dear friend," Guy said. "Excuse me for not having noticed you sooner...yes, I do feel better."

"Don't you think, Brother, that it would be best for Monsieur Sabirat to accompany us home?"

The physician and the young woman had exchanged glances. Norès had seen that, and smiled in spite of his anguish.

"Sabirat is always welcome in our house, if he wants to come. Besides which, I might have need of his advice."

A few minutes later the four friends left the building behind in the Admiral's spacious carriage, which he had put at their disposal."

Not a word was pronounced during the journey. Guy was meditating profoundly. Marie had reminded him at the opportune moment of the boldest project of which he had yet dreamed.

For more than two years, he had been studying a motor whose power, adapted to locomotion, would, so to speak, abolish distance, by means of a rapidity of transit that would put railway engines, and even dirigible balloons, in the shade. Its employment was on the brink of practicality thanks to discoveries realized at the Institut Aérostatique de Chalais.[10]

Marie, who had a serious mind endowed with remarkable scientific faculties almost equal to her brother's, had followed those endeavors at close range, and his success seemed certain to her.

A hundred leagues an hour!

Such a dream had never been realized.

Guy de Norès' workshop was in a large building behind the École Militaire.

A vast courtyard was attached to be buildings, and it was there that Guy completely recovered his self-mastery half an hour after leaving to Societé de Géographie.

The emotion felt by Madame de Norès, whose health was very delicate, obliged her to retire to her apartment. Norès was left alone with Sabirat and his sister.

The two young men were linked by a sincere amity, having worked together in academia, but to the same extent that Guy was audacious, enthusiastic and impulsive, the young physician was, by contrast, at least apparently, cold and suspicious of himself. He was, however, in the direction of his stud-

---

[10] The French government-sponsored Military Aeronautical Laboratory was established at Chalais-Meudon near Paris in 1877; it was to play a leading role in the development of both airships and aircraft long into the 20th century

ies, one of the boldest of innovators in the wake of the likes of Bernheim, Luys and Charcot,[11] whose works had brought about a revolution in therapeutics at the end of the nineteenth century, obtaining results by means suggestion and hypnosis that the ignorant still consider to be miracles, but which were nothing more than the applications of principles now universally recognized.

His sole fault was an excessive timidity, not in his laboratory in his clinic, but in social relationships. Thus, having loved Norès' sister for a long time, he had not yet admitted it overtly. It is true that his secret was so poorly guarded, in spite of his efforts, that neither Norès nor Marie was unaware of it, and Norès was only waiting for an opportunity to urge him to speak.

The affection that bound the three of them together, and their mutual interest in one another's activities, is comprehensible.

The prostration that had briefly afflicted Guy de Norès had now disappeared.

"In the face of danger," he said, "it's necessary to stand up straight; you understand my anguish, but I don't have the right to abandon myself to it. It certainly seems heartless to think of lending assistance those one loves when the peril that threatens them is two thousand leagues away, even if the telegraph lines had not been cut, but who knows? So long as communication exists, one can attempt the impossible, but here the problem is quite different; it's almost madness to search for a solution."

He interrupted himself and passed his hand over his face. "And even if I found it, even if I were to risk that supreme experiment, I'd need...how long?—twenty-five, thirty, perhaps forty hours to get to China, and death is there, imminent and pressing. And yet, can I despair?

---

[11] Hippolyte Bernheim (1840-1919), Jules Bernard Luys (1828-1897) and Jean-Martin Charcot (1825-1893), three of the significant pioneers of French neuroscience.

His brow furrowed, his features contracted. It was evident at that moment that he had been griped again by the demon of invention. He was silent, plunged in meditations so profound that he seemed to have forgotten where he was. The other two respected his silence.

"Let's go," he said, eventually. "Whatever the risks, it's necessary."

He headed for a door, beckoning to his companions to follow him.

They went into the aforementioned courtyard, along which there was a lengthy hangar. The courtyard was surrounded by high walls that defied the curiosity of the neighborhood.

Norès took a key from his pocket and opened the large battens forming the entrance to the hangar and stood aside.

"Go in," he said to the doctor and his sister.

It really was a workshop: tools of every sort, of carpentry or the locksmith's art, a forge, chemistry equipment—nothing was lacking to give the room a quasi-fantastic aspect, characterized above all by the semi-darkness due to the enormous blinds carefully lowered over the large windows.

What was most astonishing of all, however, was that in this vast space, which bore no resemblance at all, in its extent or disposition, to a mistress' boudoir, an atmosphere reigned that was saturated with a singular and exquisite odor, whose nature it was impossible to determine, so much did it seem to be compounded out of multiple perfumes synthesized into one alone.

Finally, in the middle, under a tightly-sealed tarpaulin, was an object of considerable size, rounded in form, the nature of which it was impossible to determine.

Guy had carefully closed the door behind him, not without having ordered a domestic to call him as soon as Admiral Trécourt arrived.

It was evident now that the young scientist had all his mental capacities.

"My dear friend," he said to the doctor who was looking around curiously, "no one except my sister has yet been in here, not because I'm afflicted by the stupid suspiciousness that sees every visitor as a potential stealer of secrets, but because, I confess, I devote myself here to research whose result is to bring into action unknown forces whose manipulation might well have caused the death of more than one imprudent individual. Marie is battle-hardened and more prudent: do as she does and, I beg you, don't touch anything, even objects that seem to be quite inoffensive.

"Don't worry; in our physiology laboratories we run similar risks, and employ similar precautions."

"I don't doubt it, but the warning was necessary. In chemistry, the forces are even more hidden, and one can awaken them just when one least expects it. Now, I'll come to the subject that interests me. Do you believe, Sabirat, that it's possible to construct an apparatus that, launched through the air, would have a velocity almost ten times that of our railways?"

"The problem was posed a long time ago," said the physician. "At the end of the last century, one of our greatest scientists declared that the future belongs to heavier-than-air craft, but on the condition a motor compressing the maximum power into the minimum weight and volume could be constructed."[12]

"That's the very principle from which I started," Guy said. "But in your opinion, what sort of motor would that be?"

"Research has so far been directed toward electricity, but they've only partly succeeded. The results are already marvelous, though, since an airship moved by accumulators can be

---

[12] The reference is probably to Charles Richet, who was a neuroscientist, litterateur and pioneer of parapsychological research as well as an aviation pioneer, whose attempts to adapt steam power to heavier-than-air flight were frustrated by the problem in question.

steered, provided that the wind velocity does not surpass a certain limit..."

"Even so, the speed doesn't seem able to exceed thirty leagues an hour—a figure almost obtained by our new locomotives with five-meter wheels. I'm talking about a minimum, you understand, of a hundred leagues an hour: a speed that can be indefinitely increased, provided that the resistance of the human organism can stand up to such lightning-fast transport."

Sabirat simply said: "Everything seems possible to me, especially after the experiments of which you gave us a demonstration a little while ago."

"That was mere child's play," said Norès, shrugging his shoulders. "From the moment when one has at one's disposal a conductive wire, the transportation of all physical effects is possible: after movement, sound; after sound, force; after force, light. In that I only had to follow in the tracks of my forebears...but this...!"

He stopped, as if frightened by his own thoughts.

"Brother, Brother," said Marie, "you've often told me that you'd reveal your secret to me when the day came. I know very little about it, but I have confidence."

"Dear Sister!" said Guy. "You don't know, my friend, what a precious collaborator this child has been. She has spent long nights here, preparing blueprints, and copying sheets of calculations and equations before which an astronomer would recoil. She's seen me working, knowing vaguely that every move I made might kill both of us, and never so much as quivered or hazarded an indiscreet question. If she saw me hesitate in discouragement, she re-stimulated my energy. I tell you, Sabirat, that it's to her that I owe the little that I am..."

"Oh, Guy, how can you say...?"

"But Norès is right," exclaimed the doctor. "Who can aid us in our work, encourage and inspire us, if not a good, devoted, faithful companion...?"

Sabirat was getting positively carried away. A little more and there would be a declaration that Marie was awaiting, almost smiling as she was.

Suddenly, however, timidity got the upper hand again, and the rest of the sentence was lost in an almost incomprehensible babble.

"Go on," he said to Norès, "and forgive me for having interrupted you."

Norès shook his hand, and said: "You're right. Today I have to be an egotist. I'm in a hurry to say everything, but first, I'll show you my apparatus and its mechanical structure. Help me to remove this tarpaulin. And above all, no abrupt movements."

Taking infinite precautions, the two men slid away the great leather sheath.

A kind of angular box appeared, about the side of the body of a large carriage deprived on wheels, but whose prow was equipped with a kind of steel spur forming a blade, which had to serve for cleaving through water...or air.

To either side of what would have represented the ear of the vehicle, two flat steel wheels were disposed like the sails of a windmill. Finally, above the box, there was a kind of helix placed directly in the center.

The box was hermetically sealed, with the exception of a door on one side, and a window-fame in front fitted with a very thick but immobile pane of glass.

"This is the vehicle," said Norès. "Its appearance is quite simple, and I expect you'd have no difficulty guessing the purpose for which it had been designed. It is, however, in that little box that I might shortly attempt the utopian project of going to China after a journey of twenty-four hours at the most."

In spite of his confidence in his friend's science, Sabirat looked at him with some incredulity. "Where's the motor?" he asked.

"There's the motor," said Guy, opening the door and pointing to an apparatus that resembled one of these machines with a double globe used in making Seltz water.

The doctor uttered a cry of surprise: that definitely surpassed the bounds of the possible, and he wondered whether the emotion suffered by the young man a little while ago might have disturbed his mind somewhat."

Norès smiled, like a man whose demonstrations are all prepared. "Wait," he said.

He went to a corner of the room and came back carrying something in the palm of his hand. It resembled a vaporizer, but had no water in it.

"You see this?" he said. "Well, now roll that cannonball you see on the ground over here."

"But it's enormous; I could scarcely even budge it."

"Try anyway."

Sabirat went to the rounded block and tried to move it, but he braced himself and drew all his muscles taut in vain. The cannonball did not move.

"Don't try anymore," Marie said to him. "It weights more than eight hundred kilos."

"Well, since you spoke, dear Sister, prove to our dear doctor that you're stronger than he is."

"What Mademoiselle! You can..."

"Oh, not with my hands," she said, "but with this."

And he indicated the pseudo-vaporizer, which Norès appeared to be adjusting minutely by means of an attached screw.

"Go on, Marie, and confound the skeptic."

She approached the iron block in her turn, and directed at the mass the short tube of that we shall continue to call, for the sake of clarity, the vaporizer...and instantaneously, the enormous boulder rolled rapidly across the entire hangar, so rapidly that it would have knocked a hole in the facing wall if Norès had not shut off the current by throwing an enormous iron lever its path.

"That's extraordinary," said Sabirat. "I'm no longer in doubt. But what is that force?"

"That force," said Norès, "is...perfume!"

At that moment, somebody knocked on the door. It was his domestic, announcing the arrival of the Admiral.

"I have to leave you briefly," Guy said. "In the mean-time, Marie, give our friend the explanations that you can."

"Oh! I know so little..."

"I'll complete it—above all, no imprudence."

"Don't worry."

He went out. Sabirat made a movement as if to follow him. That was exactly what he feared the most: not exposing himself to the risk of chemical explosions, any more he would have recoiled in his clinic from the operation most dangerous to his life, but being alone with Marie!

How many others would have blessed that circumstance, which permitted him to talk discreetly and respectfully, but positively, about the sentiment that filled his heart? But that accursed timidity! Guy had scarcely disappeared when he felt himself blushing, going pale...

She was so lovely, with her bright chestnut curls, coifed à la Titus, which put a kind of aureole around her delicate face, with its child-like pink complexion and its gracious and smiling lips...

"So," she said, gently raising her voice, "listen to your professor. Do you know, Monsieur Physician, how a particle of musk, placed in a room, fills the entire space with its odor, instantaneously to begin with, and then for weeks and months, but without the most in-fini-tes-imal—what a word!—balance being able to measure the slightest diminution of its weight? Don't answer. That proves that matter can escape in molecules so refined and so attenuated that it requires billions of them to make up the hundred-millionth part of a gram. Is that clear?"

"You're talking," said Sabirat, who was thinking about something else, "of what we call, after William Crookes, radiation."[13]

---

[13] William Crookes had invented the Crookes tube—an electrical discharge tube producing "cathode rays" in the early 1870s, and many physicists had been experimenting with them ever since, but in 1891 it had not yet been discovered that cathode rays were streams of electrons, or that accelerated

"Say molecular bombardment—the expression is more exact, if you think about the lightning rapidity with which those molecules spread out through space."

"That's right."

"Good—you'll make a very tolerable pupil. I'll continue."

She held her small finger in the air, like a little girl addressing reproaches to her doll. "That bombardment, whose rapidity is beyond calculation, is, like ordinary movement, a source of force. In its usual state, in fact, perfume displaces, parts or transpierces the constituent parts of the air, which constitutes an effort... Don't look at me like that...listen...and don't think about anything else."

Bah! It was all very well for her to say that he mustn't think of anything but the bombardment of molecules! The truth was that Sabirat heard nothing but a buzz, entirely covered by words that resounded in his brain with the rapidity of cerebral radiation: "She's adorable...I love her, I love her!"

Perhaps, in any case, she was taking a malicious joy in continuing in her professorial tone: "Now, the entire science of force consists of the two operations of compression and channeling. Compress by *ad hoc* means the billion-fold myriad of molecules that irradiate from a grain of musk or any other matter disengaging perfume, channel that formidable flow...and you have in the smallest volume the most colossal force ever imagined."

As she spoke, allowing herself to get carried away by the scientific passion with which she had been impregnated in her contact with her brother, she leaned inside the mysterious vehicle.

"Come," she said. "Do you see that sort of sand-glass, the inferior part of which is made of a metallic amalgam that can resist pressures of thousands of atmospheres? In its interior, under the action of magneto-electric power, the molecular

---

cathode rays could interact with matter to produce the kind of radiation that, when found in 1895, would be called X-rays.

bombardment of odorant atoms is compressed; it is sufficient to place a hand on this lever for such a force to be instantaneously developed that, acting on the system of helices fitted into the case, it raises it up to a prodigious height...and that, by courtesy of that tiller situated behind you, one can steer in the air with a rapidity that challenges the flight of birds...ah!"

She uttered a terrible scream.

This is what had happened.

Sabirat had come into the vehicle behind her and, still hypnotized by the gentility that was inflaming him, still prey to the timidity that made him suddenly mute, seeing the admirable little hand almost at the height of his eyes, he had been seized by a kind of folly...and on that hand his own had posed, as he said: "Oh, Mademoiselle..."

But the hand he had touched had thus been pushed down on to the lever—and the latent force, suddenly set free, had launched the vehicle into the air with such rapidity that it had passed through the roof without any shock being perceptible...

And it was lost in the blue sky, just at the moment when Guy de Norès came back in, exclaiming: "Truncated telegrams...it's a revolt of the whole of China against the Europ..."

He did not finish. The aerial vehicle had just disappeared before his eyes, carrying away his sister and his friend.

And the unfortunate scientist, conscious of the danger involved, and at the same time as his last hope was escaping, let himself fall to the floor, sobbing, half-mad with grief and fear.

II

Before following our unfortunate involuntary voyagers into the air, let us cross the two thousand leagues that separate us from China and recount the scenes that had caused such dolorous excitement in Paris.

This is what was happening an hour before the selenium mirror had entered into the action.

Two young women were chatting merrily.

"Well, Sacha, are you ready? Oh, the beautiful idler, still getting dressed! Six o'clock has already chimed, and you know that if you're any later, the streets will be so crowded by the Chinese that it will be impossible for us to get through. Listen!"

Throughout the city of Peking, the capital of the Middle Kingdom, a rumor was running, composed of discordant cries, the sound of gongs, trumpet-blasts, and—most of all—an incessant murmur of voices, with various tonalities, whose magnified echo resembled the roar of the sea.

Nonchalantly sitting in a bamboo armchair in front of a nielloed mirror in which she was admiring her admirable blonde hair, whose magnificent tresses a chambermaid was just finishing putting up, Sacha replied without turning her head: "Have a little patience, Marguerite. No matter how crowded the streets are, our servants will be able to open a path for us, even if they have to do it with whips...what are you doing, you clumsy girl?" The last remark was addressed to her maid. "You pricked me with a pin."

The person addressed by the mercurial Russian was a tall, young woman of Manchu origin, with a suntanned complexion and hair that was almost woolly, retained as it was by a red silk headscarf. One could not say that she was ugly, but her physiognomy had a certain quality of cunning and hypocrisy that did not dispose one in her favor. What no one had noticed was that she had shivered at the moment when her

44

mistress had mentioned the word "whips," while her little hooded eyes had flashed. She apologized, but Sacha had already passed on to another topic.

"Is your father here?" she asked the young Frenchwoman who was trying to hurry her along.

"No, I came with my cousin Albert."

"The valiant Albert de Mesnes! Oh! He won't let you venture out alone, even to go from the French Legation to the Russian Embassy?"

"But he isn't constituting my escort alone," Marguerite continued, with a certain impatience, "and the handsome Alexandroff..."

"Oh, he's turned up again!" said Sacha, a trifle disdainfully. "I was beginning to believe that he wouldn't come back from Tien-Tsin. It must be admitted that my fiancé is taking things a little casually."

"Don't be unjust, Sacha; you know very well that in the present situation, European officers, especially the Russian and the French, have grave responsibilities."

"Bah! That's attaching a very great importance to trivial scuffles. What does it have to do with us that the Chinese have substituted the Ming dynasty for that of the...? I forget the names."

"The Tai-Tsing," said Marguerite, softly. "A name that, as you know, signifies *very pure*."[14]

"Which didn't prevent the Celestials from overturning it...but look—I'm ready," the young woman added, rising to her feet.

Elena Batowna—Sacha was only a familiar abbreviation—embodied one of the most admirable types of the pure Russian race, simultaneously delicate, aristocratic and yet en-

---

[14] The dynasty that followed the fall of the Ming dynasty in 1644 is nowadays known as the Qing dynasty—which eventually collapsed in 1912 to be replaced by the Republic of China—but Tai-Tsing was a more familiar designation when Lermina was writing.

45

ergetic, beneath an indolent appearance. Her tawny blonde hair formed a crown, whose gold pins could hardly contain her abundant tresses above her face, which was brightened by two eyes with a steely gleam. Her nose was small, her complexion very pale, and her mouth so small as to make it a marvel, if her lips had not been a trifle thin.

In the supple and rounded figure, however, the well-proportioned corsage and the arms, half-bare under the fur mantle that was wrapped around her, all revealed an uncommon vigor allied to all that female delicacy, and also a pride that was perhaps justified by the position of her father, Prince Batow,[15] who had been covering the Chinese Empire for ten years with an almost-completed network of railways, struggling against both nature and the ill will of the Chinese authorities. He was a veritable tamer of men and things, which had won him an enormous reputation throughout the Orient and Europe.

Marguerite Sametel, her friend, presented a perfect contrast with her; several thousand leagues from Paris, she was the typical Parisienne in all her exquisite delicacy. Small, brunette, gracious and as lively as a bird—the classical comparisons remain the best—the daughter of Robert Sametel, the great French physicist, was as mild as her friend Sacha was impulsive, as modest as the Russian was infatuated with her nobility and her father's authority.

The two of them liked one another in spite of those differences of temperament, because they met one another on the same terrain: that of true generosity and firmness of conscience.

---

[15] Lermina is not consistent in his rendering of Russians surnames, sometimes employing "-ow" and sometimes "-off" where other writers might use "-ov." I have mostly left them as he gives them, except to unify the usage where he accidentally uses both versions in the same name, using the more frequent "Batow" for this character, who occasionally becomes Batoff in the original.

Moreover, what Sacha did not admit to herself was that Marguerite, very learned and in possession of a reasonable coolness that did not exclude energy, exercised an influence over her to which she submitted without resistance. The little Frenchwoman, as she called her, had, above all, the imposing quality of common sense, and more than once the beautiful Muscovite's paradoxes had had to show the white flag before the just simplicities of her companion.

They had grown together, having arrived in China in 19 , after the famous Treaty of Nanking, which had given France and Russia the monopoly on great industrial enterprises in the Middle Kingdom. They were both orphaned of their mothers, Princess Batowna having died some time after her arrival in Peking and Marguerite having lost hers while she was still in the cradle.

Between the two fathers the difference was as great as between the two daughters.

Prince Batow was a kind of colossus, who was past fifty but still as lively, as ardent and—let us not mince words—as violent as in the full impetuosity of youth. Reckless to the point of imprudence, he had mastered—his word—the most recalcitrant and broken all the resistances that opposed the realization of his civilizing projects, to which Chinese routine had opposed an evident ill will.

Perhaps he had not always remained within the limits of sufficiently diplomatic action, but his nature, impatient with delay, was exasperated by the slowness of Chinese bureaucracy, and more than one mandarin—even those sporting the most honorific buttons—had felt the weight of the irritable Russian's whip on his shoulders.

Charged with completing the Chinese telegraphic and telephonic networks, Robert Sametel had primarily employed the means of persuasion, and, in reality, he had succeeded, all the more so, as it was to be believed, taking into account Chinese hypocrisy and that he had earned the favor of the highest dignitaries of the empire.

During the events to which Sacha had alluded to a little while before, the Tai-Ping insurrection, the taking of Peking, and the substitution of a dynasty of Mings for that of Tai-Tsing, Sametel had contributed more than anyone else to safeguarding European influence at a moment when it was seriously threatened.

In the year that Han-Ming had been ruling, under the guardianship of Prince Kong, it seemed that all the difficulties inherent to governmental commotion had been ironed out. The new king had even seemed impatient for the telegraph finally to link the various parts of his empire, and thanks to French capital, which had found large remunerations in those operations, the last line, from the vicinity of the Red River in Canton, had just been inaugurated, at the same time as the Mongolian branch of the railway had finally rendered possible the nineteenth century dream of a direct voyage from Paris to Peking.

The two young women were preparing to go out. That day there was a great festival: on the first day of the month of Li-Chun, the equivalent of our 5 February, the Commencing Spring was celebrated.

Guy de Norès, in Paris, had recalled that circumstance. For a long time, with Sametel's consent, he had maintained a correspondence with the young woman who was to be his wife, and he had chosen the date on which to carry out the supreme experiment that we have witnessed with the complicity of the great physicist.

The whole morning had been spent, as is common practice in China, in visits and polite exchanges between families, but it was in the evening, most of all, that the fête took on its truly popular character: a costumed procession with an ox with gilded horns on a cart was to traverse the entire city from the Bell Tower to the Temple of Heaven.

It was well-known that the immutable Peking consists of three cities enclosed within one another: at the center, the Forbidden City, the abode of the Emperor, a residence inaccessible to anyone, which is only open twice a year—and only for the last thirty years—to the representatives of foreign powers; then the Imperial City, a kind of immense secondary enclosure; and finally the Chinese and Tartar cities, the last two combined into one since the advent of the Mings, by the opening of new gates in the walls that had once separated them.

These few ameliorations had had the effect of isolating the foreign Legations—French, Russian and English—whose grounds now extended over the open Chinese city. The German Legation—which had lost its importance since the war of 189 , the revenge of France, again the mistress of the banks of the Rhine—had been installed far from its peers on the far side of the Tartar city, near the Convent of the Thousand Lamas.

The French minister had kindly offered his drawing rooms and pavilions to the Russians of the Diplomatic Corps and the colony, and it was to take her there that Marguerite, whose father was lodged at the Embassy, had come to fetch Elena Batowna.

When the two young women appeared in the waiting room, Alexandroff Wintscheff and Albert de Mesnes advanced to meet them. Both of them, in the capacity of military attachés to their national Legations, were in uniform: Alexandroff, vigorous and above medium height, superb in sky blue with a gilded semi-breastplate and a spiked golden helmet; Albert, a simple naval officer, with the braid of a lieutenant. Both were young, with honest faces and a pleasing physiognomy.

Mesnes was in love with Marguerite, but, knowing that she was practically engaged, merely served as a courteous and discreet escort.

"Will Mademoiselle Elena deign to accept us as cavaliers?" asked Mesnes.

"Is there any need for such a valiant escort to cross a single street in Peking?"

"One can never be too prudent," Sandorf began—but then, as if changing his mind, he added: "I mean that this crowd is intolerable."

"Bah!" said Sacha, laughing. "A crowd of Chinese is a herd of cattle, dispersible with a prod."

As if moved by a secret thought, Marguerite and the young Russian exchanged glances.

At the same moment, a boy, about twelve years old, emerged from one of the lateral doors and ran to Sacha. "What about me?" he said. "Have you forgotten me?"

He was a handsome child with blond hair and exquisitely delicate features. He had thrown himself into Sacha's arms. She kissed him, and her gaze lit up with a gleam of profound affection.

André was Sacha's brother. After their mother's death, the poor child had redirected all his love to Sacha, who had valiantly accepted the task of protection incumbent upon her, and had found a precious aide in Marguerite, whose natural generosity fitted her for the role of pseudo-aunt.

"Since when have big boys like you wanted to see masquerades?" said Sacha, laughing. "They're only good for little girls, like us."

"Oh! Don't you want me?" said André, ready to burst into tears.

"I'll look after you," said Albert, who never missed an opportunity to find a road to Marguerite's heart.

She smiled, as if to confide it to him.

"Tzu! Let's go," he said, employing the Chinese language, with which he had become familiar.

And the five people went out on to the perron of the pavilion.

In the broad streets, a flood of people was passing by, running, waving flags in the air, holding up cut out images of monsters and dragons on the ends of long poles: a multicolored display that dazzled the eyes.

There was a vast palanquin in the first gravel courtyard, sustained on the shoulders of eight porters.

A cold wind was whistling although the evening was fine, perhaps in great haste to celebrate the spring.

Marguerite and the young Russian sat side by side.

"Well?" she asked, in a low voice. "Do you still have the same anxieties?"

"They have only increased," Sandorf replied, in the same tone, "and I'm not alone in fearing some cataclysm. I think that there are thoughts in all these Chinese heads that we can't divine. I can admit to you, who are so cool-headed, that I'm afraid—yes I, Sandorf Wintscheff, am afraid."

"But of what?"

"How do I know? Since the Mings have recovered the throne, a wind of revolt has been blowing here, and a hatred of foreigners. At Tien-Tsin, from which I've come, I thought I could see on the paving stones the blood of the massacres of yore, fresh again."[16]

"Oh, shhh! If Sacha heard you..."

The young Russian passed his hand over his brow. "You're right...today is a festival; let's leave everyone to their insouciance...but tomorrow..."

He did not finish.

Thrown from the crowd, a projectile—a ball of paper— had just fallen into the palanquin and had bounced over Sacha's knees.

She started, pale and shivering. "What insolent...?" she began.

But the ports had accelerated their pace, and they were already approaching the gates of the French Embassy.

Without affectation, Marguerite had picked up the piece of paper and slipped it into her pocket. No one had noticed her action.

The palanquin stopped; they had arrived. The gates of the courtyard closed again on the crowd, from which a kind of

---

[16] Lermina had no way of knowing that Tsientsin would become a key focal point of the Boxer Rebellion of 1900, when a fierce battle was fought there by a multinational force against the insurgents and the Imperial Army, the victory in which created a base from which aid could be sent to the foreign nationals besieged in the Legation Quarter.

snigger rose up. But they did not have time now to reflect on certain strange things observed on the way.

A company of lackeys ran forward, helping the young women to get down. Then they went into the drawing-rooms, marvelously decorated, veritable winter hothouses in which spring had been forced to appear already, with heaps of flowers of dazzling colors, with exquisite scents.

The two fathers had come to meet their children, with Prince Batow cheerful and loud, something of a Cossack with his jovial Tartar face and his long beard, whitened by fatigue. He said to Sametel: "Who would believe that this magnificent creature is the daughter of an ugly brute like me...and look at this masterpiece!" As he added the latter comment, he picked André up in his arms.

"Bonjour, Father," said Marguerite, offering her forehead to Sametel.

"You know that I think you're the prettier one," he whispered in his daughter's ear.

"That's because I resemble you," she said, smiling.

In fact, she was the very image of her father, whose fine features made a singular contrast with the rude physiognomy of the Muscovite. What brought the two men closer together, however, were a similar energy and a similar devotion to their homelands, as an indissoluble alliance cemented on the battlefield had made the two men into siblings.

Let us say right away that in the last thirty years, profound changes had taken place in Russia's governmental regime, which was now submissive to a constitutional monarch—but we shall have other opportunities to return to such questions.

The French minister did the honors of his palace with traditional urbanity. In recent years the French and Russian colonies in Peking had increased considerably. The French Republic, freed by victory from the charges that had once been imposed upon it and the necessity of formidable armaments, had finally been able to direct all its vital forces to great industrial and commercial questions. The colonies of Tonkin and

Annam had acquired an extraordinary impetus, and the civilizing expansion of our homeland had extended usefully into the central provinces of China.

Germany, reconstituted as a confederation and liberated forever from Prussian autocracy, was slowly recovering from the crisis in which the Hohenzollern Empire had perished. Still somewhat peevish, and more especially jealous, she kept to herself, leaving Europe to be penetrated by Latin genius and Slavic vigor.

The drawing rooms of the French Republic, here as everywhere, were the center of civilization and life; the pavilions, put at the disposal of the guests, the balconies of which overlooked the Tartar city and the Chinese city, were crammed with an excited crowd, in which the most celebrated names in French and Russian diplomacy, art, and science were mingling.

Julien Pasteur, a great-nephew of the man who had vanquished cholera in France[17] and one of the most eminent members of the Académie Française, was in Peking at that moment, having gone there to study certain celestial phenomena whose interest had been augmented by the recent discovery of the inhabitants of the planet Mars. The editors of the *Journal Français de Pékin*, who were passing on the latest news from Paris, were surrounded. A fuss was also being made of one of the most original Parisian artists, who had arrived by the first train linking the two capitals, and curious young women were pillaging his albums, already full of interesting sketches.

Night had fallen completely, and our ambassador, offering his arm to the wife of the Russian ambassador, had led his

---

[17] Louis Pasteur developed a treatment for chicken cholera, but made less progress with his studies of the human disease; the great man was still alive in 1891, however, and the Pasteur Institute, founded in 1887, was in full swing, so Lermina's anticipation would have seemed perfectly reasonable at the time.

guests into a marvelous room enveloped by rare plants, with an immense aviary overhead filled with exotic birds. A table with two hundred places had been set up, streaming with lights, crystal and silverware, a thousand masterpieces of French artistry, which a murmur of admiration had saluted.

The ambassador was alone for the moment, his wife having been obliged to return to the south of France for the sake of her health. It was the wife of the Embassy's First Secretary that was doing the duties of hostess.

The English had decided to celebrate the solemnity in their own Embassy: a somewhat maladroit reserve that was attributed to some jealousy on the issue of the great industrial progress accomplished by France and Russia. In spite of the regrettable attitudes of the English and the Germans, however, the true fraternity that reigned between the ambassador's guests was no less cordial. People felt that they were part of a family; a current of sympathy united all the guests, and as the artist Jean Durtal had been obliged to talk about Paris, everyone listened and applauded.

"I've been in Peking for a fortnight," he said, "which means that it's exactly twenty-one days since I quit the Boulevard de l'Opéra. What changes must already have occurred!"

"What! In such a short time!"

"I'm talking about Paris, Madame. Let's see—let's only go back thirty years. Two million inhabitants then…today, four million! A few miserable electric candlesticks pitifully following the line of the boulevards then…today, the great electric central sun of the Hôtel de Ville lighting the entire city. Paltry stoves whose emaciated flues measured out microscopic degrees of hypothetical heat then…today, the electric heater at Les Halles warms the entire city, where snow has become a myth. Public Assistance organized in such a way that every man is assured his daily loaf of bread…a month ago, the first omnibus balloons of the Renard system—you haven't forgotten the name of the man to whose dirigible balloons we owe the greater number of our victories—began to circulate, and they're about to be obliged to double the service…until they have to triple it. When I think that there were plans for a Métropolitain railway! In the arts, three flourishing Opéras at which one is entertained, which is hardly believable; a literary production reduced to fifty novels a month, augmented by three hundred scientific books; the *Petit Journal* printing three million copies and only fearing, as serious competition, that the *Terre Illustrée*, now daily, will soon appear twice daily with news of the entire world brought by telephone.[18]

"Paris is the kaleidoscope always in movement; it's living progress; it's ceaseless effort; it's…" He interrupted himself, looking in the direction of the wife of the Russian ambassador, before concluding: "the pearl of the world of which Moscow is the diamond."

At that moment a lackey brought Sandorf a note sealed in an envelope. He opened it rapidly and as soon as his eyes had scanned it, he went pale.

"What's this?" he murmured. "What does this advice, simultaneously mysterious and frightening, signify?"

No one had noticed the incident, with the exception of Marguerite, whose eyes were fixed upon him.

She saw the young man get up discreetly, in order to go out without being noticed.

What's happening? she thought. *Nothing serious, undoubtedly… and yet, I can't get these dolorous presentiments out of my mind…*

And her hand settled on the note that had been thrown into the palanquin, which she had deciphered a little while ago.

It only contained these words, in the Chinese language: *Kieou Ming. Fan Kouei. Yang komitze.* Get out, foreign devils, demons from beyond the sea.

---

[18] By the time the novel was reprinted in *Le Matin*, that newspaper was appearing twice daily and boasting in its masthead that it was receiving news from all over the world by telegraph and telephone.

Was it a threat, or only one of those banal insults that the common people often shouted at foreigners?

"Messieurs," said the ambassador, "I can hear the fête outside becoming animated. The moment has come to offer your arms to the ladies and conduct them to the balconies. Oh, I forgot—I have a visit to announce. Our friend Dr. Li-Sin, the director of the Observatory, the only Chinaman who has adopted European fashions, will be here in half an hour. Permit me to recommend him to your generous welcome, for in recent times it has seemed that a Celestial almost requires courage to cross the threshold of our dwellings."

As he pronounced the final words his voice dropped slightly; it was evident that he was attempting to hide preoccupations that the ever-attentive Marguerite understood.

No one was thinking about anxiety, however; The French wines, especially the great sparkling wines of Algeria—which had dethroned champagne ten years earlier—had disposed all souls to insouciance.

At that moment, Sametel approached his daughter and whispered in her ear: "I'm going up to the Ambassador's electricity station—you know why."

"Oh, Father, how good you are. Success is certain, isn't it?"

"Yes, yes—don't worry. Go on to the terrace. I have an idea that you'll give someone great pleasure..."

This rapid conversation, as will be understood, was alluding to the experiment that Guy de Norès was carrying out in Paris. It was Sametel who had set up the *camera lucida* and the reflectors on the roof of the Embassy, and he knew that far away, in Paris, it would be the Ambassador's visage that would appear to the amazed French audience.

When everyone had gathered on the balconies, a cry of admiration escaped from all throats. The spectacle was marvelous; as if by enchantment, the entire city had been decked out with lanterns suspended from every floor of every edifice. Everywhere, there were clouds of multicolored stars—

thousands, perhaps millions. And the effect on the deep blue sky was magical.

There was no gaslight, not a single electric bulb. For that evening, doubtless in honor of the national festival, no appeal was being made to the sciences of the Occident; it was Chinese illumination in all its routine purity, but also with all its Oriental poetry.

In the streets, the crowd had become so dense that the people seemed to be one creature with a thousand feet, like a gigantic glow-worm undulating through the boulevards, losing itself in the side-streets, surging forth on every floor of the houses.

"The procession!" shouted a voice.

Indeed, advancing along the road that passed in front of the three great Occidental legations, a crowd could be seen, in the middle of which there was some agitation.

At the same time, a fiery spray burst forth from the heart of the Forbidden City, at the summit of the promontory known by the name of Coal Mountain, illuminating the entire city.

And from the throats and mouths of all those guests, happy and confident a few moments before, a cry of horror and terror erupted.

Yes, it was indeed a procession that was approaching, in the midst of furious, howling vociferations hideous to hear...but it was not a festival procession, for in the forefront, men were marching who were carrying, suspended from an iron hook lodged in his back, the corpse of an old man, whose silvery beard hung down, a patch of which was white and bloody at the same time.

Someone shouted: "The poor fellow! That's Li-Sin, a friend of the Europeans."

And as if that name were a signal, the crowd responded with a clamor:

"Death! Death to the devils from beyond the sea! Death to the foreigners!"

III

It was a frightful spectacle, that of the still-palpitating cadaver against which a furious crowd, maddened by rage and cruelty, was venting its fury. By virtue of a refinement of torture, his wrists had been bound to his ankles, and that triangle of quivering flesh recalled the most sinister imagination of the painters of Hell.

All around, a mass of people was swarming, brandishing sharp weapons, each trying to rip that blood-stained rag, whose form was gradually disappearing under the thrusts. Lanterns were agitating, casting their red, blue and yellow glare over the multicolored groups, giving that scene of death bizarre and startling glimmers.

The grimacing faces, the lungs exhausting themselves in demonic howls...

What had happened, then?

The venerable Li-Sin, one of the scientific glories of China, a man whose influence had contributed a great deal, under the last emperor—prior to the revolution fomented by the Tai-Pings—to dragging the Middle Kingdom into the great current of European civilization, was too absorbed in his research and too confident in the justice of the cause of progress that he was defending to have taken heed of certain symptoms of hatred that were gradually increasing in the people against everything that was affected, intimately or remotely, by the Occident. He had only paid distracted attention to a few pamphlets distributed to the crowds and a few furious sermons preached at crossroads, which the Chinese authorities tolerated, if they did not authorize them.

Li-Sin loved Europe, and France in particular, so he had gladly accepted the invitation sent to him by the Ambassador. At the appointed hour, in his half-national and half-European costume, he had set out on foot for the Legation, preoccupied with his calculations and not paying any attention to what was happening around him.

As he passed before the solid arch of the Gate of Chakaomene,[19] which opens on to the highway leading to the Legations, the stroke of a gong had caused him to shudder. At the same time, the crowd that had been following him for some time without him having noticed had drawn close enough to be almost touching him.

As his way was blocked, he had raised is head and asked, in his calm voice, to be allowed to pass.

A man had touched him on the shoulder and pointed with his hand to a sort of poster hanging next to the frame of red wood from which the gong whose chime had disturbed him was hanging.

"What's that?" he asked.

"Can't you read, O literate scientist?"

Curious but not fearful. Li-Sin had moved closer, for his sight was weakened by old age, and had considered the characters traced on the piece of paper.

Then he took a step back.

"This is bad!" he said. "A curse upon the man who has written these lines!"

What he had read was:

The Fathers have spoken, the Ancestors have ordained.

The foreign dogs have insulted our gods and outraged the majesty of the King of Heaven.

Let it be by fire and the sword, in blood, that they are punished.

---

[19] I have retained the spelling from the original here, as I cannot be entirely certain which of the several Gates to the Legation quarter is indicated by the reference. I have followed the same policy with other names, although Lermina is sometimes inconsistent in his orthography, but I have used more familiar versions where practical.

At that furious appeal to massacre—the suggestion of a cruel fanaticism that was not the first—Li-Sin had experience a surge of anger.

"This is a crime," he repeated, his hand rose toward the incendiary poster, his head held high, his gaze clear.

"You're nothing but a dog, like the *Fans*!" shouted a voice—*Fans* meaning "foreigners."

"He's insulting the Emperor, outraging the Son of Heaven..."

On looking for a second time, Li-Sin had just noticed something that had escaped him at first: that below those criminal lines, a vermilion streak had been traced.

It was the imperial mark, the seal of the State appended to that act of criminal hostility.

"It's a fake!" he shouted. "The vermilion brush could not have sanctioned such a lie."

"He's saying that the Son of Heaven is a liar!"

"Strike him down! Let him prostrate himself before the Emperor's seal. Put him to death!"

The clamors increased, more audacious and formidable.

With his arms folded under his mantle, he replied softly, without anger. He explained that the foreigners were the friends of the Empire, and that they had brought their industries and scientific progress to the Land of Flowers, but the longer he spoke, the more the vociferations increased.

Armed men were slipping through the crowd now, their faces ferocious, and the circle had tightened to such an extent that Li-Sin could no longer take a single step forwards or backwards.

In the face of the mob, Li-Sin did not weaken. He believed that his age was sufficient to impose respect, as it had been previously. Suddenly, however, a club fell on his head. He dropped to one knee, instinctively raising his arms over his head—but the brutal whirlwind had been unleashed.

A hundred men threw themselves upon him. Weapons pierced him, and clumps of his hair and beard were ripped out.

It was a savage fury, in all its hideousness. The executioners stimulated one another with their clamors, to which howls responded from all directions. Li-Sin disappeared under the feet of the crazed mob.

Suddenly, there was a stir; a butcher was cleaving through the crowd armed with a hook, and with a brutal laugh, he had stuck the sharp point into the unfortunate man's back. Then, with an effort of his wrists, he had lifted him up: a horrible trophy of which the wild animals made a standard.

In his death-throes, he was still struggling; a voice cried: "Tie him up!" And cords tied his hands and feet together.

Then, drunk on cruelty, preceded by that infamous burden, the Chinese ran forward along Hatamen Road, leading to the former Tsing-Kong-Fou palace, which had been occupied by the French Legation for more than half a century.

At the same time, as if in response to a signal from an invisible leader, a frightful racket had burst forth everywhere, compounded by the banging of gongs, trumpet-blasts, drum-rolls and raucous voices. To understand what that extraordinary din was like, it is necessary to imagine a city of two million inhabitants—that was the population of Peking in 19 — suddenly giving voice, crazed with instant rage, as if in a fit of epilepsy.

In all the streets and alleyways, at all the crossroads, at the great southern entrance Tchien-Men, the eight gates of the Tartar city, The Tong-Tche-Men Gate that opens in the Oriental rampart, everywhere that a temple stood, in all the sordid corners of the city and the avenues bordered by palaces, everywhere, an innumerable crowd emerged and spread, torrentially, as if drunk, howling...

The great Hatamen Road, a kind of unpaved boulevard bordered by shops—or rather stalls—surmounted by multicolored parasols, extending for a kilometer, disappeared under the swarm of that moving mass, illuminated by lanterns held on the end of poles, overhanging the hideous trophy of the still-twitching body of the murdered Li-Sin.

Meanwhile, from the heart of the Forbidden City, from the imperial residence into which no one penetrated, fireworks were launched into the sky, the evident signal for some cataclysm ordered by the emperor himself, the chief of the Tai-Pings, effectively declaring war on Europe.

Such was the frightful cortege that the guests of the French Ambassador saw approaching the Legation.

At the same time, fearful lackeys precipitated into the main hall of the pavilion shouting: "The Chinese! They're breaking down the doors!"

Facing the balconies, the crowd was massing, shouting ferocious threats, waving the cadaver like a flag of death.

Stones began to fly, still poorly aimed by reason of the distance separating the pavilion from the exterior walls.

There was a moment of indescribable chaos.

Sandorf had taken a stand in front of Marguerite and Sacha, and had fired his revolver into the crowd.

The women, dressed for a party, insouciant and joyful a few moments earlier, had been gripped by an indescribable terror, and had rushed inside madly, seeking exits through which to flee. Very soon, however, the Ambassador and the Russian and French officers had recovered their composure.

What was the exact extent of the danger? They did not know, but they all knew enough about Chinese treason to understand what was happening; several of them still had the memory of the massacres of Tien-Tsin, the more recent riots in Nanking, and the ambush of Tchang-Cha in Hu-Nan.

A single moment of hesitation would be an encouragement given to the cowardice that was only waiting for a sign of weakness.

The French Ambassador was guarded by a detachment of marine infantry, hardened seamen and elite warriors. In the blink of an eye, in response to the voices of their officers, they were under arms.

The telephone linked the French Legation to those of Russia, England and the United States. By virtue of an unqualifiable imprudence born of latent malevolence, only the German Legation had not permitted that precaution to be installed.

In a matter of minutes, appeals had been addressed to the other legations, whose good will was not suspect—but how amazed the French were when they learned that the others had been besieged at the same time as the French Embassy.

The situation had become critical: were they confronted by a popular revolt, a mob born of drunkenness, or had the signal really come from higher up?

"Messieurs," said the Ambassador, "We're going to do our duty. I beg a certain number of you not to follow me, to stay here to protect the ladies." Smiling, he added: "In any case, the danger is only apparent. We know the Chinese…a great deal of noise for nothing."

His pallor belied his words, however.

Albert de Mesnes had run to him, wanting to be one of the first to brave peril by his side.

A group of French and Russian officers, on the Ambassador's orders, had gathered at the door of the pavilion, weapons in hand. A deathly silenced reigned in the drawing room, where all the women, save for a few, were petrified by fear and half-fainting.

First, a word about the palace of the French Legation, a brief description being necessary to make the events that are about to unfold comprehensible.

A former imperial abode belonging to the Tsing family, the palace was situated at the corner of two major streets, or highways, the Tai-Ti-Chang to the right and the Toun-tian-mithian in front of the palace. Its external appearance was monumental. A broad perron gave access to it: a stone stairway surrounded by boundary-posts linked by iron chains. To either side, on pedestals, were two enormous lions hewn in solid granite. In front of that perron was a vast courtyard extending to the external gate, formed by the central block and two lateral wings, occupied by the servants.

The perron gave access to the palace, properly speaking, and the reception rooms; then, beyond those, there were the various pavilions occupied by the embassy's dignitaries, which were divided into several groups by two spacious courtyards, one known as the Red Courtyard and the other as the Green Courtyard, denominations borrowed from the color of their architectural ornamentations. At the extremity were the Ambassador's private apartments, parallel to the strictly-defined palace.

Around these buildings extended vast gardens, enameled pavilions, summer-houses and hothouses. To the right of one of these gardens, known as the Lilac Garden, a gate opened on to a broad avenue where the barracks of the marine fusiliers was situated, along with the stables, the lodgings of Dr. Bivert, an embassy attaché, and a small Catholic chapel.

Finally, the entirety of the grounds was surrounded by thick walls six meters high, equipped several years before with an interior gallery, permitting defense against any assault. It should not be forgotten that the wall in question enclosed an area of more than two hectares.

The Ambassador, surrounded by his own officers and the Russians, had advanced as far as the aforementioned perron. Albert de Mesnes was carrying the French flag. A hundred fusiliers formed a hedge to either side of the entrance.

Then, very calmly, ordering those who were accompanying him to remain a few paces behind him, with the exception of the flag-bearer, who was to march by his side, the ambassador advanced toward the door.

On the other side of it the vociferations increased. Pieces of wood and iron objects could be heard banging on it.

The Ambassador had the bugler sound the flag, and then, resolutely, gave the order to open the door. He advanced toward the mob.

The fusiliers, with bayonets fitted, were ready to go to his aid.

When the door opened, there was formidable pressure, but as the Ambassador took a step forward, the mob instinctively recoiled, jostling one another in brutal disorder.

"Who are you and what do you want with me?" the Ambassador demanded. "This is French territory, guaranteed by treaties and Imperial decree. I demand that you leave."

Audacity produced a sure effect even on the most furious. There was a moment of profound silence.

The Ambassador continued: "France is the friend of China; our governments have exchanged sacred promises; respect them as we respect them ourselves."

Perhaps that energetic attitude was about to triumph over that still-inexplicable fury, but from the ranks of the crowd a voice shouted: "Death to the dogs from beyond the sea! Throw the French out of China!"

At the same time, with a kind of ferocious vanity, the wretches carrying the cadaver of Li-Sin, having frayed a passage to the first row of the crowd, held it up, insultingly, a few paces in front of the Ambassador.

Coolly, he marched toward them and placed his hand on the shoulder of one of them.

"In the name of your father," he said, in Chinese—for nowadays, our representatives abroad all speak the languages of the countries in which they reside—"I summon you to set that cadaver down."

Was it the temerity of the order that stupefied the brute? He lowered his arms, and set the body of the unfortunate Li-Sin at the ambassador's feet. The latter, taking hold of the flag, lowered it over him.

"This cadaver is my guest," he said. "I shall defend it to the death. Now, go away, all of you!"

That scene had such a grandeur in its simplicity that the rioters stepped back once again. But the same voice, as monotonous as a knell, shouted once again: "Death to the French! Kill! Kill!"

At the same time, detonations burst forth in the vicinity in all directions: the other Legations were under attack, and were mounting a vigorous defense.

The racket seemed to awaken the assailants from the torpor of the cowardice that had made them hesitate in the accomplishment of their crimes.

An arrow flew through the air and struck the Ambassador full in the chest. Tottering, he leaned on the flagstaff in order not to fall.

"Fire!" shouted Captain Lambert, who launched himself forward to support him.

"No, no!" cried the Ambassador. "No blood!"

But it was too late.

At the sight of the wounded representative of France, everyone had lost patience. The soldiers threw themselves upon the rebels, bayonets extended.

But the ranks opened and a volley coming from outside raked the courtyard of the Legation.

There was a danger of an immediate invasion. They threw themselves at the doors and, in spite of the formidable pressure from outside, succeeded in closing them.

At the same time, however, cries rose up from the rear, and a red light was seen that expanded over the buildings, rising into the profound sky. The wretches had thrown incendiary bombs from outside, on the other side, with such skill that almost all the pavilions had caught fire simultaneously.

In spite of his wound, the Ambassador had drawn himself up to his full height.

"Monsieur," he said to Albert de Mesnes, "above all, take care of the flag I've entrusted to you."

"Don't worry, Monsieur, I'm a soldier and will do my duty."

"And now," the Ambassador went on, making energetic efforts to remain upright, "remember that our honor is at stake here. France expects that we will all die at our posts."

The vociferations redoubled.

A rain of fire fell upon the Legation, while heart-rending screams were heard from the pavilion in which the women had been left.

What was happening there?

IV

It will be remembered that the Ambassador had begged a certain number of Frenchmen to remain with the women in order to protect them.

The cries that the initial surprise and terror had drawn from all throats had been succeeded, at first, by a bleak silence full of anguish.

In the vast drawing-room, the ladies, wrapping themselves up in their evening dresses, had huddled together, heaped up, so to speak, hiding their faces in their hands. The most fearful—and could one consider their emotion criminal?—put their hands over their ears in order not to hear the horrible clamors from outside.

Everywhere, in the Occident as in the Orient, popular furies give rise to sinister echoes, but in those countries so distant from our mores and our civilization, in which the last vestiges of our own made follies subsist, such violence takes on an even more savage character. The wild beast reappears within the man and roars with strange, sonorous and profound voices, like the raucous screech of the tiger.

With that growling—for which there is no better comparison than the echoes that make children hurry past the sheet-metal walls of fairground menageries—was mingled the infernal din of the gongs, trumpets and drums that had burst forth with unprecedented force from one end of the city to the other: a frightful orchestra of sharp and ear-splitting dissonance.

In addition, from one moment to the next, detonations crackled, along with prolonged screams in the distance, all the more terrible for being inexplicable.

Marguerite and Sacha were perhaps the only ones to maintain their composure. In Sametel's daughter there was reasoned, positive courage, a resolution that nothing could bend to confront peril with determination, whatever it might be. In Sacha, there was, above all, the feverish excitement of anger.

The Russian professed the most profound scorn for the yellow race, the hypocritical baseness of which she had observed many times, and the rancor of which she disdained. In spite of her genuine generosity and kindness, there was within her, by virtue of her education as a princess, an inveterate horror of inferior races.

If anyone had asked her, she would have replied in all sincerity that for her, a Chinaman was less than human, scarcely more than an animal. Too often, in chastising her indigenous servants, she had obeyed a regrettable prejudice and had not divined that the desire for vengeance was brooding in all those resentful hearts.

If she was pale at the moment, if her lips were taut, it was primarily because of the irritation caused her by the audacity of those she considered as slaves, and whom, for reasons of pride, she did not want to fear.

Holding her brother André, who was shivering, closely, she had said in a low voice to Marguerite: "Nothing serious to dread...a scuffle, with which the soldiers of our Legations will soon reckon."

But Marguerite had shaken her head without making a reply.

For some time, she had observed symptoms of an ill-concealed hostility toward Europeans on the part of the Chinese.

It is necessary briefly to recall its causes.

Toward the end of the nineteenth century, the Chinese, amassing their numbers in America, had been expelled by force. Mass executions—a kind of Chinese Vespers—had even taken place in the large cities of the United States. A massacre of several thousand Celestials had bloodied the streets of Chicago, and in New Orleans and Florida hatred against the yellow race had revealed itself to be as ardent—we might even say as ferocious—as that once directed against black people.

The veritable cause of that antipathy resided, as is well known, in the astonishing competitions that the Celestials offered to the natives, and in accepting such low wages for their work that they had become derisory. The Chinese could live for a day on the equivalent of two *sous*; an income of half a dollar—two francs fifty—was sufficient for them to accumulate considerable savings. At that rate, however, white men died of starvation, and they had resolved to rid themselves of those dangerous rivals at any price.

Under that general pressure, the Chinese, hunted like animals, had been obliged to flee the continent of North America. They had retreated to Brazil, but the young Republic had too much need of its own resources to abandon any evident fraction to foreigners, and once again a *cordon sanitaire* had been formed against the Chinese invasion.

They had attempted to fall back to Europe, not to mention Algeria and the new States of the Congo, but there had been a complete incompatibility between the black race and their own; the persecutions had recommenced with a character of ferocity against which nothing could prevail. Europe, without heaping ill treatment upon them, had been content to expel and repatriate them.

The resistance that the Chinese had encountered in their desire for expatriation had only served to excite them further; fatality had determined that in recent years, famine had ravaged the Middle Kingdom, while earthquakes had toppled entire cities and devastated immense territories.

Very rapidly, as superstition was added to the mix, the Europeans and their diabolical inventions had been covertly accused of unleashing those horrible scourges upon the Chinese—and in any case, what right did the Europeans have to flood into China when they expelled the Chinese from their own empires?

The Chinese who were expelled from America and Europe described those countries to their contemporaries as veritable paradises; they became the promised land on which all their dreams converged.

Prejudices and instincts of anger and revenge were the sentiments that the Ming conspirators had exploited against the dynasty of the Tai-Tsing; the ancient secret association of the Tai-Pings had spread the word of resurrection from the north of China to the south: *Death to the foreigners!*

Strangely enough, however, with the exception of a very small number, the Europeans had not understood the profound causes and consequences of that movement; they had only attributed the revolution that had suddenly substituted an ancient dynasty for the one occupying the throne to palace intrigues. A grave error! The evil had roots in the very entrails of the people. It was the eternal struggle of races reappearing, in opposition to the spirit of internationalism of which the recent Chinese emperors had given so much proof, and opening the doors of their kingdom wide to the progress of Occidental science.

That was what Marguerite Sametel suspected and, in a way, divined; that is why Sacha's disdainful insouciance made such a painful impression on her. She would have reproached herself, however, for saying anything that would have frightened the young woman. Only with Sandorf—who, for reasons she did not understand, seemed to be well informed about the dark doings of the conspirators—had it been permissible for her to exchange a few words about the complications she feared, without believing them to be imminent—but which had suddenly become manifest.

She looked at the pale face of the young Russian who, looming over the group of men by virtue of his tall stature, seemed to be waiting, pistol in hand, for the sudden appearance of some unknown adversary.

Suddenly, there was a loud cry. Rifle shots had just been heard, fired in the Embassy courtyard. Had the battle already begun, then?

"Messieurs," Marguerite shouted, "we don't have the right to detain you! Think that a few paces away, your friends, you brothers in arms, are being murdered..."

She did not finish.

A sinister noise—a kind of brutal whistle—had just drowned out her voice. At the same time, in a dazzling radiance of red light, a kind of igneous ball flew across the room and, having collided with a wooden corner, exploded with a formidable bang, spreading a blizzard of debris around it along with a stream of flame that suddenly extended over the parquet and transformed into a sheet of fire.

What happened next?

How can that scene of hideous terror be described? The women fled randomly, bumping into walls without finding any exit, the flames licking their skirts, enveloping their corsages, snapping at their bare arms and shoulders.

The blast of the explosion had extinguished the lights, and it was the fire alone that was illuminating those frightful agonies, from which heart-rending screams and desperate appeals for help erupted.

Fortunately—if anything could be reckoned fortunate in that dire catastrophe—a second bomb thrown from outside smashed into a section of wall and rebounded into the courtyard, leaving the way free to an interior terrace, and through that exit the women threw themselves, lamentable specters, in a paroxysm of panic, bumping into one another and jostling one another, as in the corridors of a theater on fire.

Fierce egotism recovered its empire. Everything was forgotten except that death as there, horrible and implacable—and that it was necessary to flee, to flee at any price.

The men—those, at least, who were still standing, for several had been grievously wounded by the shrapnel of the projectile—strove to defend the unfortunate women against their own despair, to bring a little order into that mortal chaos.

But how could they succeed?

Thanks to his height, Sandorf had perceived Sacha, dragged away by the whirlwind, courageously carrying little André in her arms, who seemed to have fainted—but that was all. He had not been able to pierce the compact flood in order to reach her.

Cries of impotent rage escaped him.

Suddenly, someone shouted: "The Chinese!"

It was true.

From outside, the wretches had grabbed onto balconies and climbed over the balustrades. Now they were appearing at the extremity of the external gallery, on the side opposite the one where the women were pressing.

When they perceived the women by the light of the blaze, they uttered a cry of triumph—for, perhaps even more than the men, they hated European women, whose beauty, luxury and charm were, in their view, insulting to the superiority of yellow women. And among the attackers, frightful harpies could be distinguished, as ugly as hags, whose sharpened fingernails were threatening their enemies. Oh, with what joy they would soon be lacerating them!

Sandorf, meanwhile, had been the first to understand the danger. Through the bloody light of the blaze he saw the ever-increasing flood of assailants—and those who had the duty of closing the path to that horde were little more than a handful: twenty at the most.

"Let's go toward death, Messieurs," said Sandorf, "and let's hold them off as long as possible."

The Europeans gathered in a part of the gallery forming a broader balcony, and from there a first volley of revolver shots lashed the crowd of assassins. But if the first ranks might have hesitated, they were pushed from behind with a furious vigor, and the troops raced toward Sandorf and his friends.

The gunfire crackled, Chinamen fell, but the others trampled the wounded and the dead. Armed with long harpoons, they hurled themselves upon the group of Europeans, and it was necessary for all of them to do their utmost to prevent one another from being dragged away.

Their revolvers were empty, and what were the swords in their hands worth against an enemy that was not within reach?

Suddenly, there was a flash in the air; other Chinese were arriving armed with tubes filled with some kind of incendiary matter, and from a distance, they projected a jet of fire at the intrepid defenders, who, horribly burned, nevertheless did not recoil, wanting their cadavers to compose a supreme barrier against the assassins.

Intense smoke prevented anything from being distinguished.

Sandorf was now backed up against the balustrade, arms folded, awaiting death with a fatalistic stoicism—and yet, until now, as if by a miracle, he had escaped danger. He was virtually the only man still standing; Prince Batow lay at his feet, his skull fractured, his body half burned.

Suddenly, he uttered a cry that was almost joyful.

In the glare of the conflagration he had just seen Sacha below him, disheveled but alive, running with André in his arms...but a sob rose into his throat, because he had also seen the Chinese a few paces behind her, who were chasing her.

"I'm here! I'm here!" he shouted—and, leaping over the rail of the balustrade, he launched himself into the air.

A drop of a few feet, and he would be beside her.

But he did not reach the ground. Something—a rope, a lasso—had just coiled around his body. He felt himself being lifted up, and carried away in his turn, while a hand put a kind of hood over his head, which, half-stifling him, prevented him from seeing anything more.

Chinamen carried him off on their shoulders, while a woman, running after them, seemed to be giving them orders.

Meanwhile, the attackers, masters of the terrain, had launched themselves after the group of European woman, who, not having found any way out, were massed at the extremity of the terrace, palpitating.

Another instant, and the filthy hands would reach them.

A detonation burst forth.

"Vive la France!" cried a voice.

It was the Ambassador's fusiliers who were arriving, under the orders of Albert de Mesnes.

The thunderstruck Chinese recoiled. A further discharge, almost at point-blank range, filled them with terror. It was a matter of every man for himself. The wretches rushed toward the exterior balconies.

"Sacha! Marguerite!" shouted Albert.

Among the voices of the women who replied, however, those of the two young women could not be distinguished.

Sametel leapt over, hanging onto the balcony, and reached the gallery.

"Help!" cried the women.

He was the first to arrive beside them.

"Marguerite! My child!"

Marguerite was not there

At that moment, the battle resumed, fiercer than ever, at all points.

The Legation was invaded from every direction.

The fire was spreading everywhere. Buildings were collapsing with a sinister sound.

It was necessary not to think of defense any longer. Particular interests and intimate colors disappeared before the peril run by the flag.

Sametel came back to Albert de Mesnes.

"If they're dead," he said, in a dull voice, "all that remains for us is the horrible joy of avenging them."

Marguerite Sametel was not dead.

If she had not replied to her father's appeal, it was because, at the moment when the French soldiers appeared at the base of the terrace, the courageous child had just discovered a means of salvation for her companions.

The extremity of the pavilion enclosed a long gallery that served as a library, and she had often shut herself up there with her father, for whom she performed secretarial tasks.

That gallery, she remembered, terminated at the wall that separated the Tartar city from the Chinese city, which had not been demolished when the final work had been done that had isolated the Embassy almost completely. A thought had suddenly occurred to her: she had often visited that wall and knew that there were subterranean corridors within its flanks, able to offer a temporary refuge in case of danger.

Marguerite was courageous; she had no fear of death, but she knew that while the women were not safe, the most valiant men would be paralyzed in their defense.

She thought about her father, who, she was not unaware, would not survive her; it was for him that she wanted to live, and also for the man whose name she pronounced in a whisper, Guy de Norès, whose wife she was before her conscience.

So, fraying a passage through the middle of the fearful women, while encouraging them with her vibrant voice, she had attained the extremity of the gallery and had attentively examined the wooden partition that closed the way to them.

At first she saw nothing.

Set on a pedestal was one of those bizarre monsters, of which the Chinese love to sculpt the forms, more grotesque than frightening. With its huge belly, which was surmounted by a frightfully horned, grimacing head, the vermilion tongue sticking out of a wide-open maw, it was obstructing the passage. The mass was solidly embedded in the wall. It was folly to think of moving it, and yet, thinking that salvation might perhaps lie behind the obstacle, Marguerite clenched her slender fingers on the idol of gold and jade, as if she hoped to tip it over.

Suddenly, her finger slipped and, without the young woman intending it, pressed down on the demonic tongue. She felt it yield under the pressure. She pushed down with all her strength, and suddenly uttered a cry of joy.

The monster rotated on its axis, moved by an invisible mechanism, and the much-desired exit had appeared.

Radiant, Marguerite ran back to the nearest of her companions and shouted to them: "Come on, come with me! We're saved!"

A few launched themselves after her, but the greater number, paralyzed by terror, had not budged.

"Sacha!" Marguerite appealed—and a voice that she took for that of the young Russian having replied to her, she bravely pushed on, convinced that they were all following her.

Ahead of her the darkness was profound; only a slight red glow projected by the fire filtered through the high windows of the library, obstructed by blinds, but Marguerite knew the way well. In the middle of the long room, two sets of shelves formed a kind of alley, at the end of which was a sphere mounted on a bronze foot; it was there, she had not forgotten, that the exit to the wall was located.

She was in haste to reach it, and when she did so, she opened a door.

A gust of cold air lashed her face.

And she found herself outside.

Stopping there, she looked behind her. In the indecisive light that transformed the women who had followed her into shadows, she thought once again that they were all behind her, and, renewing her appeal, she set off along the stone rampart.

"Let the last one through close the door behind her," she added.

She found that she was on a kind of narrow round-path enclosed between high walls, through the crenellations of which the flashes of the blaze were sparkling, but she did not pause, impatient to make sure that her European sisters were safe.

Soon, she felt a declivity underfoot; it was there that the slope led to a subterranean passage. She hastened her pace, and soon arrived at a door formed by a grille, which her father had once opened out of curiosity, and which it was sufficient to push. She did, and reached a staircase. She went down, still hearing behind her the footsteps of those in whom she had been able to inspire confidence and who had abandoned themselves to her direction.

After thirty steps, the terrain leveled out, and after a few minutes more, Marguerite stopped, knowing that she must be in a large chamber.

She rummaged in her pocket and brought out one of those charming jewels that all well-off Chinese carry on their person, and which encloses a lantern in the small central cavity. The young woman's however, fabricated by her father, enclosed a series of minuscule facets that illuminated a microscopic electric bulb.

She switched on the beam, which stood out white and bright on the black wall.

She was not mistaken; she had reached the place with which she was familiar. No noise could any longer be heard; the thick stone structures stifled every echo of the din that was resounding in the city of insurrection. Marguerite's reasoning was sound; this was a refuge into which no one would think of pursuing them.

"Sacha," she said. "Come here to me, with your brother."

But there was no reply.

She directed the beam at the group, and perceived for the first time that only half a dozen women had followed her. She did not see her friend—the one she would perhaps have saved first—among them.

"Sacha! Sacha!" she cried. "Say something...haven't you see her? She must be there, a few paces behind us...and you've left her..."

"No, no!" exclaimed the poor women. "We swear to you, Mademoiselle Batowna didn't come with us."

"That's impossible! My God! But then...she's doomed! And she'll accuse me of having abandoned her, like a coward, to save myself!"

One of them, still shivering with fear, explained to her that Sacha, as if mad with terror, had jumped down to the bottom of the terrace with her brother, and had fled.

"Which way? Speak! I need to know. I beg you..."

Someone affirmed, however, that Sacha had fled in the direction of the main courtyard—which is to say, to the point at which the Embassy's forces were concentrated. Evidently, she was safe.

"Well then!" cried Marguerite, "I need to know, at the risk of my life, and I shall."

As she took a step to retrace the route she had already followed, however, the women threw themselves at her knees, sobbing and pleading.

Could she abandon them? Where were they? Did they even know? She could not have brought them to this sinister place only to leave them there, however. That would be cowardice, a crime...

And they clung to her garments, with pleas that almost resembled threats.

Marguerite reflected.

It was true that she had taken charge of these poor women, and that it was forbidden for her to leave her work incomplete. And then again, what could she do now for Sacha? Either the young Russian had succeeded in putting herself under the protection of her father or the Ambassador, assuming that Sandorf had not already saved her, as was his duty, in which case Marguerite's intervention, even if it were possible, would be unnecessary; or...if she had fled at random...how could she find her? Which way could she go? In what part of the city should she look for her?

Marguerite said all that to herself, and her heart was constricted by a grip so painful that she feared that she might die of it.

But no! It was necessary to stiffen herself against any weakness. She owed it to those who were there, and whom she had promised to save. She owed it to her father, to Guy.

Recovering her composure, she said: "Listen to me. Time's pressing, and we don't have a moment to lose. At the far end of this room a long subterranean tunnel opens, which I've never explored to the end, and from which I don't know the exit. However, I have reason to believe that it must end a long way from here, in open country, outside the city. If we can get that far, there's hope that you'll be out of danger. Perhaps our people will already have put down the revolt"—as she said that she shivered internally, for she did not believe her own words—"and all peril will be over. If not, the city will be in the hands of the insurgents, and it will be necessary to look for other means of salvation. Have no illusions: the eventualities are terrible, but there's an old French saying: *Help yourself, and Heaven will help you.* Are you ready to do as I say...and to be courageous?"

At that moment, a singular phenomenon occurred. The women, convinced a little while before that they were safe, believing that there was no further effort to make, and far from being encouraged by Marguerite's words, found all their anguish revived...and only replied with lamentations.

Only one very young woman, almost a child, came toward her resolutely, and said: "Mademoiselle Sametel, I'll do as you say, and I promise to have courage."

Marguerite looked at her. She was a little brunette with short-cropped hair and keen and intelligent eyes.

"I don't recognize you," Marguerite said to her, softly. "What's your name?"

"Oh, it's the first time I've come out into society," said the young woman. "My father has only been in Peking for six months. He's a photographer. He had an invitation, but he felt ill when it was time to leave, and let me go to the Embassy on my own." Laughing, she added: "I didn't have much luck on my debut, did I?"

"But...your name?"

"Rose. My father's name is Nivet—Nivet, photographer of Batignolles, who came to China to make his fortune. A bad idea. Poor Papa!"

In spite of her anguish, Marguerite could not help smiling. Rose was typical of those pert Parisiennes who sometimes support bad luck better than good.

"Well, my dear Rose," said Marguerite, "I'm appointing you my aide-de-camp."

"Thank you," said the photographer's daughter. "That's quite a promotion. So, with your permission..."

She turned to the others, who were still sobbing. "Come on, girls," she said. "Haven't you finished wailing like that? A

79

little courage, damn it! Since you've been told that we'll get you out of this, stop weeping all the time…you'll make the road wet."

In fact, on hearing that youthful and mocking voice, the others suddenly felt gripped by a kind of shame.

There was a vigorous woman of about forty, Madame Perrotti, whose husband, French although originally from Lombardy, had set up a bank in Peking and was presently very prosperous. There was also the widow of an engineer, in company with her daughter, and finally, an old lady, deaf but still alert, a governess in a highly placed Chinese family.

In less familiar terms, Marguerite repeated her instructions. It was necessary to march, even to march at hazard…but they had no choice.

"Forward march!" said Rose.

And, swinging her hips like a drum-majorette, she went on ahead.

That Parisienne impertinence, which was a trifle suburban, to tell the truth, nevertheless introduced a note of energetic insouciance into the midst of that despair, which did not fail to revive a little courage.

Could they abandon themselves while that child was providing an example of resistance?

It was with a livelier step that the women set out to follow the bends of the subterranean corridor.

"I can't tell which direction we're taking," Marguerite whispered in Rose's ear. "Are we going north or south?"

"Bah! What does it matter? We'll still arrive somewhere."

"Doubtless we're going under the walls, but where will we find an exit?"

"Don't worry about it. When we've been walking for two or three hours, there'll still be time to be disturbed. You know, it reminds me of the catacombs in Paris…"

"You're very cheerful. Aren't you afraid, then?"

"What's the point? It doesn't do any good. You say that, but you have for more courage than me, for when you called out to those you wanted to save, it was just in time. Honestly, I was about to faint—yes, faint, like an aristocratic lady..."

"How old are you?"

"Me? Don't tell anyone, but I'm old, although I don't look it. Nearly sixteen."

"But what do you do here in China?"

"Eh? I help Papa...I take photographs. Poor Papa is on his own—it was when Mama died that he had the idea of going abroad. He wanted to leave me in Batignolles. I know that it's the capital of Paris, which is the capital of the world, but I said to him: 'Not a chance! I only have one father and I'm hanging onto him...so let's get going to the land of the apes.' Tell me, Mademoiselle, is it true that they often roast Europeans?"

In truth, Marguerite admired her. In addition to the fact that she seemed charming with her little turned-up nose and mischievous eyes, the girl's tone was suggestive of an innate generosity and a devotion, proof against anything.

"If we get out of this safe and sound," said Marguerite, taking her by the hand, "would you like us to remain friends?"

"Would I! How could it be otherwise, since I like you and you like me? You've no need to tell me that, you see...you're from Paris, too, near Pantin...that's obvious right away. We aren't going to die this time, take my word for it...and we'll give the Chinese a hard time if they cut up rough."

The thought of two young women fighting against an entire people made Marguerite smile sadly. She did not know that those words were almost prophetic.

Meanwhile, the route seemed interminable. The poor women had protested several times already.

Having come to a party, they were not wearing shoes made for walking. Some had bare feet, and a glacial damp was now falling from the subterranean walls.

While they were complaining, Rose had briskly taken off her skirt, made of a rather thick muslin, and had divided it into four scarves, which she wrapped around their necks. And when the old lady declared that her feet, too cramped in her luxurious shoes, could not carry her any further, Rose had presented her own shoes to her, saying: "These aren't brand new, Lady, but they're all the more supple for it."

In the face of that benevolent good humor, everyone found a little more energy.

"Do you know," Marguerite said to her, "that you have the best heart in the world, and that I'm simply going to adore you."

"At your service, Mam'zelle."

How long had they been on the move?

"Look at your watch," said Rose.

"I'm afraid of exhausting the power of my little lantern." So saying, but also pressed by a perfectly natural curiosity, she switched on the white light. Scarcely had she uttered the exclamation: "It's one o'clock in the morning," then the spark went out, however. She had foreseen what would happen correctly; the battery had not been charged for a long time, and had not been replaced.

"Don't be afraid," Rose said to her, divining her anxiety. "I can cope; I'm a real cellar rat."

"You're quite simply a little providence."

"With two feet and no feathers."

At that moment Marguerite stopped abruptly. "Listen!" she said.

They all held their breath.

A singular noise reached the fugitives. One might have thought it an external slithering that was following them.

"My God—there's an animal there, stalking us."

"A snake!" proclaimed someone else.

In fact, it was impossible to come up with a reasonable hypothesis about the nature of that monotonous, regular sound, with a kind of muted modulation.

"Don't move, as Papa says," sad Rose. "I'll go investigate."

And without waiting for a reply, she ran forward.

82

The darkness was profound; it seemed that she had eyes like a cat.

Accepting her devotion, so frank and so useful, Marguerite stopped the little troop. She did not know why, but in her turn, she had confidence in the cleverness, and perhaps the luck, of little Rose.

A few minutes went by, during which they could hear their hearts hammering.

Suddenly, a bright light illuminated the tunnel, and Rose appeared, with a torch in her hand.

"This way, quickly!" she shouted. "We're saved!"

And as they all raced in her direction, they saw an open bay in which, by the light of other torches, the silhouettes of European sailors stood out.

Saved! It was true! But where were they?

As Marguerite had understood, the tunnel extended along the wall that surrounds the Tartar city. The city of Peking is surrounded by a canal known as the Tung-Chao, whose eastern branch joins the Pei-Ho.

The tunnel in question ended at the junction of the great canal and the branch.

The sailors were French. They quickly brought the young woman up to date with what had happened.

The decisive battle was taking place at that moment within the walls of Peking. All the Europeans, having recovered from their initial stupor, had grouped together under the leadership of Monsieur Sametel.

Thus, the first name that Marguerite heard was her father's.

They had occupied a part of the city located between the Eastern triumphal arch and Hatamen, based in the Catholic mission and the Yamen,[20] the Chinese Ministry of Foreign

---

[20] The Tsung-li Ya-men had been established in 1861 by the then-regent Prince Kong (Lermina renders it Kong and Koung in different places, but I have unified his references) to serve

Affairs, of which they had taken possession so effectively that they controlled two of the gates of the city, the Chi-ho-Man and Tchien-Men.

Numerous European barges were in the Tung-Chao canal at that moment, and by that route, the Ambassadors had evacuated the women and children who had survived the massacre during the first few hours of the battle.

An officer alerted by the sailors came toward Marguerite Sametel.

"Oh, Mademoiselle," he cried, "your father has made himself a hero."

"Do you think he will succeed?" the young woman asked him.

The officer shook his head. "As the soldier said at Waterloo," he added, "there are too many of them. But don't lose any time, I beg you. Come aboard, you and your companions. A tug is waiting for us at the entrance to the Pei-Ho, and we have to get to the quay at Tsien-Sing-Fu as quickly as possible."

"Take care of my companions first," said Marguerite.

The supreme joys are egotistical. The women and the two girls who had just been saved ran to the barge, almost shoving one another to get there sooner."

"You turn, Mademoiselle," said the officer to Marguerite.

The young woman looked at him and said: "Monsieur, if you knew that your father was risking his life for the defense of the flag and the honor of the fatherland, would you abandon him?"

"Mademoiselle?"

"Go, Monsieur, do your duty. I'll do mine; I'm staying."

"Oh, Mademoiselle, you're a worthy daughter of France."

---

as a Ministry of Foreign Affairs. Lermina was not to know that it would be abandoned in 1901.

"I only ask you for one sailor to serve as a guide. Oh, don't worry—I'll send him back to you promptly."

"No need—there's no shortage of brave lads here who are burning with desire to go fire a shot with their compatriots. For you he'll be a guide, and for your father he'll be one soldier more."

"Thank you."

The officer called: "Kroarec!"

"Present, Lieutenant!" said a male voice. And a vigorous sailor came to within arm's reach.

The officer explained the situation.

"Perfect, Lieutenant—and you're doing me a big favor. I've been itching to have a crack at these Chinese apes."

"Don't forget that you need to be prudent, until the moment when you've taken Mademoiselle to her father, Monsieur Sametel."

"Mademoiselle is Monsieur Sametel's daughter! Damn it! Beg your pardon—but if she wants. I'll get myself cut in four for her father."

"That's good. *Adieu, mon brave*—and good luck!" He turned to Marguerite and bowed profoundly. "*Au revoir*, Mademoiselle...see you soon, at Tsieng-Sing."

Marguerite extended her hand to him. "Once again, thank you. I commend these poor women to you."

The young man uttered a cry of surprise. "What about this one!" he exclaimed, taking Rose—who had not budged—by the arm.

"*Au revoir*, my dear Rose, to you, too," said Marguerite. "I'll never forget what you've done for us...for me."

The girl planted her fist on her hip.

"You're sending me away, then, just like that! You're getting rid of me. That's a fine way to carry on!"

"What do you mean? The officer's waiting for you—it's necessary to hurry."

Rose took a step toward the officer, bored with comical reverence. "If you're only waiting for me," she said, "don't delay for so little."

"What do you mean?"

"It means that in there—in that cave where we spent a good while—I swore that I wouldn't quit Mademoiselle; that I'd stay with her. That's understood, isn't it?"

"But think, Rose!" Marguerite exclaimed. "It might be going to your death!"

"Don't know...and I like to learn." Then, very softly, she said to Marguerite: "Let me go with you. My father isn't a great man, like Monsieur Sametel, but he's Papa...and I want to find him."

"Come on then, my good and charming Rose...and let's not waste time."

And they drew away in the direction of the city, under the guidance of the sailor Kroarec.

VI

It will not have been forgotten that when Sandorf had jumped down from the gallery, at the risk of breaking his limbs, in order to run to help Sacha, whom he had just seen fleeing with her brother André through the fire and smoke, he had been suddenly seized, tied up and carried away. In that brief shock he had lost any capacity for resistance, and, almost at the same time, any notion of the course of events.

Furthermore, his carriers, excited by the voice of the woman who was running after them, had adopted such a rapid pace that the jolts felt by the Russian officer were certainly of a nature to provoke a very natural loss of consciousness.

Before going any further, however, in order that the story can be better understood, let us give a brief description of the mysterious city that was only known, at the end of the nineteenth century, by virtue of the accounts of a few voyagers, and that, even at the time when the events of the story we have undertaken to relate were unfolding, conserved the greater part of the original characteristics of its ancient isolation.

Peking is situated at a longitude of 114° 7' and a latitude of 39° 54. [21] The city is constructed in the middle of a vast plain; one might think that the sentiment guiding its sovereigns was the same one that engaged the Spanish monarchs to place Madrid in the middle of a desert.

---

[21] The former figure does not correspond to English citations because it is based on the Paris meridian rather than the Greenwich meridian. The data cited by Lermina are derived from *La Nouvelle Géographie universelle* by Élisée Reclus, which was still incomplete in 1891 although the Asian sections had been in print since the late 1870s. Reclus was the most famous of all France's pioneering Anarchists, and compiled the book while in exile. He served a brief term as editor of *La Science Illustrée*.

The sea, in the gulf of Petchili, is seventy kilometers to the east. The Pei-Ho, which traverses the entire province and has its source in the King-Tan Mountains, traverses Mongolia and then separates into two arms. The Pei-Ho passes 24 kilometers from Peking; the place where it is closest to the city is the location of Fort Tung, the terminus of the Tung-Chao canal, which envelops the entire city outside the walls, thus forming a double circle of water and stone. Water is, moreover, abundant in Peking; lakes and ditches are fed by canals drawn from the pools of Iung-Min-Yen, the ancient Summer Palace once sacked by Anglo-French armies.

The name Peking signifies "northern court," in opposition to Nanking, which signifies "southern court." The latter city was once the residence of the Emperors.

Within the double girdle that encircles it, Peking cannot increase in territory, although its population has increased since the end of the nineteenth century by more than half a million inhabitants.

It is thirty-three kilometers around and covers six thousand hectares.

We have already said that Peking is composed of three cities, two of which, the Tartar city and the Forbidden or Imperial City are enclaves within one another; to the south is the Chinese city, a city of commerce and industry, an cluster of shops of all kinds and merchandise of every provenance.

The topography of the Tartar or Mongol city is very easy to understand, the gates being orientated precisely at the cardinal points: to the north, the gates of Peace (Ngan-Ting-Men) and Victory (Tai-Tchang-Men); to the west, the gates of the West (Tsi-Tche-Men) and Submission (Pin-Tse-Men); to the east, the gates of the East (Tong-Tche-Men) and the People (Rchi-Koua-Men); and finally, to the south, the gate of the Aurora (Tien-Men), plus Hai-Lai-Men and Tchuen-Tche-Men, which take their names from ancient emperors.

The southern gates communicate with the Chinese city, and it was near one of them, it will be remembered, that the unfortunate Li-Sin was massacred.

Long before American cities, Peking had understood the utility of straight lines for circulation, and from all the gates, broad roads had been traced, intersecting at right angles, and dividing the city into great squares, themselves subdivided by small straight roads into smaller squares, the former analogous to the avenues of New York and the latter to the streets.

One singular detail, however, which can in itself explain the distance that has always separated the Chinese lords and literate individuals from the population, is that on the great avenues or boulevards there is not a single edifice or rich house. On both sides, there are low constructions, shops, or walls allowing nothing to be seen but the parks and gardens belonging to elegant houses hidden in the side streets.

In the center of the Manchu city is the Yellow City—in China, that color is attributed to the Emperor, and honor it shares with vermilion. Thus, in the middle of Yellow City, reserved for high functionaries, is the Red City or Imperial Palace, Huang-Chan-Ti-Kong.

In the Yellow City, remarkable for its roofs, which, under the sun's rays—or, at the time when the revolt broke out, under the reflections of the fire—seem to be covered by a golden dome, the most magnificent edifices include the Pagoda of the Literate, the Pei-Thasse, a monument elevated to the memory of the last king of the Mings, the new dynasty of which recovered the heritage after two centuries.

The revenge of the Mings had given rise to a bizarre ceremony of an almost fantastic character.

In the imperial garden, the tree could still be found from which the unfortunate Ming monarch had hanged himself when the Tartars took possession of the capital. His Manchu conqueror, unable vent his anger on the man he had wanted to keep in his power, but who had escaped him via death, had covered the culpable tree that had robbed him of his prisoner with chains, and since 1644, the date of the event, the withered trunk of the tree had borne the yoke of infamy.

Scarcely a year before, the new Emperor, who belonged to the Ming dynasty, had broken the chains of the old tree in a solemn ceremony, and then had it clad in gold armor, surmounting its top with a crown of the same metal. The strange rumor had been spread through the people that, rehabilitated and revivified by the honors that had compensated it for the odious unmerited punishment, the tree, in one last effort and as if to salute the new emperor, had put out a young and fresh branch—only one—which had dipped in order to bow to the Son of Heaven.

Also in the Yellow City, on the edge of the Middle Sea, itself a vast and admirable lake, is Coal Mountain, a steep hill surmounted by a pavilion of marvelous grace and elegance. What gives that hill, which is not very high, its curious character, unique in the city of Peking, is that if you stayed in the capital of the Middle Kingdom for twenty years, you would not find a single blade of green grass in its streets, squares or even the banks of its canals, as the humblest growth is pitilessly stifled by the sand that blows from the Mongol deserts, and yet the hill of the Yellow City is always green: a fresh, bright emerald green, giving the illusion of an eternal spring.

What accounts for this phenomenon? It is claimed that in times long past, an emperor who was fearful that his capital might be besieged had an enormous heap of coal transported to that location, which was to serve as fuel for his engines of war. The siege did not happen. The coal stayed there, and gradually, under the action of the weather, an enormous layer of vegetal earth, of incredible fecundity, formed over the heap. Is it the heat locked in the bosom of the coal that gives the earth that vegetative force? This explanation is not implausible.

Those two marvels, the Pei-Thasse and the Coal Mountain, dominate the city with their pavilions with delicate tapering horns. When the wind blows from that direction, an exquisite perfume born of plants cultivated by the monks spreads over the city, in consoling contrast to the less satisfactory scents that emanate from the rest of the Chinese city.

To the northwest of the Red City, at the corner of the square, rises the Pagoda of the Literate, the temple of examinations, and the point on which all gazes, from every part of the empire, are fixed. It is from there, in consequence of the examinations on which all Chinese civilization is based, that graduates emerge to occupy the highest positions in the administration and the government.

Of the Red City, Europeans, even in the recent years when the conquests of occidental civilizations have penetrated the country, only know the golden roofs looming above the walls.

At the moment when the last dynasty had been overthrown, the Emperor had invited the European ambassadors to the Imperial Hall built on the summit of five superimposed terraces. That was a veritable triumph for French diplomacy, which had finally overturned the last obstacle opposed to progress by age-old prejudice. The audience had not taken place, however, and death had punished the Emperor for his sacrilege. That condescension had been one of the most powerful motives for the revolution that had carried away his throne.

A magnificent bridge, entirely made of finely sculpted marble, traversing the Middle Sea and leading from the Yellow City to the Tartar City, seems to be guarded by the great monastery, with its immense buildings of white marble, its colonnades of black marble, its chapels populated by grim gods, symbolic animals with terrible faces, and the heads of lions that seem to be jealously defending the entrance to the Fu, the palace of high dignitaries.

Above it looms a high tower, an enormous and menacing mass.

South of the Marble Bridge is the Imperial Pagoda—Kwang-Mi-Tien—all white beneath its roofs of lapis tiles, resonant with the sound of a thousand little bells incessantly agitated by the wind, streaming with flags that flutter like the wings of brightly multicolored butterflies. And yet that graceful edifice is empty. Once, the dethroned Emperor had gone there to offer a respectful homage to the gods of Confucius, but the Mings, who had re-entered the Imperial Palace, abandoned it. Bats had taken possession of the pagoda, and when

91

night fell, their wings brushed the little bells and made them vibrate as if at a funeral.

By contrast, another edifice, once abandoned, had been reconstructed and luxuriously ornamented; that was the Temple of the Elephants, in the western corner of the wall that separates the Tartar City from the Chinese City. The Tai-Tsing, the dynasty of the Very Pure, had renounced the Asiatic luxury of which the elephants seemed the monstrous symbols under the Emperor Han-Ming, who had reigned for two years under the regency of Prince Kong. But under the most ardent representative of old Oriental ideas, the Elephants had taken possession of their palace again—and, training for war, they often hurled at night the sinister racket of their long and funereal cries.

At the moment when murder and fire were raging in the Chinese capital, in response to an order issued from the Imperial City, from the same Imperial Hall that the European ambassadors had failed to penetrate, but where Asiatic despotism had established itself again with all its hateful ferocity, the city took on a fantastic appearance.

There were four colossal fires on the four sides of the horizon. It was the Catholic missions that were burning: to the north, the Peh-Tang, within the boundary of Yellow City, whose magnificent woodwork was no more than a immense furnace; to the south, the Nam-Tang, with its cathedral, whose towers, seen through the red smoke resembled the writhing of two arms imploring the aid of Heaven; to the east and north, the schools, large constructions whose walls were crashing down.

An uninterrupted spray of fire rose from the Coal Mountain, not that of a blaze but a signal of death, incessantly maintained.

On all sides there were explosions, and the dull sounds of collapses. The city seemed to have been shaken by a demonic fury. Gunfire mingled its distressing echoes with the coppery resonance of gongs, and incessantly struck at the doors of monasteries, while the Chinese horde ran through the streets, the swarm of assassins, sacking the European shops, dragging the unfortunates into the streets, over the paving stones, through the mud, until the moment when, weary of torturing them, they finished them off with thrusts of swords or spears.

Never had the folly of human brutality, unleashed in all its savagery, affirmed itself so hideously. Women fled, pursued by troupes drunk on blood, and from the bridge of Pin-Tse, children were hurled into the ditches. On the western side, the Tung-Chao Canal flowed red.

It was as if there were whirlwinds of bestial fury in the air: howls added sinister punctuation to the great clamor audible throughout the city. Sometimes, a strident scream burst forth, like that of a slaughtered animal, or there was a slow, interrupted wail like that of an animal being made to suffer. This time, however, it was the human beast that was in agony.

Vaguely, under the oppression of the gag that was half-choking him, Sandorf perceived these atrocious realities. He was unable to understand, to reason, but it seemed that he was being carried away in the vertiginous whirl of a nightmare.

It went on; the porters had gone past the English Legation, which was now surrounded and invaded, at a run, going around the coal warehouse, and had headed obliquely into the Yellow City, following along the walls of temples where the hammers of gongs were launching deep and ferocious roars; then, following the southern shore of the Middle Sea through the grounds of the Imperial Pagoda, without pausing for a second, they had reached the Si-Hua Gate, and from there had threaded a path through the narrow streets of the Tartar City.

They had passed under the western triumphal arches, made of bamboo with triple openings, decked with steamers that were bright in the gleam of the conflagration, like tongues of fire. There, the crowd had stopped briefly, because the popular furor was overwhelming and hectic.

An Englishman, one of the most important commissioners in the city, had been tied to a stake and was plunged into by sword-thrusts, playing the horrible game of death by a thousand cuts, which consists of slicing a victim into shreds.

One does not disturb executioners at work. But the woman guiding the escort had moved forward.

She was a creature of tall stature, quite beautiful in spite of her Mongol type. She had the simultaneously harsh and intoxicating beauty of Oriental almas, with something akin to the hieratical character of a priestess in the sculptural regularity of her features.

Her gestures had a solemn grandeur. She approached the group of torturers, and with her hand raised and holding two fingers straight while the others we folded over her palm, she pronounced a strange word in a loud voice, composed of two sounds that melted together in a kind of soft and prolonged growl: "Aum!"[22]

The torturers were so preoccupied that they did not seem to hear it the first time. Then her hand came down on the shoulder of one of them, as he was drawing breath, weary of slaughter.

"Aum!"

This time the man shuddered, his eyes looked up, and he saw the hand, still raised in a gesture of incantation.

Then he shivered, and, looking at the woman, he recoiled in a kind of superstitious terror. He shoved aside those who were with him, repeating the mysterious syllable.

This time, the effect was immediate; the ranks opened, and while the majority, ceasing to strike, put two fingers to their foreheads and bowed, the band resumed its course. Behind them, the murderers compensated themselves for having been interrupted.

Finally, they came into the long avenue of Chuen-Che; then, heading northwards, they ran for several minutes through a maze of uninhabited streets.

---

[22] This mantra is normally rendered Om in English. Lermina renders it Aoum in this passage, but subsequently substitutes Aum when it takes on a key role in his *deus ex machina*; I have unified his references. In Hinduism it is the Word that began creation, and thus symbolizes the manifestation of God.

There was a wall, black and mute. Suddenly, the woman uttered a slight whistle and the men stopped dead.

There was a door in the wall.

The woman approached it and knocked, spacing her raps in a particular fashion. The door opened.

There was an abrupt change of scene. They were in a garden of tall, bushy trees, the tops of which were reddened by the reflections of the conflagration, while their bases were lost in obscurity, only pierced by the indecisive glimmer of a few almost-opaque paper lanterns held by men clad in long tunics and armed with naked curved sabers.

The woman went in first.

The fateful syllable "Aum!" was murmured between her and the men who were there. They bowed to her, and then two of the strange guardians detached themselves, preceding her, while the porters followed her meekly with their burden.

They walked through alleyways, narrow to begin with, but which gradually broadened and eventually ended at a stone stairway.

She climbed the steps slowly—seven of them—to arrive on a first platform, from which a second stairway of fourteen steps rose up. On the second landing, a third flight of twenty-one steps commenced.

"From seven, which is shadow, to fourteen, which is dawn—which is to say, light," the woman murmured, punctuating each of her phrases with the sacred word "Aum!"

At the top, a vast pavilion loomed up, superb in its colors and decorations, illuminated in the light of two vast fires that were burning in bronze basins, where an alcoholic liquid was boiling, as odorant as sandalwood, with an additional penetrating acidic flavor.

A vast door the color of emerald sealed the pavilion. Beside it, a gong was suspended, the sculpted copper of which displayed the head of a fantastic chimerical animal.

She seized the hammer and struck it, gently and mutedly, in a rhythmic numerical pattern, akin to a language.

No one came in response, but the door swung on its hinges silently, as if moved by an invisible force.

She turned and invited the porters to go forward, which they did—and the door closed silently behind them.

They had entered into a large room, almost dark. At the back, however, a gleam was visible that was gradually accentuated, and it became evident that light was filtering faintly from the next room through some kind of metallic curtain, which doubtless permitted sight without being seen.

She pointed with her hand toward a kind of sofa set along the wall and ordered that the prisoner should be set upon it. Then she made a sign, and the porters disappeared.

She was alone with Sandorf.

She went to him, gliding over the paving stones without awakening the slightest echo.

Having arrived close to him she leaned over and gently removed the hood that was covering his face. Then she crouched down beside him and placed her hand on his heart.

Her features contracted under the influence of a profound anguish.

Finally, the young man uttered a sigh, and she had difficulty repressing a cry of joy. He was alive.

An intense delight lit up the face of the mysterious woman, who, bending over, kissed him on the forehead.

Then she stood up.

"Mine," she murmured. "Mine forever, in life as in death."

She went to a small sideboard, took out a jade pitcher and a cup; then, having filled the cup with a liquid as colorless as water, she returned to Sandorf and put the cup in his hand.

Mechanically, in the first awakening that makes the throat dry, he raised the cup to his lips and swallowed the liquid in a single draught.

She made a triumphant gesture—and as the young man became agitated, trying to stand up, she withdrew to a darker part of the room, put her fingers to her lips and, having blown him a kiss, opened a little door and disappeared.

VII

Meanwhile, the young Russian gradually came round. Since he had drunk the liquid, it seemed to him that fire was running through his veins, but it was not painful—far from it.

On the contrary, it was life that was circulating in him, active, warm and comforting, while his mind was illuminated by a bright light.

He raised himself up with his wrists, his eyes still closed, unconscious of his own existence, in the singular state that follows lethargy.

At that moment, a singular chant began, strange, monotonous and soothing, which seemed to be coming from a long way away, softened and, in a manner of speaking, filtered by distance.

It acted upon his nerves like an intoxicating song. It seemed that he felt a soft breath passing over his forehead.

Slowly, he stood up and then opened his eyes.

At first he closed them again, as if surprised, not understanding and not remembering. Where was he? A great laziness dulled his curiosity.

The chant was becoming louder, as if getting closer, vibrating in his ears with a penetrating charm.

Meanwhile, there was a sudden relaxation in his nerves, and he found himself upright.

We have rapidly sketched a portrait of the young man: tall, very vigorous, broad shouldered, features imprinted with a character of violent energy. Sandorf bore no resemblance to the Russians of high society who, having strayed onto Parisian soil, seemed to be searching, in mad prodigality and facile amours, for a means of escaping an eternal ennui.

Alexandroff Wintscheff, in terms of his ancestry, belonged to the Kirghiz[23] race—which is to say that he had, in spite of the refinement of a sojourn in the north, the southern characteristics of the Caucasus; but it was not only physically that something of that still semi-savage race subsisted in him. Sandorf—as he was normally called, by way of abbreviation—had in his soul a singular mixture of brutality and naiveté.

Although, in the elevated milieu in which he lived, he had gradually acquired the delicate and slightly feline manners of the aristocratic society of St. Petersburg and Moscow. Though sometimes, as soon as he was delivered once again to his personal instincts, either in the distant provinces of the Empire or in the army, the instincts of violence, impetuous anger, and unreflective enthusiasm that were dormant within him reappeared.

Thus, his passions were ardent, and more than once, already, he had almost compromised himself in adventures of a gallantry that were more than soldierly, and which would have compromised his future markedly if his family and friends had not been able to attenuate the scandal.

As it was important to prevent the recurrence of those eventualities, however, the decision had been made to marry him off, and negotiations had begun between his noble parents and Prince Batow.

---

[23] The Kirghiz are mentioned in early Chinese documents as northern neighbors, whose territory embraced a part of the ancient trade route known as the Silk Road; after a war with the Uighurs in the ninth century A.D., they occupied the Mongolian steppe, but by the time they were absorbed into the Russian empire in the nineteenth century, they had become indistinguishable from the Kazakhs. The modern Kirghizstan has China to the east and southeast, Kazakhstan to the north, Uzbekistan to the east and Tajikistan to the southwest— nowhere near the Caucasus, although the so-called Kirghiz steppe extends in that direction.

Without arguing, perhaps understanding himself that the time of the follies of youth had finally to run out, he had allowed himself to be engaged to Elena Batowna, whose beauty had, in any case, made a deep impression on him. To employ a familiar expression, Sandorf had found himself something of a small boy before that creature, proud of her race as she was and whose attitude contrasted with that of the women of whom he had made facile conquests. She sometimes indulged in disconcerting mockery, playing with him like a cat with a mouse...and if, by chance, he showed signs of rebellion, a glance or a word quickly sufficed to master the turbulent cavalier.

A long posting had been imposed upon him, and the marriage was not due to take place until Prince Batow's return from China to Europe. Sandorf had not accommodated himself very well to that delay, inasmuch as constancy had never been his dominant quality. He felt that he was still an independent bachelor, and the yoke of betrothal often seemed difficult to bear.

One day when he had been prowling the streets of Peking, having nothing else to do, wondering how long he was going to remain imprisoned by the wall of China, he had seen, in a strange cortege that was passing by, in the midst of Buddhist monks, a woman dressed like an idol, her forehead hidden beneath a kind of tiara, draped in a white cloak constellated with strange signs. The eyes of that strange woman had met his own, and within an instant, a kind of bond was established between those two beings who had never met, which was to tighten into a decisive intimacy. How that had happened, and how such a vivacious, dominating passion had been established in Sandorf's heart, the ardor of which invaded him more every day, only the profound mystery surrounding new loves can explain.

The woman had passed by, and while looking at him, had raised to her lips a lotus flower, a golden jewel that she had detached from her cloak. Then, an hour after she had disappeared, Sandorf received a mysterious note: would he like

99

to see the woman who had appeared to him in that rapid vision again?

Was it one of the banal strokes of luck that the handsome Sandorf had so often encountered in his life? What did it matter, after all? The unknown woman had seemed beautiful to him, with a strange and captivating allure. A man has curiosities against which reason cannot prevail.

Sandorf had gone to the location indicated in the note.

Too courageous to hesitate, he had plunged by night into the labyrinth of the old Chinese city, the bizarre quarter surrounding the Passage of the Bimbelotiers,[24] a vast and long avenue entirely populated during the day by ambulatory merchants and sellers of Chinese antiquities.

Did the unknown woman belong to the scorned class of those petty people? Once again, Sandorf did not bother to ask himself such questions; he was carried away; he was not reasoning.

Then, a new life had commenced for him. The unknown woman had taken possession of him, had enveloped him instantaneously with seductions all the more powerful because they were complicated with quasi-marvelous peculiarities by which Sandorf's imagination, poorly educated in sum, and still imbued by old Oriental legends, had been troubled.

And that woman, who had the passionate energies and also the intoxicating languor of the Asiatic, revealed to his eyes a kind of strange, apparently magical power. Sometimes she appeared at the moment when he was least expecting her; sometimes, by contrast, when he found himself beside her, it seemed as if she suddenly disappeared, like a nocturnal vision.

Their rendezvous had always taken place in singular, unexpected locations, and everywhere, even in the quarters from which luxury seemed to have been banished forever, he saw

---

[24] The word bimbelotier is occasionally imported into English because it has no ready translation. A *bimbelotier* is a manufacturer and trader in *bibelots*: trinkets, "knick-knacks" or imitation antiques.

Sithreva—that was the name under which she revealed herself to him—surrounded by a dazzling luxury.

Sometimes, in the street, he shivered, perceiving her in the garments of a pauper, lost in a crowd of beggars; then, a few hours later, he found her again in some sumptuous dwelling, served by slaves who treated her like a queen, sparkling with gems.

When he interrogated her, she smiled with her sphinx-like lips...and made no reply.

Gradually, however, as her empire over her lover had become established more despotically, she had begun to speak to him in less enigmatic terms of an immense power of which she was the recipient. And with an astonishment that was soon transformed into admiration, Sandorf heard her talk as if in a dream about the conquest of the world.

Was she betraying herself, or voluntarily letting escape those semi-confessions relating to a plan pursued for a long time? Sandorf, in the grip of a kind of intoxication, which almost robbed him of any notion of the present and the future, did not even try to find out.

Sithreva's voice and eyes, her simultaneously hieratic and regal attitudes, all contributed to maddening him further...and yet, sometimes, when he was calmer, he remembered certain words he had heard, perceived as if in a dream, which frightened him.

Sithreva did not belong to the Chinese race; she had been born in Tibet, in a country almost unknown to Europeans, where, it was said, the secrets of ancient times were hidden in monasteries perched above the region of snows, on the summits of the Himalaya.[25]

---

[25] Lermina's eldest daughter was married to Henri Chacornac, a bookseller and publisher specializing in the occult, to whose operations the author provided useful capital, and via whom he became closely, albeit skeptically, involved in the French occult revival. Lermina was therefore familiar with the mythology of the Tibetan Shambhala, which was later to inspire

"Who is your father?" he had asked her once.

In an indefinable tone she had replied: "I'm the daughter of the Master of Masters, the one who, ten thousand years ago, was called Ram..."

Ram! What did that name mean?[26] And what did that mystical affiliation signify?

But there was one undeniable fact. Sithreva had, anchored in her most profound depths, a hatred of Europeans. As a Hindu, she hated the English, the masters of her homeland, and with them all the peoples who claimed to be civilized, who, she said, came from thousands of leagues away to despoil the Orient, to consume its flesh and its blood.

"But I'm European, and you love me!" he exclaimed.

Then she looked him full in the face, and replied: "I want you to take Europe, to give it to the Orient."

At other times, in the night, she led him through the city, into the wretched quarters where the population swarms are driven by hunger by the thousands toward the Occident, and which the Occident has rejected. And she told him about the curses launched against the whites, against the egotistical and greedy race extending beyond the Urals, all the way to the confines of the Atlantic.

In vain Sandorf tried to combat the nightmare of sorts that was oppressing his brain. Without confessing to Marguerite the source from which his information came, he had drawn her attention to the alarming symptoms that had been manifested to him.

James Hilton's Shangri-La. Like many popular writers of the day, however (lent encouragement by such syncretic occult theorists as Madame Blavatsky), Lermina makes no distinction between Hinduism and Buddhism, and also includes Islam in the same "Oriental" grab-bag.

[26] In this instance, it refers more closely to Madame Blavatsky's theosophist pseudo-history than to the Rama of the Hindu epic *Ramayana*.

Often, he told himself that he was playing a singular role in all of that. How, as a European, could he tolerate the woman he loved spreading maledictions against the great family to which he was proud to belong? Could he deny, in the profoundest depths of his conscience, that Sithreva was accomplishing, before his eyes, almost with his complicity, a nefarious endeavor that threatened his European brethren?

But soon, passion resumed its empire; he felt himself borne away as if by a whirlwind that he could not resist.

It was also the case that Sithreva repeated to him that he would be the greatest of the great, that she dreamed of elevating him to a throne so highly placed that before him, the kings of the world would be lower than slaves...

He listened, stunned and hallucinated...and the savage within him got the upper hand again, and he surprised himself by dreaming about those Asiatic empires of which the leader was almost a god. His memory recalled legends of the Caucasus, in which the Sars, whose citadels of Van were an impregnable refuge,[27] had overlooked the steppes from outside and above the world, according to the songs of the ancient Caucasians.

Pride is an alcohol, as is ambition, and in response to the inflamed speech of Sithreva, all the ancient rancor amassed by the vanquished against the conquerors of the people of the Urals and the Caspian region had risen into Sandorf's mind, and he listened ardently to the enchantress as she was pouring those hateful aphrodisiacs into him.

Such as the man who, on that disastrous day, had been transported to the strange place in which he had now wakened

---

[27] The Citadel of Van is a stone fortress build some 800 years before the modern era in what is nowadays eastern Turkey; it still stands, although somewhat dilapidated. The "Sars" to whom Lermina refers are an invention of one of Lermina's acquaintances in the occult revival, Joséphin Péladan, who liked to style himself Sâr Péladan, claiming that the title was descended from ancient Babylonia.

under the influence of the liquor that had been poured for him: a kind of ferment that recalled in its composition the Soma of the ancient Aryans.

He looked around. No lamp illuminated the place where he was, and yet it was filled with a soft light, with which the vague and mysterious chanting that seemed to be emerging from the depths of the earth harmonized.

He started walking back and forth, listening.

Strangely enough, in those distant, seemingly muffled harmonies, filtered after a fashion by distance, he recognized a melody. Where had he heard it before?

Yes, he remembered: he had been nursed by a woman who had come from the Lesghian lands,[28] and it was from her lips, when she had cradled him while giving him her breast that he had heard that song, with its monotonous chorus, the words of which said:

"The Kirghiz is the master of the desert; to him belongs the extent, to him, from top to bottom, the domination. His horse bounds over the steppe, further on, ever further; he leaps over the highest mountains, ever higher, and he gallops forever and ever, launching himself higher, until, with his bit in his teeth, he touches the stars."

That was the song, conserved by his ancestors, which spoke of heroic epochs closed forever.

But why? In millions of years, can the sons of the Caucasus not recover their liberty? Russians, no! Conquered but not submissive, the Kirghiz, Caucasians and Kurds might, on the day they wished, re-conquer the empire of which the Caspian is the great sea.

---

[28] The Lesghians were one of the major groups of Caucasian tribes identified by 19th century ethnologists, along with the Circassians and the Chechens. The notion that they might be descended from the Kirghiz, although based on Mongoloid features resulting from the empire-building ventures of Genghiz Khan and Timur, is fanciful.

More than ever—was it the effect of the beverage he had drunk?—those ideas of hectic battle against the Muscovite colossus took on substance in his mind. He felt himself carried away, as if destiny had placed a hand on his shoulder, crying out to him: "Forward!"

But at that moment, the simultaneously intelligent and aristocratic face of Sacha passed before his eyes. There was a kind of oscillation in his consciousness.

He remembered exquisite evenings in St. Petersburg, when luxury deployed all its seductions...the mountains, the steppes are certainly grandiose and limited horizons...but silk curtains illuminated by the gleam of electric flowers, the divine music of the great masters vibrating in that frame of silk and lace...white shoulders beneath the scintillation of diamonds...was there not an all-powerful magic in civilization?

At that moment, a bright light struck Sandorf's eyes.

He turned abruptly in the direction in which the source suddenly seemed to have been illuminated, and uttered an exclamation of surprise and admiration.

One might have thought that the wall had suddenly opened in front of him; in a vast bay solely closed by a kind of silvery gauze that allowed everything to be seen as clearly as through a sheet of rock crystal, Sandorf witnessed the deployment of a marvelous spectacle.

It was a temple, sustained by colonnades that were lost in a vault strewn with luminous tars, at the back of which was a golden altar, to which steps of marble or onyx led up, surmounted by flowers in sparkling colors, in the midst which stood a tall statue of an unknown substance which projected a radiance: a splendid idol in which all the seductions of the Orient were personified, an image of a woman raising her arms in a gesture of benediction, with slender hands articulating the sacred sign of the Hindus, with the middle and index fingers raised while the other three were folded over the palm.

The statue—was it really a statue?—seemed to be palpitating like living flesh, and one might have thought that a breath was emerging from its parted lips, murmuring the fateful syllable.

Songs burst forth, triumphantly, in a vocal purity that penetrated to the depths of the soul, causing the most intimate fibers of the organism to vibrate.

At the foot of the altar, men were standing in two rows—perhaps priests...or rather warriors, for they were all wearing golden helmets and breastplates, their hands grasping swords whose points were directed upwards toward the idol.

And further back, under the pillars, in a profundity that was lost in limitless shadow, was a crowd clad in white, hands extended toward the altar.

On every step columns rose up, supporting exquisitely wrought cassolettes, veritable marvels of patient Hindu art, which exhaled delicious perfumes and vapors rising in spirals all the way to the vault of the temple.

Sandorf leaned forward, stupefied, but filled with a profound, almost superstitious emotion. He was unmoving, though, as if hypnotized, his will enchained as if in a dream.

Suddenly, the chanting stopped. There was no longer anything but a soft murmur, like a susurrus, on closed lips.

The ranks parted; the tips of the swords, pointed toward the altar, came together, forming a golden vault. And over the brightly-colored carpet, gliding rather than walking, with her forehead circled in gold with a carbuncle in the center and her figure hidden beneath a long mantle of red and white linen, Sithreva appeared, admirably beautiful, with her marble pallor, her large eyes wide open and fixed upon the idol, her lips smiling as if in ecstasy, and her right hand partly raised with a freshly-blossomed lotus flower in her fingers.

She went straight toward the idol, and when she was no more than a meter away, she bowed, throwing the flower onto the steps of the altar.

She remained there for a few moments, motionless; then she slowly turned around and, facing the faithful, raised her arms and pronounced the fateful invocation:

Buddham saranam gacchami
Dhammam saranam gacchami
Sangham saranam gacchami.

Which signifies, in the Pali language: "With Buddha as my guide I go; with the law as my guide I go; with the brotherhood as my guide I go."

They all repeated the lines, one by one, and when she had finished, the clouds of perfume rose more densely into the temple, enveloping her from head to toe and placing a kind of aureole around her head.

Sandorf, dazzled, nailed to the spot, did not take his eyes off her; the daughter of Tibet had never seemed more beautiful to him, and the mad love that he had conceived for her had never imposed itself more victoriously upon him.

She was speaking now; she did not employ the Chinese language, but a kind of Tamil, used in Ceylon, which almost all Orientals understand. Sandorf could speak that language, and he did not miss a single one of the words she pronounced in her vibrant and inspired voice, every echo of which penetrated into the utmost depths of his soul.

This is what she said:

"Orient, Orient, it is from you that everything comes; you are the source, you are the fountain of truth and light...

"In you, and from you the sunlight emerges, to spread over the world. Orient, you are life...and you are justice!

"It is in the bosom of your children, throughout eternity, that the fire has been lit that created science and conscience.

"Sons of the Tien-Ti, have you forgotten? Sons of the Wu-Wei-Keaon, sons of the Ko-Lao, have you abdicated?"

What did those strange names and those mysterious appeals mean? Before going any further, we ought to explain briefly.

For hundreds of years, secret societies have existed in China that bear the names Tien-Ti (Heaven and Earth), Wu-Wei-Keaon (White Lily) and Ko-Lao (Beloved Brother). These societies, whose origins are even more ancient than that of which Freemasonry is proud, in communication with all the mysterious associations of Hindustan, Tibet and the Caspian, count their affiliates in the thousands, perhaps—who can tell?—in the millions.

The crowd knows nothing about them; they are not known to one another; submissive to the authority of the group-leaders, they only know this: that a day will come when all the oppressions of Europe upon Asia will be broken.

The society of the Tien-Ti was the richest of them all; it is affirmed that one member of its council possesses fifty million francs.

In the Philippines, in Burma, in San Francisco and in Melbourne, in spite of the expulsion of the Chinese; in Hindustan, in spite of the persecutions on which the English have attempted, since the recent revolts, to base their tottering power; in Turkestan, where the leaven of revolt increasingly ferments since the trans-Caucasian and trans-Siberian railways have, in a sense, drawn a circle around old Asia; everywhere, the phrase circulated: "The Orient for the Orientals; death to the Europeans!"

Sometimes, a movement erupted at some point in immense Asia, Europeans were massacred, blood was shed, the murderers were ungraspable, and the reprisals fell upon the innocent; the Europeans thought they had stifled the sedition. On the contrary; their vengeance had only served to alienate new enemies. And thus the hatred of the races brooded everywhere, more ardent and cruel, until the day when they would burst forth in a cataclysm of such proportions that no one would have dared to imagine it.

The Tien-Ti had been founded—or, rather reorganized—in China in the middle of the seventeenth century, in the following circumstances.

In 1644 the Tartar Manchus had expelled the indigenous dynasty. Twenty years later, the Tartar Eleuths invaded China and conquered a large fraction of it. The Emperor made a desperate appeal to his subjects, and a Buddhist monk—Kuu-Tat or Hok-Kien, those two names being identical in Chinese and

Pali, and signifying "Profound Root"—set himself at the head of his sectarians and drove out the invaders. But a traitor denounced Kuu-Tat as an aspirant to supreme power, and the ingrate Emperor put him to death; his monastery was burned and most of his closest associates perished, but five of them escaped and took refuge in a temple.

As they were walking along the bank of the river Sampo, they saw, floating in the water, and incense-burner which bore a sculpted inscription which they deciphered, and read: *Expel the Chang; restore the Ming*. The Buddhists then organized a vast conspiracy, and the battle was engaged. The society of the Tien-Ti had ramifications throughout the kingdom and the entire world; Hindus as well as the Chinese spread the word that the re-establishment of the Ming would be the signal for Asiatic domination of the entire world.

For two centuries, history registered Tai-Ping revolts, marked by horrible massacres and even more terrible reprisals. But that perseverance of more than two hundred and fifty years was finally about to attain the desired goal...

We have said that the Ming had resumed their place on the throne of the Middle Kingdom. Where the Europeans, always ignorant of the true instincts of the people they scorned, had only seen a change of dynasty, a palace revolution that was only of mediocre concern to their interests, the entire Oriental world had shuddered. It was the epoch fixed by destiny, by prophecy. It was the hour of Oriental revenge that was sounding.

All fanaticisms were ready to be unleashed at the first signal.

And that was what Sithreva, the inspired oracle of hatred and wrath, was saying to those men who had come from all parts of Asia to hear the fateful word that was about to unleash the old world of monsters and chimeras upon civilized and scientific Europe.

"Out of China, the Europeans!" cried Sithreva. "Out of India, the English! Out of Java, the Dutch, and out of Sumatra,

Tonkin and Cambodia, the French! Out of the Caucasus and the Caspian lands, the Russians, Muscovites and Poles!

"Rise up, the Orient! From Peking to Baghdad, from Edo to Samarkand, from Aden to Tobolsk, from the Himalaya to the Ural, from the Pei-Ho to the Volga, let the immense flood rush, let the formidable inundation flow and engulf! In millions upon millions, let the sons of the Aurora drive the terrified Occidentals before them, like vile flocks, and precipitate them into the Atlantic, which was their cradle and shall be their tomb...and let the victorious standard of the five hundred gods extend over the fearful world, as black as night, as white as light, as yellow as gold, and as red as blood!"

At the moment that she named the four banners, men brandished them, fluttering, above Sithreva's head. In her exaltation, sublime with fury and a sort of religious rage, she seemed magnified and to be floating above the fanatics that her words were intoxicating.

Then she addressed each of the chiefs individually.

"King of the white Nenuphar," she cried, "are you ready?"

And an ascetic with emaciated features and sparkling eyes cried: "Death to the Occidentals!"

"And you, king of the Mendicants...you, the pariah who, as a tzigane, Bohemian, gypsy or zingari, has dragged you suffering through the cities and the fields of our enemies, are you ready?"

And the king of the Bohemians, the same one who had been seen only six months before in the heart of Paris, followed and acclaimed by the idlers, stood up and said: "I have sworn death!"

And all of them replied in the same fashion: the Lama of Homuch, the Fakir of Madras, the Buddhist monks, the Magi, the Brahmins, the Marabouts, the Great Dervish of Mecca and the Master of Fire, the Great Parsee of the Guebres, all, with a unanimous impulse, swore with their hands extended, brandishing swords.

With a gesture, Sithreva imposed silence upon them, and then, slowly, with an infinite softness in her voice, which had musical incantations, she said: "And who, then, will bring us the word of the Great Mountains, the oath of the Summits? Is the Caucasus alone cowardly? Lesghians, Kirghiz, Moguls, Kalmuks, Chenchens—is there no one who will reclaim the position as your head of the great Shamyl?[29] From the fortress of Ghunid, is there no longer a voice that will cry to the slaves of Russia their shame and their infamy?"

She had come down the steps of the altar, and solemnly headed toward the silvery veil that separated the hypnotized, maddened Sandorf from the temple.

When she got there, she lifted the veil and extended her hand to him.

In order to understand the strange and deadly process that was taking place in Sandorf's mind, it is necessary to remember that, as soon as he had been deposited on the sofa by his kidnappers, Sithreva had poured him a cup of liquor that he had raised to his lips and swallowed in a single draught.

It was the Aryan Soma, the liquor of the priests of Agni, which burns the breast and exalts thought, with multiplies energy tenfold and, like hashish, multiplies the passions a hundredfold.

And as Sithreva spoke, it seemed to the descendant of the Kirghiz that he heard voices resonating in his ears—better than that, in the utmost depths of his being—that had pieced

---

[29] The Chechen Imam named Shamyl, Shamil or Schamyl (1797-1871), who led the resistance in the Northern Caucasus against the invading forces of the Russian Empire during the long Caucasian War, which resulted in a conclusive conquest in 1864, is also extensively celebrated in Hippolyte Mettais' *L'An 5865* (1865; tr, as *The Year 1865*, Black Coat Press, ISBN 9781612271002), a pioneering immersive fantasy in whose future history his descendants are credited with the liberation of the Caucasus from Russian rule and the founding of a successful nation.

him before: the songs of the woman who had nursed him, ancestral tales heard while he was still a child in the mountains.

It was true, however, that it was cowardice on his part and that of his brethren to have submitted and accepted Russian domination. Would they never shrug off that shameful yoke? Were they no longer free children of the glaciers, accustomed to roaming the precincts of the enormous Caucasus without masters?

Then a name had vibrated in his ear like a clarion call: Shamyl.

Was it, then, so distant, that memory of patriotism and heroism?

No—not even a century. It was in 1824 that the valiant Shamyl, imam and sultan of the mountain folk of the Caucasus, had engaged with his ally, the Mullah Kasi, a war to the death against the Russians. At Gimry, when the old fortress had fallen amid fire and blood, only the imam had escaped slavery, and had reached the steppes on his horse. Did no one any longer remember the victories of 1842, when Shamyl had invaded the land of the Avars, and Woronzoff had been obliged to retreat, and the Kabarda and Gerghebil fell into the power of the Caucasians? And still, although the Russians had crushed their enemy, he had escaped them, ungraspable, protected as if by a magical power...and then reappeared more ardent, more vigorous and more determined to fight.

In 1859, had Shamyl not entered into Tiflis as a victor? But treason lay in wait for him, and a year later, in the fortress of Ghunid, Shamyl, sold to his adversaries, launched this supreme imprecation: "The Russian Ogre will consume the world!"

And it was both the succession and the revenge of Shamyl that was being offered to Wintscheff—and in what conditions! With the aid of thousands of allies...

What did Europe matter to him? He was, he felt himself to be, a son of the Orient. He hated the civilized people who had corrupted and bastardized his soul...and his ears were ringing with the fanfares of battle.

The Kirghiz is the master of the desert; to him, from top to bottom, domination.

"Friend," Sithreva said to him, "are you ready? Do you want to give liberation to our superb hordes? Would you like to seize the scepter along with the sword? Would you like to be great, to be noble, to be a king?"

And Sandorf Wintscheff bent his knee before Sithreva and said to her: "Through life and through death I am yours...I love you."

And with a cry of triumph, she drew him into the temple.[30]

---

[30] Sithreva is by no means the first Oriental *femme fatale* featured in French popular fiction, but it is worth noting that similar characters became a staple of melodramas of this stripe; Sax Rohmer's Fu Manchu had a seductive daughter, and Ward supplemented the Fu Manchu series of books with another featuring the exotic *femme fatale* Sumuru.

VIII

Let us return to the battle sustained inside the city by the Europeans. The attack, as we know, had been mounted simultaneously on the various Legations, which, in total, had no more than eight hundred men to defend them.

At the English Embassy, the battle had been fierce, but as the English maintain mostly naval forces, they had only kept a very limited number of soldiers in Peking—a hundred at the most—whom the populace had soon dispatched. The Ambassador had not wanted to abandon his post and as he too had invited guests to his palace to celebrate the first day of spring, a horrible massacre had taken place.

Men and women had been surrounded by fire and had perished in the flames. Lord Gordon had been seen, mounted on the highest terrace, brandishing the flag of his nation, before a sudden collapse had precipitated the nobleman and his unfortunate companions into the very heart of the fire.

Several ladies belonging to the highest aristocracy of the United Kingdom had found death in that catastrophe, which it seemed no one had escaped.

The German Legation, which, as we have said, affected only to entertain very frosty relations with the representatives of other countries, although warned of the revolt before it had reached the part of the city where it was located, had not taken any precaution of resist an attack that everything must have caused it to anticipate.

The *chargé d'affaires*, General Otto von Schuld, one of those defeated in the last French campaign, had remained an irreconcilable enemy of the French and Russians who had conquered his homeland. Respectable as patriotism might be, even among enemies, it can sometimes, in its excesses, lead to grave complications.

Von Schuld, informed that the French and Russian Legations had been attacked simultaneously, had forgotten the solidarity that ought to unite all Europeans in Oriental countries. The roads were open before him; he had more than a hundred and fifty men. It would have been natural for him to go to the aid of the embassies in danger, and perhaps, by attacking the Chinese from the rear, he would have greatly facilitated their defense. But his narrow and rancorous mind did not show him his duty in that light.

Let them defend themselves! he said to himself.

And who knows whether, with the conviction that it was only them to whom the Chinese were enemies, he might have experienced a kind of malevolent joy in knowing that they were in peril.

However, when he saw the red light of the conflagration sparkle in the sky and envelop he city like a frightful shroud, when the formidable howls and jeers of the crowd, already gorged on blood, resounded at the gates of his Legation, he understood that he had emitted a grave imprudence with regard to his own interests.

In vain he tried to negotiate, declaring that whatever the grievances of the Chinese were, his nation at least was not involved in a conflict whose causes he did not even know. It was only when he heard the cry: "Death to the foreigners!" that he appreciated the full extent of the danger.

Perhaps he regretted his egotism then, but it was too late, and nothing any longer remained but to sell his life dearly.

At any rate, he put up a valiant defense; the buildings of the Legation, which had once been a Jesuit convent, were constructed in solid stone and did not lend themselves, like the others, to rapid destruction by fire.

The siege lasted five hours; the Germans were masterful in courage and tenacity, but what can valor do against numbers, against a crowd fanaticized by hatred and by successes already achieved?

The assault was mounted from all sides at once. Rather than surrender—and what would have been the point of a capitulation that the enemy would only have accepted in order to make it a means of treason?—Von Schuld set fire to the powder stored in the cellars of the Legation. There was a frightful explosion that made the old Chinese city shudder all the way to its foundations and killed several hundred Chinese along with the Germans who had survived the battle.

Strangely enough, by a sort of miracle, the Minister, who had remained at his post of honor, was the only one spared by the frightful blast, and it was certainly a bizarre scene to behold him standing, alone, on a section of wall whose collapse had bypassed him, still alive.

Either out of respect for his courage or by virtue of a kind of superstitious sentiment that showed him to them as an invulnerable being or one saved by the gods, the fanatics did not butcher him. He was captured, taken prisoner and disappeared, dragged away by the crowd to the gates of the Yellow City.

Scenes of atrocious savagery unfolded all over the city. All the houses occupied by Europeans had been identified long before and marked in advance for Chinese vengeance.

At the first signal, from the center to the most distant extremities of the Chinese city, all the way to Chiang-Tsu-Men and the Hai-Tien road, the unfortunate Europeans had been attacked unexpectedly, and for the most part, had not even had time to put up any defense. Some had been massacred in their beds, while others had been dragged onto the public highway and murdered with the most ignoble savagery.

Execution Square, in the Chinese city at the exit of the Tshun-Chih Gate, merited its terrible name that night; a hateful crowd filled it, seething and howling; at every moment its ranks opened before some unfortunate who was driven forward with blows of bamboo rods or dragged by the hair. Then the circle closed around him again and for several minutes, sometimes for a long quarter of an hour, madness and the application of torture were pushed to the point of frenzy.

Occasionally, a voice rose up, dominating the crowd, uttering a name: someone forgotten who was being identified to the fury of the wild beasts. Some of them broke away and ran to the designated place; entry was forced into the European's house, his wife and children were seized, half-naked and thrown as fodder to the untiring assassins.

By going along a narrow and obscure side-street that opens onto the right-hand side the right of the Passage of Bimbelotiers, one arrives at a little crossroads of about forty square meters, a kind of open courtyard, at the back of which, during the day, a shop is perceptible that would have seemed very ordinary to us, but which was genuinely exotic in the Middle Kingdom.

It is necessary to know that Chinese shops, like those which garnish both sides of the major roads, are wooden stalls similar to the temporary buildings that are established in fairgrounds, striped with red, green and yellow, ornamented with dragons or chimeras in carved wood, with streamers of a doubtful cleanliness and indescribable hue at the corners of the roofs. They are, in brief, establishments that the meanest tenant of the spiced-bread fair would not want.

The shop to which we are referring was brown in color, with gold threads heightened with red, but delicately drawn with a brush that was simultaneously skillful and distinguished. Two panes of glass framed a door, similarly glazed, on which the following inscription stood out in gold letters:

Eustache Nivet, Professor, Qualified Chemist and Photographer.

Chinese characters translated the marvelous inscription for the benefit of the profane, uninitiated into the finesse of the French language, and we can affirm that in the Chinese language, the photographer had emphasized his titles no less warmly.

Higher up, on a panel that extended across the entire width of the shop, a picture was displayed, a work of art due to some house-painter of the great city of Batignolles, which represented the following:

The sun, wearing a short jacket and coiffed in a bowler hat, arriving from one side, valise in hand, like a traveler getting off a train, while running from the opposite direction was a person wearing a pointed hat and a long beard: a typical art student of the 1830s, whose mouth, wide open, was allowing words to escape enveloped in a black ellipse: "Come on, then, my collaborator; we're only waiting for you."

This mystical painting, which, following the example of the hieroglyphs dear to occultists, presented a meaning that was simultaneously mysterious and practical, caused amazement to the worthy Chinese, who, holding the sun in great esteem, revered it all the more in the scarcely ordinary form of a belated commercial traveler.

Eustache Nivet, who had tired of Batignolles, had abandoned everything, including friends and fatherland, but he would have cut off his hand rather than not take with him that superb work, of which he had been the inspiration, and was for him a talisman.

To begin with, Eustache Nivet adapted very well to the Chinese climate and had no complaints about business. He had devised a system of double exposure that surrounded the photograph of a Chinese person with little angels—an innovation that, no one knew why, had had the greatest success and brought a clientele of amorous individuals to his door.

What, after all, did he want? To amass a dowry for Rose, whom he loved with all his heart, and, if possible, to reserve a few years of leisure during which he could pursue in depth certain researches in chemistry, of which he was very fond, and which were fairly closely related to the eternal quest for the philosopher's stone.

If he had employed the pretext of an indisposition to send his daughter to the Embassy on her own, it was with the sole aim of devoting himself, alone in his laboratory, to certain manipulations from which he expected marvels.

It would be necessary never to have been possessed by the demon of invention not to understand that, if a cannon had been fired close at hand, Nivet would not have paid to slightest attention to that circumstance, absolutely secondary as it would be for a mortal who is scrutinizing the arcane of nature.

Now, Nivet was scrutinizing; that much is undeniable. He had closed and bolted the shutter of his shop-front solidly, and had installed himself in a large room garnished with materials that would have made an alchemist's mouth water: retorts, alembics, furnaces, conical and round-bottomed flasks filled with various liquids; nothing was missing.

Nivet was a man of forty-some years, tall and commendably bald, his head being like a knee to which a narrow crown of hair served as a garter. He had a long nose, a broad mouth and overlapping teeth, plus two other physical characteristics—not to mention his moral qualities, the number of which surpassed his faculties of calculation—of which he was particularly proud.

First of all, he had a booming voice, something extra-human, tubal and trumpet-like. He flattered himself that he could crack a windowpane with a single burst of his throat—a talent useful to glazers but sometimes inconvenient in family life.

Then, the masterpiece, the marvel of marvels, was a long beard: one meter ten centimeters, not mentioning the millimeters, and so artistically shaped that it formed a point tapering almost as far as his knees, and so beautifully black!

When he was working, he threw it over his shoulder.

Such was the man—a worthy fellow, in sum, a trifle self-important, vain at times—who dreamed of transforming the world by means of marvelous inventions that he could not define very well to himself, but which he declared to be stupefying.

Having only received a very limited education, he had already succeeded in "inventing" things that had been known since Pythagoras, but that was of little importance to him; each discovery was only a step on the limitless road that he was following.

That night, the was on the point of making a compound that was nothing other than bicarbonate of soda, of which housewives have been making use for more than a hundred years, and he had not heard anything—neither the furious clamors of the assassins nor the sounds of explosions and beaten gongs.

He was tranquil; his daughter—the dear child—was having fun at the Embassy. He was quite alone, quite tranquil.

In Execution Square, however, a Chinese illuminator, to whom photography provided a disastrous competition, decided to cut it short by reminding the executioners that somewhere in the vicinity there was a Frenchman by the name of Nai-Vao, that being a Chinese onomatopoeia of the bourgeois name off Nivet.

A cry of joyful rage saluted this communication, and twenty of the bandits, armed with pikes, axes and other malevolent devices, had raced away, howling, to the little square of which we have spoken.

The Chinese, being only twenty against one, were prudent, all the more so because Nivet by virtue of his amicable liaison with the sun—and also his beard, which gave him the appearance of a lama—had contrived to inspire a kind of superstitious esteem in the brigands.

They believed him to be something of a magician—which did not alter the fact that he had to be killed, like all the rest; on the contrary.

Except that, after having consulted one another momentarily, the assailants decided to act with a certain precaution.

It was decided that the man would be drawn out of his home by friendly words; that would be safer than penetrating lightly into his lair, where a demon might come to his aid.

One of the Chinese, therefore—a big fellow who had served with European sailors and spoke a kind of Oriental pidgin, comprehensible even to a child of Batignolles, would go to the door and knock gently to begin with.

There was no reply; Nivet was supervising the cooking of some ingredient, an operation too close to his heart for him to pay any attention to trivial noises from outside.

He knocked louder, but as the silence persisted, it was decided to emphasize the blows, which became violent enough, as the saying has it, to wake the dead.

Nivet was very much alive. This time, he heard, and listened.

Who was that? He was not a physician to be woken up at such an hour. As for Rose, it had been agreed that she would stay the night with a friend, a French shopkeeper, who had been charged with taking her to the Embassy. It could not be her. Who was it, then?

The blows increased their force, and the bandits, in spite of their intentions, increasingly carried away by their wrath, became less effective in dissimulating their intentions.

Nivet had moved away from his furnace, and he leaned toward the door, listening.

The Chinese believed that they were talking in whispers, but in fact, a kind of furious growling escaped from their furious throats, which was not at all reassuring.

The Batignollais had only a very limited confidence in Chinese gentility; he too, for some time, had been noticing symptoms that had caused him some anxiety—to the extent that he had had a presentiment that, one day or another, there would be some kind of squabble.

One of the assailants, more imprudent that the others, launched a very explicit insult; another growled a threat.

"Well," murmured Nivet, "these people don't seem very friendly to me."

He went up a small staircase to an upper floor, where there was a kind of grain-loft.

At that moment, through one of the skylights that opened in the direction of the Tartar city, he perceived the reflection of the conflagration, and heard the rumor of the infuriated city.

With a gesture that was habitual to him when the situation took on a grave character, he tucked his beard under his arm. Then, resolutely, he advanced toward the other skylight overlooking the narrow square, which the twenty assassins filled almost entirely.

He leaned out.

"Who's there?" he asked, "And what do you want with me?"

He spoke Chinese with a suburban Parisian accent, of distinctly bizarre effect.

"Come down," shouted a voice, "We have to talk to you."

"Talk to me about what? I can hear you very well, tell me what you want. You know that I don't take photos at this hour."

"Are you coming down, swine?" howled one of them.

That made things much clearer—all the more so as Nivet, now entirely awakened from his transcendental meditations, could hear the frightful howls of the torturers who were killing people in Execution Square, and the victims that they were torturing.

Doubt was no longer possible; even though he could not take exact account of what was happening, they could only be abnormal and terrible events.

In a matter of seconds, Nivet, who was no fool, had made his plan.

Very mildly, he negotiated for a little while longer, explaining that he would like nothing better than to open the door to his good friends the Chinese, but that they would have to give him time to get dressed...five minutes...three minutes...a few more seconds...

The others, not very intelligent, were delighted with the success of their ruse. In a moment, Nivet/Nai-Vao would open the door, and just as he was stepping outside, they would grab him...and three minutes later, in Execution Square...

But the Batignollais photographer, who understood very well what was at stake, and was very fond of his life—which, according to him, was one of the most precious in the world—had not remained inactive.

He had gone to the back of the grain loft in quest of a kind of pump, similar to those that were used in the nineteenth century to water gardens, a copper cylinder equipped with a piston and a nozzle—except that the nozzle was rather long, about fifty centimeters, and terminated in a copper plate pierced with holes, the purpose of which was obviously to spread the water jet out into a fan over a perimeter of more than two meters.

While preparing the object, Nivet said in a loud voice: "My friends, my excellent friends, don't be impatient...here I am...I'm coming down...there...I'm ready."

The others extended their claws toward the door in order to grab him before he could put up a semblance of resistance.

He picked up a flask, filled a bucket with a colorless but singularly odorous liquid, and then let slip the remark, addressed to no one but himself: "Let's go, my Greek fire!"

The inventor reappeared under the photographer.

Suddenly, the Chinese felt themselves inundated by a liquid that rained down on their heads and shoulders.

They uttered cries of rage. Water! The imbecile had the pretention of driving them away with a cold shower! It was too stupid, in truth.

Deciding to finish it immediately, they hurled themselves at the door.

In order to proceed more rapidly, Nivet picked up the bucket and emptied it over his assailants in one go.

"Death to the Frenchman!" The cry trailed off into frightful lamentations.

This is what had happened:

Nivet had taken a little box out of his pocket, had taken out a dozen matches, had struck them—with a very Parisian gesture—on the back of his trousers, and then had dropped them on the assembled group.

Eustache Nivet's Greek fire was purely and simply the volatile liquid long known as mineral essence, luciline or other more or less elegant names,[31] endowed with rapid inflammatory qualities. Right when one of the matches touched one of the points where the liquid had fallen, flames instantaneously

---

[31] In this context, "luciline" refers to a petroleum extract marketed by Alfred Guérard, who called his petrol refinery La Luciline because it manufactured lamp oil. It was not sufficiently refined to contain a single organic compound—hence such vague terms as "mineral essence"—but consisted mostly of ethanes like the butane used in modern cigarette lighters.

sprang forth everywhere: on the garments, on the head, in the hair, on the skin...and so bitter, so mordant, eating away the flesh with such rapidity that the wretches, enveloped by flames, were writhing, throwing themselves on the ground, and rolling over, without being able to extinguish the terrible conflagration.

In the narrow space where they were confined, they collided with walls, crushing one another and jostling one another, falling and rebounding: a veritable demonic dance.

Very proud of the result of his chemical combinations and comparing himself secretly to the priests of Dodona who, as everyone knows, defended themselves against the Gauls with thunderbolts,[32] Nivet did not hang around to enjoy his triumph, for a terrible thought had just surged forth in his mind, suddenly illuminated by a poignant anxiety.

Rose! His dear Rose! If the order these wretches were following was "Death to the French!" there was no doubt that the first effects of their rage would have been exercised on the French Embassy.

A good patriot and an excellent father, Nivet did not hesitate. He ran to the far side of the grain loft and, opening the skylight, he looked down.

Behind the house there was a little garden adjacent to waste ground that extended as far as the Hai-Tai Gate. If he could escape, he would have reached the ancient rampart in less than a quarter of an hour, and the Legation would only be a short distance away.

"Come on, Latude!" cried Nivet.

He called by that name, famous for nearly a century and a half,[33] an engine of his invention that bore an unmistakable

---

[32] Dodona was the site of a famous oracle in Greece, originally devoted to a mother goddess who was supplanted by Zeus (hence the defensive thunderbolts). How the Gauls got into the story in Nivet's version is anyone's guess.

[33] Jean-Henri Latude (1725-1805) was imprisoned in the Bastille after stupidly offending Madame de Pompadour, and be-

resemblance to a knotted rope, but the knots of which there were many, appeared to be tightened in an entirely new fashion that would have amazed the most cunning of our mariners. In addition, it was equipped with a hook—another new and very ingenious invention—that permitted it to be suspended from the windowsill. While, on the other side of the house, the wretched Chinese were howling, writhing and fleeing, Nivet let himself slide into the void.

In a few seconds he had reached the ground, and without further reflection, he launched himself across the empty space and reached the gate. Fortunately, the crowd was busy elsewhere, and the few people who were there gave no thought to stopping the man who went past them with the rapidity of an arrow.

As he turned the corner of the old wall, he saw, a few paces away, an old monk who was in a hurry, doubtless going to spread the word of death far and wide. He had a long beard that gave Nivet an idea, and he was wearing a long kaftan that enveloped him entirely, with a sort of miter on his head.

The place was deserted—and he had little choice in the matter of means.

Nivet recalled the good old days when he had played as a boy in the Place de Clichy and engaged in friendly wrestling matches with his comrades. He still remembered a certain kind of throw that, with his usual industriousness, he had perfected. He hurled himself upon the servant of Kong-Fu-Tseu— otherwise known as Confucius—and administered a blow of the fist to the back of the neck at the same time as he took the legs from under his adversary with a skillful thrust of his foot, which laid the monk out flat.

---

came famous for his escapes from that prison and others; after the Revolution the Convention ordered that he be paid compensation for his tribulations by his persecutor's family, and he was able to die rich as well as legendary.

Stripping off the cloak and hat took but a moment, and without apologizing, while the monk, completely stunned, was wondering what devil had just fallen on his skull, Nivet fled.

It was as well that he had thought of effecting that transformation; without it, he would not have gotten ten paces further. Scarcely had he found himself on the main road leading to the French Legation when he was caught up in the turbulent flux of assailants running in all directions. Fortunately, his costume and his beard, which were entirely appropriate to the situation, granted him free passage everywhere.

He drew nearer to the Legation, and now the poor man was prey to inexpressible anguish. Everything was ablaze, everywhere there were cries of agony and despair.

Suddenly, there was an enormous surge.

The gate of the main courtyard had just opened, and all the soldiers that had not yet succumbed, with Albert de Mesnes at their head and the injured ambassador, laid on a stretcher, in the middle, along with a few women who were being carried, ran out, launching vigorous gunfire into the road that had just opened up.

The Chinese rushed them, but our soldiers were armed with repeating rifles. The Chinese fell, and it was necessary to advance by marching over their cadavers.

It was, however, also necessary to fear that the ammunition would run out, or that the ever-increasing crowd might succeed by the sheer weight of numbers in overwhelming a handful of valiant men already exhausted by long efforts, for whom discouragement would almost have been permissible.

Fortunately, at the moment when the situation of the French was about to become critical, and when Nivet was regretting not being able to play in Chinese the priestly role of an appeaser of discords, he suddenly heard a volley of bullets whistle past his ears, while vibrant trumpets resounded with an ear-splitting blast.

It was the Russians, running to join up with the French— and Nivet's tall stature was serving them as a target at which to aim.

He scarcely had time to throw himself flat, face down—a position that presented serious inconveniences for a few moments, because the surprised Chinese were seized, for the most part, by an indescribable panic, and started fleeing, treading on his body as they went.

The French, roused by Albert de Mesnes' cries of "Forward," took advantage of the unexpected respite to contrive a gap, and succeeded in joining up with the Russians.

The leaders of the two troops exchanged a few rapid words. It was obvious that resistance was impossible in the Legations, as they were poorly constructed to resist a siege. It was necessary, as soon as possible, to identify and reach a point where they could regroup and take the decisive measures that the situation demanded.

Suddenly, Nivet, who had slid forward on all fours, stood up between the two leaders.

"Swine!" cried the Russian, raising his saber.

"I'm French—don't be stupid! It's me, Nivet, the inventor, the successor of Archimedes!!"

That name was known throughout the French colony, somewhat as an item of ridicule—but it was not a moment for equivocation.

"What are you doing here?"

"I've come to give you an idea of genius. The Yamen—the Chinese Ministry of Foreign Affairs—is a short distance away. There are never any troops there. Take possession of it; it's a veritable fortress."

"The man's right and the advice is sound," said Albert.

The Russian immediately acquiesced, and the order was given to head for the Yamen.

In good order, holding off the attackers, who were gradually recovering from their terror and reforming more menacingly, the two small Russian and French contingents beat a retreat in the required direction.

The crowd did not understand the movement; they thought that the foreigners were heading for the canal in order to embark, and rushed in that direction in order to cut them off. That error was, at least for the moment, the salvation of the Europeans. They reached the Yamen, which was only protected by an insignificant guard-post. In a matter of seconds the doors were forced and the French and Russians found themselves sheltered in a vast stone building, which did, indeed, constitute a veritable fortress, and which possessed the further advantage of being adjacent to the Catholic Mission, another monumental and solid building.

It was a temporary respite, of which they took advantage to fortify the position.

The engineer Sametel, who had death in his heart because he did not know what had become of his daughter, and had every reason to think that she had been massacred, nevertheless did not fail in his duty for an instant.

Curiously enough, the Chinese, as imprudent as all Orientals, had evacuated the Yamen completely, and the a few subaltern employees that remained were put in a safe place. The Minister was with the Emperor, in the Council where the massacres had been decreed.

The Yamen was indeed a fortified location, equipped with cannon, and also with an electrical network, which, although international communications had been severed, was at least functioning internally and could be usefully employed for the artillery.

Nivet, asking in vain for news of his daughter, had begun sobbing when he learned what everyone believed to be the absolute truth—which is to say, the death of the majority of the women, young and old, who had been in the Embassy. On hearing the scientist Sametel giving orders and disposing of electric detonators, he suddenly felt gripped once again by the demon of invention. As timidity had never been one of his faults, he approached Sametel deliberately, and demanded to talk to him.

It must be admitted that the moment was ill-chosen, especially when one thinks of the almost comical reputation that the photographer had acquired by his vainglorious pretentions, so Sametel initially told him, rather harshly, to go away—but

Nivet was tenacious, and by force of importunity, he succeeded in dragging the engineer into a corner and whispering a few words in his ear.

At first, the engineer shrugged his shoulders, but then suddenly became still, listening. He had suffered often enough from the intolerance of others realizing that there is sometimes something useful to be found even in the ideas of a lunatic. And it appeared that Nivet's communications were not without interest.

Suddenly, Sametel seized his arm.

"Your idea is insane," he said abruptly, "but we don't have any choice. Do you know how deep the network you're talking about is located?"

"I confess that in matters of detail," Nivet stammered, who, like all semi-scientists, was ignorant of most of the elements of the question that he pretended to know in depth, "I'm not fully informed."

"It doesn't matter—we'll have to try. I'll give you ten men who'll dig a trench at the point I'll indicate to you. But I have to ask for your word of honor to follow my orders."

The worthy Nivet, who still had a very heavy heart in thinking about Rosette, said, gravely: "Monsieur, I know that, compared to you, I'm ignorant. Give your orders, and I'll carry them out."

"Good. I order you, them, to press the workmen, and encourage them…but don't do anything else. Don't attempt an imprudent and premature application of an idea that might, after all, bring grave dangers in its wake."

Nivet felt rather proud of the responsibility that was about to weigh upon him. "I'll obey," he said, in a tone full of dignity.

While he drew away with the soldiers who were to serve as ditch-diggers, Sametel went back to Albert de Mesnes, and the two of them went to the French Ambassador, still lying on his stretcher, whose features were agonized.

The surgeon had attempted everything indicated by his science, in vain. The representative of France was mortally wounded, but as the two men advanced toward him, he made a vigorous effort, and succeeded in propping himself up.

"Above all, no recklessness!" exclaimed the surgeon.

"Yes, yes, I know," said the Ambassador. "Well, Messieurs—or rather, my dear friends—I've been waiting for you impatiently."

"I've been obliged," said Sametel, "in association with Monsieur de Mesnes, to take all the measures suggested by the horrible danger we're in."

"And you've done well. It's to you, and you alone, that I leave the frightful mission that death will prevent me from accomplishing."

"Death is not yet here."

"What's the point of trying to deceive me?" said the Ambassador, shaking his head. "You know as well as I do that I'm finished, and that my life is only a question of hours, perhaps minutes." As they all tried to protest, he stopped them with a gesture. "Who do you think you're talking to? Here, I represent France, and no mission has ever given me the right to be prouder, but I also know the duty that is imposed on me. Here, a thousand leagues from the fatherland, I am and must be a soldier: not a man who fights with a weapon in hand, but a man who must carry out his obligations with an impassive heart, until death. Well, Messieurs, in your amity, you'll become accomplice to a fault if, by virtue of a fault common—alas!—to many dying men, I gave any credence to your words of consolation. I know that I'm dying; I repeat it to you because it's the truth, and a worthy man does not lie. Dare you contradict me, Doctor?"

The surgeon looked away.

"Thank you," said the Ambassador. "That's the gesture I expected, which dictates my supreme duty to me."

"At least don't exhaust yourself—conserve your remaining strength."

"Oh, I also know that I still have some vigor at my service; I'll prove that to you shortly. And to obey you, to conserve the energy I need for as long as possible, I'm going to talk to you in a low voice. Come closer."

The three men obeyed. In truth, they were paler than the moribund.

"Help me to sit up...that's it! Now listen to me, and remember that what you're about to hear are the supreme orders of the man who speaks in the name of France—and that, no matter what, you must obey me."

"Count on us, Monsieur. We'll obey."

"I am counting on it. So, it's to you, Monsieur Sametel, and you, Monsieur de Mesnes, that I delegate all my powers. It's a matter to taking the gravest resolutions, without hesitation; in order to save the French—the Europeans, for France is the fatherland of all fatherlands—there is no sacrifice before which you ought to recoil. I'm not talking about your lives; I know you won't bargain with them, but it might be that you'll have to risk even more. Some eventuality might be produced that will oblige you to forget all personal sentiment, all pity for yourselves or those dear to you. Accept the sacrifice, whatever it might be, and for the salvation of others, if it's necessary for you to surrender a shred of your flesh, or, which will be more horrible, the flesh of someone else, someone you love..."

Sametel interrupted him. "We understand. Yes, you're right; at this moment, there are those among us to whose patriotic anguish is added the torture of intimate despair...don't worry. If you have to die, go in peace; not one of us will fail in his task."

"I don't doubt you, my friends...and in the dolor in which I'm quitting the combat post, it's a consolation to me to leave in my place men like you. So, everything for France and for humankind...let that be your motto. But that's not all. Come closer I beg you."

It did indeed seem that his voice was weakening—but his eyes were shining with a metallic gleam.

"Monsieur Sametel, how long do you think the Yamen can be defended?"

131

"Even against the hordes of wretches who are going to come at us, I'm counting on five or six hours."

"Oh, that's more than enough. Now, Messieurs, understand that this is an order: "I want to go to the Imperial Palace.""

A triple explanation responded to that statement, so strange that, in truth, they were wondering whether the man who had proffered it was still in his right mind.

As they looked at him I amazement, he relayed: "I'm not mad. I want to go to where my place is. Am I not the Ambassador, the man who has the right, in the name of his country, to talk to sovereigns face to face, who has the duty to remind assassins, even if they are crowned, that crime is all the greater when one has the power to oppose it? Yes, yes, I want to go to that man. I want to tell him, in the presence of his ministers and his slaves, that no potentate, despot or Son of Heaven can violate with impunity the sacred rules of justice, and if I have to fall down dead in front of that man, at least I want my dying breath to be one last protest in the name of France and humankind."

"But you know full well," exclaimed the surgeon, "that to make such an effort is to break the last link attaching you to life."

The Ambassador held out his hand.

"Remember, Messieurs, that you have sworn an oath. Is it having pity on humankind to have pity on one man? You don't understand, then, that I might—who knows?—be able to stop the massacre. The voice of France can be heard. Come on, Messieurs—to hesitate to obey me would be to deny your word of honor."

The three men looked at one another. Evidently, it was madness to attempt the impossible...and it would further abridge that life already condemned...but the Ambassador was right. A representative of France could not recoil before anything, before any consideration; when duty speaks, France has the right to heroic madness.

"But how do you expect to get as far as the palace?" asked Sametel.

"You can't even stand up," the doctor added.

"I'll be carried. I need to get as far as the threshold of the room where the chief of the torturers is sitting." In a firmer voice, he said: "Monsieur de Mesnes, you have the command of your troops here. Monsieur Sametel, you're in charge of the technical aspects of the resistance. Your places are here, and I order you to remain here."

"But what about you?"

"Me!" said the Ambassador, in a voice that was still strong. "You'll place me in the middle of forty of our marine soldiers, with the flag at the head, and they'll have orders to open a way in order to obtain passage for my stretcher."

At that moment, Nivet appeared, red-faced, his features convulsed. He was oblivious to any orders.

"What do you want?" shouted Sametel, angrily. "Get out!"

"Wait!" cried the photographer. "Listen to what I have to say. I've found the subterranean passage that I'd heard about."

"And where does it go?"

"To the Imperial Palace!"

The Ambassador uttered a cry: "You see!"

"But once again," said Sametel, still angry, "how does he know what he's saying?"

"I got it from an employee of the Yamen whose tongue I loosened with my boot. You know what I told you, Monsieur Sametel—that I'd noticed that when the electric beacon on the Yamen was switched on, a beam of light immediately emerged from the summit of the Imperial Palace...so a communication had to exist. And it occurred to me that perhaps we might even be able to blow up the Imperial Palace from here. But it's much better than an electric wire...there's a vast network of subterranean tunnels."

"Well, Messieurs," said the Ambassador. "You were asking how you were going to get me to the palace. This brave man has resolved the problem. Now, don't waste time—I'm in a hurry to do my duty." And he added, in a whisper: "And to have the right to die."

There was no reason to hesitate—and after all, was it not a chance of salvation? Who could tell whether that magnanimous temerity might not change the face of things? Perhaps the Emperor of China was human.

Sametel hastened to give orders. Four men would carry the stretcher, while marine fusiliers accompanied them, ready to open a path by force.

In truth, it was going to certain death, but no one thought about that.

In a few minutes, everything was ready.

The functionary who had given the information to Nivet—whose methods of persuasion had made a particular impact on him—was instructed to place himself at the head of the little cortege, between the soldiers, to whom the order was given loudly to shoot him at the first suspicion of treason.

The photographer insisted on serving as one of the stretcher-bearers—a favor that, in truth, could not be refused to him.

Sametel thought it his duty, however, to remind him that he was a father.

"Don't I know it!" cried the poor man. "Haven't those wretches killed my beloved Rosette?"

Sametel turned his head away, for he too had a tortuous anguish in the depths of his heart.

The route that the Ambassador had to follow passed under the Tartar city and ought to come out somewhere in the imperial gardens. A surprise was, however, possible.

"If any misfortune occurs," said Albert de Mesnes, "how can we be notified in order to send help?"

"See these telegraphic wires?" said Nivet, pointing to the black cables that ran along the wall, illuminated by the torches. "I'll find a way."

"All right," said Sametel. "In any case, our task is commencing here."

Indeed, furious destinations were audible above, as the attack recommenced, more ferociously than ever.

The Ambassador, propped up on his pillows, said: "Remember, Messieurs—and adieu!"

"We'll see one another again."

"Who knows?"

And the cortege moved off into the tunnel, while Sametel and Albert ran to help the Europeans under attack.

The Russians and the French were a single company, acting with admirable unison.

Thanks to the cannons abandoned by the Chinese, they succeeded in keeping the horde at bay, and had succeeded in saving a number of Europeans who had run to the Yamen in search of refuge.

The Russians were commanded by an old Cossack general with a fearsome moustache, courageous to the point of folly. His name was General Butowieff.

As he knew the city well, having lived there for many years, he was the one who had succeeded in rapidly establishing communication with the canal; the gardens of the Yamen almost extended as far as the wall, and it had been possible to take possession of the gate almost without firing a shot. That ensured a retreat for the women, children and anyone not in a fit condition to bear arms. Fortunately, barges with decks had been numerous, and hundreds of Europeans, belonging to all the nationalities represented in Peking, had already found refuge aboard the ironclad *Suffren*, moored at the opening to the Pei-Ho.

But was that salvation?

VIII

Meanwhile, the two young women, Marguerite Sametel and Rose Nivet, guided by the sailor Kroarec, were hastening through the vast gardens of the Yamen, unfortunately designed as a labyrinth, in accordance with the Chinese mania, so effectively that in order to cover a distance of perhaps two kilometers, the walkers, having been obliged to retrace their steps ten times, had traveled nearly two leagues, and a considerable time had elapsed when they reached the buildings.

And what anguish did Marguerite and Rose not suffer when they heard the clatter of the artillery and the clamors of the assailants!

By then the glare of the conflagration had become so intense, and lit up the sky so broadly, that it was veritably as clear as daylight. Fugitives were flocking through the grounds, running at top speed in a desperate attempt to reach the canal, where there was at least a hope of finding shelter. Kroarec had difficulty opening a passage, because the unfortunates, recognizing him as a French sailor, hurled themselves upon him, surrounding him, seizing his garments, imploring him as if he could save them simply by a act of will.

It was necessary for Marguerite Sametel to name herself in order to protect him and free him—and it is even fair to say that as soon as she pronounced her name, the ranks parted in front of her.

Was her father still alive, at least? No one could give her an answer. At that moment, General Butowieff was in command. No one knew anything more, except that the battle was becoming impossible, as more than fifty thousand Chinese were storming the Yamen, in which a handful of men could not hold out much longer.

"My God!" Marguerite sobbed, dragging her companion along more rapidly. "Has my poor father been killed?"

Finally, she uttered a cry of joy: she had just perceived Albert de Mesnes, bareheaded, his clothes covered in blood, sword in hand, urging the soldiers forward yet again.

She ran to him.

"My father?" she cried.

"Ah! There you are, Mademoiselle!" exclaimed the young man. "Safe and sound. What a joy for your father…come, quickly."

And, seizing her by the hand, he drew her inside the palace.

"My father's alive!" Marguerite cried, joyfully. "But my happiness mustn't make me selfish. Rose, come with me."

"Who's the girl?" demanded Albert.

"The daughter of a French photographer…"

"Nivet?"

"You know Papa?" said the girl, charmingly.

"A brave patriot who's already rendered us a great service."

"He must have invented something—but where is he?"

"He left with the Ambassador for the Imperial Palace."

At first sight, that explanation did not present any terrifying character, and Rose dared not ask for further elaboration.

Kroarec, leaning toward her ear, said to her quietly: "Don't worry, Mademoiselle—I'll get the details." She addressed one of her finest smiles to him—which appeared to give the brave fellow a sense of appreciation.

Sametel was in the midst of the officers, giving orders. Suddenly, he perceived his daughter, and there was a sudden explosion of joy in his fatherly heart. He ran to her and threw his arms around her.

"You! You, my child! Oh, if you knew what terrors I've endured!"

"Me, too, Father. Fortunately, here we are, together—and this time not to be parted again, whatever fate awaits us."

Sametel shook his head.

"The resistance is reaching its end," he said. "What will become of us?" He turned to the French and Russia officers. "So, Messieurs—your conclusions?"

"The same opinion as General Butowieff. Within half an hour, the Yamen will be invaded. We're running out of ammunition, and more than a third of our men are dead or wounded."

"And yet," said Sametel, "We can't surrender the location until we know what's happened to the Ambassador. It's already more than an hour since he left. Has he even been able to get as far as the Emperor? Those wretches are capable of any treason."

"At that moment, a flourish burst forth outside so sonorous and so shrill that it even drowned out the din of the artillery.

"What's that?" demanded Sametel.

At the same moment, General Butowieff came in. "Monsieur," he said to Sametel, in a tone pierced by a strange embarrassment, "Negotiators have presented themselves at the doors of the Yamen."

"How many are there?"

"As negotiators, only three...and one of them..." He did not finish, as if the words he had been about to pronounce cost him too dearly. But he added: "Behind them is a crowd of several thousand men, who'll flood into the Yamen as soon as the doors are open.

"In that case, it's necessary to talk to them from the height of the gallery surrounding the Yamen. Don't you agree?"

"It's the only prudent course to adopt."

"Let's go, then, Messieurs. Monsieur de Mesnes, it's to you that the representative of France had confided the flag. Come on—and whatever fate is reserved for us, let everyone know, at least, that the Russians and the French, united once again, can look it in the face."

Immediately, they headed for the ramparts.

Marguerite and Rose hid behind the row of anxious officers.

In the large square that extended in front of the Yamen, the spectacle was magical. A multicolored crowd, noisy to the extent of howling, was huddled beneath the red light of the sky, which detached silhouettes and illuminated the bright hues of their garments. But more than that: the crowd had suddenly opened up, and through the middle of it a cortege of monks and warriors had advanced, sparkling with steel and dazzling tints.

A phrase ran over all lips, pronounced with a double emphasis of dread and veneration: "The Tien-Ti."

For a long time, the people had known about that secret association, the power of which, multiplied a hundred times by the mystery surrounding it, assumed colossal proportions.

They were all there: all the men we saw a short while ago in the Temple, swearing an oath of hatred and extermination against Europe.

And in the first row there were three individuals:

A man dressed in a long white tunic, coiffed with the Persian tiara of the Magi, servants of Zoroaster.

To his right side, Sithreva, impassive in her hieratic rigidity as a priestess, rendered more beautiful still by the fiery reflection that illuminated the antique regularity of her features.

On his other side...there was another man, of tall stature, dressed in the steel armor of the Circassians, a helmet on his head and a chainmail gorget falling over his shoulders, his face almost hidden by his visor, the three holes of which allowed his crazed eyes to be seen.

That was the one that General Butowieff had not wanted to recognize or name: Alexandroff Wintscheff, traitor and renegade.

Meanwhile, Robert Sametel, with Albert de Mesnes on one side, carrying the French flag, and the Russian general on the other, next to whom an officer was deploying the Muscovite flag, had advanced onto the rampart. On his order, the

French bugles had replied to the Chinese trumpets that had launched the appeal for negotiations into the air, and repeated three times.

Robert Sametel spoke fluent Chinese.

"Who are you and what do you want?" he demanded. "Having attacked us in cowardly fashion, have you come to offer your repentance and bring us the first reparations to which we have a right?"

The monk raised his hand.

A deathly silence descended upon the square.

"Foreigners," he said, in a deep voice, so vibrant that it could be heard in every corner of the vast square, "to what treason do you refer? Who, then, has come to invade our country, to wrench us out of the profound peace that has been ours for centuries, to insult our mores, our customs, and our gods? Who, then, has brought the accursed sciences that are nothing but sources of pride and ruination? You and you alone.

"If, on the contrary, we, the Sons of Heaven, the subjects of the only and true master of the world, have wanted to take our place in the lands that our emperors have condescended to yield to you as a privilege, you have expelled us, pursued us, tortured us. You are the enemies, you are the accursed...

"And after having worn away magnanimity to the ultimate limits, we have come to tell you: the time of forbearance is past. The Sons of Heaven refuse to tolerate your insolent vanities and ruinous fantasies any longer. Out of China, Occidentals, out of our territory, barbarians! And listen to that which has been written by the one who is the Light of Worlds..."

All these words had been pronounced in a strong voice, in a rhythmic cadence, in a bizarre and gripping chant. He had unrolled a long strip of yellow silk, one with characters traced in bright vermilion.

"The Son of Heaven," he read, "whose all-powerful hand has fallen upon the culpable, says: To the barbarians, one sole path is still open to salvation, and that is the path of submission. Thus, on the reading of this inscription, marked by our seal, which is the word of Heaven, the barbarians, belonging to the nations of Europe, will place themselves in our hands as prisoners in order, on their knees, to implore our magnanimous pity; they will immediately surrender all their arms, their flags, and their archives.

"At this price alone, the mercy of their lives will be granted.

"If not, the veil of death will be extended over them, and the great Emperor, Han Ming, will go to their capitals to impose his will, which no human power can alter or deflect.

"Thus said by us, Sons of Heaven, representing the Great Dragon and Master of Worlds. Let everyone bow down!"

And at the moment the voice of the monk died away, the thousands of Chinese who were there bowed down, almost touching the ground with their foreheads.

Then the shrill commotion resounded once again.

Sametel had listened with his arms folded and his head held high. When the blasts of the brass instruments had subsided, he spoke, in a voice in which tones of profound indignation resounded.

"Man," he said, "is it true that your master has sent you to bear such insolent words as those you have uttered? By the most cowardly of crimes, the subjects of the Son of Heaven have massacred the Europeans, thus covering themselves with a shame whose memory will never be extinguished. And when you still have the blood of so many innocent victims on our hands, you dare to come to dictate conditions to us that would be odious if they were not insane.

"To surrender ourselves, to lay down our arms, dishonor our flags, which no shame has ever soiled! That is what you dare to demand? Man, go tell your master that, though your miserable torturers tear our bodies into shreds, not one of us will bow down before him. From this day forward, he is at odds with civilized nations; he is the barbarian that will be scorned and chastised. We might all die, but let him remember that beyond the deserts that form a wall for him, there are nations that are able to avenge murders, and inflict a punishment

141

on him so terrible that all trace of him will be effaced from the earth.

"Man, have you nothing more to say to us? In the name of humanity, in the name of human rights, in the name of the eternal principles of Justice, I beseech you to return to the one who sent you and report my words to him...and let him know that every drop of blood shed will be paid for a hundred times over..."

"Is that your final word, Foreigner?"

"That is my final word."

"Well, to your insolence, this is the response of the Son of Heaven."

The monk made a gesture. A man clad in red advanced, holding a severed head by the hair, and threw it against the wall of the Yamen.

A cry of horror and anguish escaped all the European throats. The head was that of the French Ambassador.

"Fire! Fire on these wretches!" cried Sametel.

And from all parts of the rampart, a fusillade burst forth, cutting through the filthy crowd of torturers and assassins who no longer had the right to call themselves human.

At the same moment, Sithreva, drawing herself up to her full height, uttered a cry of war and hatred, and all the bandits rushed the walls, hooking their fingernails and grinding their teeth: a veritably demonic attack.

"At least," shouted General Butowieff, "the traitor will be punished first!"

And with a prodigious bound, the old Cossack launched himself to the foot of the wall, and sword held high, ran at Sandorf, who had not pronounced a single word during the long scene, or even motioned a gesture.

Before the brave Russian could reach Wintscheff, however, the crowd closed round him. He could still be seen for a few moments, towering over his assailants by virtue of his colossal height, striking and killing, but then he fell, and the wretches tore him apart with savage cries.

As for Sandorf, Sithreva had taken him by the arm—and the negotiators had disappeared as if the ground had swallowed them up.

The work of slaughter recommenced...but this time, without hope.

"Russians and Frenchmen," cried Sametel, "Are you ready to die rather than surrender?"

"Yes! Yes!" cried all voices.

"Well then, use every last cartridge and charge! Then I shall be able to do my duty."

Marguerite had also recognized Sandorf. At first she had thought he was a prisoner, but she had quickly observed the more-than-strange attitude of the Russian officer; with her feminine intuition she had divined that he was under the absolute control of the exceedingly beautiful woman whose fanaticism had a character that was both grandiose and terrifying.

But Sacha? What had become of Sacha?

She asked the question, but no one was able to give her an answer. She had fled with her brother André, and no one had seen her thereafter. She was doubtless dead.

And Rose, sobbing, said to her: "As my father is dead. My poor father, so good..."

"Not yet," said a voice behind her.

She turned around swiftly. Nivet was there, laughing and weeping at the same time...taking her in his arms...kissing her with eager lips.

An innate temperament immediately regained the upper hand: "One doesn't kill a Nivet as easily as that," he said. "When I saw that it had gone bad, I made myself scarce, without being noticed...and here I am. But that's not all. I've brought my invention. Where's Monsieur Sametel?"

"Here I am, my friend," said the engineer, whose face was horribly pale—for he understood that the minutes were counted, and that he was about to be required to put his own hand to the powder-keg that would save the honor of the flag, burying all its defenders in its folds—and with them, his daughter. "Tell me what happened."

The story was brief. They had gotten into the palace and reached the room where the Council was sitting, under the presidency of the Emperor. Immediately, however, all the men had been seized and dragged before the Son of Heaven, who had demanded that the French Ambassador offer his submission, in the name of his country.

What Sametel had replied a little while before were the same words that the representative of France had pronounced. He too, in the name of justice and civilization, had reproached the crowned executioner for his crimes—who, mad with rage, had struck him with his own scimitar. The others—the great dignitaries and Ministers—had finished the work, falling upon the injured man, who was soon a cadaver.

It was at the moment when their rage was at its paroxysm that Nivet had been able to slip away.

"But Monsieur Sametel, I've brought you a means, if not of saving everyone, at least of creating a diversion of which we can take advantage."

"Speak, quickly."

There are people over whom the comical never loses its rights. Nivet struck a dramatic pose in order to speak, rounding out his punctuation to the point that Sametel, seething with impatience, spoke a little rudely to him.

And yet, it was true that he had brought an idea of genius.

While traveling through the tunnel that led from the Yamen to the Imperial Palace, he had come across vast bunkers full of powder, dynamite and explosive engines. The idea had occurred to him to detach two of the electric wires that communicated with the Yamen and wind them together, and then he had put them in contact with a powder barrel.

"You understand, Monsieur Sametel. Connect them here to a powerful battery...and the powder will catch fire, and the dynamite will explode, and the Imperial Palace will blow up...and during the confusion..."

"Yes, yes!" cried Sametel. "Nivet, you're a brave man, and I thank you in the name of France. To work! To work!"

In an instant, the piles were ready.

"Hold hard!" shouted Sametel to Albert de Mesnes, who was running back and forth, facing up to the enemy on all sides. Fortunately, not one of the assailants had yet been able to force an entrance into the Yamen.

And Sametel, aided by Nivet, brought the electric batteries into play.

A frightful detonation ripped through the air. At the same time, a column of fire rose up. In the crowd, there was a formidable clamor.

The ground shook, as if in an earthquake.

The Imperial Palace had just blown up.

At the same time, the walls of the Yamen collapsed,

In that catastrophe, the furious attack gave the Europeans a moment's respite.

Sametel and de Mesnes rallied their men, and the decimated troop, in the midst of which Marguerite and Rose were marching hand in hand, beat a retreat toward the canal.

Honor was saved, and the French flag had not been soiled.

PART TWO
THE BARBARIAN INVASION

I

Let us return to Paris.

You have not forgotten the emotion, the despair, and the terror experienced by Guy de Norès at the moment when, returning to his laboratory after a brief absence motivated by Admiral Trécourt's visit, he had seen the aviation apparatus, the enormous power of which was well known to him, projected through the roof and plunging into the atmospheric depths of the sky, carrying away his sister and Dr. Sabirat.

At first he remained motionless, as if thunderstruck.

That accident—that catastrophe—adding to the one that his experiments at the Sorbonne had revealed to him, and which the admiral had confirmed, troubled the young man's reason momentarily, to the point at which he fled, running, and shouting for help.

His mother had come in response to his cries. At first, she did not understand; she thought that her son, overexerted by incessant work, had fallen prey to a fit of fever.

When he recovered his composure, he explained. To be sure, the poor woman could not understand what the formidable apparatus might be that had been able to carry two living beings into space like that, but she knew her son's genius too well to doubt the reality of a fact whose strangeness did not, in sum, surpass that of the revelation she had witnessed a little while before.

Both of then returned to the laboratory, and the hole in the ceiling left no doubt as to the reality of the accident.

"My God!" cried Madame de Norès. "My poor daughter! She's doomed to an atrocious, terrible death!"

Guy shook his head and made no rely.

How could the catastrophe have happened? No doubt it was possible. It was evident that, having gone into the machine in order to examine the mechanism, they had activated the engine. And although Marie de Norès knew the principle on which the new mode of locomotion was based, Guy was convinced that she did not know how to manipulate the various controls.

"You're not answering me, Guy," said the poor mother. "Do you have any doubt, then, about the result of this frightful accident?"

He was stammering, trying to give her a reassurance that he did not share, when the door opened.

It was the Admiral who came in.

"What's happened?" he exclaimed from the threshold. "My carriage had scarcely traveled a hundred meters when I heard a sort of explosion; at the same time I saw some sort of shell rising into the air, which was lost in the clouds. The idea occurred to me that you had had some kind of accident."

"That's only too true," Norès replied, and related what had happened.

The Admiral uttered a despairing groan. "Poor things!" After a moment's reflection, he added: "Is this the invention that you obliquely mentioned to me, then?"

"Yes, Monsieur. I've been working on it for many years, and I curse the day when I finally found the solution to the problem."

"Science should never be cursed," said the Admiral. "I certainly sympathize with the pain that the catastrophe is causing you, but tell me, on the one hand, are you sure that your sister won't be able to steer the apparatus?"

"How can you ask me that question? If she were able to control it, she'd have come back already."

"That's true—unless astonishment and a momentary but very natural fear have prevented her from acting immediately. On the other hand, do you only have one model of the apparatus?"

"I was going to carry out the decisive experiment in a few days' time," Guy explained. "Only then would I have finished the construction of two machines that are presently in the workshop of the company that financed them."

"Can't you finish them right away?"

"What's the point?"

The Admiral looked at the young man in surprise; he divined a profound depression, quite explicable given that in a matter of hours Norès had had to fear, if not mourn, the death of the two people he loved most in the world: his fiancée and his sister.

The valiant officer felt, however, that he ought not to allow that privileged soul to abandon himself thus, so it was in a most energetic tone that he replied: "What's the point? In truth, is that really you speaking, my dear Norès? What's the point of science, then, except to repair that which seems irreparable? It's necessary to react, to fight. Don't you understand that, thanks to your invention, it will be possible to fly more rapidly to the aid of our compatriots who are struggling at this moment under the blow of barbarians? Also, won't you be able to launch yourself to the rescue of your sister and your friend? Where are they now? Are they lost in limitless space, or have they been transported to some place where it might be possible to find them? There's more than one of our mariners, damn it, who'll agree to pilot your machine. Come on, Norès, lift your head up and get a grip on yourself again. You must, I implore you, in the name of those you love and in the name of the fatherland."

That forceful and vibrant voice extracted the young man from the torpor into which he had sunk. He passed his hand over his brow, and said: "You're right. I no longer knew what I was doing—those two consecutive blows had knocked the stuffing out of me, but I need to get a grip on myself. First of all, where are the unfortunates?"

"Can you determine that?"

"Wait."

Norès' features were suddenly mobile; the pallor of anguish had suddenly been succeeded by the animation of research: he had been seized by a triumphant idea.

He ran to a corner of the workshop.

"Provided, he murmured, "that the apparatus hasn't been destroyed by the explosion!"

The Admiral followed him anxiously. Now he was wondering whether the young scientist was really in his right mind.

What could his last words signify? Was he claiming that he could see into the upper atmosphere? By means of what telescope did he think he could follow the voyagers into space?

No, it was not a matter of some kind of telescope.

With a cry of joy, Norès had discovered, beneath a muslin veil, a small apparatus, singular in form, seeming to be made of thousands of juxtaposed mirrors, each one orientated in a different plane. The whole thing might have weighed two or three kilos at the most.

The Admiral looked at it uncomprehendingly.

Norès said to him: "Would you care to accompany me, Monsieur?"

"Gladly—but what's that?"

"You're going to leave me again!" cried the mother, who had been hiding her face in her handkerchief, weeping, until then.

He went to her. "Mother," he said, "I love you and I live for you—no, I'm not leaving you, but, as Monsieur de Trécourt says, so long as a glimmer of hope remains, a worthy man doesn't have the right to despair. Have no fear, I'll be back momentarily."

"At least swear to me that you aren't going to carry out some dangerous experiment..."

"Oh, this time I can swear it to you, Mother. Come, Monsieur de Trécourt."

They went outside, and once they were in the courtyard, Norès started climbing a small staircase going up to the top of the house. He was carrying his apparatus carefully, and moving slowly.

Naturally, the Admiral was most intrigued, having no idea what the young man planned to do.

They arrived on the roof, and followed a pathway contrived between the gutters.

"Where are we going?" asked the Admiral.

"To the chimneystack that you can see there. We need to get up as high as possible, to a point where we can see the whole of the broken roof of my workshop."

They had arrived. The platform sustaining the chimneypot was large enough for both men to stand on it without danger.

Norès reached it first and extended his hand to his companion, who joined him.

Norès set down his apparatus on the highest point.

It consisted, as we have said, of a kind of a spherical mirror formed of innumerable plates fitted together, which had the approximate appearance of a revolving mirror used to catch skylarks. The color of the mirror was not, however, the one ordinarily given to silvering by mercury or silver; it was grayish, but simultaneously very bright.

Beneath the hemisphere was a kind of very short telescope, about the same size as one branch of a pair of theater opera glasses, the ocular lens of which was outside while the other end disappeared under the reflective surface.

"As long as it's not too late," Norès murmured. "Why didn't I think of it sooner?"

He looked around; the air was remarkably clear.

From the position where the two men were standing, a large periphery of the sky was visible.

"That's good," said Norès.

He had knelt down in front of the instrument, and, peering through the ocular of the lorgnette, he rotated the demiglobe as if he were calibrating it.

A few minutes passed thus, during which the Admiral held his breath, so excited was his curiosity.

"Yes, yes!" Norès suddenly cried. "The apparatus rose up to my right, with an incredible velocity…a hundred, two hundred, four hundred meters…the door was closed and no fall had taken place…then…ah! A cloud! I can no longer see anything…wait…is that possible? I can see it again…it has ceased climbing and has departed eastwards with the rapidity of a shell…still no exterior accident…but… There's the horizon…it's lost, disappeared."

"But how can you see all that?" exclaimed the Admiral, who was increasingly doubtful about the young man's state of mind.

Norès straightened up. "Look for yourself," he said. "Concentrate all the force of your will and vitality in your eye. I'll maneuver the apparatus, which you don't know how to operate for yourself."

Indeed, throughout the time he had been gazing, he had kept one hand free to operate a lever that displaced the axis of the mirror.

The Admiral had taken his place—unconvinced, it must be admitted, that he was going to see anything. But he was a sensible man and he did not reject anything *a priori*.

Suddenly, he uttered a cry of surprise. "That's strange. I can see a kind of vehicle being carried away at dizzying speed, a sealed wagon, above which a propeller is rotating so rapidly that one can't follow its movement. Then everything disappears…to reappear a little further away…as you said, heading eastwards…then nothing more. I don't understand."

"That," said Norès, "is the telescope of the past."

"Of the past?"

"Let's go back down. I know what I wanted to know. My dear sister, although she can't control the apparatus completely—for I don't remember having given her a complete demonstration—has at least understood that the greatest danger on departure was rising up to the limits of the atmospheric layer, where respiration would be impossible, and where the apparatus would, in a sense, be quartered. She's stopped it, to depart horizontally. At least that's one danger avoided. Furthermore, I'm aware that my dear Marie hasn't panicked. Sabirat, who's with her, has a cool, precise intelligence. I still have some hope that they'll succeed in getting out of this dangerous adventure."

While talking, they had come back to Madame de Norès, whom Guy did his best to reassure—which, to tell the truth, was not at all easy, for the good woman did not have a very scientific mind.

Finally, she calmed down, and Guy was able to go out with the Admiral, with the aim of collecting the available information on the subject of events in China, and also of taking all the necessary measures that the situation required.

"Can't you explain to me briefly," while the vehicle escorted them away, "what the strange apparatus is that you showed me—the telescope of the past, as you call it."

"My dear Monsieur de Trécourt," Guy replied, "That might be difficult. The apparatus is based on principles so new I'm afraid that if I explain them to you, I might seem to be mad."

"My dear Guy, I hold your mind in too high esteem not to admit that you know a great many things I don't. I didn't believe in your selenoscope, but when you were kind enough to demonstrate its application to me, I yielded immediately."

"That's true—so I can take the risk of explaining to you what I haven't yet revealed to anyone else. Listen, then."

"With all my attention."

"When one places the objective of a photographic apparatus facing an object, the image of that object is fixed on a sensitive plate, is it not?"

"That's a banal observation."

"But have you ever wondered where the image was between the moment when it is, as it were, disengaged from the object that one is photographing and the moment when it reaches the plate?"

"Eh? I confess..."

"That you don't get it. You're not unaware that, according to the data of science, every illuminated body emits luminous rays, the beam of which comes to blossom, as it were, over the sensitive plate."

"That's right."

"Those rays transport the image through space, so to speak, and only stop at the moment when they strike the plate; but a thousandth of a millimeter from the plate, they don't yet exist in a condensed state, and are continually renewed by the emission of the body whose image is being projected."

Monsieur Trécourt was listening attentively. Norès, when he made such demonstrations, spoke in a soft, slightly muffled voice.

"So," he continued, "if you've understood me, you've already grasped the notion that images of everything there is exist, floating, as it were, in space, invisible to our normal senses, but visible when we stop them, conquering them, if one might put it like that, by some development of the personal faculty."

"In sum," said the Admiral, "the idea is logical...but when the object is moving...?"

"Its image moves with it."

"But what becomes of the image previously projected?"

"It endures for some time; then, gradually, it fades away, becoming increasingly imperceptible. And look, this idea that seems so new and strange to you was nevertheless admitted for thousands of years by millions of people."

"What do you mean?"

"The Hindu religion recognizes the existence of an enveloping fluid penetrating the entire universe, to which it gives the name of Akasha, or astral light. It's in that fluid that the images of everything are condensed, numbering in the billions, mingling and overlapping...and their totality produces the visible world—which is to say, in sum, the illusion, Maya."

"Decidedly, my dear chap, you seem to me to be a little lost in the...astral light. Shall we come back down to earth? I prefer, I confess, your comparison borrowed from photography. I'm a positive man, and in matters of hypotheses I demand that one only accepts the minimum possible number."

"You're right, and I apologize for letting myself get carried away further than I intended. There is in these hypotheses a question of intellectual level, of which it's necessary to take account. So, I told you that the images of everything exist in space before being fixed by photography or some other process, and that they remain durable for a certain interval. Well, at the moment when my aero-perfume—a provisional name, of course—is launched into the air, it projects its captured image into space, and it is found there in the various positions taken by the material object. The problem is to arrive in time to be able to capture it before its dilution and its complete volatilization, so to speak.

"My optical apparatus, then, which is based on the principles of photography and microscopy, permits those images to be seen during the time that they remain perceptible. Do you understand, for example, that in an empty room, one can photograph a person who has just gone out? The clarity of the subsisting image depends on the quantity of light and the timing of the pose. Thus, our observation of a little while ago was favored by the bright light of broad daylight. In the same way that the eye sees much more clearly in daylight, the universal retina of the immensity projects images more clearly. Thus, we were able to follow the image of the aerostatic apparatus through space, as Monsieur Marey was once able to photograph the various phases of the flight of a bird."[34]

"All that seems very strange to me," said the Admiral, after a pause...and yet the fact is there. I've seen it."

"Yes, you've seen it. Oh, Admiral, how the ideas seethe in my brain! They'd make me pass for a madman if there weren't men like you, to understand us—the reckless questioners of infinity. But we're arriving at the Ministry. I feel my

---

[34] The scientist and photographer Étienne-Jules Marey published his book *Le Vol des oiseaux* [The Flight of Birds] in 1890, shortly before Lermina began serializing his feuilleton.

anguish gripping me again. Come, Monsieur, and may we learn some reassuring news!"

While Norès and his companion go in search of information, let us try, for our part, to discover what had become of Dr. Sabirat and the young woman. Had the scientist's extraordinary apparatus revealed the truth?

Certainly, Dr. Sabirat was a cool-headed man, and he had given unequivocal proof more than once of the civilian courage that is perhaps more rare than military valor.

When he felt himself carried away into the air, however, by that formidable leap, especially when he had heard the cry of distress uttered by Marie de Norès, and had seen the poor young woman's face convulsed by an anguish all the more terrible for being mute, he had been thunderstruck for a few moments, as if incapable of making any movement.

Fortunately, however, he was one of those men in whom the mental reacts to the physical, and the notion of real danger had promptly imposed itself upon him, along with the necessity of reassuring his companion.

"Don't be afraid, Mademoiselle!" he cried. "I'll answer for everything!"

It was evidently a very hazardous cry, but in those ultra-perilous circumstances anything was preferable to prostration, to self-abandonment. Before even knowing whether a struggle was possible, it was necessary to recover the will to fight. Sabirat understood that so well that, when the first moment of stupefaction had passed, he was no longer thinking about anything but taking action. How, and in what direction? He had absolutely no idea, but the idea that dominated him could be expressed as: *Something has to be done, even so.*

He had scarcely had the opportunity to examine the interior of the compartment in which he found himself, a parallelogram whose two sides were closed but whose two extremities were open to space, fitted with thick panes of glass. Through one of those fixed windows a helical propeller could be seen that was presently immobile; through the other, the immensity was visible and of unusual profundity.

There was no reference point. Where were they? It was impossible to hazard any hypothesis—but it was easy to observe that they were climbing with lightning rapidity. Clouds were passing by; they were passing through them like a shell. Then there was the profound blue, and then, once again, an intense vapor that enveloped the apparatus and plunged the unfortunate couple into a kind of darkness.

Sabirat understood what was happening; they were rising, still rising at a velocity of hundreds of meters per second…so it would not take them long to reach the limits of the respirable air; that was death with brief delay.

"Mademoiselle," he said, "I'm not asking you to forgive me. We're both victims of a fatality that nothing could doubtless have avoided. Now, do you know your brother's apparatus? It's necessary that we cease to rise with this alarming rapidity. There is one way, which is to break one of the sides of the box—that pane of glass, for example—but that would lead to a brutal fall, perhaps death by crushing. It's necessary to act upon the engine, to deflect it. Don't you remember any information given to you by your brother?"

And as the young woman, as if emerging from sleep, opened her eyes and looked at him, as it were, without seeing him, he continued softly: "Come on—we only have a few more minutes. Look, Mademoiselle: this is the lever we pushed down which determined our departure. There are two others forming a triangle with it, of which that one is at the apex. I confess that I hardly dare hazard a hypothesis. I beg you, try to remember."

But Marie, her arms hanging down in an attitude of discouragement, only murmured: "I don't know."

Sabirat shivered; it was obvious that the shock suffered by the young woman had momentarily robbed her of her faculties; the nervous distress had been too powerful for that essentially delicate nature.

157

What could he do? She seemed to be asleep; her vague eyes had no focus…and yet, the peril was becoming increasingly urgent.

Already, Sabirat could feel the first effects of the increasingly rarefied air.

He could hear an ominous creaking in the walls of the hull. At the same time, it seemed to him that breathing was becoming more difficult. Was that an illusion? But he was experiencing the preliminary symptoms of vertigo.

He was confronted, as we have said, by a system of levers, one of which, occupying the upper apex of the triangle, had been depressed by the involuntary pressure and had determined the ascent.

There were two others, one to the right and one to the left. What did the most elementary logic indicate? Evidently, that the right-hand lever produced an easterly direction, and the left-hand one a westerly thrust. And yet, at the moment of action, Sabirat felt a profound anguish.

There are times when one's arm, during a movement of which can determine the life or death of those one loves, feels heavier than lead.

He stiffened himself, however, against the weakness that was invading him.

It was a life-or-death gamble; he had logic in his favor, but how little human reasoning weighs in such moments.

It seemed to him that he saw Marie going pale, and divined that she was having difficulty drawing breath, that her lips were gasping in vain for the air they lacked. Very gravely, as resolute as a pilot adjusting a tiller, he placed his hand on the right-hand lever and pulled it down with a single thrust.

There was an abrupt shock throughout the carcass of the machine, and then an oscillation.

Sabirat was frantic.

Suddenly, he felt the equilibrium, momentarily disturbed, re-establish itself—and the helix, which had been immobile thus far, began to turn with enormous rapidity.

The aerostat flew through the air like an arrow, in a horizontal plane.

It was salvation; they were no longer rising. Sabirat uttered a cry of joy and hope.

"We're saved," he pronounced, with a clarity all the more emphatic because he wanted to imprint that as-yet-unjustified certainty in the mind of his companion.

And, indeed, Marie, straightening up slightly, repeated the word: "Saved!"

"Yes, Mademoiselle. Listen to me: recover all your composure. You must have courage; the moment has come to show it. We have obtained a first success; I'm convinced that it only depends on your energy to escape the dangers that threaten us."

As he spoke, with his voice becoming calm again, Marie gradually came round. The young doctor was telling the truth; there was an uncommon energy within her. But in fact, the adventure had been so abrupt, so stunning, that more than one man among the most impassive would have lost his composure.

"I beg your pardon, but to tell the truth, I no longer knew where I was," said Marie, striving to smile.

"Well," replied Sabirat, "we're quite simply fifteen hundred or two thousand meters above the level of Paris."

"But if we're still rising, we'll soon be asphyxiated."

"Have no fear," the young man continued, smiling. "I believe that I've succeeded in avoiding that painful extremity."

"Really...how?"

Sabirat explained to her what he had done and how: by simple intuition, he had succeeded in carrying out a saving maneuver. "But haven't you learned from your brother how the levers work?" he asked.

"No, in truth. He couldn't imagine that I would embark first and alone in this terrible machine. But in your opinion, what should we do now?"

"I'm not too sure. However, on seeing the clouds pass by through that glass, it appears to me that we're traveling horizontally."

"Very rapidly?"

"I can't measure it, but I believe that our speed is very rapid."

"If we could find out where we are..."

Sabirat looked around. In fact, there was a total lack of reference points.

Suddenly, Marie uttered an exclamation.

"What is it?" Sabirat asked, fearing another unforeseen complication.

Here on the floor, this key...that copper handle..."

"Hmm!" said the young man. "I confess that I'm not without suspicion. In touching any of the components of this unknown machine, we'd be risking producing a result that might be injurious to us."

"However," said Marie, who had now recovered her self-control completely, "it's not plausible that my brother has installed some means of destroying his own machine."

"That's true."

"Let's put ourselves in his place and suppose that we were the inventors. We'd have the idea of providing a means of rising up and descending, of hovering, of going forwards or backwards, of steering our flight...so this copper handle might serve to obtain one of those results. We already know how to go up..."

"Alas, yes!" sighed Sabirat, who had not yet forgiven his imprudence.

"Well, there still remains one lever in the console; it must be something other than going up or steering to the right. It can only be to go down, or..."

"Would you like us to try it?" asked Sabirat.

"Why not? It's necessary for us to try everything, until we've found something."

The doctor was not entirely reassured; he divined that the life of the woman he loved more than ever—for it seemed to him that the peril shared put an even stronger bond between them than before—might depend on one false move.

And the excellent young man, instead of replying, instead of acting, lost himself in his reflections, wondering whether he would ever return to earth with the woman he was already calling, in the depths of his consciousness, his fiancée.

"What do you think?" asked Marie, naively. "Doesn't my reasoning seem to you to be unassailable?"

"Yes, yes, in truth...and I'm ready to do as you say. So very ready that I'll risk everything."

And he advanced his hand toward the third lever determinedly.

"Not too quickly!" exclaimed Marie. "A little prudence is always necessary..."

Sabirat had placed his hand on the lever; obedient to Marie's advice, he pressed down gently, and then a little more heavily.

The two young people felt the very clear impression that the aerial vessel turned around, slowly and without any shock.

"We're going the other way!" exclaimed Sabirat. "We're retreating—or, rather, returning to the departure point."

Marie shook her head.

"At the height we're at," she said, "It scarcely matters whether we're going in one direction or another. The best thing would be to find a means of descending. Then, if the movement isn't too rapid, we can do our best to land."

"Descending!" Sabirat replied. "But you've seen that we've made use of the three levers, and none of them had that effect."

"With the result that we'll be condemned to wander perpetually, like souls in torment, between earth and Heaven."

"And as we're not souls, we'll inevitably be doomed to a frightful death...of starvation."

The two young people remained silent momentarily.

They were beginning to despair, although, in fact, each of them was thinking about the other. Marie accused herself of having brought the doctor into the aerostat, while, for his part,

Sabirat could not help blushing as he recalled the involuntary movement that had led to such a disastrous catastrophe.

What were they to do? They could not resign themselves to going back and forth eternally in the sky. That was poetic, but dangerous in the long run.

"I've got it," said Sabirat. "There still remains the brass handle in the floor."

"That's true—we forgot that. There's no reason to hesitate, since, having found the means of climbing and going forwards and backwards, it only remains to find that of descending. Except, remember that it's necessary to guard against falling too rapidly, for fear of smashing into the ground."

"Don't worry," said Sabirat. He almost added: "I know what I'm doing."

He knelt down and put his hand on the lever in question.

"It rotates," he said.

In truth, they were holding their breath.

This is what happened:

Gradually, a circular opening was uncovered, which initially adopted a form something like the crescent of the new moon, and then a semi-circle, and then a whole circle about the size of the brim of a hat.

Sabirat uttered two exclamations, one of disappointment, because he understood that it was merely a porthole, and the other of admiration.

"Look, Mademoiselle," he said. "It's marvelous!"

Like a large optical lens, the circle allowed the ground to be seen, but with such magnification that the mountains, valleys and rivers appeared in the clearest fashion. It was like a telescope of unusual power aimed at the earth.

Sabirat had knelt down, peering with all his attention. Marie did likewise, and the two of them, head to head, their hair in contact, examined the miraculous spectacle that was unfolding before them.

They could not make out the details, to be sure, but what they saw was like an immense relief map unfurling in an endless scroll.

They both tried to recognize the places above which they were passing, but it was not easy—almost impossible, in fact—because of the rapidity of their progress.

After a few moments of contemplation, Sabirat stood up again.

"Alas, Mademoiselle," he said, "it's quite beautiful, but what good does it do us? We're observing all the more evidently that we're moving with amazing rapidity. Where are we? We don't know, and if we did know, what use would it be, since we haven't found the means of landing?"

He was right; even supposing that they had recognized France, their city, their house, would it not have been a further torture to fly forever without being able to stop? It was enough to drive them to despair.

Sabirat, who was vigorous by nature, and famished, was beginning to experience strange cramps in his stomach. Two or three times already Marie had stifled significant yawns; it was obvious that hunger was coming—and what means did they have of satisfying it?

A bird flies well too, but not in a hermetically sealed cage; it can settle on a tree to catch some insect by the wings, after which, ballasted, it sets off again for the sublime regions. But here there was an excelsior without a term, without a pause, without the hope of alighting on some hospitable branch.

No, no—it was not impossible that Norès, the inventor and genius, had forgotten that essential part of the mechanism, the descent.

It is true that great architects have built edifices in which they have forgotten the staircase, but those distractions are rare, and when it is a matter of an apparatus that rises up thousands of meters, it would be implausible that, having desired to rise, one would not remember the line from old Corneille: "He aspires to descend..."

Sabirat prowled around the wooden box like a wild beast in a cage. He inspected every corner, placed his hand on the knots in the wood, palpated the slightest patches in the hope of finding some secret button, like those for the mysterious doors in the châteaux of the Middle Ages.

But there was nothing; he always found himself facing the three levers again, repeating the observations already made. By lowering the top lever, they rose, and by touching the levers to the left or the right they went north or south—nothing more.

But in that case it was necessary to renounce all hope; nothing remained but to cover the head and await death: slow, frightfully painful death from starvation.

Oh, if Sabirat had been alone he would have smashed the locomotive apparatus. There would have a brutal fall through space, the crash—but at least his bones would be broken on the ground and would not have to circulate eternally in the immensity.

But Marie was there, gently and resigned, not uttering a word of reproach. Poor dear child!

And in a surge of despair, the doctor fell to his knees to beg her pardon.

Marie uttered a small cry of fright; it seemed to her that her companion was suffering a fit of madness.

"What are you doing?" she cried.

"What can I do, except tell you that I'm a wretch, unworthy of pity? Isn't it me who has snatched you away from your mother?"

"Get up, please, I beg you."

She had spoken so curtly that Sabirat, fearing that he had displeased her, stood up abruptly, stepping back slightly. His head bumped into the topmost lever, which had been lowered for the departure, and which rose up again in response to the impact.

It is necessary to understand that in the rest state, the three levers projected horizontally. Thus when the excellent Sabirat had put pressure on the young woman's hand, he had provoked the depression of the lever, while now, his skull, touching the extremity, had raised it above the horizontal.

At the same movement, there was a vibration throughout the apparatus; then there was a moment's pause, as when the brakes are applied to a vehicle, before it resumes its course.

That was exactly what had happened.

Yes, the aerostat had stopped; yes, it had resumed its flight...but...

"We're going down!" cried Marie, pressing herself upon the window that permitted an outside view.

Sabirat could not believe his eyes, and yet, nothing was more real. The superior propeller had changed direction, and it was now drawing the aerial vehicle toward the earth.

Marie experienced a sudden revelation.

"Do you understand?" she cried. "Each lever is susceptible to two contrary movements, according to whether the arm is above or below the horizontal. To go up it's necessary to lower that one...and to raise it in order to descend."

"With the result," Sabirat continued, "that according to the greater or lesser angle that the lever makes with the horizontal, the upward or downward effort varies in violence."

"And we didn't think of that! Oh, what a good thing it was," the young woman added, naively, "that you threw yourself at my knees."

"You're not angry with me?"

"Certainly not. But Monsieur Sabirat, instead of gazing at me with your wide eyes, you'd do better to remember that by descending too rapidly, you're now risking shattering us into a thousand pieces on the ground. Come on, pilot—to the helm! Try to slow down the velocity of the fall, so that we arrive without too much damage."

"I'll do my best...but how can I judge?"

"Look through the porthole in the floor, watch the earth becoming more and more magnified. Judge the speed of our descent for yourself. Keep lowering the lever—but always keeping it above the horizontal, of course. That's right! We're descending more slowly...but in what country are we coming down?"

As Sabirat made a moment to look more closely, she added: "Above all, don't move. I'll tell you everything I can see. Mountains...yes, and in the middle, a sort of amphitheater, a ring, which seems to be divided up like a chessboard. It's no longer very bright; it's evident that dusk is approaching. What do you think, Monsieur Sabirat?"

"In your opinion, is it an inhabited country?"

"Oh, certainly. I can see a sort of city...there are towers...minarets..."

"Then we're in the Orient...in Turkey, perhaps. Should we go down?"

"What do you think? You're a better judge of that than me."

"I think that the Turks are good people," said the doctor. "Hospitable enough. Perhaps it would be better to land among them than more civilized folk."

"For my part, I have no objection...decide for yourself."

"Let's go down," said Sabirat.

In a matter of moments, he felt that he had acquired a mastery of the lever and that it was possible to increase or decrease their movements at will. He was even beginning to put a certain brashness into it, like a pilot confident of the tiller in his hand or a horseman sure of his mount.

"We're getting close," said Marie, kneeling on the floor, "but it's getting darker and darker...I can't make anything out. Oh! Crows..."

"Birds of ill-omen," said the doctor.

"Oh! Do you have such weaknesses, then? Then again, in truth...we have to make a decision...we're still arriving somewhere."

"So be it."

There was a silence. They felt themselves descending further, and the physical impression was rather painful, rather like the first symptoms of seasickness.

Then there was a sudden shock.

"Be careful," said Marie. "We must be touching."

With a rapid movement, Sabirat had set the lever horizontally. The vehicle had stopped.

The two voyagers remained motionless for a moment, listening.

No noise reached them.

"As long as we haven't come down in a desert!"

Marie could not repress a shudder.

"I'm going to open the door," said the doctor, "And take a look outside."

"I don't want you to risk yourself on your own. What if you are attacked?"

"Bah! I'm unarmed—that's the best way of not causing umbrage to anyone."

"It doesn't matter. I'm coming with you. Are we not bound together in ill fortune?"

"As in good, I hope," said the doctor—who felt, in truth, that he was taking a risk in that clear declaration.

Marie put her hand in his. "As in good," she repeated.

Sabirat leaned over to kiss her hand.

"Be careful," said Marie, laughing. "You'll cause another accident. Come on, make up your mind—open up and let's go."

Sabirat did not hesitate any longer. He was delighted. It seemed to him that in the last minute he had lived more than in entire years. Had not Marie accepted the frank, honest, durable alliance that he had offered her?

And to think that, without that adventure, he might never have dared to say anything. There are, it appears, people who can only admit their love two thousand meters above sea level.

So it was with a light heart that the young doctor resolutely opened the door of the aerostat, now perfectly immobile.

"I'll go take a look around," he said, turning to Marie.

"And leave me alone? No. The apparatus might be seized by some new caprice and carry me into the air on my own. I confess that such a voyage doesn't tempt me…all the more so as the moonlight is superb. We'll surely find someone who'll offer us hospitality."

"So be it," said Sabirat—and gallantly offered his hand to his companion to cross the threshold.

They took two steps outside.

"But where are we, then?" said the doctor, with a hint of anxiety.

They were walking over dry grass that crackled underfoot and sank beneath their weight.

Facing them, they saw a large sheet of dazzling whiteness, like a circular wall in which they could not see an exit. Then they saw a large step of white stone in front of them. Sabirat climbed it first; it was a foot above the ground. He uttered a cry of surprise. A ditch opened in front of him, in the form of a parallelogram about two meters long and barely a meter wide.

Courageously, Marie came to stand beside him.

"One might think that it's a grave," she said, shuddering slightly.

She took him by the arm and, with a very feminine curiosity, in haste to obtain the solution to the enigma, she drew him to the edge of the ditch. But there was another adjacent to it, and then another: it was like a checkerboard of tombs.

Suddenly, Marie stopped, shivering in terror. "Look!" she said, extending her arm. "There! There!"

Sabirat was an energetic man, but in truth, he could not suppress a shiver that shook him in his entirety.

In one of the graves, directly in front of them, a body lay—or, rather, was curled up and on its back—the face blackened beneath the white hood that partially hid it. The hands were protruding from the shroud and were convulsed in a frightful pose, while the legs, folded up over the body, gave the horrible appearance of a monster like those one sees on Indian pagodas.

The two young people had taken a step backwards, but they stumbled and nearly fell into another ditch, from which a flock of filthy crows escaped, croaking.

"My God, it's horrible!" sobbed Marie. "Let's get out of here, I beg you. I feel that I'm going to die."

In truth, the spectacle was horrible, of a nature to cause the strongest to falter.

What was this atrocious charnel house? Tombs everywhere, to the right and the left, in all directions, from which macabre forms surged, nameless beings, all in poses that the most boldly imaginative of artists would scarcely have dared dream: some with their arms raised toward the sky, seemingly threatening some invisible enemy; others half-kneeling, seemingly at prayer...but the most hideous, without a doubt, were those tipped backwards, lying on their backs, displaying their fleshless heads, their bony masks in which two holes were like eyes devoid of pupils, gazing into infinity.

Habituated to the amphitheater as he was, Sabirat had difficulty resisting the horror that invaded him. He felt Marie pressing against him, unsteadily, on the brink of falling.

And yet, it was necessary to act: an insipid, nauseating odor was rising, throwing disease-ridden miasmas into the air, every one of which contained death.

"I beg you, Marie," he said—he no longer thought of calling her Mademoiselle—"be brave. This is an Oriental cemetery. I remember having heard mention of peoples who bury their dead in this fashion."

She made no reply; the fear had been stronger than her willpower, and she fainted.

Then Sabirat took her in his arms, like a child, and started walking slowly over the edges of the ditches, not finding the direction that would take him out of that horrible labyrinth in which any fall would have been frightful. The carrion birds were flying around him with raucous cries, as if furious at being disturbed in their funereal nocturnal feast.

He went on, without knowing where, stiffening his muscles in order not to weaken, feeling that his soul was burdened.

Finally, by dint of searching, he ended up encountering a wider pathway, along which it was possible to walk without fear of stumbling.

The young woman's head was resting on his shoulder, and he saw by means of the moonlight that she was as white as a corpse.

Finally, he perceived the wall, which was only a few paces away from him, and found the bed of dry grass beneath his feet that evidently surrounded the central checkerboard of graves.

He reached the wall and began to follow it, telling himself that there must be an exit, since people came in here to bring in their dead. But he made a complete circuit twice, in vain. Nothing: there was no trace that indicated any kind of door.

What should he do? Had they, then, escaped one horrible danger only to risk perishing now of an even more frightful death?

The young man felt his arms becoming numb under the weight he was carrying. His muscles were weakening, but he did not want to set Marie's inanimate body down on the ground, which was doubtless impregnated with contagious mists. He stiffened himself against the pain that was gradually invading him.

Suddenly, he shuddered; it seemed that he could hear the sound of footsteps. Where was it coming from? For a moment, he had the crazy idea that it was the dead who were about to rise from their tombs in order to surround him and draw him into a horrible *danse macabre*, as in the lurid legends of the Middle Ages.

He leaned over, cocking his ear.

They were muffled human footfalls, the echo of which reached him as if stifled by an obstacle. Just then, the moon was covered by a cloud, and Sabirat remained motionless in profound obscurity, not knowing which way to look.

Suddenly, the sound of footsteps ceased, and voices became audible. Then, it was as if something scraped against the wall, on the side opposite to where the young doctor was standing. The profound emotion he felt somehow increased the acuity of his senses, and he realized that that there were men a few paces away from him, who had just applied a ladder to the wall.

He was not mistaken, because he could hear the creak of the rungs. Someone was climbing up.

Perhaps they were filthy night-prowlers, grave-robbers who did not recoil before sacrilege and had come to despoil the cadavers. He did not budge; all in all, it was still better to find himself facing human beings, even bandits, than to remain in this sinister solitude.

Black forms appeared on the crest of the wall. The moon, although hidden behind the clouds, illuminated them slightly and gave them a fantastic aspect. What struck the doctor first of all were their tall bonnets, which elongated their heads in fantastic oblong forms.

Two of them sat astride the wall. They were looking outwards, so they did not perceive the young man leaning against the wall, still carrying his cherished burden.

They leaned over, as if drawing a heavy weight toward them, and words were pronounced that seemed, by their intonation, to be orders. A dark mass soon appeared on the stone rim, folded up. It was a human body in a sack.

Sabirat remembered then. Although his memory was incomplete, he was sure that he had read somewhere that, among Oriental peoples, burials took place at night. He was, therefore, really in a cemetery, and these men had just brought a new cadaver, which the crows would soon be tearing apart like the others. They were not bandits, not committing sacrilege, but believers of a singular and exotic religion.

Indeed, behind the cadaver, two more men had climbed up. Then the ladder that was outside was drawn up, and now, with violent efforts, it was being dragged over the top of the wall, where it was soon balanced. Then, the heavier part having been slid over, it was lowered into the cemetery and carefully adjusted. Two men came down, reaching the ground a few paces from the young man, while the others, still on the crest, lowered the sack slowly toward the ground. It was received, and the rope supporting it was untied and the two men walked away, carrying the cadaver, over the boundary of the white checkerboard.

Sabirat followed them with his gaze, wondering how the adventure was going to conclude.

He saw them stop and drop the cadaver into one of the ditches, tipping it out of the sack. Then they raised their arms into the air, uttering guttural exclamations that might have been prayers.

A quarter of an hour went by like that.

Finally, the strange ceremony ended, and the men slowly retraced their steps.

This time, there was no hesitation; it was necessary to take advantage of this unique opportunity to get out of that funereal location. Sabirat marched toward them resolutely.

As he approached, they stopped abruptly, frightened.

Evidently, they took the sudden apparition for a fantastic manifestation—perhaps the soul of a dead man that had re-animated a cadaver, perhaps a vengeful god who wanted to punish them for an unknown sin.

After a second of hesitation, they prostrated themselves onto the ground, their arms folded over the top of their head, uttering stifled moans.

Sabirat knew several Oriental languages; he took the risk of speaking the one that, in his estimation, was understood by the greatest number, Persian.

"Don't be afraid," he said in that language. "I'm not a demon, I'm a man: an unfortunate, who is asking you for help."

There was no response at first. He was about to address them in Arabic when one of them raised his head. Sabirat repeated what he had said. "I beg you," he continued, "in the name of the god of your forefathers, help me."

This time, he had the satisfaction of seeing that he had been understood. The two strangers stood up and came toward him. After taking a few steps, however, they uttered a cry for help. Sabirat, who had not thought of looking behind him, suddenly felt himself seized by his shoulders and pulled to the ground.

"Profane dogs! Sacrilegious wretches" cried furious voices. "To death! To death!"

The situation became increasingly perilous. Marie, still motionless, was lying on the ground. Sabirat, stunned by his fall, could no longer find the words of the language that was being spoken.

But what point was there in arguing? Obviously, these people believed that there had been an odious profaning of the sepulchral location.

Sabirat was lifted up and carried away. The men ran toward the ladder. A rope was looped beneath his armpits. He was lifted up as the cadaver had been a little while before. In a kind of nightmare, he found himself on the crest of the wall.

He wanted to cry out: "Marie! Marie!"

But vertigo gripped him while he was slid down the other side of the wall, where he lost consciousness.

II

When Sabirat came to, it was broad daylight. At first, he did not remember what had happened to him, and he looked around fearfully, blinking in the bright light that was descending from above.

To tell the truth, what he saw could hardly orient him to his present situation.

Immense walls surrounded him, topped, above their crumbling, breached summits, by a large expanse of blue sky, profound and immobile: a tower, in fact, with a ruined summit, but still solid in its enormous blocks of stone, strongly cemented. One might have thought it a vestige of one of those cyclopean structures that were said to have been constructed by giants, ancestors of the pygmy humans of today.

It is true that in the nightmarish state of mind the young man was in, everything took on gigantic and somewhat frightening proportions in his eyes.

He moved and let out an involuntary groan.

His entire body seemed to him to be aching atrociously; he feared that one of his limbs had been broken by a fall or violent blows.

Having shaken himself in order to regain is self-possession, he told himself that the best means of making sure of the state of his bones was to get to his feet, and with a thrust of his hips he tried to stand up—but he fell back with a veritable cry of pain.

It was then that he perceived a large ring sealed around the middle of his body, which was connected to the wall by an iron chain.

He was a prisoner—and in what a prison!

Suddenly, he thought about his companion.

"Marie!" he shouted in an anguished tone.

But no voice replied to his, and the sound came back to him in an almost dismal echo.

174

He could not suppress a shudder, because he now remembered the frightful accident that had launched him through the air with the young woman, and then the frightful descent into that sinister and accused place.

What had become of Marie? Had she only escaped one danger to be delivered into one that was even greater?

A prisoner? Of whom? Of some ferocious and savage people. Collecting his memories, however, Sabirat recalled that the men had appeared to understand Persian.

Among the Orientals, the Persians were, after all, those whose sovereign had the closest relations with Europe; it was said that he had imported the seeds of modern civilization into his Estates.

And yet, this brutal captivity and these exaggerated precautions taken against an unarmed foreigner did not testify to a well-developed spirit of humanity.

What could he do? Wait! But perhaps every minute augmented the perils that Norès' sister was encountering. Sabirat told himself that it was his duty to make any sacrifice for the salvation of the woman he loved.

He twisted in his chains, hoping madly that he might break them, but he became increasingly convinced that it was a vain struggle. With his legs and his torso shackled, his arms could not exert their full leverage. He was weaker than an infant, and, reflecting that Marie might be subject to similarly horrible treatment, which her delicacy certainly would not survive, he was gripped by a rage that soon dissolved into the bleak despair of impotence, and large tears ran down his cheeks.

I addition to the fact that he could not make a single useful movement, he could not see anything around him but worn stones, debris fallen from the top of the tower—not even a fragment of iron that he could seize, with which he might kill himself—for, in truth, in the despair that imposed itself upon him, he thought about ending his life. But he stiffened himself against that cowardly thought. So long as he could suppose that Marie, his beloved Marie—for now he no longer hesitated

to admit the love that the young woman had once accepted—
was alive, he owed it to her, until his dying breath, to think
about the chances that might yet remain of saving her.

Very remote chances, it was necessary to admit.

Hours went by while the unfortunate felt his strength ebb
away, and a kind of intoxication, doubtless that of hunger,
invaded his brain.

So, it was finished. He would die slowly, horribly, in that
in pace into which fate had precipitated him. He would not
even have the supreme joy of looking his torturers in the eyes,
insulting them, spitting his hatred and scorn in their faces.

For a Frenchman, to be able to confront one's murderers
is to die less dolorously.

Suddenly, it seemed that he could hear a noise. He raised
his head abruptly. A shadow was profiled against the sky, at
the crest of the wall.

Breathlessly, he waited, thinking that perhaps one of his
torturers was about to appear before him.

But it was an illusory hope. From the summit of the tower a rope unfurled, at the end of which hung a basket. The
basked came to rest beside him, within arm's reach, and by
means of some ingenious mechanism, the rope was detached
from it, which rose up again alone, hissing against the wall.

Already, Sabirat, half-standing, was shouting, appealing,
using all the Persian vocabulary he had been able to learn at
the Oriental school in Paris, where he had once attended lec-
tures, with no suspicion of the unusual circumstances in which
he would be enabled to test his knowledge. But the rope had
reached the crest of the wall; the human shadow was once
again outlined against the sky, and then suddenly disappeared,
without paying any heed to the desperate cries of the unfortunate prisoner.

He had a fit of rage, clenched his fists and howled—but
what was the point?

Around him, there was nothing but silence, and he was
quite certain that his torturers, if they had heard him, were
firmly resolved not to make any response. But if they wanted

him dead, why not abandon him completely? Why come to add to the initial cruelty the even more cowardly ferocity of bringing him what he needed to prolong his miserable life?

Well, he would cheat them, frustrate their calculations of cruelty. No human power could force him to touch the food that had been offered to make his agony more prolonged. He would not eat, and thus his torturers would no longer have the hideous satisfaction of hearing his impotent imprecations. In their turn they would be irritated that their victim was escaping them so rapidly.

And the unfortunate, closing his eyes, lay down resolutely on the ground, determined to let death come without making the slightest effort to escape it.

How, an hour later, did he surprise himself by avidly devouring the watermelon and the maize cakes and drinking from the pitcher of water in long draughts? Is any other explanation necessary than the will to survive, to struggle against the final destruction that lies in the obscure depths of every consciousness?

Now, his decision was very different—and also much more reasonable.

While a breath of life remains to a truly energetic man, it is cowardly to confess himself vanquished. He will live, attentive to the slightest circumstance, relentlessly on the lookout for an opportunity of salvation. Once again, as long as he had no proof that Marie was dead, he owed it to himself to fight for life.

And the hours passed…

Then a day, and then another…

Every morning, the shadow appeared at the top of the tower. Then, with the same precision, the basket of provisions descended beside him, within arm's reach.

He shouted, he appealed, but there was the same silence, the same heart-breaking impassivity.

But Sabirat stiffened himself against the despair that sometimes took possession of him. What was most atrocious of all was the immobility to which his shackles condemned him. He could scarcely raise himself up on his knees; he could not stand upright—but what was the good of having studied medicine, especially anatomy, if he could not apply his science to himself? The young doctor exercised his ingenuity in creating a kind of gymnastics for his benefit, which exercised his limbs one by one, so well that, even in that more than critical situation, he had nothing to fear from ankylosis.

But the silence!

To tell the truth, during those interminable days, it was a terrible torture not to hear any sound. Above him, always the same sky, bright and bleak; around him, always the same mute stones.

There, too, his willpower triumphed. Sabirat had the courage to work his mind even so, constraining himself to resume his studies and pose himself problems that had not yet been resolved. Then, when evening came, he hypnotized himself and succeeded in going to sleep.

He counted twelve days like that. He did not know how long he had been unconscious to begin with, and certain clues caused him to suppose that a narcotic had been administered to him…to the extent that, in his estimation, he had been isolated from the rest of the living for an entire fortnight, without having obtained any other result than conserving his strength and his mental faculties.

Then, one evening, when the stars were commencing to sparkle above in the hollow of the tower, as if in the field of a gigantic telescope, Sabirat suddenly heard a burst of resounding commotion, the feeble echo of which reached him amid a cacophony that was both harrowing and terrible.

In the situation he was in, it was not an insignificant event. He listened more attentively and became gradually better able to discern the multiple sounds that were reaching him through the thickness of the walls.

Along with the vibration of the instruments—more or less barbaric trumpets, bugles and buccinas—there were the hoof-beats of thousands of horses, and the increasing murmur of a crowd uttering savage cheers. And all of it was getting closer, concentrating, after a fashion, around the opening of the tower.

What was about to happen? Had the barbaric tribe into whose hands he had fallen suddenly been attacked? Was it the exodus of an entire people expelled from their homes? Was it a battle?—for he had heard the detonation of firearms...but they did not seem to be numerous enough to indicate a battle...

Breathless, stretching his neck, he listened, and waited.

Suddenly, there was a noise at the top of the tower; shadows, more compact than those that ordinarily appeared, loomed up on the crest, and the young doctor saw something long and narrow descending into his *in pace*.

A ladder! Then men, balanced on the rungs.

Perhaps they were coming to murder their victim...but what did it matter, after all? It was better to put an end to the uncertainty.

"What do you want?" he shouted. "Do you intend to kill me?"

Without replying, two men came down to him and immediately set about freeing him from his chains. Then, one of them said a single word in Persian:

"Up!"

It was not death, but a semblance of liberty. Sabirat was finally able to stand up—tottering, it is true, for in spite of all his efforts, he had not been able to preserve his limbs from a relative numbness. Summoning up all his energy, however, he straightened up, gripped the ladder, and started climbing vigorously.

He did not reflect; he enjoyed the exquisite pleasure of movement, and if he were to encounter an executioner at the top of the latter who would strike him down, at least he would have experienced an almost joyful sensation in not dying enchained like an animal under a butcher's sledgehammer.

He finally set foot on the top of the tower, but at the same moment, he felt himself dragged forward. The men surrounded him; he was hoisted onto a horse, which departed at a gallop, in the midst of other horsemen, who were racing with a tremendous speed.

The night was profound, although the stars were casting a pale gleam over the landscape that was sufficient to distinguish objects.

Sabirat felt such joy in his relative liberty that, without allowing himself to be dazed by the open air, he succeeded in reacting against the intoxication of sorts that was agitating his brain, and examining attentively what was happening around him.

He was being transported amid a multitude of disparate costumes and brutal physiognomies, whose most evident characteristic was an Oriental appearance. He had, therefore, not been mistaken in his initial rapid observations; he was, if not in Persia, at least in one of the bordering regions

Of the men galloping around him, some were of the very pronounced Kalmuk type, with prominent cheekbones and flattened noses; others, on the contrary, had almost regular features and long, slender noses. One might have thought them a strange mixture of different nationalities, connected by an accidental bond.

Some were dressed in superb costumes, armed with rifles with sculpted butts and sabers in sheaths sparkling with ornaments; others, by contrast, with their shoulders scarcely hidden beneath fur cloaks, were brandishing spears of the most rudimentary form.

Sometimes, however, identical harsh and guttural cries escaped from their throats, like exclamations of anger and hatred. He did not understand their significance.

The ride had something fantastic about it; for as far as he could see, he could only make out the host; even those who doubtless had the mission of ensuring his safety, carried away by their mounts, often left enough free space around him for him to be able to run away. But what would be the point? Not knowing where he was, he understood that it was in his interest to continue following the multitude—which, he observed, did not exhibit the anxiety of a troop of fugitives but, on the contrary, the enthusiasm of an attack force.

Sabirat was not unaware that the tribes occupying the immense territories of Afghanistan and Khorasan are frequently at war with one another, lacking unique leaders whose authority can group and direct their forces; perhaps he was witnessing an armed assault by one village on another. In fact, all reasoning was still impossible; it was necessary to submit to chance and wait for some unforeseeable opportunity to seek information.

The gallop was unrelenting; fortunately, Sabirat was an excellent horseman, and now, completely in control of himself, he boldly followed those whom he considered as guides rather than jailers.

Hours passed without any relaxation of the furious pace—but Sabirat sometimes saw, along the roadside, new groups launching themselves into the midst of the troop, joining with it, and then galloping on in the whirlwind, which extended and elongated—multiplying, visibly.

Already, the first glimmers of daylight were arriving, and, as if they were on a ridge, the doctor saw a vast plain before him, black with horsemen. In the distance were the towers of a city. Evidently, they were nearing their goal. The horses were urged on, while the cries thundered more loudly.

In the distance, a troop was advancing, comprised of men whose armor was sparkling in the light of the rising sun.

It was a marvelous spectacle. One might have thought it a scene from the ancient crusades, when knights advanced ahead of vanquished Muslims.

Here there were evidently neither victors nor vanquished, however, but soldiers proceeding ahead of a leader. That was what Sabirat understood, from a few words overheard by chance.

The group of new arrivals stopped in front of a ruined but admirably imposing mosque, which stood on a small hill in the middle of the arid plain.

Like true cavaliers in a fantasia, all the others launched themselves toward that goal at a rapid gallop, uttering cries of "Inshallah!"—Glory to God—while firing rifles. Then they stopped, forming an enormous circle around the central point of the mosque, in the middle of which the tribal chiefs were standing.

Sabirat, whom no one was any longer thinking of keeping under surveillance, pushed his horse forward and arrived in the first row.

Suddenly, he uttered an exclamation: the man who, in the middle of a troop of warriors, was standing at the foot of the ruined mosque, looming over those surrounding him by virtue of his height, was Alexandroff Wintscheff.

Sabirat thought that he was saved; how could he divine that he was confronting a renegade of civilization?

III

The spectacle that Sabirat had before his eyes was both splendid and frightening. The plain was black with horsemen, and beneath the dazzling sun there was an amazing riot of colors, of sparkling banners and immense flags, on which monsters of every form displayed their grimacing faces.

What struck the imagination above all, however, was the enormity of the swarm, conveying the impression of a multitude of which any calculation seemed to defy human reason.

Sandorf had raised his hand, which bore a standard striped with a hundred colors, but which was cut through by a traversal green bar.

In the other hand, he was brandishing a heavy sword.

As if by enchantment, the cries died down, and Sandorf took a few steps forward, climbing a mound, from which he could overlook the plain.

He was not alone.

Next to him marched a woman clad in the long robe of an Oriental priestess; it was Sithreva, who, her arms folded over her chest, was reminiscent of a statue descended from its pedestal.

When he reached the top of the mound, Sandorf began to speak, in a resounding voice.

"Glory to God!" he cried. "Brothers, the hour of vengeance has sounded. For long enough and too long the false gods of Europe have insulted the grandeur of the prophet. His voice has echoed through your solitudes and has ordered you to gather around his sacred standard, and to come and chastise insolent Europe. You have obeyed; that is good.

"Already, from every corner of the ancient world, from the seas where the sun rises, the peoples have set forth toward the accursed Occident. From north to south there is one army, a hundred innumerable armies, on the march. What is your first enemy? It is Russia, which has stolen your lands from you, which has dared to violate your customs and outrage your beliefs. Death to the Russians!"

And like a clap of thunder, the cry, repeated by a hundred thousand throats, resounded in the air with terrible echoes that seemed to resonate from one end of the earth to the other.

Sabirat listened, stupefied, wondering whether he was asleep or awake. What! Was it really the young man he had met in Paris, who, seeking pleasure above all else, had declared himself a hundred times over to be a friend of Europeans, of France, who was speaking, exciting the savage passions of these fanatics, who were responding to his exhortations with clamors of death? And these threats, these cries of hatred addressed to those who had been his hosts, who had given him a new fatherland...

It was impossible.

Sabirat, unable to control his wrath, urged his horse forward with an abrupt surge and found himself alone at the foot of the mound that Sandorf had made into a pedestal.

"Wretch!" he cried. "What crimes are you meditating? Are you mad or infamous?"

He had shouted those words in French, a language that no one around him except Sandorf understood. By his gestures, however, and his exasperated attitude, those surrounding him had divined that he was insulting their leader, and they threw themselves upon him.

But Sithreva had leaned over the ear of her lover and whispered a few words into it. He raised his hand and ordered that the infidel be brought to him. His orders had an omnipotent effect. The raised arms fell back, and Sabirat was dragged toward Sandorf. Although he was solidly held, Sabirat, fully determined, struggled with the courage of despair.

Sandorf said to him: "Who are you, and what do you want with me?"

"You don't recognize me?" Sabirat said. "Is that because the bandits you command have detained me in a cruel jail for weeks? I'll tell you my name. I'm Dr. Sabirat, Sametel's friend, Prince Batow's friend, the friend of all those you have betrayed."

At the names of Sametel and Prince Batow, Sithreva had stiffened, in a movement of anger. The name of Batow, which was Sacha's, was no longer ever pronounced. "Is it here, Sandorf," she said, "that you ought to listen to this miscreant?"

"You're right, Sithreva. Let him be taken to Bukhara...and I'll make my will known later."

To Bukhara![35] So Sabirat was separated from his homeland by the Caspian deserts! But this land belonged to the Russians, who had extended their empire from Khiva to Samarkand!

He tried to protest, but as Sandorf, having given his orders, had turned away, Turkmen threw themselves upon him and, with a furious brutality, dragged him toward the designated city, the Rome of Islam, as Vambery[36] called it.

But to the question he had asked himself, a prompt response was given.

Alongside the road by which he was taken, he saw groups of wretched men in chains, some of them bloodied and mutilated. They were Russian soldiers. Then, further on, heaps of corpses were strewn by the roadside, still wearing European uniforms.

There was no doubt about it; it was the crusade of the Orient against the Occident; the first battles of the invasion preached by Sandorf had been fought. And by means of a kind of sudden intuition, Sabirat connected these facts with the

---

[35] Bukhara is now the capital of Uzbekistan, on the old Silk Road. It is separated from Persia (i.e., Iran) by Turkmenistan to the south. Kazakhstan lies to the north, including the "Kirghiz steppe," which extends a long way to the northwest of Kirghizstan.

[36] The Hungarian writer Arminius Vambery (1832-1913), who published a memoir of his extensive travels in Central Asia in 1865.

185

Chinese mob whose first eruption he had seen at the session in which Norès had shown what was happening in Peking.

Bukhara was full of soldiers, if one could give that name to the terrible hordes that had invaded it: Uzbeks, Tajiks, Kalmuks, Kipchaks, even Multanis and Hindus! There were Tartars from Yaksu, Yarkend and Kashgar, Khalks from Shandur, Ersari, Kara, Teke and Yomut.

Vagabond troops that saw a European pass by hurled furious obscenities at him. Fortunately, his guards, fanatical servants of Sandorf, the Pir—the Chief—as they called him, intended to carry out his orders to the letter. Twenty times it was necessary for them to respond with force to those who wanted to take their prisoner from them in order to tear him apart. They carved a passage with sword-thrusts, and more than one person paid for his resistance with his life.

Finally, they reached the center of the city, and Sabirat was thrown into one of the cells of the Teke, the great seminary of Islam, today transformed into a citadel occupied by thousands of Turkmen.

So these peoples, fiercely independent, true brigands who lived by plunder and pillage, who hated one another to the point of setting the most perfidious ambushes in the desert, had suddenly been united by this criminal mission preached to them by a fanatic…madman, rather…for Sabirat, alone now in the dark damp cell where they had locked him up, wondered if he had really understood, if it could be true that a man who had appreciated the benefits of civilization, who had enjoyed them, who had left sympathies and affections in European society, had really come to profess such hatred against that which he had seemed to love.

Scarcely an hour had gone by when they came to fetch Sabirat on the Chief's behalf.

He was taken through subterranean passages, perhaps to protect him from the fury of the wretches whose formidable clamors he could hear outside.

Introduced into a room with a high ceiling and a floor covered in rugs, he saw before him Sandorf Wintscheff, standing up, waiting for him.

The Kirghiz—whom Sandorf had believed to be of pure Russian blood—was pale. "Monsieur," he said, in a voice that he strove to render firm, "give thanks to our former friendship, which persuaded me to save your life—but remember that I'm not disposed to listen to insulting words. I am the master here, and your life is in my hands. I am also your judge, and I order you to reply to me."

Sabirat had completely recovered his composure. He considered Wintscheff attentively, and in spite of the calmness the other affected, dissimulating his agitation beneath the rudeness of his language, the doctor understood that his conscience was far from restful.

"Monsieur," the doctor replied, "I don't know who says that you're the master, nor by what right you constitute yourself the judge of a man who has no crime for which to reproach himself, but enlightenment might spring forth from this interrogation of which I have need, so I consent to submit to it. Speak then, and I shall see whether it pleases me to respond."

Wintscheff made a gesture of anger; he thought that he had inspired fear, but he saw that he was dealing with an adversary who was difficult to intimidate.

"How do you come to be in this country?" the Kirghiz demanded, brusquely.

"That first question," Sabirat replied, "appears to me to be singularly ironic. Does one normally demand of a prisoner why he is in his dungeon?"

Wintscheff drew closer to him.

"Prisoner! What does that mean?"

Sabirat had not lost sight of the slightest play of the physiognomy of the Kirghiz, and he remarked that he seemed sincerely surprised as he asked the question.

"Prisoner, I said," Sabirat confirmed, "and I'm astonished that a gallant man should feign ignorance, when he finds himself facing a man whom a single word could doom."

"Monsieur!"

"Do you not know—or are you pretending not to know—that I've been held captive by your followers for more than two weeks?"

"You! On my honor, I had no idea."

Coldly, Sabirat went on: "I heard you just now proffering words of hatred against Europeans, against the Russians…which proves to me, Monsieur, that perhaps you and I do not attach the same meaning to the word *honor*."

Wintscheff became livid. He plugged his hand inside his jacket, and his fingernails dug into his breast.

There is a banal phrase, which alone can explain the sentiments seething in his brain: *God, how annoying it is to be wrong and to know it.*

To be sure, he only had to make a sign to impose silence on the little physician who permitted himself to cast doubt on his word, but the fashion in which Sabirat had pronounced the word "honor" had been, if one might put it thus, essentially French. Wintscheff had understood the nuance in all its finesse, and he sensed that the honor that was being invoked was not that of his interlocutor.

He contained himself and continued: "Monsieur, I urge you, in our own interest, not to try to push me too far. You're right; we're not of the same race. We have neither the same beliefs, nor the same aspirations."

"You have had them."

"I deny them!" asserted Wintscheff. "Oh, you thought, Messieurs of the Occident, that you would pose as eternal masters of the Orient; you thought that with your great words, civilization and progress, you would forever be the exploiters of those millions of people who have their faith, their past, their strength. Those times are past, Monsieur. Yes, I, Alexandroff Wintscheff, deny the Europe that has enslaved my fatherland, which has debased us to the point that we have even forgotten the names that our forefathers left us. No, I'm not Russian; I'm not European; my name is not Wintscheff—a barbaric name with the ring of slavery. Curbed for too long, I have stood straight. Today my name is Tamir the Kirghiz, the descendant of Timur,[37] who was the master of the world. I am the revolt that raises its head, the slave who breaks his yoke. And tomorrow, the master will avenge himself on those who have had the imprudence to declare themselves his masters."

Sabirat considered him attentively. On that overexcited face he had seen the flame of fanaticism gradually ignite. An entire atavism of savagery became visible through those pupils, as ardent as those of wild beasts.

For the young doctor, that was a revelation; he understood what the alliance of enemy peoples, united by that bond, signified: the hatred of the Occidental. A revolt rose within him, but he succeeded in conserving his composure.

"All right," he said. "I won't argue with you. Let's go back to our point of departure—which is to say, the cowardly act that was carried out against me and a defenseless child."

"What do you mean?" exclaimed Wintscheff, whom we shall permit to retain his European name. "Do you believe that Occidentals have the privilege of generosity?"

"I don't know about that," Sabirat replied, "but I don't suppose that when you came to Paris, for example, with…a woman, anyone separated you violently from your companion and threw you into a dungeon."

"Explain yourself clearly!" exclaimed the Kirghiz.

"Gladly." And Sabirat recounted what had happened to him. He passed over in silence, of course, the fashion—eccentric, to say the least—in which he had arrived in the Turkmen region. It was merely a matter, he said, of a scientific

---

[37] Timur (1336-1405), often known in the West as Tamerlane (i.e., Timur the Lame) was a Turko-Mongol conqueror who attempted to restore the Mongol empire of Genghiz Khan, terming himself the Sword of Islam for political reasons. He conquered most of Central Asia and much of northern India, but did not succeed in conquering Ming China or the Ottoman Empire.

exploration, something analogous to the mission once undertaken by Madame Dieulafoy and her husband.[38]

"But you weren't alone?" Wintscheff objected. "You had an escort?"

"I beg our pardon. Our men had remained some distance away. We could not have appeared dangerous, and the brutality of your…Orientals…did not seem in the least justifiable."

"Who is the woman accompanying you?"

"I could, Parisian as I am, reply that it's none of your business, but since you seem curious, I'll satisfy you." He took a step toward the Kirghiz and looked him straight in the eyes. "The young woman who accompanied me," he said, was an intimate friend of Nathalie Batowna, Mademoiselle de Norès."

At the name of Nathalie—of which Sacha, it is well-known,[39] is only an abbreviation—Wintscheff took a step back. In the young man's tone, he had understood everything that the name in question suddenly evoked: the sense of reproach, not to say scorn.

A hundred times, Wintscheff had declared himself to be the fiancé of the young Russian woman.

"Now," said Sabirat. "I demand that you tell me what has become of Mademoiselle de Norès…whether you have had her murdered."

"Monsieur!" exclaimed Wintscheff, again, in a tone of outrage. He made a move as if to throw himself at the young

---

[38] The ardent feminist Jane Dieulafoy (1851-1916) adopted masculine dress in order to travel with her husband Marcel in Europe, Egypt, Morocco and Persia, keeping an elaborate diary and engaging in studies of a broad archaeological and theological scope. The Dieulafoys obtained permission to lead an official archaeological mission to Persia in 1884; she published the first of her several novels in 1890.

[39] In fact, Sacha or Sasha is usually a contraction of Alexandra, and Lermina seems to have forgotten that he has previously given Sacha's forename as Elena.

man, but the latter had folded his arms disdainfully and was looking him in the face.

The Kirghiz passed his hand over his face. "In truth," he said, in a voice that anger caused to tremble, "you're wrong to challenge me, as I am the stronger of us, but in spite of my…Oriental savagery"—he emphasized the phrase ironically—"I'll remain calm. Listen to me carefully: I know nothing about your arrest and detention. I only learned two days ago that a European had been detained by a Turkmen tribe. I gave orders that he be set free and brought to me. I therefore do not know what has happened."

"*A* European, you say? But what about Mademoiselle de Norès?"

"I was only told that a man had been arrested."

"Which is to say that the wretches have killed her! That would be the most cowardly and infamous of crimes."

"And the most futile," murmured Wintscheff. He added: "Monsieur Sabirat, we shall know the truth."

He went to the window. In front of him, a vast square extended, covered with horsemen, who, while waiting for the signal to depart, were engaging in one of those strange fantasias in which riders and horses seem to form a single entity, bounding, turning, and wheeling like a cloud of fantastic animals.

Wintscheff was spotted, and formidable cries burst forth, saluting the leader who was about to lead those furious hordes in the pillage of Europe. For all of them, those lands of the Occident were a mysterious region where gold flowed in streams, where always-gilded crops covered immense areas, where the cities contained immense riches stolen from their forefathers—for it was revenge, above all, that these bands wanted to take; their imams, lamas, and monks had repeated a thousand times over that their miseries were due to the Europeans who had robbed them. It was the patrimony of the Orient that it was a matter of recovering; it was their sufferings of old, their famines and even their plagues, that it was necessary to avenge. All the scourges that had fallen upon them were due to the spells and crimes of the Occidentals: those magicians who adored the demon Shaitan, the enemy of Allah, Buddha, and Fo; it was their gods, too, that they were going to defend.

And Wintscheff, absorbed in his dream of power, told himself that he was the master of all those men, who were only waiting for his signal to rush upon the enemy and constitute for him—for him—the vastest empire that had ever been united under the hand of a single man.

Impatiently, Sabirat waited.

"Well, Monsieur," he said, finally, "have you forgotten once again what you have promised?"

Wintscheff shivered, as if suddenly awakened. Then, without answering, he opened the window and made a sign.

The acclamations had redoubled. With a gesture, he gave thanks.

Then he summoned a servant and gave him an order. Sabirat did not understand it.

The silence between the two men was heavy now.

Although Wintscheff took pleasure in proclaiming himself a savage, hating the civilization he had enjoyed for such a long time, there nevertheless subsisted within him more than one vestige of the delicacies that the policed life put into the conscience of a man. He was irritated that, at the very outset of his career, hazard had put him in the presence of one of the people he had known before—and in what circumstances! When he had loved to proclaim himself a Parisian *par excellence*, when he had thrown money out of the window to provoke the admiration of those of whom he now declared himself to be the implacable enemy!

Then again, what did all that matter now? But he had met the doctor at Norès' house in Paris, when he had been the assiduous cavalier of Nathalie Batowna, whom he had loved and had abandoned, treacherously, in the midst of horrible circumstances in Peking.

What had become of her? Had she perished in the torment? In vain, Wintscheff tried to drive those thoughts out of his mind, which now haunted him again, and he dared not turn to look at Sabirat—who, with his eyes fixed upon him, seemed to be reading the utmost depths of his soul.

Suddenly, the door opened.

The two men shivered involuntarily, snatched from their meditations, and a double exclamation escaped their lips.

Sithreva had just come in.

Wintscheff's cry was merely one of surprise; it was not her that he had expected to see. But on the part of the young doctor it was an exclamation of astonishment, admiration, and a vague dread that he could not yet explain.

Now, the young Hindu with the velvet eyes and the warm complexion, with features of an admirable perfection, was no longer the priestess that we once saw fanaticizing the Orientals arranged under the banner of the five hundred gods. She had abandoned the long tunic and the hieratic coiffure that gave her the appearance of a sphinx descended from a granite pedestal.

The woman had become a warrior. A breastplate of metallic mesh, so fine that it seemed to be woven like silk, molded her vigorous bosom, while on her head, a kind of helmet surmounted by a chimera with deployed wings increased her height almost to superhuman dimensions. A darker fire shone in her eyes, and her hand rested on the hilt of a naked sword, attached to her side by a red sash.

She was the very image of War, and more: the goddess of Vengeance, a messenger of death, ignorant of pity.

"You, here, Sithreva!" exclaimed the Kirghiz. "I had ordered that Ko-Hor, the Turkmen chief, should be sent to me."

"But it's me who has come."

"Why?"

"Because I know what questions you desire to address to Ko-Hor, and it's me who will answer you."

Sabirat's eyes went from one to the other, and in an instant, the young man had understood the drama that he was witnessing. He had divined that the man, so proud, so ambitious for an empire, was the slave of the woman, whose fanaticism doubled her superb beauty.

"All right," said Wintscheff, suppressing a gesture of impatience. "The prisoner tells me that he was not alone when he was arrested."

"That is true," said Sithreva.

"A woman was seized at the same time."

"That is true," the Hindu repeated.

"We don't make war on women," said Wintscheff. "The woman is a European, it's true, but she's harmless, and it would be particularly agreeable to me..."

"If she were set free," said Sithreva, smiling ironically.

"Yes...yes...I've interrogated the doctor"—he pointed at Sabirat—"And he's given me very clear explanations. We have no interest in keeping him captive."

Sithreva was looking at him intently, and Wintscheff, stammering in spite of himself, seemed to be pleading rather than giving an order.

"Madame," said Sabirat, intervening, "I don't know what your authority is here, or whether your consent is necessary for a simple act of justice to be done, but I can assure you that we did not come here as enemies..."

Sithreva interrupted him, turning to Wintscheff. "Do you know the name of this young woman?"

"Yes; it's Mademoiselle de Norès, I believe."

"Which is to say," said Sithreva, "the sister of the man whose name is on everyone's lips today—who, it appears, is preparing engines of destruction against us that will frighten the world."

"Monsieur de Norès," said Sabirat, "is valiantly defending his homeland."

Sithreva did not reply to him; it was still Wintscheff that she was addressing. "This Norès, if I'm not mistaken, is the fiancé of Mademoiselle Marguerite Sametel?"

Wintscheff blushed: to mention Marguerite was to make allusion to his previous engagement to Sacha.

"Sametel!" the Hindu continued. "Another name that it is necessary for us not to forget, for it is that of one of our most ardent adversaries—the Sametel who was the most active agent of the invaders who had sworn to enslave the Orient."

"But this young woman is not their accomplice."

"You think so?" said Sithreva, shrugging her shoulders. "You have for these people, our most dangerous enemies—for they belong to the accursed nation of France, which claims to be at the head of the civilizing movement—a very singular indulgence of which I don't seek to know the cause. But it's of no importance; people, as you like to tell me, are only responsible for their own actions. So be it! And it's for their actions alone that you ought to demand that this man and woman account."

"Our actions?" exclaimed Sabirat. "Are you claiming that we've committed some crime?"

"How do you treat spies in your country?"

"They're put to death."

"Well," said Sithreva, extending her arm toward Wintscheff, "to you, who have accepted the supreme command and who answers for the security of our soldiers, I denounce this man and I denounce Mademoiselle de Norès as spies and traitors."

"Infamy!" cried Sabirat. "Ah! Since it's a woman who proffers that insult, it's from you, felon and true traitor, that I demand account for it!"

And the young doctor, carried away by anger, threw himself at Wintscheff, arm raised.

Before it could come down, however, men had appeared who threw themselves upon him and knocked him down.

"Yes, spies," Sithreva continued, "And more than that. Wintscheff, occupied with military organization and the thousand cares of command, you cannot watch over everything—but have no fear; I am here…and I know how to defend you."

She went to Sabirat, whose guards were now holding him firmly.

"Frenchman, friend of Norès," she said to him, in a wrathful voice that hissed between her teeth, "what is the diabolical machine you have transported into the cemetery of Yeni-Khosroul?"

Sabirat started in surprise. What did she mean?

"Oh! You're feigning ignorance," Sithreva continued. "These Occidentals are audacious in their hypocrisy." To the guards, she said: "Take this man to that window." She went on: "Look now, and tell me if you understand me better."

The window to which Sabirat was taken overlooked an interior courtyard, and there, on a cart drawn by yaks, the doctor recognized Norès' aerostatic apparatus.

Was that, then, what the Hindu called a diabolical machine?

He could not help smiling. He now divined the errors inspired in these ignorant people by the sight of an apparatus with which they were not familiar and of which they could not deduce the marvelous usage.

"What's that?" cried Wintscheff—who, better versed in Occidental sciences, was nevertheless unable to imagine the purpose of the curious machine. "Is it true that you've transported that into this country?"

It would be more accurate to ask, Sabirat thought, *how the machine transported us. In any case, I have no intention of replying.*

"You remain silent!" exclaimed Sithreva. "Your silence is a confession in itself. In any case, do you think that we have not recognized one of those engines of death, formidable destroyers, that your Norès and your Sametels devise for the ruination of their adversaries? It is veritable audacity to have transported such an instrument of murder to this almost unknown region, but the more difficult the action is to comprehend the more we suspect some infamy and monstrous invention. It has fallen into our hands; it belongs to us."

"And what can you do with it?" Sabirat could not help crying. "I defy you to discover its secret."

Scarcely had he spoken than a smile of triumph brightened Sithreva's face. "So," she said, "you admit that there is a secret?"

Sabirat shut up, understanding that he had said too much.

"Oh, you won't keep silent forever," she said, in a singular tone, in which Sabirat detected a threat. "You're not forgetting that you're a prisoner, and I don't suppose that our chief will insist now that you are set free."

"With the consequence," Sabirat replied, "that because you're ignorant, I'm condemned to perpetual imprisonment."

"Ignorant? At last we're asking to be educated. Explain the usage of that machine to us, and you're free."

"So it's a treason that you're asking of me?"

"If the secret of that machine is inoffensive, if it doesn't conceal some means of warfare and destruction, why refuse to speak? And why would you be a traitor, if it's not a weapon of war?"

Sithreva, sure of herself, was speaking with a calmness that was no longer deceptive. And, indeed, the logic of her words was unassailable.

Strictly speaking, Guy de Norès' machine was not a weapon of war, but Sabirat was not a man to make use of sophistry in order to avoid what he knew to be his duty. Whatever it was, the secret did not belong to him, and he did not have the right to reveal it.

"Do with me what you wish," he said, in a firm voice. "I won't speak."

"We'll soon be able to vanquish your resistance!" cried the Hindu.

"Which is to say that you'll appeal to your torturers and you'll tear me limb from limb. Do it. I swear to you that you won't extract a word from my lips."

"But you're not the only one who possesses the secret," retorted Sithreva, after a pause.

"What do you mean?" exclaimed Sabirat. "Do you dare to talk about Mademoiselle de Norès? Would you have the infamy to employ means unworthy of civilized beings on her?"

"You know full well that we are not civilized."

"Wretches!"

Sabirat writhed, attempting to escape the grip of his guards. Sithreva's last words had filled him with fear and horror. Certainly, he knew Marie too well to admit for a moment that she would yield to threats, but if these bandits were to torture her…!

Sithreva had approached Wintscheff and whispered something into his ear.

The Kirghiz had nodded his head in assent, without saying a word.

Sabirat understood that it was his fate and Marie's that was being decided at this tragic moment, so he summoned up all his strength to recover his composure and to be ready to support all the physical or mental ordeals that it might please these bandits to inflict upon him.

But would the young woman have the same strength?

At the thought of what these torturers might make her suffer, he experienced a horrible anguish.

Meanwhile, Sithreva had made a sign, and Sabirat's guards, dirty Turkmen, mere contact with whom disgusted him, took hold of him more tightly and dragged him toward the door.

He turned his head. Neither Sithreva nor Wintscheff was following him. Where were they taking him?

He was obliged to go down long staircases, and then to follow long, narrow, and damp corridors, of which his eyes could scarcely make out the eroded walls, over which water was streaming. Evidently, he was being taken underground to some dungeon, in which he was about to be locked.

Eventually, however, he felt the ground underfoot rising again. A door suddenly opened wide in front of him…and the sun was so ardent, the passage from darkness to light so abrupt, that he was constrained to close his eyes momentarily.

When he opened them again, he saw before him a vast courtyard, closed on three sides by buildings, but open on the fourth to an arid and bare plain.

Around the courtyard, soldiers with ferocious faces were massed, armed with rifles and sabers.

A company, in response to an order, came to surround him, and his guards then ceased to hold him. It was like a deliverance.

But in that movement, the troop that now guarded him had revealed a corner of the courtyard, where Sabirat recognized Norès' aerostat, on the cart as he had already seen, with its shiny propeller, reminiscent of the wing of some fantastic bird.

It was very difficult to divine what was happening now.

The soldiers had drawn their swords and were putting the points to his breast.

As he raised his head, in a movement of pride and disdain, as a true Frenchman, who does not fear death, he saw Sithreva on a balcony, leaning on Wintscheff's shoulder, watching.

He smiled scornfully and folded his arms, taking pleasure in defying the renegade and his fanatical accomplice.

"Frenchman," said Sithreva's voice, full and sonorous, which reached him distinctly, "are you ready to surrender de Norès' secret to us?"

"No," he replied, resolutely.

"Well then, look."

Then the group of soldiers that had their backs to the palace, opposite the side open to the plain, stepped aside, in order to reveal...

Sabirat uttered a fury and desperate cry.

This is what he saw:

There was a cannon—a bronze monster—and in front of it mouth, attached to it, was Marie de Norès, pale but equally impassive, holding her head high.

A prisoner since the moment when Sabirat had been separated from her, Marie had borne the miseries of her captivity courageously, but what dangers she had run in the midst of those brutes with human faces! Fortunately, from the first day, a kind of dervish had been attached to her heels...

He had been the first to divine that the machine, whose purpose he could not determine, constituted an invention for whose secret the Chief would pay dear. Far from employing violence, he had attempted by means of hypocritical kindness to capture the young woman's confidence. She had divined the trap, but, taking advantage of the dispositions of the man who had constituted himself as her benevolent jailer, she had not given him a formal refusal. By means of procrastination and promises, she had succeeded in gaining time, hoping that an unexpected circumstance might furnish an opportunity to escape.

She knew that Sabirat was alive. The night before her departure, she had even convinced the dervish that before speaking she had to confer with the prisoner, who was the only one, she said, who knew the entire secret—and in the fever of his curiosity, the Oriental had consented to attempt to establish communication between them.

Unfortunately, the order to join the main body of the army had arrived abruptly, and the plan had been aborted. And Sithreva, informed of the young woman's captivity and irritated by the hazard that put her in the presence of someone she still considered as a rival, had demanded that she be handed over to her. She had come to interrogate her and had demanded treason, as she had of Sabirat.

Marie had only replied to the infamous proposal with scorn. And the Hindu had sworn to exact a pitiless vengeance.

A little while before, Marie had been taken from her prison and now she was here, attached to that engine of death, which they had had the cruelty to load in front of her. One gesture would provoke its explosion.

She was resigned, fortified by her patriotism and her honor.

Suddenly, she too had perceived Sabirat, surrounded by soldiers, threatened by death, and had allowed a cry of fear and sadness to escape.

The young doctor had raised his furious fist toward the balcony.

"Wretched woman," he shouted, "and you, even more cowardly man, I wish I were near enough to you to spit all my hatred in your face!"

Wintscheff made a movement of rage. Sithreva restrained him.

At the same time, she made a sign, and a man emerged from the ranks of soldiers: a kind of priest with a long white beard, enveloped in a green kaftan, indicating that he had made the pilgrimage to Mecca. He was a Hadji from Chinese Tartary, as evidenced by his white turban.

He had undoubtedly received preliminary instructions, because, without asking what the mute order meant, he advanced slowly toward the young woman, and, when he was a few paces away from her, said in French, in a deep and guttural voice: "You know what Nasib"—Destiny—"has decided for you? Death is touching you. If you have any power over this man here, hasten to use it, for pity is ready to remove you. Let him reveal to the Pir the secret of the mysterious machine, and both of you will be free. If he refuses, you will die first. Then, for a second time, he will be summoned to obey, and if he does not submit, the Angel of Death will take him. Do you understand?"

For all the spectators of the sinister scene, Marie de Norès, very pale, offered the image of proud resignation and nothing more—but a Parisian who had observed her at close range would have noticed something at the corner of her lips resembling a smile of mockery and bravado.

When the Hadji had finished, she replied: "First of all, what influence do you think my voice can have on the Frenchman, my companion, at this distance? He could scarcely hear me, and there is, I believe, a Turkmen proverb that says: *Persuasion murmurs, but does not shout.*"

Thus, while her torturers thought they had crushed her strength by means of terror, she had not lost her composure for an instant, had not weakened for a minute. Since the moment when she had been separated from the man whom she now considered to be her fiancé, as her husband, she had not lost the hope of finding him again and of escaping with him. Even when she had been attached to the mouth of the cannon, the bronze of which was bruising her, her indomitable hope had not abdicated.

She was on the lookout for an opportunity, ready to profit from the slightest circumstance, and, to tell the truth, had a kind of intimate conviction, irrational but instinctive, that she had nothing to fear, and that Sabirat would be saved along with her.

How? By what miracle? She had no idea; she only knew that it was so—and that certainty, which had no basis but was unshakable within her, gave her intelligence and incredible acuity.

The Hadji had remained still momentarily, his clenched hands on his breast. He too had expected tears and supplications, but the young woman he believed to be broken by fear was replying to him clearly, with the most perfect logic.

And furthermore, she was quite right.

They hoped, in order to extract a secret, to abuse the affection that they assumed to exist between the two people; was it on terror alone that it was appropriate to speculate? Would the supplications of the lover not be more powerful?

The Hadji had understood, and in Marie de Norès' tone he thought he had detected the intention to obtain the desired sacrifice from Sabirat.

In truth, the lives of the two strangers were of no importance; one interest overrode all others: the knowledge of the machine, which the Oriental imagination had endowed with fantastic virtues—which was perhaps the case, although not in the sense that they supposed.

"What did she say?" demanded Sithreva, who had not heard.

The Hadji replied in a loud voice, but in Chinese. "She says that if she is allowed to speak to her lover, she has the power to persuade him."

The Hadji was embroidering slightly, but who would not have done so in his situation?

"All right," said Sithreva. "I'll give them five minutes. Let them be detached and brought together."

Sithreva had spoken in French in order to be understood by Marie; there was still a certain vanity among the foreigners in proving to the French that they could speak their language.

Marie shivered with joy.

Was she really thinking of betraying her brother's secret? The death that was confronting her was one of the most horrible the imagination can conceive. Was it not possible that her feminine nerves might be unable to resist that agonizing anguish?

The order had been given, however, to reunite briefly the two young people. Untied, Sabirat had run to Marie, and, my God, forgetting completely what propriety would have demanded in a Parisian drawing room, had taken her in his arms and clasped her ardently to his heart, so forcefully that, greatly troubled, she struggled like a captive bird and freed herself, blushing deeply—but not sorry.

"Before all these people, Monsieur Sabirat!" she murmured.

"That's true—I beg your pardon, but what do you expect; it was stronger than me. I beg you to forgive me."

"Oh, I don't hold it against you—but let's talk and talk quickly, for these people don't seem to me to have a great deal of benevolence toward us. It's understood, isn't it, that you have no more intention than I have of telling these miscreants what my brother's invention can do?"

"Certainly not; it would be a betrayal, which would horrify me."

"On the other hand," Marie continued, "it's very evident that if we don't give them satisfaction, we're doomed."

"Obviously. For myself, I'm not unduly concerned; a Frenchman is a soldier of his country, and owes his life to the fatherland…but you…"

"I'm a Frenchwoman; know that I love my country with all my heart, and am ready to die for those I love."

She had said that so valiantly, with a gaze so frank and expressive, addressed to Sabirat, that he had to restrain himself very firmly in order not to repeat his indiscretion of a few moments before.

"We have no hope, then!" he exclaimed, suddenly.

"Who can tell?"

"Didn't you hear what that woman said?"

"Of course: either we surrender our secret, or we die."

"And what a death! When I saw you at the mouth of that cannon just now…"

"I assure you that it wasn't as uncomfortable as all that."

"You have the courage to joke?"

"It's necessary to have every courage."

"Except that of seeing those one loves suffer. Do you think I'm afraid to die? That's what I want to shout at them…let them take my life…but let you go."

"Do you think that I could live without you?" said Marie, holding out her hand to him. "Perhaps it's not very correct, but I'm sure that Maman won't blame me for getting engaged without consulting her. They're already getting impatient. Will you do as I say?"

"What do you mean?"

"I want you to obey me in everything…as if you were already my husband."

"Can you doubt it? What could I do that would be sweeter for me than obeying you?"

"Well then, step back two paces. There, that's good! Now, pay attention, and above all, look very emotional."

The recommendation was superfluous, for Sabirat was utterly amazed when he saw the young woman throw herself at his feet, while she cried: "I beg you, I implore you…tell them what you know…I don't want them to kill me…mercy, my friend, mercy!"

And she threw her arms around him, whispering: "Push me away and shout: *no, no!*"

He had no clear idea where the comedy was going, but he did as he was told, making grand gestures and trying to free himself.

"So," Marie continued, in a tone of high drama, "you were lying when you told me that you loved me?" Between sobs, she murmured: "Weaken. Begin to be shaken. Say: *But what about the Fatherland.*"

"But what about the Fatherland?" repeated Sabirat, bewildered. "The Fatherland!"

"What does the Fatherland matter? You should only think about me…about me, who loves you." In a low voice, she added: "That's me compromised!"

In sum, the scene had been well enough played for Sithreva to be following it breathlessly, leaning over the balcony with profound attention.

She had a ferocious idea, which, she did not realize, completed the effect that Marie was attempting to produce.

"We need to finish this," she shouted. "Soldiers, seize that woman and carry out my orders!"

The soldiers advanced toward Marie in order to grab her—but the young woman had had time to whisper to the doctor: "Consent now…don't worry, I'll answer for everything!"

And Sabirat, who had begun to glimpse the objective at which Marie was aiming, shouted: "No, no! Stop! I consent…I consent!"

Sithreva uttered a cry of triumph. She had, therefore, crushed the pride of the damned Occidentals, so proud of their patriotism! She could hold them in scorn!

"Bring them here," she ordered.

And a few moments later, Sabirat and Marie appeared before Wintscheff and the Hindu again.

In the long dark corridor through which they had passed, Marie had explained everything to Sabirat.

"I knew full well," said Sithreva, sniggering, "that fear would weaken with your resistance. So much for the courage of the French in the face of death."

Sabirat opened his mouth to reply, but Marie squeezed his hand and threw herself at the Hindu's feet. "He consents, Madame, he consents to everything, but I beg you, don't make him pay too dear for the sacrifice he's making for the woman he loves! You're a woman, don't you understand what he's suffering? Are you not loved—you, so beautiful—sufficiently to admire love in others?"

"Let's not discuss ridiculous sentimentalities!" cried Wintscheff, who could not help feeling ill at ease before the young woman that Sithreva was torturing. Monsieur, have you decided, yes or no, to demonstrate the use of the machine to us?"

Sabirat felt a strong desire to leap at his throat, but he had strength to contain himself. "I'm ready," he said.

"First tell me what the machine's purpose is."

"It's an instrument of war."

"I knew it!" cried Sithreva. "And how did you bring it here?"

"By means of a dirigible balloon," Sabirat replied, earnestly.

"What!" cried Wintscheff. "The trials I witnessed have succeeded already?"

"Almost completely," said the doctor. "And the proof is the presence of the machine in a place where no one saw it arrive."

"But I repeat, what does it do?"

"It's a military televox." While pronouncing that barbaric term, Sabirat maintained a perfectly serious tone.

"Tele…?" queried the Kirghiz

"Televox," Sabirat completed. "Compounded from two words, one Greek: *tele*, rapid; and the other Latin: *vox*, voice."

"But we already have the telephone."

"Oh, it's not at all the same thing. The telephone transmits the voice of the person who speaks into it..."

"Indeed...and the televox?"

"Transmits, by contrast, the voice of another. Which is to say that at ten, twenty, fifty or a thousand meters, once can hear the voice of someone speaking as if one were beside them. It's surprising...and you understand that on campaign, being able to overhear the secrets of the enemy..."

It was not very clear, and Sabirat was becoming slightly confused. Marie had told him to invent some kind of apparatus and implant the desire to have a demonstration right away, but that it must not be an apparatus of locomotion or a weapon. The specification was not one of the easiest to fulfill, especially when one only had five minutes to come up with a good plan—but human vanity has incredible resources to come to the aid of brave individuals.

In his capacity as a semi-European, Wintscheff wanted to appear before Sithreva to be well up in matters of modern science, and although he did not really understand, he said: "I get it. It's a kind of loudhailer."

"In reverse," Marie put in. She added: "It's my brother's latest and most marvelous invention, and it's very simple. Now that we've decided to save our life at any price, we can tell you everything. Thanks to that machine, we can hear from here what's being said in St. Petersburg."

"That's impossible."

"It's the case," Marie repeated, boldly. "You don't know then, what electricity can do in the hands of a genius like my brother. Inside the machine there's what we call an orientator. One places the needle on the city to which one wishes to be instantaneously connected, in terms of sound, and it's extraordinary: one can hear the noise of the streets. Then one steers toward the houses where something of interest is being said, and one eavesdrops on the conversations, so to speak. Would you like us to prove it to you?"

"Of course I would," said Sithreva.

"If you'd care to accompany us to the machine, the demonstration will soon be made."

"I'll come with you. Come on, Wintscheff.

The Kirghiz—we could easily say the ex-Russian—torn between his ambition and his memories of being a civilized man, uttered a sigh of relief. To be sure, he was under the absolute empire of Sithreva, but the Hindu's fanaticism sometimes frightened him, and he felt himself being drawn down a slippery slope at the bottom of which he glimpsed an abyss of blood and terror. If Sithreva had given the signal condemning Sabirat and Marie de Norès to death, he would not have raised a hand to halt the executioners, but it was a veritable joy for him not to be forced to ratify a action that he would have considered, in the depths of his soul, to be brutal, cruel, and unworthy of the man he had been.

Thus he hastened in response to the Hindu's summons, and the group now returned to the vast courtyard where, in the midst of the soldiers, the cart carrying the machine was. Solid ropes secured it to the vehicle.

Marie was able to exchange a few words with Sabirat, who had nodded his head as a sign of acquiescence.

"Monsieur," said the doctor to the Kirghiz, "it's necessary, for the demonstration to be useful, for the machine to be taken down from the cart and placed on joists that hold it off the ground.

"All right."

Orders were given and groups of men set to work. Sabirat supervised the operation carefully, making sure above all that none of the external mechanisms were damaged in the process. Sithreva and all the Orientals followed the operation with the profoundest attention. Marie kept very close to Sabirat, and, in truth, the two now gave the appearance of two professors about to make a demonstration of their own accord to docile and attentive pupils.

The most curious of all was the Hadji who had kept Marie prisoner, and who was biting his fists in rage at not having constrained her by force to surrender the secret to him. So, thanks to his holy garment, he had gradually slid into the first row, and was almost touching the machine, wanting to grasp more rapidly than anyone else the key to the enigma that might have made him rich had the known it before anyone else. Even if one has made the pilgrimage to Mecca, one is nonetheless a man, and the worthy dervish would not have disdained a few significant rewards.

Hazard served him marvelously. He found himself placed in such a way that he was half-hidden behind the shell of the machine and could speak to Marie without being seen.

"Frenchwoman," he said to her, "you don't suspect treason. When you've spoken, you and your companion will be killed. I alone can save you by saying that your life has been placed under the protection of Allah. Only give part of the secret to the Pir and reserve the complete knowledge of it for me, and I'll save you. If not, I'll let the executioners do their work."

It was a commission of a new kind that the worthy man was demanding, and it would not have taken much for Marie, on hearing his petty conditions, to give way to involuntary hilarity. She replied in the same tone: "Agreed, but you have to swear to take us under your protection."

"I swear."

"By the beard of the prophet?"

"By the beard of Mohammed."

That was a binding contract, and the Hadji, joyfully, moved even closer to the machine, placing his hands on the doorway that Sabirat had just opened, and plunging his gaze inside. At a glance, the latter had observed that, by an incredible hazard, no damage had been done; the Turkmen, fearful of an explosion, had handled the object with the utmost care, and everything was intact.

Sithreva advanced and, leaning on Wintscheff, asked what experiment they were going to carry out first.

Singularly enough, at that moment, the violence she possessed, with all her Oriental finesse, caused her to abandon all suspicion. She knew—or, rather believed—that she was the absolute mistress of the life of the two fiancés, and that was sufficient for all anxiety to have disappeared. In addition, the scorn and hatred that the Europeans inspired in her caused her to find it perfectly natural that they would purchase their survival with treason.

"The best thing to do," said Sabirat, "is to offer you a preliminary proof of the ability of the machine. Say something into Wintscheff's ear that only he can hear, and we'll listen to it from inside the machine and repeat it to you."

That did, indeed, seem impossible, in spite of the short distance separating the two groups.

"Do it, then," said Sithreva.

"But for that," Sabirat added, "we need to close the door of the box."

"Obviously," said Wintscheff, very interested in the experiment, and wanting to be sure that the words could not be heard by ears alone.

Sabirat and Marie de Norès found themselves inside once again.

"Marie," said the young man, "you're not unaware that we're going to risk a terrible death again?"

"I know—but anything rather than remain in the power of these barbarians."

In the meantime Sithreva put her lips close to Wintscheff's ear.

"Are you ready?" shouted the doctor's voice from the interior.

"Yes," replied Sithreva, and added, in a very low voice, in the Kirghiz' ear: "I love you."

But the response to her was a furious cry of rage from Wintscheff, complicated by furious clamors from the crowd, and a horrible howl of terror.

For this is what had happened:

"God's will be done!" Sabirat had said, pressing Marie's head to his bosom—and resolutely, he had pulled down the lever, trembling lest the anticipated effect might not be produced, by virtue of some unknown accident.

As in de Norès' workshop, however, the apparatus, after oscillating for a hundredth of a second, had shot up vertically into the air more than two hundred meters.

Wintscheff had shoved Sithreva away so violently that he had almost knocked her down. Then, raising his arm, he cried in a thunderous voice: "Fire! Fire at the wretches!"

A few detonations burst forth, but at the same instant, the marabouts, hadjis, and other holy mendicants threw themselves toward the soldiers, imploring them not to shoot.

Out of generosity? Hardly.

In consciousness of the futility of that fusillade? Not that either.

For the strangest and most inexplicable of reasons.

It will not have been forgotten that the Hadji who had proposed a sub-treasonous treaty to Marie de Norès had positioned himself in such a way that he was in the best place to divine the secret of which the young woman, he believed, was only going to reveal in part to Wintscheff and the Hindu. As it was a matter, however, of striking a sufficiently indifferent pose not to be suspected of espionage, the worthy Hadji, whose name was Ben-Borouk, had perched himself on the external edge of the hull and, in order not to slide off, had grasped one of the blades of the external propeller.

In that fashion, his head was adjacent to the wall, and he would hear what was being said and done inside.

It was well planned—but then, without any warning, the machine had risen into the air with an incomparable velocity.

Ben-Borouk howling—and surely no one would be sufficiently unjust to think it a crime—wanted to hold on, but to what? To the ground, which was fleeing beneath his feet with dizzying rapidity. Illusion! In brief, he let go, and would have fallen headfirst if, by a freak of chance, his camelhair tunic had not been caught up in the propeller, as if by an iron claw.

Have you ever seen a horse being loaded on to a ship? A large strap is passed under its belly, and attached to a crane. Hoist away! And the animal is suspended, its feet in the air, rotating above the quay, looking stupidly bewildered, as old Corneille put it.

The case of the unfortunate Ben-Borouk was absolutely identical.

He was suspended by his back, his arms and legs hanging down...a uniquely delicate situation, not to say uniquely ridiculous, and exceedingly dangerous, for however solid a camelhair garment might be, its resistance has its limits, like everything human.

And the servant of Mohammed howled more and more loudly.

It is now explicable why Ben-Borouk's colleague had stopped the soldiers who were about to fire. Hadjis do not eat one another.

When Sabirat and Marie de Norès had felt the machine leave the ground, and when, through the pothole, they had seen clouds envelop them, they had—forgive them, Lord!—thrown themselves into one another's arms as if they had been married with all the civil and religious sacraments.

It was deliverance; it was escape...and from what a horrible death! They remained motionless momentarily, enjoying that return to life, to hope.

And through the opening, rays of splendid sunlight enveloped them like an halo. It was marvelous, and the children can be forgiven for having lost sight momentarily of the clarity of the situation, inasmuch as Sabirat, who could feel Marie's hair against his breast, was not in the least disposed to philosophy. It was sufficient for him to be alive, and he wanted the moment to last forever.

Women being more reasonable than men, however—that is an axiom we must accept, whether we like it or not—Marie was the first to remember the danger they had run before, when the aerial vessel had previously transported them into space.

"Friend," she said, disengaging herself from his arms, "where are we? Don't you remember?—first, it's necessary to level off."

"That's true," said Sabirat, stifling a sigh. "I forgot everything—forgive me."

"Oh, I forgive you," Marie said.

After a moment's reflection, Sabirat gently raised the lever again, in accordance with the lesson of past experience, and he felt the movement of elevation fade away.

"Fly horizontally," breathed Marie. "Now we need to get our bearings."

And as Sabirat obeyed, she knelt down and uncovered the orifice in the floor.

"The ground can no longer be seen distinctly," she said. "We're out of range, but it's necessary not to remain over this accursed country. You know the two levers that permit eastward and westward direction."

"And also north and south, for now I understand the principle of the movement of the levers above and below the horizontal. Each of them produces two directions, which correspond to the four cardinal points. If we at least had a compass! Which direction should one chose when one doesn't know where one is?"

"Bah!" said Marie, with a small gesture of obstinacy. "Let's go first, and see later. I'm confident."

The fact is that, having escaped Sithreva's clutches, they had a perfect right to rely on Providence.

"Westwards, then," said Sabirat, resolutely. "We're in the Orient, and logic dictates that we should try to get back to our homeland if we can."

"So be it—westwards."

Sabirat collected himself quickly, studied the levers like a pianist before his keyboard, and lifted the one on the right.

There was a formidable purr outside, accompanied by a howl so savage and so strident that Marie went frightfully pale.

"What's that?" she exclaimed. "One might take it for a human scream!"

"I'll find out," said Sabirat, and moved to open the door.

"Be careful!" cried Marie. "If you stumbled..."

"No, no, I'm sure of myself."

Resolutely, Sabirat opened the door and peered out.

What he saw surpassed all description.

It will be remembered that the Hadji had been in the situation of a sack of wheat hanging from a hook—a stable position, although paralyzing—and in the panic caused by the very elevated placement, far above sea level, he had no longer been able to utter the slightest sound, abandoning himself to the will of the prophet, who, as everyone knows, keeps an accurate record of future events: what is written is written. He remained motionless by instinct, moreover, understanding that the slightest agitation might provoke the tearing of the camelhair, his only hope and his only safeguard. Oh, if the goods were shoddy...[40]

Thus, it was still supportable...until the moment when Sabirat had, so to speak, set a westward course. Because the tiller was linked to the propeller to which the holy man was so unfortunately attached, the propeller had begun rotating.

A sickening rotation! A desolating gyration, for it carried the unfortunate Ben-Borouk with it in its whirl, and he was now spinning like one of those artificial fireworks that are the joy of idlers.

And that as what Sabirat saw: a rotating mass in which he could only distinguish something long that was in circular movement, like the sails of a windmill under the pressure of a strong wind.

Marie had leaned out behind him, also looking with a curiosity mingled with terror.

Suddenly, she recalled the scream she had heard, and launched herself toward the lever.

"We have to stop!" she cried. "It's a man!"

"Not too abruptly!" Sabirat had time to shout.

---

[40] There is an untranslatable pun here by virtue of the accidental relationship between *camelote* [shoddy goods] and camel. Lermina was not to know that *camelote* would also become, in due course, a slang term for cocaine.

Indeed, he had understood that the object, whatever it was, would fly off at a tangent, like a stone from a sling, if the interruption were too abrupt.

Marie had heard, and lowered the lever gently to the horizontal.

Now Sabirat could see the Hadji, who was rotating more slowly.

The propeller finally came to a stop, while the aerial vehicle hovered.

Sabirat, who had leaned out, hanging onto an external handle with one hand, succeeded in seizing hold of the wretch, who was hanging inertly, stunned and hypnotized by the rapidity of the gyration.

Fortunately, the young doctor was exceptionally vigorous; otherwise it would have been impossible to carry out the audacious and difficult maneuver by means of which he succeeded in bringing the suspended man over the platform that formed a step outside the door, and finally rolling him inside.

The Hadji collapsed like a bag of damp rags.

"Let's head westwards again," Sabirat said to Marie de Norès. "I'll try to get this excellent savage back on his feet."

And while the propeller, freed from its burden, throbbed with a formidable roar, Sabirat knelt down next to the unfortunate Turkmen and massaged him vigorously.

Success soon crowned his efforts, and he had the satisfaction of hearing the holy personage sneeze vigorously—which is always a good sign.

Ben-Borouk opened his eyes very wide, only to close them again more rapidly. Perhaps the worthy Hadji thought that he had crossed the bridge that takes pious Mohammedans to Paradise, and had experienced a disagreeable shock on seeing, instead of the expected houri, the bearded face of Sabirat—who, moreover, in a voice that had nothing feminine about it, said to him: "Come on, stir yourself—show a little energy."

The holy man was literally bewildered; anyone would have been. Fortunately, Sabirat spotted in his belt something that had all the appearance of a water bottle, doubtless filled from some sacred spring.

He detached it and, before putting it to the Hadji's lips, took a sniff. He could not suppress a burst of laughter; it was barley liquor, something like prime quality raki. Admittedly, its effect would be all the more sure and even more immediate.

The holy man took a long draught—so long that Sabirat had to wrench the bottleneck from between his teeth.

The panacea quickly took effect, and the Hadji, widening his eyes, demanded in a surly voice that proved the complete reestablishment of his lungs: "Where am I?"

"My dear Monsieur," said Sabirat, "It would be impossible for me to inform you very precisely. All that I can say for sure is that you're between one thousand and two thousand meters above sea level.

"What!" said the Hadji, bounding to his feet.

"It's the simple truth, and since you seem to me to be quite well, if you'd care to take a look out of this porthole, you'll soon be convinced that I'm telling the truth."

He had opened the lower viewport, and the Hadji leaned over, shivering in every limb. He invoked Allah an appropriate number of times—after which Sabirat thought it useful to give him a few explanations.

Ben-Borouk had some difficulty understanding what had happened, in so far as his knowledge of aeronautics was somewhat limited, but he was obliged to yield to the evidence. It was not by courtesy of the Prophet that he was suspended in a box hundreds of feet above the mountains. Admittedly, as soon as the notion had entered his head, he was gripped by an intense terror, and, while shivering from head to toe, he begged Sabirat to descend to the ground.

"It's easy for you to say that," said the young man, laughing, "but it would displease us greatly to become involved in an adventure similar to the one from which we've just extracted ourselves so fortunately. Tell us where we are, and I promise to take your request into careful consideration."

Marie intervened. "We must have traveled a long way," she said. "We can't know any more as long as we remain at this height. Don't you think, my friend, that it would be prudent to move closer to the ground and try to get our bearings?"

"Right," said Sabirat. "This time, it's broad daylight, and there's no danger of descending into a place as sinister as the first time."

"But how can you go down?" exclaimed the Hadji.

"You'll see that nothing is simpler," Sabirat replied, who was not reluctant to put on a demonstration of an experiment so dearly acquired. "This is what we do."

He put his hand on the descent lever. There was a slight shock, as when one applies a brake, and the voyagers felt themselves descending.

"All's well," said Sabirat. "Let's moderate the movement in order to remain at a range from which we can inform ourselves precisely."

He knelt down in his turn and gazed attentively through the downward viewport.

"It's bizarre," he said. "It seems that I can see little white clouds rising up in the direction of our vehicle and then suddenly separating and dispersing in the air. What can it be? At the very bottom, I can see a very large white cloud, with jets of smoke at its extremities..."

Suddenly, a crackling sound became audible.

The aerial vessel was going downwards with disorienting rapidity.

Other abrupt noises, similar to explosions, ripped through the air.

"Go back up!" he cried to Marie. "I understand everything—we're being bombarded."

Indeed, as Marie, still a novice in the operation of the apparatus, did not return the lever rapidly enough to the vertical position, shells of enormous dimension began to burst around the airship.

Sabirat had stood up in order to accelerate the maneuver.

Either because the movement was too abrupt, or because some component of the apparatus had suddenly broken down, he sensed that the vessel was no longer obedient.

"My God!" cried Marie. "One might think that we were out of control!"

It was true; a moment ago, the aerial vessel had started spinning, like a wounded bird. It rose up, descended, and headed north, only to veer southwards a moment later. Sabirat tried in vain to regain control, bringing all the levers into play one by one, with infinite precaution, but the expected effects were not produced.

Suddenly, Marie cried: "Look, my friend, at that enormous mass heading toward us!"

He leapt to the lateral porthole and saw, a hundred meters away, a quasi-fantastic form: that of a gigantic fish swimming in the air, which seemed to be heading straight for them.

At the same time, with a shrill whistling, long, thin projectiles cleaved through the air, not hitting the apparatus but flying past it and bursting some distance away with formidable bangs.

"Aerial torpedoes," said Sabirat. "We're doomed if we can't get away. I understand now: we've been spotted by the observers of an army, by some captive balloon, perhaps a dirigible cruiser. We're being pursued, and as we have no means of defending ourselves..."

An enormous voice shouted through the air: "Surrender!"

That was easy enough to say. What could they do to obey? In truth, any thought of flight was insane. Sabirat was beginning to realize that the apparatus, already charged for a long time, was exhausted. Norès' ship was fluttering its wings like a wounded bird, and the moment was doubtless close at hand when it would no longer have the force to sustain itself in the atmosphere. Then there would be a horrible, hectic, crashing fall.

But then—the call had been issued in French!

All these reflections had passed through Sabirat's mind with lightning rapidity.

Marie, very pale and ready for anything, even death, looked at him, wondering what decision the man she had made the master of her life was about to make.

The Hadji, mad with terror, had fallen flat on this face and was imploring Allah, who could not do anything.

Resolutely, Sabirat opened the door of the apparatus and leaned out, waving his handkerchief, the white color of which seemed to him likely to be deemed peaceful. "Don't shoot!" he shouted. "We surrender!"

There was a great silence. The dirigible balloon was drawing closer by the second, circling like a vulture about to fall on its prey.

The detonations had ceased.

Suddenly, an enormous shadow enveloped the voyagers, and coming to a halt, the balloon drew alongside them.

The nacelle—or, rather, the armored suspended chamber that served that purpose—was occupied by three officers.

"Russians!" Sabirat shouted. "We're saved."

"Russians!" howled Ben-Borouk. "I'm doomed."

"Who are you?" demanded a Russian officer, while grappling irons settled on the airship.

"We're French," replied Sabirat. At the same time he uttered a cry; he had just perceived that the hull of the apparatus had been pierced by a fragment of a shell—damage that had almost reduced it to incapacity.

"Save my companion first," Sabirat shouted, seizing Marie in his arms and imploring the aid of the officers.

In a matter of seconds the young woman was transported to the nacelle.

"Your turn, Monsieur," said the officer who seemed to be in command.

"But I'm not alone; there's an injured man here.

"Can't you embark him too?"

"I can't get him to move."

In fact, the Hadji, who regarded the Russians with a horror increased by a terror carefully maintained by the fanatics, had such a fear of falling into their hands that he was clinging onto the levers, from which Sabirat could not succeed in detaching his hands.

By virtue of that action, however, he brought one of the mechanisms into play, and the airship suddenly started to fall vertically.

Sabirat scarcely had time to throw himself backwards. He leapt with all the might of his legs toward the nacelle, and succeeded in grabbing hold of it.

The officer, perceiving the danger, cut the grapples still retaining the airship, whose fall would have dragged them down.

They saw it disappear with alarming rapidity.

"Poor fellow!" exclaimed Sabirat. "He'll break all his limbs on the ground.

Suddenly, Marie uttered an exclamation. "Look, Monsieur Sabirat, at the name inscribed on the balloon!"

Sabirat obeyed and uttered an exclamation in his turn: "The *Norès!*"

"So what?" asked the officer.

"But I'm Guy de Norès' sister!" said Marie.

The officer bowed. "In that case, Mademoiselle, I'm very glad that our encounter didn't have fatal consequences for you. In an hour, you'll be with your brother."

"Where are we, then?"

"At Borovichi, on the road to St. Petersburg."[41]

---

[41] Borovichi is in the north of the Valdai Hills, not far southeast of St. Petersburg. It is not only an extremely long way from Bukhara, but it is very difficult to imagine how the airship could have gotten there by following a westward course, which would have taken it over the Caspian Sea and Turkey, Greece and Italy, more than twenty-five degrees of latitude to the south of Borovichi. On the other hand, it is equally difficult to imagine how the airship got to Uzbekistan, if one con-

"But this dirigible balloon you're manning..."

"Is one of the scouts tracking the movements of the enemy army?"

"What army?"

"What! Don't you know? All Asia is hurling itself upon Europe. It's a struggle to the death." The officer added, sadly: "And who can tell who'll emerge victorious?"

"You're scaring me. Give me the details."

"This is where we're landing. Behind that hillock you'll find the advance guard of one of the corps that's defending Russia. Monsieur de Norès is there with the Council of War."

While he was speaking the balloon descended to the ground.

As soon as they were solidly moored, the officer helped Mademoiselle de Norès and her companion down.

At that moment Russian officers appeared some distance away. At a sign addressed to them from the balloon, they hastened their approach. The commandant of the balloon entrusted the doctor and the young woman to them. When he pronounced Marie's name, the officers made a military salute.

"The sister of Guy de Norès is most welcome. If you'd care to follow us, we'll take you to your brother."

---

siders the manipulations of the controls described in the course of the outward journey.

IV

In a tent before which Russian officers were standing sentinel, naked swords in hand, three men were chatting around a table on which a map was spread.

One of them, clad in a white tunic whose breast as embroidered with a two-headed gold eagle, was named Louis-Alexandroff Romanoff; he was the Tsar of All the Russias, to whom his people had awarded the title of the Great Protector.

Some years before, the internal situation of Russia had been completely modified. On his deathbed, the father of the present Tsar[42] had ordered his son to give his government a new direction. For pure autocracy, which tended simultaneously to tyranny and theocracy, he had been enjoined to substitute a constitutional regime appropriate to Russian mores and habits.

It is well known that under the despotic regime of the old Romanoffs, liberty had been entirely resident in the organization of the commune, the Mir, a sort of fraternal municipal group in which the citizens considered themselves to be bound by an absolute solidarity. Thus far, however, that solidarity had only prevailed as a defense against the demands and the prevarications of the central authority, avid and brutal tyrants who exploited the people and stifled their complaints with the knout, or by depopulating the Mirs and sending the most intelligent and active of those whose determination might cause trouble for them to Siberia.

One phrase always ran through the people like a cry of protest and hope, however: "If the Tsar only knew!"

---

[42] When Lermina serialized his story, Alexander III was still the Tsar; he was to be succeeded in 1894 by Nicholas II. Neither had a son named Louis, but Nicholas' actual heir apparent, Alexei, was not born until 1904, so there was plenty of time, from Lermina's viewpoint, for him to have other sons.

And Louis-Alexandroff, faithful to his father's wishes, had wanted to know. He had ordered an investigation in every part of his immense empire, entrusted to reliable men chosen from among the most active representatives of the liberal party, those who had until then posed an unrelenting challenge to autocracy. That investigation had been carried out secretly. Two year later, the Tsar had said, smiling: "For two years I was the chief conspirator against my own empire."

And the Tsar had known. Suddenly, between him and his people, there was something like the opening of a great door, through which the light penetrated as far as the throne, previously enveloped by egotistical advisers, shadow, and ignorance.

The Tsar had known...and he had understood that he had a duty to fulfill valiantly his role as a pastor of humans, and that power was not and ought not to be an egotistical satisfaction, but that a man who placed himself above others assumed superior duties in consequence. And Louis-Alexandroff had resolutely undertaken the endeavor of the liberation, regeneration, and education of his people.

How many obstacles he had encountered at first!

All the satisfied, all the exploiters, the entire gilded whirl of courtiers, functionaries, devourers of the budget, from first to last, had risen up, frightened, divining that they were threatened by catastrophe, that the time of enriched idleness, satisfied hatreds, and conquering injustices was about to elapse.

From one end of the immense Muscovite empire to the other, there was a formidable raising of shields against the prince who wanted to be a human being. Bitter struggles were engaged; a permanent conspiracy, all the more powerful because it was supported by means sanctioned by age-old routine, had covered the empire with an inextricable network. Some of its members had even succeeded in recruiting ignorant peasants suspicious of all innovation to the cause of the past.

The Tsar had not weakened. Escaping assassination attempts as if miraculously—it was the so-called nihilists who had then constituted themselves as his voluntary defenders—he had fooled them by courses he had mapped out. He had marched with a firm and sure tread, without deviating by an inch, and a day had dawned when an entire series of ukases had established the new order: municipal liberty definitively founded, federation established between all the communes, represented in great municipal councils to defend their interests, then delegating to the national council men carefully chosen to discuss and settle major questions in the interest of the security of the entire empire.

Above the whole, the Tsar, a kind of pontiff of humanity, took charge of carrying out the decisions, appointing the men to whom executive power had evolved, respectful to all, a veritable father of a still-youthful people, simultaneously a sovereign and a philosopher.

We cannot go into detail about the innumerable reforms with which the sovereign's initiative had endowed his people. Europe, astonished at first, habituated as it was to the immutability of Tsarism, had been enthused by the young emperor who was the first to provide an example of disinterest for the love of justice. It was like a continuation of the great French Revolution, completing the regeneration of Europe, and that thought was further affirmed when universal suffrage, functioning from the Urals to the shores of the Baltic, had been seen to give Louis-Alexandroff something akin to a new and solemn investiture in conferring the title of Great Protector upon him. From that day on, the union between France and Russia had been better than a political treaty; it had been, so to speak, a pact of fraternity, and with all its voices, France had saluted Russia with the name of Big Sister.

Such was the man who, at the moment when we resume our story, was in his tent, studying a map of the Oriental countries.

He was tall in stature, a trifle stooped, as if the weight of his thoughts had curved him into a meditative attitude. He had the vigorous features of the Romanoff family with, in addition, something luminous, vivid, and human that gave a strange and superb gleam to his Russian eyes.

"Ivanoff," he said, to the man who was standing next to him, whose father had once perished on the scaffold of the nihilists, "you've heard Monsieur de Norès; it's your turn to speak."

Indeed, the third person was Guy, the Frenchman, who was looking at the Tsar with an inspired gaze, with his hand on his chin.

Ivanoff placed his finger on the map. "Let's sum up," he said. "It's agreed that Monsieur de Norès knows exactly what our situation is, what we can do and what we hope to do. We're men speaking as one man; there must be no misunderstandings or reticence between us."

The Tsar nodded in assent. "Speak in all frankness."

"So," Ivanoff went on, "we've been surprised by the most frightful cataclysm that has ever fallen upon the civilized world. Suddenly, without any forewarning, by reason of an organization that has been going on for a long time, which we have not detected, the entire Orient has risen up; in a single day it has risen up against us, with colossal forces at its disposal—poorly balanced, it's true, but terrible by virtue of its mass, which might be sufficient in itself to crush us."

He moved his finger over the map. "Here," he said, indicating with broad gestures the reference points of his demonstration," from the polar circle to Ceylon, and entire world is rising against us; from the mountains of Verkhoyansk, the Stanovoy mountains and the Yablonovy mountains, hordes of Ostyaks and Kamchatkites have descended: Yakutsk and Kirensk burned, then Yeniseik; Tomsk sacked, Omsk taken, Berezov set ablaze. The whole of Manchuria is vomiting its hordes on Ourga. China, the colossal volcano, is vomiting its lava from Peking to Canton, from Hang-Tcheo to the Karakorum mountains, from the frontiers of Burma to Lake Baikal the yellow avalanche is rolling its floods of mud and blood. Is that all?

"Here, in the Sea of Japan, the European fleets have been burned by means of the most infamous of treasons. Oh, we were trusting, and we had taken aboard Chinese pilots and sailors. They made us pay dearly for our stupidity. But then, is there not a heroic folly in this fanaticism? These men, these brutes, in order to obey the orders of secret societies, burned themselves along with our ships. From Formosa to Sakhalin a sheet of fire has extended, closing the way to European vessels. From Japan to Luzon Island, dynamite has blown up the seabed, displaced the reefs, and caused unknown banks to emerge, reducing all our geographical science to redundancy. Borneo and Sumatra close the circle.

"We're proud of our science! What are we, though, compared to these malignant wills, which, by destruction, summoning all the most redoubtable forces of nature, not to mention the lives sacrificed, the cities destroyed, the continents dislocated, the islands sunk, have been able, in a single day, at the same hour, to declare a war to the death against the old world Europe, terrified of its own impotence. Let's not mince words: we're afraid!"

Ivanoff stopped, breathless. That sinister invocation had made him pale, although he was not a coward.

Immobile, the Tsar, his hand on his forehead, was staring into space at some vision of blood and death.

Only Guy de Norès seemed to have conserved all of his composure. There was only a slight flush in his cheeks. "Go on, Ivanoff," he said, simply.

The latter ran his hands through his hair, and then passed them over his face, as if to recall himself to reality.

"We're afraid," he said, in a dull voice, "because we doubt ourselves, our strength, and even our energy. On what can we count? In a few days, with the admirable organization of mobilization that we've borrowed from France, we've dispatched three hundred thousand men to the Oriental invasion. Where are they? Swept away, vanished. And yet, haven't we had nature for an accomplice? Have you forgotten the Gobi cataclysm?"

The event to which Ivanoff was alluding was one of the strangest and most terrible of which humanity ought to conserve the memory.

It was the day after the battle that we have witnessed in the streets of Peking.

As Ivanoff had said, the conspiracy of which Sithreva had been the organizer, and which had been preparing for years in the shadows the decisive explosion of which Europe was to be the victim, had burst forth at a single moment from north to south and east to west.

Revealed at that time, in all its terrible grandeur, was the organization of Chinese secret societies about which we said a few words at the beginning of this story, and to which me must return momentarily.

Let us recall certain facts that had been forgotten for a long time in the era in which the facts we are recounting occurred.

In 1876, terror reigned in Hang-Chow, from Nanking to Shanghai; an implacable and mysterious fatality seemed to be weighing over the black tresses that are the most beautiful ornament of the Celestial Empire.[43] The mandarin, who had been asleep in an dream colored by the enchantments of opium, observed fearfully, on waking up, that the pigtail of which he was so proud had disappeared; the merchant at his counter, the passer-by on the public highway, and the artisan in his workshop suddenly perceived that they had just lost the most precious appendage of their toilette; no social condition escaped the scourge, and the crystal button of the literate was no more spared than the black skullcap of the street-porter. The invisible hand that exercised its ravages indiscriminately over

---

[43] The "pigtail panic" in Hang-Chow was reported in the *North China Herald* in May 1876. At the same time, legislators in California were attempting to pass laws compelling Chinese workers to cut off their pigtails as a means of trying to force them to leave.

the most humble and the noblest heads did not even respect wigs.

The authorities issued proclamations; solemn prayers were said in the pagodas; the good Spirits received fervent invocations from all directions and the evil Spirits saw themselves heaped with presents designed to deflect their wrath. All the manifestos of the public powers, the ceremonies celebrated in accordance with the rights prescribed by the decrees of Li-Pu,[44] and the supplications and the offerings were futile; the evil continued to make further progress every day. Sometimes the pigtails vanished as if they had been carried away into the air by a diabolical breath, and sometimes they fell gently of their own accord, as a ripe fruit drops from an overladen branch.

Finally, by chance, two men were caught *in flagrante delicto* at the moment when they were cutting the tress off a literate man who was engaged in a lively controversy with a group of passers-by outside the door of his house. They were armed with a pair of scissors so small that they could be hidden in the palm of the hand. The blades of those minuscule instruments were as sharp as razors. While accomplices were charged with deflecting the attention of the victim, the malefactors approached the pigtail quietly and, in accordance with the opportunity, sliced it off with a single sweep and contented themselves with an incomplete amputation that left intact an extremely thin wisp of hair destined to break in a short while under a weight it could not sustain.

The Chinese police oscillated between unbridled curiosity and extraordinary discretion. Let us add quickly that the mandarins charged with watching over the security of the Celestial Empire do not have a monopoly on abrupt changes of pace; there are delicate affairs in which the same vacillations are produced among their colleagues in the Occident. When the authorities in Shanghai and Nanking learned, from the confessions of malefactors fallen into their grasp, that they

---

[44] Presumably the 9th century Tang emperor of that name.

were in the presence of a secret society, they did not take their research any further, stopped dead as they were by the terror that was excited by the mere name of the White Lily.

What, then, was the White Lily? Originally, a religious sect, at least in appearance, but before anything else a society of hatred against progress and against the Occident. As means of propaganda it employed magic and stirred up fanaticism. Here are a few details that we found in a periodical, *Harper's Magazine*:[45]

In 1810, an insurrection directed by the leader of the redoubtable organization almost overturned the emperor Kin-King and the Manchu Tartar dynasty of the Tsings.

Fang-Yung-Tcheng, the grandmaster of the Order, when he was vanquished in a decisive battle, the imperial troops took such a large number of prisoners that, for perhaps the first time in history, highly-placed Chinese mandarins were seen having recourse to clemency.

The viceroy of Nanking, who knew the secret statutes of the White Lily, offered to spare the lives of all the rebels who would consent to eat meat. It was an ingenious means of putting to the proof the members of a sect whose rules ordered its faithful only to nourish themselves on vegetables. A fairly large number of captives did not resist the temptation, but they only escaped the rigors of the official government to be judged, condemned, and executed by the authorities of the occult society, whose vigilance could not allow an oath to be violated with impunity.

Persecuted unrelentingly by the decrees of the Son of Heaven, the White Lily changed its name; it is now known as No Hypocrisy, but it remains just as formidable.

---

[45] Frederick Boyle's article on "Chinese Secret Societies" appeared in the September 1891 issue of *Harper*'s, not long before this episode was penned. Lermina's decision to import its substance into his story, further breaking the back of Ivanoff's already-interrupted narrative, appears to have been made on a sudden whim.

Popular imagination attributes to the members of the society the power to work miracles. They only have to blow on a paper bird to give it life. Educated and enlightened, Chinese have gravely affirmed to an Englishman, Monsieur Balfour, that they had witnessed these marvels.

Those are the simple affiliates; the dignitaries of the congregation can do magic tricks that are even more fabulous. They are masters of holding their breath for hours, entire days if necessary. Their faces turn black, their limbs take on a cadaverous rigidity, and during that period of apparent death, the soul leaves the body and draws away to collect information that it is charged with bringing back. As soon as it has fulfilled its mission, its master recalls it and it resumes its customary place.

One day, it happened that, having neglected to bring back his soul at an opportune moment, one of the highest dignitaries of the Order did not wake up again. That accident, which was potentially capable of compromising the prestige of the sect, caused a suspicious emotion among the initiates. But what did an accident matter that was soon transformed into a miracle? For the people were convinced that the dead man had been resuscitated and that it was now his spirit that would remain eternally the head of the Conspiracy.

The Society took the name of Tien-Tai. The war of the Chinese pigtails recommenced with a new ardor.

The pigtail worn by the subjects of the Son of Heaven is the emblem of the subjection of the Chinese by the Tartars. To cut off with scissors that mark of servitude was to protest against foreign domination and to reveal the national sentiment deep in the heart of the true children of Han. In the same way that the Muscovite awaited with impatience the advent of the bearded Tsar who was to deliver him from the razors brought by German civilization, China would only become free again on the day when its sons ceased to braid their hair.

The Society took on an increasingly considerable development. The forms of initiation took on a progressively solemn and mysterious character.

According to an English author, when a neophyte wants to be admitted to the Tien-Tai—which is to say, "the Society of Heaven, Earth, and Human Being"—also known by the names of the Triad and the Universal League, he must go to the camp of the faithful and present himself at the Eastern Gate. It is there that the executor of noble works resides, whose naked blade is ever ready to fall upon the head of any profane individual audacious enough to introduce himself into the sacred enclosure without authorization.

The newcomer is clad in white; in principle, he ought to wear a new robe, but if he is too poor, the Society spares him that expense on the sole condition that he has his ordinary costume cleaned with the greatest care. His right shoulder and his knees are bare; instead of braiding his hair, he allows it to hang down freely over his nape, in order to demonstrate that he protests against Tartar domination.

Before crossing the threshold of the sacrosanct Gate, the neophyte pays his subscription, which is the equivalent of 17 francs 50. Once that indispensable formality has been accomplished, eight members of the League cause him to pass beneath an arch of overlapping blades. By a curious coincidence, one of the French paintings that has had the greatest recent success represents the aldermen of Paris crossing their swords over the head of Louis XVI to render him extraordinary honors on his arrival at the Hôtel de Ville.[46] Are the Occidentals, then, so proud of their civilization, merely plagiarists of the Chinese?

Let us return to our fanatic, who is advancing tremulously into the mysterious enclosure. Here he is arriving at the Pavilion of Red Flowers, where the faithful purify their souls in waters drawn from the river Sam-Ho, on the banks of which the "Five Ancestors" persecuted by the ingratitude of the Em-

---

[46] A painting by Jean-Paul Laurens depicting the reception of Louis XVI at the Hôtel de Ville in 1789 was exhibited in Paris in 1891. The alleged crossed swords are not obvious in the rather poor reproductions currently available online.

peror and the intrigues of his unworthy favorite Tan-Sing took refuge.

The neophyte then proceeds to the Circle of Heaven and Earth and traverses the bridge of two planks guarded by the Red Young Man armed with a spear destined to pierce any profane individuals who have escaped the vigilant eye of the guardian of the Eastern Gate. On the far side of that fearsome passage is the Market of Universal Peace, the Temple of Happiness, the City of Willows, and the Garden of Fishermen; this is the seat of the Grandmaster.

At the moment when the ceremony begins, the spectacle become even more imposing. The arch of swords is formed again over the neophyte's head. He kneels down, swears an oath of thirty-six articles and declares that all his relatives are dead. In the language of the initiates, that formula signifies that a member of the League no longer recognizes any earthly ties.

After having made that declaration, the fanatic prostrates himself at the foot of the Grandmaster's throne, and the eight swords that were interlaced above his head are placed on his bare shoulder.

He is presented with a cup of arrack; he mixes with that beverage a few drops of blood that he causes to run from his arm, on which a slight cut has just been inflicted; then he drinks it all in a single draught, and the Tien-Tai count one faithful follower more.

And that was the association that had sworn the fall of the Tsing dynasty, which had brought to the throne the descendant of the Mings, previously expelled by the revolution of 1644.

That descendant, who lived unknown to anyone, was designated by the mysterious name of Elder Brother. Government officials denied his existence, as they also mocked the secret society whose ramifications nevertheless enfolded them in stifling fashion.

One day, the Elder Brother had suddenly reappeared and had entered the palace of his ancestors under the name of Han-Ming.

On the same day, throughout the Oriental world, prophets had emerged among the Muslims, the fire-worshipers, and the Mazdaists. Everywhere, whatever the particular confessions were, all hatreds had been suddenly forgotten, to melt into a common, unique, and furious hatred against the Occidentals. And thus, on every part of the globe, at a signal whose point of departure no one could determine, but which had traveled to the four corners of the Asiatic world, innumerable masses of men had launched themselves forward.

The immense Chinese territory, from the Yellow Sea to Hindustan and Russia, had vomited forth millions of soldiers, and that multitude, whose force resided primarily in numbers, had spread like a monstrous flood through Mongolia and Tibet, incessantly augmented by new recruits who seemed to spring from the earth.

It was a frightful human avalanche, devoid of discipline, devoid of cohesion, but linked together by the fury of fanaticism, the worst of all follies. From all breasts the same cry of hatred rose up, so formidable that the echoes reverberated all the way to the extremities of Asia and caused Europe to shiver with an unexplained anguish.

It was not fear; the military engines at its disposal, the presumed cowardice of the adversaries, the consciousness of a strength that had multiplied tenfold in the last fifty years, all contributed to reassuring the most pessimistic.

And yet the Orient had conserved a mysterious, almost fantastic quality that troubled Occidental consciousness.

Meanwhile, at the first news of the massacres in China and the invasion that had followed it, Russia had not faltered in its duty. Was it not the advance sentinel of Europe? Was not its mission, ethnological in a way—the first—to halt the torrent that was threatening Europe with a formidable submersion?

For a long time, in any case, the Tsar had dreamed of exporting civilized ideas into those barbaric lands, and all his cares had been directed toward the means of transportation penetrating all the way to the extreme frontiers of his immense empire. The engineering works of the Transhimalaya were in the process of being carried out, and the principal tunnel of the Devalagiri was due to be pierced within two years.

The mobilization of Russian troops had thus been relatively easy, and a hundred thousand men had been hurled at the Asiatic hordes.

Never had the comparison of a bar of lead melting in a furnace been more apt.

In a matter of days, those hundred thousand men had disappeared, as if swallowed up, devoured by the tide that continued to surge and did not stop.

A cry of pain had emerged from all throats, and for the first time, people in Europe had become conscious that something frightful and inevitable was happening, like an earthquake, or a flood destroying all dykes.

When the news arrived in St. Petersburg, the Tsar did not want to believe in such a disaster, but doubt quickly became impossible. The catastrophe was complete and irremediable.

At the same time, other news no less terrible reached Europe.

The French and the English had combined forces in an operation to go by sea to attack Peking itself and avenge the massacre of the Europeans. All the ships stationed in the seas of China and Japan had received orders to rally and attack the coast of Petchili. But there a further disaster awaited the Europeans.

What had happened? The reality of the event was scarcely believable, but as soon as our ships had approached the Chinese coast, the sea had caught fire around them, and they had been devoured by the conflagration.

The Chinese had found a means of setting fire to the sea. What means? There was mention of blocks of potassium anhydride that had been precipitated into the waves. The force of

234

projection due to the immediate dehydration had been such that the particles of potassium had been distributed over several leagues, transforming the sea into an immense furnace. Water on fire! Is there any dream more terrifying and more sinister?

At any rate, France and England had lost their most formidable ironclads in a matter of hours. The submarine boats had not reappeared. It was a veritable maritime cataclysm.

France, with her usual energy, had told Russia that she would join forces with her.

But then an incident had occurred that had compromised the situation further. At the news of the disaster of Petchili, Germany, in response to the voices of a few agitators who formed a previously-incoherent party around Adalbert von Bismarck, the grandson of the famous Iron Chancellor, had broken the federal ties uniting the various parts of Germany and had given its support once again to one of the Hohenzollerns; it was a brutal *coup d'état* that threatened to change the entire face of Europe. It was Prussia crushing Germany once again under its iron heel, and the first act of the new government, directly inspired by the emperors of old, had been a proclamation repeating the ancient pretentions of Germany over Alsace, Lorraine and the Vosges.

It was not yet a declaration of war on France, but it was evident that the ambitious Wilhelm could only enjoy the fruits of his usurpation by flattering the basest instincts of his people, and France thus found herself under imminent threat.

The French parliament had, in consequence, put a stop to the immense effort that it was preparing to direct toward Asia. It was necessary to ward off the more immediate danger and to be ready to respond to the insolent provocations being launched on a daily basis by the reptiles of Berlin.

Russia had been the first to engage France to leave all the weight of the Asiatic war to her. The colossal forces of the Muscovite empire ought to be sufficient for the task. Perhaps the danger from that direction might even be warded off in time for Russia to aid France, if necessary, in chastising the Teutonic insolence.

The invasion, however, was making further progress every day. It was like a puddle of oil growing ever larger.

The Oriental hordes, which the Hindus, Buddhists and Mohammedans were beginning to join, having massacred the English in Delhi, Calcutta and other great centers, and now moving toward Afghanistan to join up with Chinese forces still held up by the Gobi desert.

In spite of the explorations of new voyagers, that part of Asia was still little known; it was still almost deserted. From Yarkand and Khatan to the frontiers of Manchuria, at the intersection of the three great mountain chains of the Altai, the Kuen-Lun and the Himalaya, the Gobi desert—which some people believe to have been the site of the ancient Atlantis destroyed in prehistoric times—occupies a vast plateau made firm by the first two of those chains. Over an area of fifteen hundred thousand square kilometers, it extends from northeast to southwest over a distance of two thousand kilometers. The Tian-Shan or Celestial Mountains divided it into two parts. It is an immense plateau of moving sand, which the winds agitate into gigantic undulations.

Crossing the Wall of China at all points, the Tartars and the Mongols had gradually filled that immense area, and the crowds were compressed at the foot of the snowy mountains, akin to the advance citadels of Europe.

The Elder Brother had just arrived and had deployed before the hordes the standard of the Five Hundred Gods, causing a monstrous chorus of hatred and fury to rise up, avid for blood and plunder.

A kind of proclamation had been hurled in the face of Europe, which was a monument of savagery: "No quarter! Death, nothing but death!"

But then, suddenly, beneath the feet of that multitude, the earth had trembled. It was the entire desert that had risen up, under the effect of subterranean fires that had been believed to be extinct for hundreds of centuries; abysms had opened, launching jets of sulfur and bitumen.

Thousands upon thousands of men had perished in that convulsion of nature, which had only lasted a few seconds.

For a moment, Europe thought that it had been saved. A vain hope! From the depths of inexhaustible China, other hordes had emerged, replacing the dead, filling in the gaps, and after a sort of oscillation in the mass, which seemed to form only a single body, the forward march had recommenced.

That was the catastrophe Ivanoff recalled in the conference in which he was discussing the matter with the emperor Louis-Alexandroff Romanoff and Guy de Norès.

Ivanoff continued:

"It would be criminal to entertain illusions. This very day we've learned that masses of men coming from the depths of Asia Minor are heading for Constantinople. Will Hungary be forced, as in the days of the Hunyadis, to repel the Asiatics? Where is Sobieski? It's up to us to strike a great blow. Can we do it? Today we have at our disposal fifteen hundred thousand well-armed men, who are defending the route to St. Petersburg. But how do we know that, while we are fighting desperately here, the wave will not outflank us?

"All the peoples of Europe are and ought to sense that they are as one against the terrible peril that is menacing them, and yet, look: indolent Austria hardly seems to be stirring; Germany is taking advantage of the turbulence to think egotistically about her particular ambitions, claims condemned twenty times over...and her ill will is paralyzing France. Can Italy come to our aid? Enclosed in her peninsula, she thinks herself unassailable—as if the barbarians of old had not found a way to reach Rome, which is her heart! Fearful England is only thinking about Hindustan, which she is losing, and is directing her energies solely in that direction...and she is still under the influence of the terror caused by the burning of her ships. The picture is grim. I ask you: am I exaggerating?"

"Not at all," said the Tsar. "All that is true."

237

"So," said Ivanoff, "it's a fight to the death, and Russia will not fail in her mission. Now the human avalanche is heading toward St. Petersburg; our advance troops have been driven back, and if we had not ordered them to retreat, for the sake of prudence, a hundred thousand men would already have been drowned by that monstrous wave. The decisive hour has sounded. Five hundred thousand Russians are gathered under your orders, and tomorrow, or this evening, the battle will begin. We shall say: *For civilization and for the Tsar...*but what does the future have in store for us?"

"Ivanoff," said the Tsar, severely, "I no longer recognize you. Are you really the man that I've seen confronting the most terrible perils without failing? Don't shake your head like that. I've told you: like you, I can take account of the immensity of the task that's incumbent upon us, but I shall be able to rise to the height of my mission. We have to combat numbers in proportions never seen before, even in the most terrible wars of which history makes mention. But you're forgetting what we call Force: no longer the brutal, irrational force that operates at hazard, but scientific, calculated force. Thanks to our dirigible aerostats, thanks to our machine-cannon that can launch five hundred melinite shells over a perimeter of five hundred square meters, thanks to the electric detonators that numb and topple, we shall reckon with this fanatical turbulence. Isn't that your opinion, Monsieur de Norès?"

The young Frenchman raised his head.

"It's necessary to submit to the inevitable," he said, in a grave voice. "You've done me the honor of asking the French government for my collaboration. Without having any more illusions about my own value than are appropriate, I nevertheless observed to Your Majesty that my place was, above all, in France, which, as you know, is threatened by grave perils. Even so, I have come, not only to render myself respectfully to the formal request, but also because it was necessary for me to obtain an exact account of the means of combating these wretches.

"Just now, Your Majesty enumerated the frightful engines of which modern warfare comprises. Let us not forget that they have been invented for struggles between civilized peoples, and that until now, that progress in the art of killing has been the principal factor maintaining peace. It requires all the mad arrogance of a Hohenzollern to think of setting two European nations at odds, when it is certain that the deaths will be counted in the hundreds of thousands! But still, it is a matter of men whose character and temperament we know; in certain conditions we can count on panic, and also on discouragement, on desperation in confrontation with the frightful hecatomb...I will even say that a Head of State, unless he is a monster, could not go to a battlefield, even after a victory, without shivering to the profoundest marrow of his bones.

"Here, though, we are dealing with individuals whose veritable character, whose consciousness is virtually unknown to us. We know that in China, in India, and in Africa, fanatics, in a sort of cerebral intoxication, endure tortures before which Europeans who are no less courageous would recoil..."

Ivanoff interrupted: "I've seen Hindu fakirs smile and sing while the bones of their feet were disarticulated one by one..."

"For those men, pain is just a word, death is not a terror. Their leaders, in appealing to their most profound hatreds, have made them all into as many fakirs, ready to endure anything. What effect will be produced in the ranks of those madmen by melinite, the most powerful explosives, or even the long electric sparks that resemble lightning? In ancient times, to be sure, the priests of Delphi defended their temple in that fashion against an attack by barbarians who fled in terror, but will it be the same today? I'd like to hope so, but allow me to doubt it. To sum up briefly, I don't believe that fear has any effect on these men; I only believe in real, effective, positive, destruction."

"We'll destroy them!" cried the Tsar.

"How many are they?" asked Norès. "Ten thousand, a hundred thousand or two hundred thousand men can be killed,

239

but can you kill a million, two million or three million? For it is in those numbers that it is necessary to count these Asiatics, accumulated over the centuries in excessively narrow limits. It's necessary to take account of the formidable pressure that is driving them forward. In brief, I can say nothing, offer no opinion, before having seen them. There is a psychology of war. That is what provides the elements of resistance and victory."

"But when you've seen?" said Ivanoff.

"Either I will be much mistaken," said de Norès, "or—I say this without false modesty—I'll be able to discover the monster's weak spot…and then, Your Majesty, I, who believed that I would never work other than in the cause of peace, swear to you that for the great cause of civilization, of European life, I will force the sphinx of Science to yield its secret to me."

"And I'm convinced of that too," said the Tsar. "How are you going to observe the battle?"

"In the dirigible balloon, undoubtedly," said Ivanoff.

Norès made an angry gesture. "Oh, why did I have to see the apparatus that would have rendered me master of the air disappear! When I think that that discovery, in which I invested all the hope and all the joy of my life, cost the lives of my sister and my best friend!"

The Tsar knew the details of that painful adventure. "Who can tell?" he said. "Perhaps your sister isn't dead."

"All appearances…I hadn't taught her the use of the controls…"

At that moment the door of the tent was lifted up and an office appeared on the threshold. As he remained immobile without saying a single word, Louis-Alexandroff understood that he wanted to talk to him alone. Without affectation he got up and went out of the tent.

A few minutes went by, during which Norès and Ivanoff exchanged their anxieties. In spite of their valor, they shivered as they thought about the next day's battle.

The Tsar came back in. "Monsieur de Norès," he said, "do you believe in miracles?"

"Outside of pure mathematics, as Arago said, the word impossible does not exist."

Norès had replied with a smile, but at that moment the sovereign lifted the flap of the tent and Norès saw his sister advancing toward him, holding out her hands.

The young man uttered a great cry, and became so pale that he seemed veritably to be on the point of fainting—but already, his sister had thrown her arms around him, saying "Brother, Brother, it's me, it's really me! Oh, how happy I am!"

"And not to displease you, there are two of us!" exclaimed a joyful voice.

And Sabirat came in, his face radiant.

"Alive!" repeated Norès. "What, it's not an illusion?" To the Tsar he said: "Oh, Sire, forgive me this emotion."

"But am I not a man, like you? I can certainly understand, and I tell you that this joy is a good omen."

Norès covered his sister with kisses; he had been so desperate that it had required an almost superhuman effort for him not to renounce the world forever.

Suddenly, the passion of the scientist regained the upper hand. "But what about the airship!" he cried.

"Wounded, but saved," said the young woman.

"What! You mean that it's in my apparatus...?"

"That we arrived here? Certainly—and I can affirm that the airship is a first-rate vehicle."

Norès looked at her in amazement. He seemed unable to understand what he was hearing. "But the controls...," he stammered.

"Do you think that I'd worked by your side for so long without assimilating a few of your ideas. I didn't know very much, it's true, but with the aid of...of Monsieur Sabirat, we got out of trouble well enough."

"And the apparatus is nearby?"

"Half a verst away," said an officer. "It fell with such force that it hollowed out a hole in the ground, where it's embedded like a ship that has run aground..."

He did not finish. Norès had already run outside, making rapid apologies to the Tsar—who, in any case, followed him immediately, propelled by curiosity.

"Oh, these wretched scientists," said Marie, dragging Sabirat away. "He cares less about us than his perfumery box."

That fashion of describing the airship was a trifle irreverent, but Norès paid no attention to it; he ran with the Tsar to the indicated spot, and set about examining the aerial vessel attentively, the entire lower section of which was embedded in the ground.

At the same time, he gave the Russian sovereign summary explanations.

"The damage isn't great," Norès said. "If Your Majesty would be kind enough to supply a jack, the ship can be refloated within the hour."

The sovereign hastened to give the orders, and while Norès directed the operation, he asked his sister and Sabirat to tell him all about their strange voyage.

What interested him most of all was the fashion in which the aerial vehicle had behaved under the action of the various controls, and whether it had not extended its atoms of perfume. All the information they gave him was concordant with his hopes.

"Who can tell?" he murmured. "Perhaps it's the involuntary experiment from which salvation will come."

Meanwhile, under the action of a powerful electric locomotive, the airship was gradually lifted up.

"Gently!" cried Norès.

This was the decisive moment for him. Would the apparatus have resisted the impact of the fall? Would it be possible to repair it and take to the air again, as one says of a ship that is seaworthy?

Slowly, the airship emerged from the hole in which it was buried, and the breathless Norès observed, joyfully, that it had maintained its shape: there were the lateral propellers, whose open gyrations had hollowed out a kind of mold without their steel blades having been broken or twisted; there was the door in place, and the floor...

But Norès uttered a cry of chagrin; he had just discovered the wound inflicted in the airship's flank by a shell fragment. That was the real peril.

It required even more precautions to complete the work. Norès supervised the action of the lifting-tackle himself. He was leaning down to the ground, waiting for the final propeller, which served as a kind of pivot, to emerge from the ground. It was gradually rising up when Norès cried: "What's that? There's a shapeless package caught up in the blades!"

As the machine was now a few feet above ground, they could see something hanging down limply, with rods of some sort flailing the air, and from it, a voice emerged crying: "Allah! Allah!"

"The Hadji!" exclaimed Sabirat. "How has that one survived?"

It was indeed the servant of Mohammed, who had as many lives as a cat—for, when they hastened to detach him from the propeller and lay him down, they observed that he was in full possession of his vital force—certainly not undamaged, but breathing and talking.

His body had been flattened beneath the enormous weight of the airship, stretched, so to speak, to the point of presenting a minimal thickness, and the slight gap that hazard had hollowed out between the propeller and the bottom of the ditch had sufficed for him not to be crushed.

He was so much alive, in fact, that, on perceiving the Russian uniforms with his wide open eyes, he was gripped by a further fit of terror, and howled: "Don't kill me! I'll tell you everything!"

Then, as if he had only expected to be returned to life in order to lose the notion of it, he shivered, threw his arms into the air and fainted.

"Who's this clown?" asked the Tsar.

Sabirat explained briefly.

"What did he mean by his promise to confess?"

"I'd like to clarify that," said Norès. "With your permission, I'll have this individual taken to my tent, and when he's recovered his senses, I'll see what profit can be obtained from his good will."

"As you wish," said the Tsar. "Now, Monsieur de Norès, would you care to explain the purpose of this strange machine to me?"

Now that the apparatus was above ground, Norès examined it anxiously. The damage it had suffered inspired serious anxieties. The entrance door had been badly twisted, and it was with infinite precaution that he succeeded in climbing into the airship. He emerged again after a few moments.

"Fortunately," he said, "the important components haven't been destroyed. I can fix the apparatus in a matter of hours. The shrapnel hasn't reached any of the vital organs. If the Messieurs of the artillery will grant me a corner of their workshop, I'll repair the damage as fast as I can."

That was done. Thanks to the benevolence of the Tsar, Marie de Norès was escorted to the care of a lady of the court who had accompanied her husband, a senior officer, while Sabirat was welcomed by the army surgeons with the extreme sympathy that was never lacking for the French.

The Tsar resumed walking back to the camp, accompanied by Ivanoff, whose pessimism was increasing by the hour.

The approach of the enemy army had been signaled, if it really could be called an army. Scouts were arriving one after another, announcing the appearances of new hordes at every point of the perimeter whose center was occupied by the Russian army.

An hour went by; the Tsar held a final Council of War.

"Messieurs," he said to his generals, "remember that to-day, it is no longer only for Russia and the Tsar that you are going to fight, but for the cause of civilization in its entirety. We have the responsibility for the great cause of old Europe, which is under threat. No weakness, and forward!"

His vibrant speech armed all hearts; the generals brandished their sabers, enthusiastically proffering the oath to vanquish or die.

The officers of the general staff launched themselves in all directions at the gallop, bearing decisive orders; then, at a signal, the frightful rumble of the first detonations of the artillery was heard. It was like a release of thunder, and on hearing that explosion, which caused the ground to shake, the Tsar said to Ivanoff: "Friend, if I die in this battle, at least I know that I didn't provoke it."

At the same moment, Norès' airship rose into the air, and, alone in his flying machine, of which he had become the master again, he set forth, as he had told the Russian sovereign that he would, to seek a key to the enigma that would permit him to combat the Chinese invasion.

V

This is what the French scientist saw.

The horrible hecatomb that bears in history the name of the Gunstloff catastrophe—the name of a small village, previously ignored, that was the center of the action—cannot be compared to any of the battles recorded in the annals of humankind.

From the height of his aerial observatory, Norès saw the Russian army extended over twenty leagues, magnificent in its attitude: the infantry massed in groups and conserving all its liberty of movement, with captive balloons above indicating the enemy maneuvers; then the cavalry, superb and marvelously mounted, from the Cossacks with horses as rapid as the wind, to the Poles, now the faithful allies of their former persecutors, proud of having become a nation again and burning with desire to show themselves worthy of their recovered fatherland, whose Lithuanian horses could sustain the fatigue of an uninterrupted march for fifty hours.

Then there were the northern contingents, from Archangel, Olonets and Vologda, and from Greater Russia, from Novogorod, Smolensk, Moscow, Nijni-Novogorod, Tula and Kursk...

The Baltic had sent its most glorious children, from St. Petersburg, Reval, Riga and Mittau.

The Finlanders were gathered in large numbers, sons of the Finno-Ugric races who were the first inhabitants of Europe, and to whom ethnic science will perhaps restore the title of ancestors of the present human race: the Estonians, the Livonians, the Lapps, the Zyrians, the Vogults, the Permiaks, the Tchermisses, the Samoyeds, the Teptiares: all those strange tribes which hate Oriental brutality and had come in response to the sovereign's voice.

Among the Tartars there had been many defections; all those that Mohammedanism had touched had sided against

Europe; only the Bukhirs and the Yakuts had remained faithful. By contrast, the Caucasian nations—the Armenians, the Georgians, the Lesghians—who had the terrible memory of Asiatic domination, had risen up to halt the flood of their ancient torturers. The Teutonics and the Scandinavians had formed well-equipped corps.

Of Siberia, nothing remained. In the first disaster, the Buryats and Kalmuks had been decimated.

Norès calculated mentally that the Russian army amounted to almost half a million men. What particularly attracted his attention as an engineer and scientist was the formidable artillery, comprising nearly two thousand fiery mouths, with all the improvements of modern artistry, from electric machine-guns to colossal mortars launching asphyxiating shells: all progress in the art of killing was accumulated in that relatively narrow space in which the forces of the two worlds were about to collide. The range of the weapons was such that, with the exception of a few groups of scouts who were distributed at intervals, the adversaries could not suspect their presence.

The balloons, in these circumstances, were doing marvelous service; by means of appropriate and clear signals, they were indicating to the Russian artillery the direction in which to aim the guns, and rectifying the force in accordance with the movements of the enemy.

And, indeed, at the commencement of the action, Norès saw two Asiatic corps, which had launched forward impetuously, annihilated without even having arrived within the range of their own weapons.

In truth, the young Frenchman felt full of hope. He was certain that the Oriental armaments were not comparable to those of the Europeans; of all the tribes that had emerged from the heart of the Iberian steppes or the depths of Mongolia and China, the greater part were only armed with obsolete rifles or even bows and arrows.

To equip that multitude, all the arsenals had been pillaged, but, in those backward countries, they are more like museums in which specimens of outmoded engines are conserved. Cannons could still be seen there whose models went back to the French Second Empire, and Norès observed that their servants lacked appropriate ammunition, and were loading those rifled guns in the same fashion as the bombards of the seventeenth century.

In those conditions, it seemed that the inferiority of the Orientals was such that the European victory could not be in doubt for a moment.

But Norès suddenly understood this:

With a depth so distant that, even from his aerial observatory, he could not perceive its limits, the young scientist saw a black stain, swarming and compact, like an uninterrupted mass, like a single animal with millions of limbs, feet, and tentacles, moving incessantly forward without pausing for a second.

The Russians, encouraged by the signals coming from the balloons, had hastened their aggressive movement, for they had noticed that no enemy projectile had yet fallen on the European ranks, while their own artillery was continually hollowing out gaps in the profound Oriental legions.

But what Norès now observed, with a momentary shiver that was like an involuntary sensation of terror, was something of which only an analogy can give a clear idea.

The dykes have broken; an enormous flood has rushed through and spread out, an immense sheet; then, suddenly, it finds a new slope that directs it toward the plains, toward the villages, toward human habitations. The slope is gentle, the river flows slowly, slowly, but under that mute and incessant flow it seems that everything disappears, everything dissolves. The edifice whose roofs rose up proudly a little while before suddenly seems to disintegrate and collapse.

Before that black advance, which nothing can stop, villages are alive; the flood passes, and they are dead, everything effaced, no longer anything but a memory.

Let humans, in a fit of desperate folly, with the aid of colossal engines, launch entire rocks against that liquid mass; let them precipitate monoliths the size of mountains in order to create an obstacle: the thing arrives, makes a hole, and then the sheet closes up again, and without any change, without the surface even being rippled, the water marches on and on.

Thus was the Asian torrent.

It was a sea in a perpetual rising tide, which never ebbed, a monstrous swell always moving always flowing.

The enormous shells, the masses of iron, the electrical discharges that hurtled into the midst of that human ocean smashed, twisted and tore; a hole was created—and then the flood continued its flow; the wound seemed to scar over instantly, and further on, always further on, without haste, with the heavy monotony of destiny, the horde advanced.

Norès saw that, and understood, perhaps for the first time, the horrible and terrifying force of numbers.

Those men, those brutes, were not doing battle, not furiously charging their enemies, ignorant and careless of danger—and what did a few scarcely-divined hecatombs matter to such masses?—they were flowing forward incessantly, without hesitation, a formidable inundation, an unstoppable creep.

And the moment came when those waves, whose limit could not be seen, which extended to all the depths of the horizon, a swarm such as the imagination did not dare conceive, reached the European corps.

There was an unprecedented spectacle of heroism and despair.

Infantry, cavalry and artillery were all unleashed against that living, moving wall.

Was there any hope? Of what? One, two, twenty gaps are pierced, but when the onslaught is continuous; when, behind every man killed, one finds a hundred more, a thousand more; when, to the right and the left, in front and behind, innumerable enemies are still standing...what charge or flanking movement can be attempted?

One recalls Victor Hugo describing, in his magical style, the furnace in which the regiments of Waterloo "melted like wax in the breath of a forge..."

This was worse; it was the sinister and relentless engulfment of thousands upon thousands of men, horses, and canons.

A magnificent regiment of white cuirassiers charged recklessly, musicians in the lead playing the Russia national anthem at full blast. Norès saw them reach the hideous host, penetrate into it like a red-hot iron...and then the music was extinguished, and the silver plumes disappeared, and the sparkling breastplates...and nothing at all remained: nothing but the Asiatic multitude passing over the cadavers of men and horses, without its march being halted for a second.

For four hours—four hours of unspeakable agony—the Russian regiments hastened themselves with stoic valor into that ever-growing tide, which swallowed them up.

The Tsar, mad with despair, had wanted to throw himself out of the aerostat that was carrying him, in order that he too might drown in that whirlpool that possessed the darkness of the abyss. His officers had great difficulty holding him back, and it had required the friendly voice of Ivanoff to bring the sovereign out of that paroxysm of madness.

"Louis-Alexandroff Romanoff," he had cried, "Russians are dying but Russia is alive! There's no more valor to deploy here. One can't contend with the impossible. It's necessary to give the signal to retreat."

"But that's dishonor! And besides, the torrent won't stop...it will continue advancing, and the engulfment will continue."

Suddenly, a voice shouted from the air: "Order the retreat, Sire, and I'll save the rest of your army!"

"Who's speaking?" shouted the Tsar.

"Me, Norès!"

And the airship drew alongside the captive balloon that was carrying the sovereign.

"You can do something?" cried Ivanoff. "But by what means?"

"Don't interrogate me—time's pressing. Let your troops fall back at once. I've seen your enemies; they're not pursuing them. They're walking, not running. It's vital that within half

250

an hour, there's a space of a kilometer between the two armies..."

"So be it," said the Tsar. "What else can be done, anyway, except trust your offer?"

A signal flare went up from the balloon. Until then, not a single Russian had recoiled, but the signal was repeated three times, visible to the entire army, and in the conventional language translated by the rockets, it was an imperative order for a precipitate retreat, as prompt as possible.

Obediently, with the precision of regiments maneuvering on the drill field, the Russian troops commenced the backward movement. There was no cowardice in the flight—and yet, how did panic not take possession of all those unfortunates, who had seen half their companions perish?

The withdrawal, since it had been ordered, was now enacted with immediate haste. Fortunately, everything had be so well calculated in advance by the military engineers that the way of retreat was free, and the directions of redeployment had been strictly designated in advance.

Of the two thousand artillery pieces that had been engaged, about five hundred still remained at the front, and they blasted the first ranks of the Orientals, who, as Norès had understood, were not launching themselves in pursuit of their vanquished enemies. Thy scarcely oscillated under that frightful machine gun fire; they continued advancing, with the same monotony of pressure, with the same fatalistic indifference that nothing could disturb.

Norès airship was still alongside the imperial balloon.

"Well," said Romanoff, whose voice was hoarse, by virtue of the humiliation that gripped his throat, "your orders have been carried out, Monsieur de Norès. In your turn, is there anything you can do?"

"Perhaps," said the young man, "if it pleases science." He added: "If I die, I commend my sister to you."

"You have my word."

At that moment the two armies had broken off all contact. The Russians were more than a kilometer away from the most advanced Asiatic lines.

"*Au revoir*," said Norès—and the aircraft headed for the ground.

It landed on a small bluff.

To understand what follows it is necessary to remember what happened previously in the young scientist's workshop, when Norès, before Sabirat's eyes, had displaced a ball of iron weighing approximately two quintals with a kind of vaporizer. You will also recall the theory provided by the engineer: it was a matter of the incredible force of expansion that is contained in perfumes, one atom of which is sufficient to fill a considerable space in a second. It was by submitting that expansive force to a formidable pressure that Norès had succeeded in constructing a motor of hitherto unknown power.

Now, one of the important properties of perfume is that its faculty of dissociation does not stop; so long as the odorant material exists, the molecules continue to spill from it with equal rapidity, in quantities so infinitesimal that one can only observe a depreciation in weight after a very long time.

Thus, as soon as the apparatus was closed and, in consequence, the external projection was no longer happening, the dissociation continued in the sealed generator and was subjected to a pressure of several thousand atmospheres.

That was what Norès had observed on retaking possession of the apparatus. The generator had exits into several storage tanks, and Marie and Sabirat had only made use of the provisions accumulated in one of them.

It was now almost a month since they had left Paris, and one can imagine the formidable quantity of molecules that had accumulated in the primary generator. Norès had doubted at first that the material of which it was constructed could resist such pressure, but experiments had reassured him, and just now he had had the joy of observing that the force of expansion at his disposal was equivalent to that of the most violent cyclone—which is to say, a wind-speed of about forty meters a second, producing a pressure of more than 160 kilograms per square meter.

According to his calculations, taking account of the quantities of radiant matter contained in the generator, that colossal effort could be sustained for several minutes.

It was then that the idea had occurred to him of attempting to save the Russian army from complete annihilation.

Now, the moment had come to act.

The airship, as we have said, was perched on a slight ridge, a black dot of such scant importance that the Asiatics had scarcely noticed it. Undoubtedly, they thought it was some abandoned artillery battery. They were still advancing, with the same movement of an unstoppable flood.

They were five hundred meters from Norès; it was the decisive moment. He, too, was not about to be engulfed by that sea to which no human force seemed able to say: "You shall go no further!"

Pale, with his eyes glued to one of the interior portholes and his hand on the handle of the great generator—a control that the aerial voyagers had fortunately not discovered, for a false maneuver would undoubtedly have cost them their lives—Norès directed a tapered tube at the line formed by the Asiatics, which he had fitted to the orifice, and which emerged from the apparatus through a kind of peephole disposed for that purpose.

The direction that he gave it relative to the line was an angle of about thirty degrees—which is to say that he was not aiming at them head-on, but obliquely.

"Let's go," said Norès, "and may the justice of our cause aid its success."

He pulled the handle.

A strident whistle-blast resounded, tearing through the air. That was the gas—we shall employ that word in order to be better understood, although the matter projected was infinitely more dilute than the most subtle known gas—escaping from the generator with extreme violence.

In ten seconds, it reached the Orientals, and Norès, whose tight chest was breathless, saw something surprising.

The mass of the assailants was now oscillating like a field of ripe wheat; the men were falling onto one another, forming an obstacle to those following behind, constraining them to turn back. The pressure was so strong that, as in a pool over which a violent wind passes, it formed a vertiginous gyratory eddy, and by virtue of a sort of mutual attraction it seemed that even those who were not touched by the wind were drawn into it. The first ranks, to a depth of more than a hundred men, were knocked down, broken, scythed like wisps of straw by a southwest wind...but the others, experiencing an unexpected, incomprehensible resistance, unconsciously changed direction.

Sir John Lubbock recounts[47] that, having once seen a field menaced by a column of ants composed of an infinite number of individuals, the passage of which had left nothing behind it but ruins, the idea had occurred to him of deflecting the direction of the head of the column by a mere two or three degrees. The entire horde of tiny creatures had followed, and the field was saved.

Under the pressure of the hurricane unleashed by Norès, the angle of the Asiatics' direction had changed by more than a quarter of a circle, and now the young scientist saw the black stain heading southwards, having lost the notion of a straight line—and heading southwards with the same implacable slowness.

He could scarcely believe his eyes. Once again, therefore, intelligence had triumphed over brute force—an ephemeral triumph, to be sure, for the leaders would doubtless return the column to its original direction; but it was an assured respite...and perhaps salvation.

The Asiatics disappeared over the horizon.

---

[47] In his pioneering study of social insects, *Ants, Bees and Wasps* (1884)

Suddenly, Norès heard a voice calling to him. He emerged precipitately. It was the Tsar, who seized him in his arms and hugged him delightedly.

"Monsieur de Norès, you're more worthy than I am to command peoples. Tell me, what would you like as a reward? Whatever your desire is, I give you my word that it will be granted..."

"I desire," Norès said "to return to France as soon as possible."

"To leave me!"

"In saving you," said Norès, gravely, "who can tell whether it might not be my own country on to which I've unlashed the danger?"

"At least," said the Tsar, "you'll do me the honor of dining at my table, as I've just been notified of the arrival of European prisoners of the Orientals, who, thanks to the disturbance you produced in the ranks of their torturers, have succeeded in escaping."

"Europeans!" said Norès, going pale. "Are there, then, some who escaped the massacre?"

"Come," said the Tsar—and they hastened toward the camp.

VI

It was in an old dacha a few versts from St. Petersburg that the staff officers who had escaped the massacre were waiting for their sovereign.

To those valiant fighting men who had braved death a hundred times in the most terrible circumstances, it seemed that they had emerged from a frightful nightmare. This was no longer war, alas; it was the folly of Xerxes wanting to fight against the sea.[48] They had seen their battalions disappear like sand in a crucible—and they remained, not frightened but exhausted, as if annihilated, with the sensation that that they had encountered something superior to any human force.

How had the torrent that was about to engulf them suddenly been turned aside? How had they been brought back to the rear safe and sound? How did they find themselves here, out of immediate and sinister danger? None of them could say. As they had obeyed the discipline that had launched them forward, so they had obeyed the signal to retreat...and that was all. They no longer had the strength to reason, or even to think.

Was that horrible catastrophe to be imputed to a crime? They did not know, but even if the most terrible punishment were to fall upon them, not one of them thought of seeking to avoid it. They felt guilty, since they were alive, and the fatherland had been defeated.

The emperor came in. All heads were bared.

---

[48] According to Herodotus, when the first attempt made by Xerxes the Great to invade Greece in the 5th century B.C. was thwarted, after his improvised bridges across the Hellespont were destroyed by a storm, Xerxes held the Hellespont responsible and sentenced it to three hundred lashes. Given that his second attempt to cross it was successful, it is not entirely obvious that the chastisement did not have the desired effect.

Louis-Alexandroff went to the first ranks, his hands extended, open. With a few words, he comforted the despairing men. No, he certainly had no reproach to address to anyone. On the contrary, he rendered them full and entire justice. They had done their duty, more than their duty, for not one had faltered, and if death had been refused to them, it was not because they had not offered themselves to it.

"But my lieutenants," he said, in a vibrant voice, "it is necessary before anything else that you know the name of the man who has saved us—yes, saved us from definitive and irremediable disaster. His name is Guy de Norès; he's a Frenchman, and once more, the pact of amity and gratitude that has so long affirmed their fraternity has been sealed between the two nations." He turned to the young Frenchman, and added: "Monsieur de Norès, the entirety of Russia thanks you via my voice. I shall offer you neither dignities nor decorations; the service you have rendered to us is not one of those that can be repaid—but I, the Tsar, offer you my hand loyally and I say to you: Your name is henceforth sacred among us."

Norès stepped back modestly, but in a few vibrant words, the Tsar recounted the extraordinary adventure, giving form to the massacre, and all the officers, for whom the new science still retained a whiff of magic, bowed to him with a kind of fearful respect.

"Sire," said Norès, "I'm profoundly touched by a gratitude that I would like to have deserved more completely. But at this moment, if you will permit me to make a request..."

"Say what you want and orders will be given."

"Well, mention was made just now of Europeans who have been brought here..."

"In truth, I forgot!" exclaimed the Tsar. "Where are they? Let them be brought here immediately."

Officers went out to carry out the sovereign's orders. A few minutes went by, during which the Tsar conversed with his generals.

Suddenly, the door opened, and an exclamation escaped all throats.

Over the threshold advanced a group of men and women so wretched and haggard in their appearance that everyone felt gripped by an inexpressible anguish.

Were these diminished, trembling unfortunates, barely clad in rags, tottering forward as if their limbs were unable to carry them really human beings?

Suddenly, a louder, more heart-rending clamor burst forth. Norès launched himself toward those who were in the first rank, astounded, unable to believe his eyes.

He had just recognized the French engineer Robert Sametel, his bloodied eyes closed, and in the woman he was clutching by the hand he had seen...who? Marguerite Sametel, his beloved, the fiancée of his heart.

And as he pronounced the same of Sametel with an accent of ineffable gravity, the blind man said: "Who's calling me?"

"Me! Me! Norès, your son!"

"Guy de Norès!" cried Marguerite, raising her head. "No, it's impossible!"

"It's me, it's really me...but please, for pity's sake, tell me that I'm dreaming, that I'm mad...Robert Sametel, my father..."

"I fell into the power of those demons," said the engineer. "Then, to avenge themselves, they burned my eyes."

"Infamy!"

"Oh, if you knew," Marguerite continued, "to what frightful tortures they've subjected us[49]...why we're not dead, in truth, is a miracle that I still can't explain. My father blind-

---

[49] Lermina must surely have intended when he began the serial to relate this part of the story in detail. Did the Sametels and the Nivets, after leaving the Yamen, manage to reach the *Suffren* before being captured? At what point, and how, were they separated from Albert de Mesnes? Did they encounter the German Ambassador, who was also taken prisoner? Who brought them with the Asiatic horde, why, and in what circumstances? We really should have been told.

ed, me thrown into a dungeon where I was up to my waist in fetid water for a week... Well, no! We're French, and we didn't want to die...then they dragged us in the wake of their hordes through the deserts of Mongolia. I felt almost glad, for they hadn't divined that for me, the worst torture would have been to be separated from my father...and there remained to us I don't know what mad hope of escaping."

"What she isn't telling you," Sametel interjected, "is with what energy, what admirable and unwavering patience, she maintained our courage...by her dignity, by I don't know what quasi-magical influence, she was able to impose a sort of respect on those brutes..."

"Let me finish, Father," said the young woman, squeezing his hand to cut short eulogies that were troubling her. When the collision with the Russian army occurred, we thought we were doomed. We knew from experience, alas, that all resistance was impossible, we had the impression of that heavy, crushing, indefatigable force against which no courage could prevail...and we had decided, rather than witness impassively the catastrophe in which the Europeans would succumb, to throw ourselves forward, into the heart of the battle, to perish there, even under the thrusts of our own forces: it seemed to us that death would be less miserable thus.

"How, after hours of anguish, at the moment when we abandoned ourselves to despair, were the Asiatic hordes suddenly struck and disorganized, as if by a miracle? From the point where we found ourselves, behind a compact mass that closed every exit to us, we couldn't see anything, we couldn't understand anything...suddenly, we heard something like the whistling of a hurricane. We saw rows of men knocked down, lifted from the ground, thrown round like wisps of straw by the north wind...and a path opened up before us. I took my father by the hand, and we ran straight ahead, without knowing where we were going. We stumbled through the midst of cadavers...finally, we recognized the Russian colors. We shouted for help...and we were saved."

"Sire," said Norès, turning to the Tsar, just now you asked me what reward I wanted for the service that I rendered your army. Let me tell you that I've been abundantly rewarded, for the man you see here, mutilated by those swine, is Sametel, the man to whom I owe the little I know…and this young woman is my fiancée…my wife!"

Sametel and his daughter were not the only Europeans to have escaped the massacre. Rose Nivet, the courageous gamine, and her father, the genial photographer, had not abandoned them for an instant—but Nivet had also suffered his martyrdom; they had cut off his beard.[50]

"But what became of Sacha Bernstorff?"[51] asked Norès, anxiously. "Was she not the fiancée of the miserable renegade Wintscheff, who has sworn the death of all those who welcomed him like a brother?"

"I can't inform you completely as to Sacha's fate," said Marguerite, "but I believe that she was saved, along with her brother, by Albert de Mesnes. I've been told that they found a means of embarking for Europe. If we ever see them again, they'll be in France."

"France," said Norès, "is now where we should be. Courage, Robert Sametel…the misfortune that has struck you is certainly horrible, but your genius will survive your martyrdom. Henceforth, I sense—I know—that it's against France that the effort of these horrible hordes will be directed. It's from the Alps to the Vosges and the Rhine that our fatherland must erect an uncrossable barrier to the invaders. All the living

---

[50] The Nivets were obviously intended to play a greater role in the story when they were introduced—and perhaps they have. Why would we have been told about Nivet's thunderous voice if it were not to play some significant part in the plot?

[51] Lermina has now forgotten Sacha's surname (Batowna) as well as her forename, but her story too should also have been recounted in detail, especially as we are subsequently told that she learned an important item of information in the course of her tribulations, although we never find out what it is.

force of our nation must stand up, to save civilization, to save the world!"

"And I shall help you do it!" cried the Tsar. "I'll answer for Wilhelm of Prussia. You won't be troubled in our heroic attempt. Count on me. Return to Paris, Guy de Norès, and tell those who are directing the destiny of your great Republic that a Romanoff has given you his hand as a sign of alliance, and that, even if it costs me my last soldier, no German will dare to attack you."

"I receive your promise, Sire. Once more the alliance will be sealed that will render us invincible. And now, there's not an hour to lose. To Paris..."

And the unfortunates who had thought themselves condemned to the most terrible of deaths a little while before, suddenly galvanized by that vibrant voice, repeated:

"To Paris! To Paris!"

EPILOGUE
THE WORLD SAVED

A month has passed since the sinister events that we have just recounted.

That short period had been rich in further disasters and catastrophes.

As Norès had anticipated, the Asiatic hordes, deflected from a straight line, had at first oscillated like a ship without a rudder. They had then spread like a sheet over White Russia to the shores of the Sea of Azof, swollen by all the torrents that were incessantly descending from Tartary and Turkestan and rising up from India and Persia.

The flood had enveloped the Black Sea, swallowing up Constantinople, and had been halted momentarily at the Danube by the valiant efforts of the Rumanians and Hungarians—but there again, numbers overwhelmed courage, and once the barrier had been crossed, Budapest and Vienna had disappeared under the frightful tide.

On their way, the Orientals were beginning to pause occasionally in centers where the pillage went on for a longer period. The brutes plunged into frightful orgies illuminated by the blaze of fires; they were hideous intoxications spiced with unspeakable ferocities.

The main body of the army, however, which had been estimated at some twelve hundred thousand men, was still pressing forward. Its supreme leader was known: it was Wintscheff, whose fury seemed to increase with every success. Before his name that of the legendary Attila paled; it was said that he marched preceded by the standard of the Five Hundred Gods, steeped in blood.

Revolting executions marked the stages of his march; everyone who attempted to resist was subjected to the most atrocious tortures; a Hungarian leader had been cut into quarters, which had been sent as a sign of menace to the great cities of Austria. The cruel theories that the Prussians had once put into action during the war against the French in 1870 were implemented once again by those barbarians from the depths of Asia. No one, including women, children, and old men, found any mercy in the hands of the monsters, whom terror preceded.

A woman, it was said, presided over these atrocities: Sithreva, the Hindu, the furious priestess of Death, drunk on blood and mad with hatred.

Suddenly, however, there was a pause in the ever-rising tide. The course of the Asiatics then turned northwards toward Dresden and Berlin. Berlin was invaded on the day the emperor had declared war on France. He fled, and came to seek asylum in France; ever generous, our fatherland welcomed him, but the terror he had suffered had disturbed his reason; he was mad.

At the center, the Orientals occupied Stuttgart and Munich. To the south, they extended from Innsbruck to Milan and Turin. It was a semicircle that was tightening around France and Switzerland; nothing any longer remained but the barrier of the Alps, the Jura, and the Vosges. Behind those immense bulwarks, France waited, breathlessly.

At present, she was the refuge of all the defeated of Europe, the shelter of all the desperate. To fugitives of all nations she had opened her doors wide; cities and villages had been improvised over the whole extent of the territory, and in hundreds of thousands, Russians, Germans, Hungarians, Austrians and Italians—even Italy contracted a new debt of gratitude toward us, which she would disclaim at a later date—camped in the rural regions, nourished by our peasants, cared for by our nurses.

In those days of peril, Paris presented a striking physiognomy. The great Council of Defense had summoned Guy de Norès to its presidency; day after day, the people were kept apprised of the situation, without any dissimulation. All the men who were able to bear arms had been called up and recruited to the active army and the reserves. The Territorial Army occupied the strongest positions.

The Parisians, calling a truce in their eternal agitations, provided an example of calm and discipline. On the boulevards, in the squares, there was not a single cry, not a single demonstration. The city was like an immense barracks of volunteers, in which no one was thinking of anything except doing his duty.

People grouped around posters put up by order of the government, serious and grave, communicating their apprehensions in low voices, with no fuss and no fear, ready to do anything for the salvation of the nation.

The style of the proclamations was sober, with none of those resounding phrases that can excite the imagination momentarily but which cannot give hearts any real confidence.

France is preparing, said the latest of these posters, *to repel the most terrible invasion that has ever fallen upon a civilized nation. All the living forces of the nation are ready for the resistance; the shock will be frightful, but the French must not lose confidence in the justice of their cause, which is that of the entire humanity. Three armies of three hundred thousand men are facing the assailants, but it is, above all, on the progress of Science that we must count. In this morning's session, Monsieur de Norès has communicated to the Council plans and projects that it would be premature to deliver to the public, but from now on, the Council affirms on its honor that victory is possible. Let the people remain calm, let the press continue its work of discretion and public encouragement. France will not abandon herself! Vive la France!*

A few imprudent individuals, moved by personal ambition, had attempted to provoke an unhealthy agitation in the name of an adventurous general once punished by his seniors for indiscipline. Attempts had been made to present him to the people as a savior whose panache would be sufficient to put the enemy to flight. He had run around the boulevards followed by a band of blowhards escaped from the capital's underworld, but a squadron of police had sufficed to dissipate the rabble; the general had been brought before a police court, where he had been sentenced to two months in prison for misappropriation of funds.[52]

People had confidence in Guy de Norès, who spent his days locked in his laboratory, not showing himself in public. It was said that the young Russian, Sacha Bernstorff, who had miraculously escaped the massacres and had been brought back to France by Albert de Mesnes, who himself was promoted to the command of an army corps in the Alps, had brought him precious information. As legend never loses its rights, much comment was made about the presence close to him of an old Muslim, who was only known by the name of the Hadji, and who, it seems, had furnished him with the most interesting revelations.

A catastrophe almost momentarily troubled the patient tranquility of the great city. Norès' electricity workshops were located on the Buttes-Chaumont, which had been closed to the public. One night, Paris was woken up by a formidable explosion; the ground shook throughout the perimeter of the fortifications.

People ran to the site of the disaster and observed that the summits of the Buttes had completed disappeared into an enormous excavation that had suddenly opened up at their base. However, no one had been killed. It was thought at first to have been an earthquake, and it was no mediocre anxiety to see nature aiding the invaders in their work of destruction, but within an hour, a note issuing from the war administration explained to Parisians that the explosion had not been entirely accidental. It had been an experiment carried out by Guy de Norès that had succeeded beyond his expectations, and above all, sooner than he had expected. It was connected with the plan for resistance and gave a near-certainty of success.

---

[52] This sly insertion satirically reflects the career of General Boulanger. Its inclusion is entirely gratuitous, and perhaps odd, given that the author is in such a tearing hurry to wind up his devastated plot. Perhaps he had a hidden agenda.

The same day, a meeting took place that excited the curiosity of Paris very keenly: the members of Swiss Federal Council had a long discussion with the French government. Although secrecy was strictly guarded, it was known that the discussion had been long and difficult. One singular phrase was widely quoted: one of the Swiss had cried: "We can't sacrifice a part of our territory!"

It seemed, however, that a definitive understanding had been produced, and the official note announced to the public that the meeting had taken place terminated with these mysterious words:

Europe cannot be too grateful to the noble Swiss Republic for the sacrifices that she has consented to make for the salvation of civilization.

The days passed. It was known that the Asiatic hordes, after being interrupted momentarily by the slopes of the Alps, as if astonished in the face of those colossi, had resumed their forward march. In fact, had they not already crossed the Himalaya, the Urals, and the Carpathians? That final obstacle could not halt them for long.

The Parisians were not at the end of their surprises.

It is well known that for the exposition of 19**, an engineer had conceived the veritably eccentric idea of constructing three more Eiffel Towers similar to the first, and then had linked together their summits—and on that platform he had built a further tower rising to a height of 450 meters, which constituted a formidable edifice of 750 meters in height. It was a whim of the constructor, whose utility was far from having been demonstrated, and the public, after having satisfied their curiosity by going up to the top of the tower, had gradually become disinterested in the spectacle, weary of its monotony.

The Espagnet Tower, as it was called, after its constructor—who, desolate at his lack of success, had killed himself by throwing himself off the top—had thus been relegated to the rank of a useless curiosity, of which no one, including foreigners and provincials, any longer took notice.

Then, all of a sudden, it was learned that Norès had had an optical apparatus of exceptional power installed on the topmost platform. In any other circumstances people would have smiled, assuming that the great engineer had the pretention of watching over the frontiers of France—but one day, a notice from the National Defense informed Parisians that they ought not to be alarmed if the sky took on an unusual appearance.

You can imagine how everyone's interest was stimulated. Was it a matter of a meteorological phenomenon, or some kind of bolide of frightening appearance? Some people talked about an eclipse, and the less brave recalled historical legends that attributed to celestial phenomena the announcement of terrestrial cataclysms.

On the night that followed the advice given by the government, all of Paris spread out into the streets, anxious and attentive.

When the darkness was at its deepest, a jet of light, of such great power that the entire city was suddenly illuminated, emerged from the summit of the Espagnet Tower. It resembled a colossal electric beam. Then, instantaneously, in the depths of the sky—and, it seemed, at a distance equal to that of the farthest stars—bizarre characters appeared: three symbols very clear and sharp, whose significance hardly anyone comprehended, stood out as if they had been traced by a brush of fire.

The news quickly spread, through that city in which everything is known, that the three characters belonged to the Sanskrit alphabet and that they formed the word AUM, a sacred formula of the Hindus, from which our occidental religions have borrowed the mysterious Amen.

What could that strange invention signify? The most singular thing was that the inscription remained immovable in the sky, as if it constituted a signal.

It can easily be imagined that imaginations were hard at work, compounded by the fact that, the morning after the curious incident, Norès quit Paris, accompanied by the Hadji. This time, the government abstained from any explanation, or any communication. One might have thought that a profound silence had suddenly fallen over the city; a sentiment of expectation and subconscious anguish gripped the population.

Something was about to happen. Was it salvation, or was it, on the contrary, the final catastrophe?

Two days later, posters with large print were plastered on the walls. They bore the following words:

Mont Blanc has blown up. Norès.

Flooding through Europe, gorging themselves on the spoils of the people, wading through rivers of blood, the Asiatic hordes had continued their fatal march, which no obstacle interrupted. Like a torrent whose dykes have been broken, the human tide was precipitated onwards, noisily.

If any sign of lassitude appeared, if the Oriental brutes, full of conquest, seemed to want to enjoy their victory for longer, the voice of Sithreva rose up, and, reawakening passions that were ready to fall asleep, rendered a new ardor to the exasperated bands.

Sithreva was personified in a terrible incarnation of the hatred of the Orient for the Occident. In her hands, Wintscheff was only an instrument. Maddened by his passion, forgetting everything else—his past and his honor—the wretch lived in a bloody nightmare. Cleverly, the Hindu maintained him in an unhealthy intoxication that no longer left him the free disposition of his faculties; he went before her, enveloped by an atmosphere of crimes, as if hypnotized, unconscious, and numbed.

Sometimes, however, in moments of calm, he had a vague notion of the infamous work that he was accomplishing. As he passed through cities once flourishing with civilization, superb with vitality and intelligence, now bleak and desolate, quivering like mutilated cadavers, a somber melancholy took possession of him; specters haunted his sleep and, like a new

Richard II,[53] he saw the phantoms of his victims surrounding him, harassing him, threatening him with their maledictions. He was afraid.

Between the furious excitations of battle and the fits of remorse, madness gradually crept in, setting its iron claw upon his enfevered brain. He had reactions of horror. But the pitiless Sithreva watched him; in moments of weakness she gripped him again.

Sometimes, however, he cried: "When will it stop?"

And, singularly enough, those words, which he pronounced incessantly, by some mysterious means, had an echo in the profound masses of those who were following him.

Stop! It seemed that the syllable suddenly became for them a kind of revelation, a latent and inexplicable desire.

Yes, they still marched even so, with the ineluctable will to crush, but the brute will in question was that of the mass. The leaders dreamed of something else. Like an ogre in a fairy tale, they had scented fresh flesh—which is to say, the joys of civilization: the music, the femininity, the perfumes, everything that forms the galvanoplastic envelope of our Occidental world. Everything was gold; everything was love. And among those brutes the appetite developed, and wanted to be slaked. The frightful pillages of treasures and women had given them a taste for them.

Now, the objective was France, was Paris: France, with its delicacies; Paris, with its exquisite elegance.

Realizing that, the monks, marabouts, hadjis and gurus— all the exploiters of that stupid humanity—were afraid. What if civilization, by virtue of a sort of osmosis, were to penetrate those wretches; if, in drinking of the Fountain of Youth that is France, they were suddenly regenerated; if revolutionary Paris, the perturber of consciousness and illuminator of reason were

---

[53] Lermina seems to be confusing Richard II, who is not confronted with any phantoms, though has a Shakespeare play titled for him, with Richard III, who is, and also does.

to take possession of those hallucinated minds, transforming and civilizing them?

It was necessary that they did not stay. The dream of the guides, the Brahmins, was to appease them to the point that, weary, having lain down drunk on vanquished civilization, they demanded to return home, to the ignorant and submissive world of the Orient.

The danger was real. One does not come into contact with our civilization with impunity. There are contagions of conscience. Already, revolt was stirring in the hordes; some individuals were talking about their rights; some, fatigued by being dogs launched forward, had remembered that they were human.

Then Sithreva, in concert with all the religious leaders, whatever name they adopted, had announced by proclamation that "the Orient must march forward, ever forward, until the sacred sign of Buddha, AUM, appears in the heavens."

Ben-Borouk, the Hadji, knew that—and that was the secret he had offered to surrender in order to save his life.

Now, one night, when the Orientals were hesitant to march forward, at the foot of the Alps, suddenly, in the sky, in the profoundest depths of the zones of the infinite, the fateful symbols had been designed!

A stupefying miracle!

Sithreva, Wintscheff, and all the liars and exploiters who had dragged the Asiatics along, who knew that the prediction was, in fact, a lie, were amazed. Aum, the sacred word of Krishna and Gautama, the alpha and omega of all knowledge, the key to ecstasy, the stairway of Devachan: that was what had appeared, really and materially, in the sky.

Lie! Magic! They did not believe it, since they had reserved for themselves the privilege of raising into the air some new banner bearing the sacred characters, remaining the masters able to halt the innumerable troop whenever they wished.

No, such a prodigy was not possible.

Can you imagine a conjurer who announces an unprece-dented trick and sees it take place before him, without his par-ticipation being required?

Sithreva and Wintscheff, and the priests of Buddha, Brahma, Siva, Fo, and Mohammed, threw themselves in front of the Asiatics crying: "It's a lie! A lie!"

But they reaped what they had sown. They had exploited ignorance by multiplying it a hundredfold. Ignorance and stu-pid superstition were stronger than they were. And toward that sign, ablaze in the heavens, all of them—the Chinese and the Hindus, the Tartars and the Samoyeds—raced forward. There, where the sign was displayed, was paradise. It was necessary to reach it, to place themselves directly beneath it, to salute it as the unique and holy banner. In the Five Hundred Gods there was no god; God was the sacred formula.

And crossing the Alps, without fear, paying no heed to abysses and precipices, the Asiatics launched themselves to-ward the location overhung by the Sign.

It was suspended in the ether directly above Mont Blanc, on the frontier of France.

There was no resistance. Switzerland, that intrepid nation which has the honor of the soil implanted in its conscience, which has the fatherland in its blood, let them pass, leaving the way open, the roads devoid of defenders.

Can you understand now what the members of the Fed-eral Council, representatives of the Helvetic Republic, had conceded to the French Republic? For the good of humanity and civilization, they had alienated their right to die as citizens and as patriots. They allowed those bandits to foul the scared lands, to dishonor the proud summits before which the con-querors had paused.

In the noble Swiss nation there was a terrible tremor, but a promise had been made; their word had been given, and it was kept.

The Asiatic passed without anyone being able to count them. They did not stop. What did the villages matter to them, the huts suspended on the mountainsides, the pastors' chalets, deserted and mute? They passed by, heading for a single goal, toward the mysterious AUM that still lit up the sky from dusk to dawn. There was the triumph; there was the eternal felicity promised by God, by Brahma, by Allah, to whom they were obedient.

And thus they arrived, some at Matigny, others at Morgex and Cormayeur.

There, miraculously, the fateful sign had suddenly stopped, as if fixed in the sky, an inscription retained by the golden nails that were the stars.

In the entire army there was a clamor, like a hymn of deliverance.

It was the goal, the triumph, the repose, and also the satiation of all the contained passions. God spoke, and he said: "Here it is!"

Sithreva and Wintscheff were astonished and irritated. It is the fate of ensnarers of men to collide with the unknown, the incomprehensible. They had allowed the legend of the sacred word to propagate through the crowd in order, on a day chosen by them, to bring an end to the surge and to signal the final victory. They thought themselves masters of the solution: by a kind of conjuring trick, they would impose their will on the credulous…eventually, when their hatred had been slaked.

Now, suddenly, the prodigy that they had invented in its entirety, of which they believed themselves to be the masters, had burst forth regardless, against their will.

In Wintscheff, who still had a savage naiveté, that surprise was complicated by superstitious terror. Were the heavens really taking a hand? Was nature ordering him to stop?

The arrogant Sithreva possessing Oriental science—the science of the past—completely, although ignorant of the science of the present, did not believe in perturbations of the laws of nature. For her, there was no miracle, but some infamous treason for whose authors she sought in vain. Why would she have suspected the Hadji that she had barely glimpsed and who, believing that he would be subjected to the most horrible tortures, had purchased his life by surrendering to Norès the secret that he had discovered.

Sithreva did, however, divine some enormous trap, some formidable peril. She tried to resist; she ran through the camps crying: "It's not true; Brahma has not spoken." But in her turn, she understood that a torrent had been unleashed and that no dyke could stop it.

She ordered, she prayed, she threatened. What did her anger and her pleas matter to those brutes? They marched, their eyes fixed on the heavens. They would have crushed her; it was necessary that she let them go.

And the craziest of all the unthinking was Wintscheff. He too had been gripped by a kind of fury. He wanted to go forward: he was caught up in a kind of monstrous dream of war against the heavens, against destiny.

Sithreva, throwing her arms around him, cried out to him: "Take care! You're going toward the abyss!"

He did not hear her. Haggard, his arm raised toward the snowy summits of Mont Blanc, he said: "It's there…I'm going!"

And the formidably numerous horde followed the same path without hesitation.

From all directions, the march converged on a single point: the mountain above which the sacred word was inscribed.

Through the Col d'Argentières, the Porte de Tiolet, via Scalèfe, Tétatête[54] and Tondu, they encircled the immobile mountain, which seemed to be calling them and waiting for them, always maintaining its fiery crown.

It was an amazing thing to see those black masses invading those white immensities. The glaciers cracked under the weight and abysses opened up that swallowed thousands of men. Were they even aware of it? No solution of continuity

---

[54] I have reproduced these names as they appear in Lermina's text, although they seem to have fallen into disuse, if they ever had any significance.

divided the innumerable cohort, which seemed to resuscitate and regenerate itself. Under the swarm, everything disappeared: the hamlets of Fratzes and Tuent, the chalets of Herbagères, Annemasse, Bonneville and Balme. At the Pont de la Dioza, which collapsed under the weight, cadavers filled the abyss. The others passed over that viaduct of the dead.

Finally, following the Arve, descending from Brévent and the Aiguilles Rouges, passing by Chapeau and Flégère, the Orientals set foot on the sea of ice.

The AUM was still sparkling in the sky.

The hastiest urged the latecomers on.

At the Géants, the Mauvais-Pas, the Egralets and the Bossons they were densely packed, covering the summits, filling the valleys, so compact that all those individuals seemed to form a single being, like a human carapace armoring the mountains.

Wintscheff was there, at the head, sword in hand. Night was falling; soon the magical sign would burst forth in the heavens, and he wanted to be the first to show it to his soldiers with the point of steel.

Pale and somber, Sithreva was beside him. She was beginning to doubt everything: her reason, her will power, herself.

Was she really mad? What! That work of destruction to which she had devoted her entire life, and of which she felt herself to be the architect, the prophetess, was suddenly escaping her, taken over…by whom?

For someone who believes herself to be the mistress of destiny, there is no torture more atrocious than finding herself confronted by the inexplicable. She knew full well that there are no miracles, since she was a maker of miracles, since she, with her priests, had mocked the heavens a hundred times over, knowing how to make them her accomplice.

She huddled close to Wintscheff, who, in spite of his strength of mind, was trembling like a child.

The Asiatics were howling joyful hymns.

The scene was monumentally grandiose. The darkness extended. The crowd could no longer be seen, but the innumerable voices of the anthill could still be heard.

Suddenly, although Sithreva still doubted, a luminous dot appeared in the sky, with the splendors of lightning.

Then other dots...then forms that were accentuated...and finally, clear and radiant, the three letters: AUM.

An enormous clamor resounded, furious and enthusiastic at the same time, in echoes repeated thousands of times by the rocks, by the precipices, by the summits, by the valleys...

The sacred sign was there, directly above the highest summit of Mont Blanc.

But that clamor, all hope, salvation and joy, was suddenly transformed into a single scream, or a death rattle...a kind of hiccup, scarcely formulated and quickly stifled...

The earth had shaken; the rocks had collapsed; the summits had been precipitated into the valleys, instantaneously and unexpectedly overturned, as if a hand, emerging from the bowels of the earth, had grabbed those gigantic masses and had turned them over.

It was more than an explosion, more than an earthquake. What was underneath was now on top, and what was on top was underneath: a leveling collapse, a paste of rocks and ice, a mincemeat of humans and things.

Mont Blanc had just blown up.

Norès' genius had triumphed.

How many thousands of men perished in that catastrophe, provoked by the scientist who had utilized terrestrial electricity for the defense of France and civilization, who had brought forth from the abysms of the globe the enormous, immeasurable quantity of force of which the two poles are the piles.

Not all the Orientals had disappeared; some three hundred thousand had escaped the disaster. They fled...but France was alert.

It was at the gates of Strasbourg, the sentinel city, that the crazed Asiatics collided with the French army. There was an atrocious, stupefying battle; there was an insensate heroism on the part of the vanquished; they fought for a week, with a savagery before which the historian recoils...but in the French army, there was not an hour of weakness, not a minute of hesitation.

The Battle of Strasbourg was the greatest work of deliverance of the twentieth century.

France had the burden of it, and the honor.

One interesting detail: Norès did not ask for any reward, and he was held in sufficient honor not to be offered any. He married Marguerite Sametel and was happy, as if he were not a great man.

SF & FANTASY

Adolphe Alhaiza. *Cybele*

Alphonse Allais. *The Adventures of Captain Cap*

Henri Allorge. *The Great Cataclysm*

Guy d'Armen. *Doc Ardan: The City of Gold and Lepers*

G.-J. Arnaud. *The Ice Company*

Charles Asselineau. *The Double Life*

Henri Austruy. *The Eupantophone; The Olotelepan; The Petitpaon Era*

Cyprien Bérard. *The Vampire Lord Ruthwen*

S. Henry Berthoud. *Martyrs of Science*

Aloysius Bertrand. *Gaspard de la Nuit*

Richard Bessière. *The Gardens of the Apocalypse; The Masters of Silence*

Albert Bleunard. *Ever Smaller*

Félix Bodin. *The Novel of the Future*

Louis Boussenard. *Monsieur Synthesis*

Alphonse Brown. *City of Glass; The Conquest of the Air*

Emile Calvet. *In a Thousand Years*

André Caroff. *The Terror of Madame Atomos; Miss Atomos; The Return of Madame Atomos; The Mistake of Madame Atomos; The Monsters of Madame Atomos; The Revenge of Madame Atomos; The Resurrection of Madame Atomos; The Mark of Madame Atomos; The Spheres of Madame Atomos*

Félicien Champsaur. *The Human Arrow; Ouha, King of the Apes; Pharaoh's Wife*

Didier de Chousy. *Ignis*

Jules Clarétie. *Obsession*

Michel Corday. *The Eternal Flame*

André Couvreur. *The Necessary Evil*; *Caresco, Superman; The Exploits of Professor Tornada* (3 vols.)

Captain Danrit. *Undersea Odyssey*

C. I. Defontenay. *Star (Psi Cassiopeia)*

Charles Derennes. *The People of the Pole*

Georges Dodds (anthologist). *The Missing Link*

Charles Dodeman. *The Silent Bomb*

Harry Dickson. *The Heir of Dracula; Harry Dickson vs. The Spider*

Jules Dornay. *Lord Ruthven Begins*

Alfred Driou. *The Adventures of a Parisian Aeronaut*

Sâr Dubnotal *vs. Jack the Ripper*
Alexandre Dumas. *The Return of Lord Ruthven*
Renée Dunan. *Baal*
J.-C. Dunyach. *The Night Orchid; The Thieves of Silence*
Henri Duvernois. *The Man Who Found Himself*
Achille Eyraud. *Voyage to Venus*
Henri Falk. *The Age of Lead*
Paul Féval. *Anne of the Isles; Knightshade; Revenants; Vampire City; The Vampire Countess; The Wandering Jew's Daughter*
Paul Féval, *fils. Felifax, the Tiger-Man*
Charles de Fieux. *Lamékis*
Louis Forest. *Someone is Stealing Children in Paris*
Arnould Galopin. *Doctor Omega; Doctor Omega and the Shadowmen* (anthology)
Judith Gautier. *Isoline and the Serpent-Flower*
H. Gayar. *The Marvelous Adventures of Serge Myrandhal on Mars*
Léon Gozlan. *The Vampire of the Val-de-Grâce*
G.L. Gick. *Harry Dickson and the Werewolf of Rutherford Grange*
Edmond Haraucourt. *Illusions of Immortality*
Nathalie Henneberg. *The Green Gods*
V. Hugo, P. Foucher & P. Meurice. *The Hunchback of Notre-Dame*
Romain d'Huissier. *Hexagon: Dark Matter*
Jules Janin. *The Magnetized Corpse*
Michel Jeury. *Chronolysis*
Gustave Kahn. *The Tale of Gold and Silence*
Gérard Klein. *The Mote in Time's Eye*
Fernand Kolney. *Love in 5000 Years*
Paul Lacroix. *Danse Macabre*
Louis-Guillaume de La Follie. *The Unpretentious Philosopher*
Jean de La Hire. *Enter the Nyctalope; The Nyctalope on Mars; The Nyctalope vs. Lucifer; The Nyctalope Steps In; Night of the Nyctalope; Return of the Nyctalope; The Fiery Wheel*
Etienne-Léon de Lamothe-Langon. *The Virgin Vampire*
André Laurie. *Spiridon*
Gabriel de Lautrec. *The Vengeance of the Oval Portrait*
Alain le Drimeur. *The Future City*
Georges Le Faure & Henri de Graffigny. *The Extraordinary Adventures of a Russian Scientist Across the Solar System* (2 vols.)
Gustave Le Rouge. *The Mysterious Doctor Cornelius* (3 vols.); *The Vampires of Mars; The Dominion of the World* (w/Gustave Guitton) (4 vols.)

Jules Lermina. *Mysteryville; Panic in Paris; To-Ho and the Gold Destroyers; The Secret of Zippelius*
André Lichtenberger. *The Centaurs; The Children of the Crab*
Jean-Marc & Randy Lofficier. *Edgar Allan Poe on Mars; The Katrina Protocol; Pacifica; Robonocchio; Return of the Nyctalope;* (anthologists) *Tales of the Shadowmen 1-10*
Xavier Mauméjean. *The League of Heroes*
Joseph Méry. *The Tower of Destiny*
Hippolyte Mettais. *The Year 5865*
Louise Michel. *The Human Microbes; The New World*
Tony Moilin. *Paris in the Year 2000*
José Moselli. *Illa's End*
John-Antoine Nau. *Enemy Force*
Marie Nizet. *Captain Vampire*
C. Nodier, A. Beraud & Toussaint-Merle. *Frankenstein*
Henri de Parville. *An Inhabitant of the Planet Mars*
Gaston de Pawlowski. *Journey to the Land of the 4th Dimension*
Georges Pellerin. *The World in 2000 Years*
Ernest Pérochon. *The Frenetic People*
Pierre Pelot. *The Child Who Walked on the Sky*
J. Polidori, C. Nodier, E. Scribe. *Lord Ruthven the Vampire*
P.-A. Ponson du Terrail. *The Vampire and the Devil's Son; The Immortal Woman*
Edgar Quinet. *Ahasuerus; The Enchanter Merlin*
Henri de Régnier. *A Surfeit of Mirrors*
Maurice Renard. *The Blue Peril; Doctor Lerne; The Doctored Man; A Man Among the Microbes; The Master of Light*
Jean Richepin. *The Wing; The Crazy Corner*
Albert Robida. *The Adventures of Saturnin Farandoul; The Clock of the Centuries; Chalet in the Sky; The Electric Life*
J.-H. Rosny Aîné. *Helgvor of the Blue River; The Givreuse Enigma; The Mysterious Force; The Navigators of Space; Vamireh; The World of the Variants; The Young Vampire*
Marcel Rouff. *Journey to the Inverted World*
Han Ryner. *The Superhumans; The Human Ant*
Pierre de Selenes: *An Unknown World*
Angelo de Sorr. *The Vampires of London*
Brian Stableford. *The New Faust at the Tragicomique;The Empire of the Necromancers (The Shadow of Frankenstein; Frankenstein and the Vampire Countess; Frankenstein in London); Sherlock Holmes & The Vampires of Eternity; The Stones of Camelot; The Wayward*

Muse. (anthologist) *News from the Moon; The Germans on Venus; The Supreme Progress; The World Above the World; Nemoville; Investigations of the Future; The Conqueror of Death*
Jacques Spitz. *The Eye of Purgatory*
Kurt Steiner. *Ortog*
Eugène Thébault. *Radio-Terror*
C.-F. Tiphaigne de La Roche. *Amilec*
Louis Ulbach. *Prince Bonifacio*
Théo Varlet. *The Golden Rock. The Xenobiotic Invasion; The Castaways of Eros; Timeslip Troopers* (w/André Blandin); *The Martian Epic* (w/Octave Joncquel)
Paul Vibert. *The Mysterious Fluid*
Villiers de l'Isle-Adam. *The Scaffold; The Vampire Soul*
Philippe Ward. *Artahe*
Philippe Ward & Sylvie Miller. *The Song of Montségur*

MYSTERIES & THRILLERS

M. Allain & P. Souvestre. *The Daughter of Fantômas*
A. Anicet-Bourgeois, Lucien Dabril. *Rocambole*
A. Bernède. *Belphegor; Judex* (w/Louis Feuillade); *The Return of Judex* (w/Louis Feuillade); *The Shadow of Judex*
A. Bisson & G. Livet. *Nick Carter vs. Fantômas*
V. Darlay & H. de Gorsse. *Arsène Lupin vs. Sherlock Holmes: The Stage Play*
Séamas Duffy. *Sherlock Holmes in Paris*
Paul Féval. *Gentlemen of the Night; John Devil; The Black Coats ('Salem Street; The Invisible Weapon; The Parisian Jungle; The Companions of the Treasure; Heart of Steel; The Cadet Gang; The Sword-Swallower)*
Emile Gaboriau. *Monsieur Lecoq*
Goron & Emile Gautier. *Spawn of the Penitentiary*
Rick Lai. *Shadows of the Opera: Retribution in Blood; Sisters of the Shadows: The Curse of Cagliostro*
Steve Leadley. *Sherlock Holmes: The Circle of Blood*
Maurice Leblanc. *Arsène Lupin vs. Countess Cagliostro; Arsène Lupin vs. Sherlock Holmes (The Blonde Phantom; The Hollow Needle); The Many Faces of Arsène Lupin*
Gaston Leroux. *Chéri-Bibi; The Phantom of the Opera; Rouletabille & the Mystery of the Yellow Room; Rouletabille at Krupp's*
Richard Marsh. *The Complete Adventures of Judith Lee*

William Patrick Maynard. *The Terror of Fu Manchu; The Destiny of Fu Manchu*
Frank J. Morlock. *Sherlock Holmes: The Grand Horizontals; Sherlock Holmes vs Jack the Ripper*
Jean Petithuguenin. *The Adventures of Ethel King*
Antonin Reschal. *The Adventures of Miss Boston*
P. de Wattyne & Y. Walter. *Sherlock Holmes vs. Fantômas*
David White. *Fantômas in America*
Pierre Yrondy. *The Adventures of Thérèse Arnaud*

SCREENPLAYS

Mike Baron. *The Iron Triangle*
Emma Bull & Will Shetterly. *Nightspeeder; War for the Oaks*
Gerry Conway & Roy Thomas. *Doc Dynamo*
Steve Englehart. *Majorca*
James Hudnall. *The Devastator*
Jean-Marc & Randy Lofficier. *Royal Flush*
J.-M. & R. Lofficier & Marc Agapit. *Despair*
J.-M. & R. Lofficier & Joël Houssin. *City*
Andrew Paquette. *Peripheral Vision*
Robert L. Robinson, Jr. *Judex*
R. Thomas, J. Hendler & L. Sprague de Camp. *Rivers of Time*

NON-FICTION

Stephen R. Bissette. *Blur 1-5. Green Mountain Cinema 1; Teen Angels*
Win Scott Eckert. *Crossovers* (2 vols.)
Jean-Marc & Randy Lofficier. *Shadowmen* (2 vols.)
Randy Lofficier. *Over Here*

ART BOOKS

J.-M. Lofficier & D. Taylor. *Tongue Lash*
Jean-Pierre Normand. *Science Fiction Illustrations*
Raven Okeefe. *Raven's L'il Critters; Rave's Faves*
Randy Lofficier & Raven Okeefe. *If Your Possum Go Daylight...*
Daniele Serra. *Illusions*